FURTHER ACCLAIM FOR
LET THERE BE LITE

'Rupert Morgan's satire of modern life is brilliant. He is like
Ben Elton at his wittiest but minus the worthiness: although he
makes salient points about our time, taking swipes at
democracy, big business, justice and celebrity – you don't feel
as if they are being rammed down your throat. His writing is
fast and his characterization superb . . . Definitely one to watch'
The Express

'Satire which takes you up to the edge of libellous – and gets
away with it . . . Nothing is spared by Rupert Morgan's
blistering pen: neither love, family, democracy, race relations,
politics, nor journalism. Atlantis is a place where logic is
dangerously inverted and morality a dangerously
old-fashioned concept. As a story it rattles along with the
pace of a thriller. As an inventive swipe at the Establishment,
it will make you wince'
Daily Mail

'Bittersweet, laugh-out-loud funny, and all too true'
Fay Weldon

LET THERE BE LITE

Rupert Morgan

BANTAM BOOKS
London • New York • Toronto • Sydney • Auckland

LET THERE BE LITE
A BANTAM BOOK: 0553 81284X

Originally published in Great Britain by Bantam Press,
a division of Transworld Publishers

PRINTING HISTORY
Bantam Press edition published 2000
Bantam Books edition published 2001

1 3 5 7 9 10 8 6 4 2

Set in 10/11½pt Sabon by Falcon Graphic Art

Bantam Books are published by Transworld Publishers,
61–63 Uxbridge Road, London W5 5SA,
a division of The Random House Group Ltd,
in Australia by Random House Australia (Pty) Ltd,
20 Alfred Street, Milsons Point, Sydney, NSW 2061, Australia,
in New Zealand by Random House New Zealand Ltd,
18 Poland Road, Glenfield, Auckland 10, New Zealand
and in South Africa by Random House (Pty) Ltd,
Endulini, 5a Jubilee Road, Parktown 2193, South Africa.

Reproduced, printed and bound in Great Britain by
Cox & Wyman Ltd, Reading, Berks.

This book is dedicated to
Ganesh,
a god of whom I know very little
except that he has a sense of humour.

Thanks to my adored wife, without whose unquestioning faith and support this book was nevertheless written, and to my parents for years of remaining calm.

PREFACE

Do you want the good news or the bad news first?

Okay . . . we are not alone. There are other intelligent life-forms out there. Far closer than any of us imagined, as a matter of fact – a tenth planet in our very own solar system, about the same size as ours and orbiting at a similar distance from the sun. But on the far side, which is why it's never visible.

Thanks to its similar chemistry and conditions, life evolved there in much the same way as it did over here. As with our planet, a temperature wobble brought billions of years of growth to an abrupt halt some time ago, wiping out its dinosaurs, most of its forests and flowers, and numerous squishy things that were not highly evolved enough to warrant a pronounceable name.

Very sad, but actually quite normal. God or no God, Creation is clearly not an exact science. It is time we faced that fact. Time we realized that the Big Answer we're always looking for, the explanation for all the bad shit blocking up our historical pipes, might just be the damned weather.

Maybe people would stop taking Life so *personally*.

The point here, however, is that such tragic annihilations open the door to other genetic possibilities that would probably never have got a foothold otherwise. And so pretty soon this tenth planet had humans.

But everywhere.

So now you know: there is another whole planet full of humans.

Still, the good news is that they're making just as big a mess of it as we are.

I

We are all in the gutter, but some of us are looking at the stars . . .

That's us all right, Susan Summerday reflected: in the gutter, looking at the stars.

Breaking our damn necks.

The previous owner of the Hotel Excelsior broke his by taking God's elevator from the penthouse terrace down to 16th Avenue. Which, it has to be said, is about the most stylish way a man could commit suicide in Entropolis. You're still just a mess on the sidewalk, of course, but a mess with an address.

Turning her back on the chattering huddles in the penthouse Banqueting Room, Susan let the velvet of the curtains brush her bare shoulder as she gazed out over the city and downed the rest of her champagne in one long, ladylike sip. The curtains, hanging long and rich from the high ceiling, were held apart like spread legs by sashes at the knees. Standing between their thighs, gazing over the city, Susan Summerday could justifiably consider herself one of the select few, sitting on top of all the humans piled up on this rock, looking down upon the world.

From which vantage point, if she was honest with herself, it made no more sense than it did from anywhere else.

It never had, and it most likely never would. Which

was probably why it came to be about making all these other things: a name, a splash, money, or at least ends that met . . . because it apparently couldn't make that one simple thing that would make everything else all right: sense.

And it came to be about cities like Entropolis, a vast beast of ambition to swallow people whole and shit them stripped of innocence. They slid out the other end looking much the same, like tinned corn, but they were almost as empty as the reflections Susan Summerday saw in the glass before her – those of her husband Michael, the fifty-odd smiling couples who comprised the élite political strata of these great United States of Atlantis, and, almost invisible but for the whites of their eyes, the unsmiling waiters.

For they did not have to smile, of course. That was where they could find superiority over these pale, cream-voiced people they were here to serve. Susan Summerday, for instance, had to smile like she was an advertisement for life itself. For eight years she had smiled the smile of a vice-president's wife, the smile of a Senator's wife for a decade prior to that, and now, God help her, she had to smile the smile of a woman whose husband should be elected President.

She sometimes believed it was only the lotions that kept her pretty face from cracking in two.

But tonight, she knew, she would smile especially brightly, a smile just for their host, should he ever deign to turn up.

The surprise in political circles had been palpable when, after a prolonged period of secrecy, the identity of the venerable hotel's new owner was revealed to be John Lockes. Why on earth would the reclusive billionaire, whom no one outside the confines of Infologix's hi-tech headquarters had seen in nigh-on ten years, want to buy the Excelsior? His field was information technology, not hotels. True, he'd branched out last year by taking over

P. S. Yorsakt, the fast-food conglomerate, but the debt-ridden Excelsior? It wasn't even a serious hotel, for that matter, being more of a political club masquerading as a hotel. What it lost in money it more than made up for in kudos, but that was of no interest to a man like Lockes, unless . . .

And sure enough, the pieces had started to fall into place. That initial surprise had mutated into suspicion as the invitations to tonight's select party arrived. It was all too clear: Lockes is one of the single most generous donators to the campaign funds of politicians across the spectrum; Lockes buys the Excelsior; Lockes invites a small band of key power-brokers to an informal get-together . . . *ergo* Lockes wanted something back for his years of generosity.

Nothing could be more natural, of course, but the frisson it had sent through their subtle community was all the greater for the fact that he had never, in all his years of fiscal support, contacted any of them personally, let alone asked anything in return. Susan Summerday knew it had everyone else in the room as rattled as Michael, coming just months away from the elections. There was nothing that a politician liked less than not knowing the price of a bargain he had already made. Not that that ever stopped them, in her experience.

But which of them could refuse their host anything now? To provoke his wrath, to make him switch his financial support to an opponent, would be suicide: John Lockes, the founder and president of Infologix, was the richest man in the world.

Quite literally the host with the most.

The actual figures involved were beyond Susan's comprehension, but it was enough for her to know that one of the country's leading collections of modern art was owned by a man who, fifteen years ago, had accepted the offer of a few Infologix shares in lieu of the price of the pizza he had been delivering to Lockes' student dorm. Lucky son of a bitch. Legend has it that it was even the wrong pizza.

She was stirred from her musings by the looming presence of a waiter beside her. She turned, holding her glass out to be refilled, and stood in silence as the huge man carefully dribbled out the champagne. It was absurd, as though the bottle and the glass were being friendly to one another while she and the waiter were the inanimate objects. She felt a sudden urge to smile at him, fixing her eyes on his dark mantelpiece of a brow, but when he finally looked up and caught her waiting grin, he did not return even a flicker of acknowledgement. Her smile popped, her spine suddenly tingling with anxiety at the lurking power of that impassive regard. She turned rapidly away to save face, only to gasp in shock as she found herself nose to nose with the booze-bloated features of Senator Jefferson Smith.

'So, my dear . . .' he wheezed, winking conspiratorially, 'do you think he really keeps his toenail clippings in a jar?'

The late Alfred Zweistein was a Tortured Artist. True, this world might have been a better place if people had been less fascinated by Tortured Artists and had spared a little more sympathy for all the Tortured Accountants, Tortured Lawyers and, indeed, Tortured Torturers, but Zweistein's is still a tale worth telling.

He was perhaps the greatest mathematical genius of the century, although unrecognized as such. Many would have objected, of course, that this meant he was a Tortured Scientist, but this, like all prejudices, was the product of ignorance: most people who liked to consider themselves aesthetically inclined were stunningly bad at maths. So mathematicians got called scientists and the modern world was arguably more barbaric in its tastes than Ancient Greece.

14

But it, unlike the Greeks, had no slaves – as such – so that was the end of any argument.

As a young man, Zweistein posited his Theory of Reality, namely that R=HA–. In layman's terms this can be explained in the following way: facts, Zweistein said, are isolated elements that are never constant in space and time, being subject to the corrosive effects of entropy. No fact is ever the same, regardless of the time or position of the perceiver. Rumour, on the other hand, is a compound substance which grows in mass and credibility the more dispersed it becomes. Divide the greater of these two, rumour, by the lesser, fact, and you have H – or History – as understood by any one individual.

So far, so simple. However, multiply this by A minus, or the fraction of seventy years that the individual has *not* lived – say, $^{65}/_{70}$ for a child of five, or $^{10}/_{70}$ for a sixty-year-old man – and you have that individual's perception of Reality (R).

This is why one becomes increasingly unsure of what one knows the longer one lives. Because R=HA–. In purely empirical terms, a child *knows* more than its parents.

The mathematics involved in proving R=HA– are fiendishly difficult, unsurprisingly, and perhaps even impossible. Certainly, the attempt defeated Zweistein himself, provoking a catastrophic nervous breakdown that did extraordinary things to his hair. Like most geniuses, his path finished in a lunatic asylum, his theory remained unpublished, and he was never recognized as anything greater than someone who spent his days pretending to break wind whenever the nurses turned their backs.

Which is a tragedy, because in an age of mass media the need for a Theory of Reality was greater than ever. It would have explained, for instance, how ideas such as the existence of UFOs had moved from wild speculation to widely perceived reality from one generation to the next without the addition of any objective evidence, barring a few photographs that, in the most charitable scenario, suggested alien craft had some form of Crap Picture Shield to thwart the paparazzi.

'Do I think he keeps his toenail clippings in a jar?' Susan Summerday repeated, her tight beauty relaxing attractively at the sight of her old ally. 'No, Jefferson, I do not. What do you think?'

'Obviously not,' the ageing Senator concurred, 'total rubbish. The jar is a dead giveaway – why would the richest man in the world have a *jar*? Do *you* have a jar?'

She nodded solemnly, keeping the edges of her lips pulled tightly down as she tried to honour the Senator's observation with the gravity it deserved. 'Can't remember the last time I even saw one. There must be jars at home somewhere, but not in parts of the building I visit.'

'My point exactly. Although it's nothing to be proud of, we belong to the jarless class. Were Mr Lockes inclined to keep his toenail clippings for posterity, he would no doubt acquire ... a casket. A rare piece obtained in an auction. I fear the story is the rather unimaginative fabrication of someone who, quite literally, has loose screws. And therefore, my dear, a jar.'

When a terrified Susan Summerday first crossed the threshold of this penthouse room on her husband's arm as a new Senator's wife, almost twenty years ago, there had been only one man who had greeted her with genuine hospitality. He remained the only man she absolutely trusted. There was something about Jefferson Smith that set him apart from everyone else in government, and their respect for him was based on more than the simple fact that he was the Senate majority leader.

For all the compromises he had been forced to make, for all the betrayals he'd suffered and the wickedness he

16

had walked with over his long career, Jefferson Smith had somehow retained a good heart. To outsiders it would not have seemed like a great heart, maybe not something that would have impressed a preacher or philanthropist, but to those who knew what they were talking about, who had seen their own integrity chip, crack and crumble with the years, Jefferson Smith's ability to withstand the whirlwinds of power and hold on to a little common sense and decency was nothing short of phenomenal. It was widely acknowledged that he would have made a great president had the Atlantian public been psychologically capable of voting for a man who was a smoker, a drunk, and fat.

'You seem rather zen under the circumstances, Jefferson,' Susan commented softly, conscious of the air of tension all around them.

'Liquid mantra, my dear,' whispered the Senator, holding up his glass. 'I'm as anxious as anyone else to know what this is all about, but my nervous system has just risen above material concerns.'

'Is it not possible that Lockes simply bought this place because it amused him to do so?' she suggested optimistically. 'The man could probably do it on his credit card, after all.'

Jefferson shrugged wearily. 'Sure. He could buy the credit card *company* on his credit card. But we're still left with the alarming question of what one's idea of fun is if one is the richest man in the world.'

'Wasn't he second?'

'Oh, the Sultan. We don't count him. Our man got there by being smart, not because some accident of geology dumped an ocean of squashed lizards under his tent. John Lockes is the richest man in the world . . . *morally speaking*.'

'Morally speaking . . . right!' she laughed.

The morality of it depended on whether one thought it was okay for one man to hold the copyright on the Return Key® of the standard computer keyboard. Susan's own sympathies lay with those who complained that in this day and age that was the virtual equivalent of holding a copyright on penises.

Yes, he'd done it legally. And yes, others could and should have realized as early as he did how important that one button was going to prove once information technology got going. But even so, the outrageous truth about John Lockes was not that he had his toenail clippings in a jar, but that he had his competitors' balls in a vice.

To be fair to the man, his wealth was not entirely the product of this one coup. Infologix, his company, was also an innovative software producer. One of its best-selling items, for example, was a program called Abstractor, the idea for which had sprung from Lockes' realization that computers were now producing so much information that what people really needed was a program capable of condensing it all to a manageable bulk.

Infologix Abstractor was that program. It could summarize any document to the length desired, depending on the time a person could afford to devote to it. At full, 100 per cent setting, it could cut almost anything down to one sentence.

Naturally some of the subtleties got lost in the process. One day a college professor had tested Abstractor's capabilities to the limit by feeding it with the entire Old Testament of the Holy Book. He set the program to 100 per cent reduction and waited. Ten hours later, having examined everything the ancient texts had to offer in the way of wisdom and philosophy, the computer produced its notorious conclusion:

Because I say so, that's why.

* * *

'Of course, you're right,' Jefferson acknowledged. 'Seen from one angle it is morally indefensible. But on the other hand, Lockes is an Atlantian and Infologix is the biggest software producer in the world, which means jobs for Atlantians and Atlantian dominance of the industry. We're the good guys. We win. That has to be moral.'

'And they say you're not cynical . . .' she sighed, squeezing his arm affectionately. 'That's how you've survived so long.'

'On the contrary – I've survived because I listen. Do you know, for instance, who your husband has chosen as his running-mate in the election?'

She lifted a dark eyebrow. 'Does my husband know, more to the point? Or have his advisers not yet informed him of his choice of Vice-President?'

'Oh . . . I think so,' Jefferson breathed with an unmistakable air of despair. 'He's talking to the man right now.'

Susan Summerday's head flashed round to check who Michael was talking to, her eyes bugging and her jaw slumping as she found her answer.

'Oh no!' she gasped. 'No! Say it isn't so.'

*

The good news, so far as Vice-President Michael Summerday was concerned, was that Governor Tyrone Wheeler had a third nipple. Because it was the revelation of this genetic excess that had just put the Conservatives' best candidate for the presidency out of the running.

Not that people held the nipple itself against Wheeler so much as they disapproved of his having lied when the rumours of its existence first surfaced. The leaking of his medical records had subsequently sealed his fate.

The governor hadn't given in without a fight, desperately trying to retrieve the situation with a sensational

19

appearance on *The Lola Colaco Show*, in which he had not only admitted the nipple's existence but had entered into a frank and open discussion of his feelings about it, laying bare his shame, his innermost fears and, indeed, his chest to the Atlantian public in a highly emotional interview. But even that could not save him from the anger of those whose trust he had betrayed by lying in the first place, particularly the members of Triple-Nipple Pride whom Lola had invited to share the stage with him.

So the Conservative candidacy had fallen to Senator Jack Douglas instead, a far less threatening opponent in that he had a reputation as an intellectual, which some folk reckoned was a mite suspicious in a man without any kids. All things being equal, therefore, Michael Summerday ought to have been just six months of public apathy away from stepping into President Monroe's shoes.

The bad news, so far as he was concerned, was that he had found himself agreeing to run with Bob Redwood on the ticket. Redwood, his advisers assured him, was the perfect demographic match for his own candidacy. He was young. He was handsome. He was a football hero. Above all, he made people feel good about themselves by not threatening them intellectually: he was a straight-talking guy who called a spade a spade – because, to be honest, he didn't have any alternative vocabulary for a spade.

Summerday's campaign team had calculated everything down to the last fraction of a percentage point, they said, and Redwood was the man. He wasn't expected to deliver whole states single-handed, but to plug the demographic gaps on a more general, subtler level.

'I have a *what*?' Summerday had exclaimed when they presented him with the conclusions of their focus groups.

'You have a Yee-Ha Deficit,' his campaign manager, Chuck Desane, had answered gently.

'Meaning what – that I think lynchings are a little *passé*?'

'Well, there you go, Mike – you said "*passé*". That's a Yee-Ha Deficit. People think you're responsible and trustworthy, but they'd like you to be a little more . . . tall in the saddle. Now Bob Redwood is Yee-Ha – he'd say lynchings were old-fashioned.'

'. . . But a good thing nevertheless,' Summerday had muttered darkly. 'Please – the man is a moron. He thinks Affirmative Action is why black athletes get to run the hundred metres in less time. It's out of the question.'

Like most people, Michael Summerday was both a better person than he thought himself and a good deal worse. Better, because he had preserved many more of his principles over the years than he felt he had, and worse, because should the right situation arise he was entirely capable of sacrificing those, too.

He accepted Bob Redwood as his running-mate. What was the point of having advisers, after all, if you weren't going to take their advice? And Redwood, although cerebrally lo-cal, was a good man in his own way.

As are psychopaths, however.

Summerday often wondered whether he himself was a good or a bad man in that fairy-tale place where all of a person's contradictions are reconciled: his heart of hearts. He tried to be, given the chance. For one thing, he wanted to make Atlantis a better place when he became President. He planned to do things. Big things. For the moment he was playing his cards so close to his chest that even he was not entirely sure what they were – never a bad strategy for surviving the jungle of democratic politics – but he was a believer in high ideals. At bottom.

His late father, Senator Thadeus Summerday, had given him some very good advice about this when he was a young man. It was hard-won advice from a dying man who felt he could finally wring a few

21

drops of wisdom out of his weatherbeaten heart:

'The truth, Michael,' he had said, 'is that no leader can be both good and wise. History shows us how, time and time again, and for all the right reasons, we do the wrong thing. That is why we have democracy – it is the art of doing the right thing for the *wrong* reason.'

His son had nodded solemnly, but Thadeus' words travelled straight to that junkyard part of the youthful brain reserved for the opinions of fathers. Had Thadeus been a wiser man, he would have known not to bother sharing his wisdom.

Furthermore, people never learn from other people's mistakes, and his son was now repeating much the same error in his attempt to give his young running-mate a crash-course in information technology before their host arrived.

'. . . And it is the programs that we run *on* the hardware, Bob, that we call software,' he was explaining when Susan looked across. 'Is that clear now?'

'Uh-huh. Uh-huh.'

'You're sure about that?'

'Uh-huh. Oh yeah. Sure.'

'Do you want me to go over it again?'

'Could you?' the young Senator grinned, pretending to mop his brow.

Summerday took a deep breath and searched for a way of rendering the subject intelligible to his colleague.

'Okay. Bob – a computer is basically like a gun, all right? You have your hardware – which is the firearm itself – but that's no use without bullets, is it now? So that's the software – the thing you have to put into your computer before you can start having any *fun* with it. And then the operating system is the firing pin – it's what makes the gun and the bullets connect. Is *that* clearer?'

Redwood's eyes narrowed subtly and he began to nod as he thought it through. 'Uh-huh . . . yeah . . . uh-*huh*! I get it. I definitely get it.' He looked up with an air of boyish enthusiasm. 'Computers are cool! Maybe I should get one, huh?'

'I think you should, Bob. That's a good idea. I mean . . . maybe you'll use it or maybe not, but at least you can truthfully say you have one. It's important we be seen as up to speed with modern technology.'

'Locked, cocked and ready to rock! So what's the . . . what's the biggest one I can get?'

'The *biggest*?'

'Yeah, I mean . . . big, you know?' the young Senator persisted, his eyes glinting, 'like don't-mess-with-me size. Big-big.' He chuckled at the thought.

'Actually, Bob, you might want to go for a compact model rather than the biggest.'

'Uh-huh?' Redwood frowned. 'Like a lady's computer? Come on, Mike – hey! I may be a beginner, but I can handle it. How much kick do these babies pack?'

Summerday went to speak, his lips opening before he realized that there were no words coming up his throat. Nothing. Redwood had short-circuited his entire speech faculty. Even his hearing had gone awry, the room suddenly seeming silent.

'Well . . . hey, I should ask John Lockes, shouldn't I?' the Senator whispered, pointing toward the door.

Summerday turned in a panic, realizing that the room had indeed fallen silent.

The richest man in the world, morally speaking, had arrived.

'No . . .' the Vice-President wheezed, clutching Redwood's arm. 'Don't . . .'

'No?' gasped an amazed Redwood. 'That's crazy – why not?'

Summerday gripped his arm with all his might, ordering, 'Because, Bob, I say so, that's why.'

The young Senator looked crestfallen, gazing imploringly

into his running-mate's eyes but seeing only absolute determination there. He was disappointed, but in a strange way also found it comforting to submit to Summerday's authority.

'Aww . . . okay . . .' he sighed.

*

In common with everyone else in the room, Susan Summerday had only the vaguest notion of what John Lockes looked like, but there was no mistaking the man who had just entered. He wasn't one of them, and he certainly wasn't a waiter, so this had to be the king of Infologix. There was nothing extraordinary about him, so those who had been anticipating hair down to the knees and a nappy were sorely disappointed, but he looked every inch the geek-made-good – the fine cloth of his suit and his immaculate shoes set off by an unflattering haircut and pre-middle-age skin that still bore the traces of pustulous teenage eruptions. He had two identical pens in his breast pocket. But overall his features were so unremarkable that Susan found her eyes sliding frictionlessly off his face.

This was a man who could pass unnoticed in an identity parade.

In the expectant silence that greeted his entry, Lockes remained still, regarding them with an air of mild surprise from the doorway. Finally, he made some minuscule adjustment to the way his glasses were positioned on his nose, and announced:

'I'm hungry. Let's eat.'

And that was it. No introductions, no speeches, not even an apology for his tardiness.

You have to be so rich to behave like that, Susan Summerday thought.

She and Michael, being the ranking couple at the

dinner, found themselves seated either side of Lockes at the head of the table. Jefferson Smith was next to her, as majority leader, but after that things got rather scrappy.

Conversation was excruciatingly muted throughout the first course. Perhaps it was the legacy of so many years of asociability, or maybe he was simply not a talkative character, but Lockes seemed happy to eat his salmon mousse with lobster sauce without the distraction of idle chatter. Every attempt the Summerdays made to start a conversation seemed to be dealt with by a simple nod of agreement or some unhelpful monosyllable until eventually, desperate to fill the silence, they ended up talking to each other. Which made a change.

To compound his discomfort, Michael Summerday found the waiters were making him increasingly nervous as they served the main course. The most alarming was the man with the *gratin dauphinois*. He filled his tuxedo like the juice in an orange, muscles bubbling under the material as he slowly moved about the table. His bald crown reflected the chandeliers, but his eyes, shaded by that mantelpiece of a brow that had so fixated Susan earlier, were darkly menacing caves. Summerday tried to reason with himself that the man's physique was no fault of his own, no guide to the possibly gentle, daisy-chain weaver's soul inside, but there was more to it than that tank of a body. His whole manner was unsettling. As he circled the table with his dish, one could see each successive guest tense at the offer of potatoes in cream. He pronounced *gratin* like 'grating', asking in a stone rumble, '*You want* gratin?' In any other circumstances there would be no doubt whatsoever that he was offering to lift you up with his bare hands and vigorously rub your face against the nearest brick wall.

From the corner of his eye, Summerday noticed Lockes was watching him with an air of mild amusement.

'Criminals, Mr Vice-President,' he announced softly, as

if sharing a rather risqué but amusing joke, 'all of them. The blacks.'

'I'm sorry?' Summerday asked, not that he hadn't heard but because he was unsure of the correct protocol when dealing with such a profoundly racist comment from someone with Lockes' wealth.

'Criminals, I said. You were looking at the waiters. They're all ex-convicts. I'm trying to give them a second chance. The least a man in my position can do. And it turns the Hotel Excelsior into a tax-free enterprise – one of your laws, I think. Thanks.'

Summerday returned his smile, but was at a loss for what to say. Lockes had staffed the Excelsior with criminals? The man had to be insane, just as the rumours suggested. That was like hookers working at the Vatican.

Looking around again, he could see that there was indeed something unsettling about each and every one of the waiters. Even the smallest ones were not the kind of people with whom one would relish being trapped in an elevator.

'Oh . . . *criminals!*' Summerday laughed as if he'd originally misheard. 'That's . . . that's . . . well, that is . . . yes . . . tax-deductible.'

Lockes regarded him flatly. 'You know, the last time I felt hurt by people doubting my sanity, Mr Vice-President, I bought the world's largest fast-food conglomerate.'

Summerday suddenly found he had preferred it when Lockes remained silent. He just couldn't seem to get a grip on this conversation.

'You bought P. S. Yorsakt as . . . comfort food?'

'What?' Lockes frowned. 'What the *hell* are you talking about? I bought it to teach those bastards on the Stock Exchange who'd been selling Infologix shares that it was not for them to worry about rumours concerning my sanity! I didn't have anything to gain by buying a

26

bunch of burger and pizza chains, did I? I'm in computers, for heaven's sake. It was an insane idea! But that was the point – it doesn't matter if my ideas are insane, only that I can do whatever the hell I please and they will accept it! Sure enough, they all started feverishly buying Infologix and P. S. Yorsakt, regardless of the fact that it was a ridiculous combination. I'm just warning you not to make the same mistake as them, Mr Vice-President.'

Seeing her husband's panicked expression, Susan Summerday dived to his rescue. 'Michael didn't mean to suggest anything of the sort, Mr Lockes. We don't read the tabloids.'

Lockes turned her way with a sudden, strange smile. 'John, please, Mrs Summerday.'

'Susan.'

'*You want* gratin'?'

'Please.' Lockes leaned aside as a pythonically muscular arm reached across, bearing a little silver spoon of potato. 'Everybody reads the tabloids, Susan. The defining feature of gossip is that it is self-promulgating – if one person reads it, everyone reads it. It's a virus. Actually, all forms of belief are viruses. God is a virus. The fact of the matter is that we know nothing, least of all about each other. What do you know about me, after all? How do you even know I *am* John Lockes?'

'*You want* gratin'?'

'Thank you.' Susan Summerday leaned aside, her heart racing from the effect of Lockes' tirade. 'Well, I suppose it's a matter of extrapolation . . . I know John Lockes bought the Excelsior, and so—'

She broke off with a yelp as something searingly hot landed where her ovaries used to be. She looked down to see *gratin dauphinois* sliding down her designer dress. 'Oh . . . my . . . *God*! My Hamaki!' Her fury was such that she momentarily forgot social niceties as she wheeled

27

on the man responsible. 'Ryuchi Hamaki! Does the name mean anything to you? What do I do now, please – wear my *plate*?' She shook her head in disbelief. The dress was a write-off.

'I am so sorry,' the billionaire whispered, rising from his chair to confront the immobile hulk who still stood with the empty spoon clasped absurdly in his melon-sized fist. 'Well? What have you got to say for yourself?'

The man shrugged softly. 'Ain't my fault,' he growled in a voice like distant thunder.

'Not your fault? I obviously missed something. How can it not be your fault? Was there an earthquake?'

'It ain't my fault,' the behemoth rumbled. 'She ain't wearing no bra.'

There was a stunned, uncomprehending silence. Lockes frowned.

'Oh, I see! You throw food over women who aren't wearing bras. Now, isn't this something you perhaps should have mentioned to your parole officer when he offered you a job in catering?'

The waiter shifted uncomfortably on his feet, turning to Susan Summerday and continuing in his slow, insistent manner. 'I couldn't understand why your breasts were so . . . it don't look natural.'

Susan stopped dabbing at her lap, a low fire suddenly sparking in her eyes as her face steeled with anger.

'They're *not* natural, dumbo,' she snapped, 'they are fake. They are guaranteed. They would not droop if you strapped me to a rocket. Wow! Just how long have you *been* in jail? Did we have the pill?'

'I was only—'

'I think that's enough!' Lockes cut in. 'Thank you, Susan – I'll deal with this now. You – what's your name?'

'Uzi,' the man replied. 'Uzi Washington.'

'Well, Mr Washington, might I ask what you did before coming here?'

28

'Armoured trucks, mostly.'

'Ah!' Lockes exclaimed. 'Well, the problem here is that waitering is not like robbing an armoured truck, is it? So your skill with a crowbar is of little use in the more delicate operation of a spoon, if you see what I mean.'

Uzi Washington was silent.

'*Do* you see what I mean, Mr Washington?'

'No.'

'I mean that I have to let you go. My people will let your parole officer know you're in the employment market in the morning. I'm sure there are jobs in demolition ideally suited to a man of your qualities.'

Washington stood in shock, his spoon trembling imperceptibly. 'You can't do that to me. You'll mess up my sheet.'

'Your sheet is clean?' Susan Summerday laughed. 'Maybe I could wear it for the evening instead of my Hamaki. Sort of a toga thing.'

'*Fuck your fucking Hamaki, lady!*'

She looked momentarily stunned, then whispered just low enough for the ears of those immediately around her, 'Fuck my fucking Hamaki. That would be in, what, his *prick-à-porter* collection, I suppose?'

'Leave us, Mr Washington!' Lockes ordered. 'You cannot imagine the mess your sheet will be in if you anger me further.'

Washington stood for a second more, shaking with rage and hurt, then dropped his silver spoon and strode off toward the kitchens.

Lockes sat down with a wide-eyed smile, regarding the harrowed faces around him. The entire table had fallen silent during the exchange. Suddenly the kitchen door slammed open again, and Washington stormed back into the room.

'Washington,' Lockes groaned, 'don't you understand?

You're fired – that's all there is to it!'

'No, man, *you* don't understand!' came the reply as Washington covered the space between them in four huge strides, producing a gun from behind his back and putting it to Lockes' head. '*You're* fired!'

II

If people thought John Lockes was mad enough to keep his toe-nail clippings in a jar, it was almost entirely due to the *Public Investigator*.

At various times the *Investigator* had reported that John Lockes was suffering from amnesia, or from a hideously disfiguring skin disease, had undergone a sex change, had been abducted by aliens, was an alien, or an android, was dying of cancer and desperately seeking to clone himself in a South Atlantian clinic and, on more than one occasion, that he was dead.

These were the stories which had ultimately brought about the hostile takeover of the largest fast-food group in the world, conglomerating Ghetty's Burgers, Meat-U-Eat and the Love 'N' Pizza chain. All total garbage.

The stories, too.

And all written by one man – the *Public Investigator*'s specialist reporter of the weird, the scandalous and the frankly unbelievable: Macauley Connor.

Earlier on the same day that the guests at the Hotel Excelsior found themselves facing a gun-wielding maniac, Macauley Connor had climbed stiffly out of his car, stretching his legs and tucking his shirt back into his crumpled trousers. He squinted in the afternoon sun as he looked despondently around the farmyard, and sighed.

What kind of a man drove eight hundred miles to come to a dump like this?

The Billson farm would have benefited greatly from an occasional dusting-down with a tornado. Between the anarchy of half-broken machine parts, dented barrels and holed sacks, the myriad pieces of rubber and wood that might one day come in handy, and their dilapidated seat of government, the farmhouse, there was an entire evolutionary tree of junk.

At the lower end of the scale were the basic inanimate objects – simple non-creatures such as paint pots and hubcaps that had just taken the first, hesitant step toward specialization by mutating into rag holders and chicken-feed trays. Above them came the more socially complex unbeasts – some old baler twine, a one-pronged pitchfork and a concrete post, for instance, had formed a mutually beneficial relationship by carving themselves out a niche as a washing line. From the primordial junk had risen chicken hutches whose ancestral elements had not aspired to greater things than being fork-lift palettes, fertilizer sacks, tyres and the occasional door. Whole sheds had come into being, lifting themselves up from the ground in an evolutionary leap that would surely lead one day to their attaining an upright stance. There was a lean-to, huge and undeniably leaning, and behind this, lording it over the yard like the whale does the ocean, an entire barn.

And then there was Brody Billson himself.

From the moment Macauley had set eyes on him, the very instant the man appeared in the doorway of his house and waved sluggishly, he suspected himself of being in deep trouble. He had a sense for this kind of thing nowadays. It was confirmed by the way Billson came lurching toward the car like a hack actor audition-ing for some low-budget horror movie.

The Creature From the Gene Pool.

Billson's claim to fame was that his chicken had been abducted by, as he so succinctly put it, space aliens from outer space. Billson, of course, was the kind of man whose mental universe was also peopled with space aliens from any urban conurbation with over fifty thousand inhabitants.

The reporter had met his type often enough before: a man so utterly disconnected, so looping-the-loop in his trains of thought that he was able to imagine that aliens from outer space – kitted out with the latest whiz-drive and galaxy-jump goober – had crossed the vast inter-galactic tracts in search of his chicken.

'See, there were nothin' ordinary 'bout that chicken, if you know what I mean, Mr Connor,' he breathed conspiratorially, as if Macauley would instantly understand what kind of chicken they were talking about here. 'They knew that. That's why they tuck 'er.'

'Sure, sure. I see, yes, they sure did.' Macauley nodded, taking notes. He had a policy: agree first, *always* agree first, and ask questions later. He never tried to reason with these people, knowing well that there was no means of changing their minds that did not involve pulling a trigger. 'Just so the readers get the picture, what would you say was particularly special about this chicken?'

Billson's tanned and wrinkled face, a face like a huge sun-dried raisin, broke into a smile. 'Frances liked it.'

'Sure, yes, I see,' Macauley answered, noting it down. 'Who's Frances?'

'Frances! Who're we talkin' 'bout, Mr Connor? The chicken!'

'Of course. Frances the chicken. Great, great – I've got the picture. And so ... for the readers, you know ... what exactly do you mean when you say Frances "liked it"?' Connor waited, pen poised, for the reply.

Billson stared murkily at him, his dry eyes unblinking and his leathery lips no longer cracked into a smile.

'We're both men, Mr Connor. I shouldn't need to explain nothin' 'bout that to you. I think you know what I mean.'

Macauley's heart grew cold on him. He'd heard right. He wished he hadn't, but the man's meaning was clear. He was talking about sex. With chickens. And how they were both men.

This kind of thing happened. Not too often, but once every few months at least. Macauley would be out somewhere in the middle of nowhere, checking up on a story for the *Investigator* – always the same absurd bullshit, but you had to get a photo of the talking dog or no one would believe it – and suddenly, with the same cold heart, he would realize that he had just shaken hands with one sick-fuck maniac. And always, like today, there would be no one in screaming distance for miles around. Nothing but flat prairie and softly giggling corn.

The *Investigator* had a record of where he was, but it wasn't much comfort. It would just give the police a better chance of finding his body, depending upon what kinds of farm machinery Brody Billson had at his disposal. For his disposal.

Billson, Macauley had noticed, had pigs.

Pigs will eat anything if it's properly ground up.

These situations required quick thinking. He knew he was alone with a crazy, but the vital questions were: How crazy? and Crazy how? He had to be able to judge what to say and how much to play along. In some ways dealing with crazy people was a question of manners like any other – how big a slice of Billson's fruitcake did he eat so as not to cause offence?

'I've never known a chicken who liked it myself.' He smiled. 'At least I don't think I have. How do you tell?'

Billson eyed him steadily. 'You just know. You ever been with a woman?'

'Sure.'

'Did she fake it?'

It would be unwise, Macauley sensed, to complicate matters by suggesting that he had been with more than one woman in his forty-four years on the planet.

'Yes. She faked it.'

'How did you know?'

Macauley let his voice flatten. Prairie flat.

'I could just tell. She was a lying bitch. Like all women. Except my mother. And yours.'

Billson kept him fixed up tight with his stare, nodding almost imperceptibly. Then he smiled.

'Well, chickens ain't any different!' he chuckled, slapping the reporter's shoulder in manly comradeship. It was just the two of them against a world of bitches, women and chickens alike. They were buddies.

A chicken was walking past, pecking the dirt in deep concentration. Billson reached down and grabbed it by the neck, holding it up between them. 'Say, them aliens di'n't get Rita here. She's pretty much up for it – not like Frances was, but you'll see the difference. What say we get our peckers out an' give her some pumpin', Mr Connor?'

This was now definitely getting beyond his control. He had to escape and soon.

'Sure, Brody! Hey, you don't mind me calling you Brody, do you? It just seems stupid being all formal now that we're going to be humping poultry together, don't you think?' He stuck his hand out. 'I'm Mac.'

Brody's face split into a black-toothed grin and he switched the pedalling Rita to his left hand so as to shake with his right. 'Well, hell, I guess you're right, Mac!' he hucked, rattling Macauley's arm joints with enthusiasm. 'But that don't mean you ain't still my guest, understand? I'd feel real bad if you didn't get first go on old Rita here! You just go right ahead now!'

'Why, thank you, Brody,' Macauley answered,

unzipping his pants and pulling out his wan penis.

'You want me to hold 'er, or you gon' do it yoursel'?' Brody asked, proffering the sprinting chicken.

'Oh . . . maybe you best hold her, since I don't know what kind of a kick she has, Brody.'

'She's a live one!'

'I bet she is. You got the Luvmatic?'

Billson's head jerked back in bafflement like a – well, probably not unlike a chicken being raped.

'Do I got the *what*?'

'The Luvmatic? You know, cream! Moisturizer!'

'Well, shit, no . . . I got axle grease – that do you?'

'Hey, if you've never porked a chicken with Luvmatic, you ain't ever porked a chicken, Brody! Hang on to Rita there for me – I got some in the car!'

He walked steadily, casually, his penis dangling in the afternoon sun. The car was only fifty yards away. The keys were in the ignition. It almost always started first time.

He turned and smiled as he reached the car. Brody was where he left him, Rita dangling sadly from his left hand. The farmer grinned and made an obscene chicken-fucking gesture as Macauley got into the car.

The last Macauley saw of him was as he began to disappear in the cloud of dust kicked up by the car's spinning wheels. His expression had turned from bewilderment to anger, and he began to shout and look around for something to throw at the car. Failing to find any stones nearby, he threw Rita.

*

Three hours later, safely holed up in a motel 185 miles away, Macauley Connor lay clothed but shoeless on the bed, listening to the trickle and *clunk* of the antique air-conditioning unit. Billson had put the creeps up him so

36

badly that he had covered eighty miles before he remembered his penis was still hanging out. It was the breeze as he stood by the gas pump that tipped him off, as much as the strange regard of the guy at the cash desk.

After six years of working for the *Public Investigator*, Macauley was heartily sick of witnessing society's malaise. For as much as people – himself formerly included – wanted to believe that the problem was an unfair distribution of money, education and opportunity, the truth was that the real inequality started with the distribution of genes. He'd seen enough of the real Atlantis now to believe that there could be no hope of a better world until college kids stopped talking idealistic nonsense, took the bull by the horns and started a mass programme of breeding with the hicks.

It was not an opinion that won him friends on any side of the debate, but that only encouraged his suspicion that he was right. If the problem is unpleasant, doesn't it make sense that the solution be more so? Forget politics, education and economics, and try Mother Nature's system: good old-fashioned fucking. Shuffle the gene pack and deal a new world.

What possible hope could there be for a better world so long as there were so many idiots roaming the countryside? How do you engage a meaningful debate with people more interested in tales of space alien penises and ghostly rapes, crossword prophecies and hi-fi devils?

For all that it had initially amused him to encounter the bizarre and pathetic individuals who inhabited the lowest rung of Atlantian society, from whose fetid imaginations the portion of the reports that he didn't make up himself was drawn, it began to depress him once the novelty wore off. He felt as though he had become a drain for all the crazy stories, all the insane theories, all the done-down sorrow and fucked-up frustration of their broken dreams, their house-of-mirrors minds, the mirages of their cultural desert . . .

Macauley Connor was typical of that sad generation of bright and talented people who, having lost faith in their own culture, took refuge in privately mocking it. A once-dedicated journalist, he had given up trying to discover the truth of things when he realized that the truth was almost always either too complicated or too mundane for people to bother reading about.

His breaking point had come during the time he spent covering the B. C. Simmons case. The irony of it was that he had fought hard to be given the assignment, knowing it was the kind of sensational, high-profile court case that would keep him on the front page for the duration of the trial. Only he wasn't to know that the trial would last 623 excruciating days.

How could he? The facts were simple enough, after all.

The prosecution's evidence comprised the murder weapon (a hunting knife found in Simmons' locker at his gym that bore traces of both the victims' blood, and was engraved with the monogram *B.C.S.*); plaster casts of footprints from the crime scene that precisely matched a pair of hand-made shoes owned by Simmons; the tape from Simmons' answer-phone on which he had left the message '*Hi, this is B. C. Simmons. I can't take your call right now, but please leave a message and I'll get right back to you as soon as I've taught my bitch wife a lesson that she'll never forget*'; and finally a home video of the murder, shot by a passer-by at the scene, in which B. C. Simmons could clearly be seen stabbing them to death with a hunting knife whilst screaming, '*Die, bitch, die!*'

The prosecution believed they had a strong case, and only took one afternoon to present it.

The next 622 days, however, were taken up by the record number of expert witnesses called by the defence. Particularly long and complex were the testimonies by historians specializing in the slave era, various professors of linguistics, several behavioral dieticians, and experts in fields as diverse as comparative mythology, meteorology, quantum mathematics and fashion.

In the end the jury was forced to accept the defence's argument that Simmons was no more responsible for the murders than the Pope (whose testimony was admirably clear and concise), and if anyone should be held *responsible* for the two tragic deaths it was either Cain or Abel, though which was unclear.

After that, Macauley had kind of lost the plot. It didn't help that he was going through an acrimonious divorce that dangerously exacerbated his drinking, but the crunch came when he assaulted a female politician during an interview. The whole affair was grossly misconstrued, leaving people with the impression that he had tried to rape her when in fact he had only been following his journalistic instinct that she was lying about not having had breast implants. Afterwards he could see that he had gone too far, but at the time it seemed like an important issue of trust.

His subsequent reputation was such that no respectable newspaper in the country would employ him. He found himself utterly alone and abandoned, the realization eventually dawning upon him that even though he was quite clearly an alcoholic in need of help, not one of his so-called friends cared to organize an intervention and force him into a fashionable clinic. It wasn't the 'rape' that chilled them so much as his having broken a much greater taboo – that of becoming a failure. He was unworthy even of redemption.

By the time he hit rock bottom, he was not only homeless and living in his car, he didn't even pay the parking.

Why bother when there's no address behind the unpaid tickets?

Spending the last of his money in cheap bars, Macauley

had finally reached that most pathetic stage of all – the one where a person feels compelled to tell their story. One day he was burdening a stone-faced barman with his tale when he began to shake with joyless laughter as the irony of the situation suddenly struck him: this, he realized, was real investigative journalism.

He had discovered the secret at the heart of Atlantian society.

There was no truth he could unearth – no scandal, no conspiracy, no villain – that was more significant than his first-hand knowledge of how, in this great and free country, anybody could become a non-person. The Atlantian Dream was a cover for the Atlantian Nightmare – for every nobody who struck big, ten thousand somebodies fell into the cracks in the sidewalk.

It was a moment of epiphany. Everyone finds something when they hit the bottom. Some find truth, some find God. The truth either kills you, sends you crazy or makes you stronger.

God, being omnipotent, does at least two out of three at once.

Macauley Connor got stronger. For the first time in months he felt a desire to return to journalism, only this time he was resolved to give society the news it deserved, rather than the news it needed. Digging out his portable computer from the trunk of the car in a giggling frenzy, he began to write an entirely fictional news story.

It purported to be an interview with a poor, single mother who had been offered $50,000 for her nose by a mysterious stranger. Desperate to feed and clothe her children, she had accepted the deal, her own nose being replaced by a silicone prosthetic. Imagine her shock, he wrote, when she subsequently saw a Messiah Jones video in which the billionaire pop star was sporting what was unmistakably her nose, and realized to her outrage how cheaply she had sold her proboscis. She was, he finished, currently claiming a 50 per cent share in royalties on the grounds that one cannot sing properly without a nose and she thus had 'organic artistic involvement' in the song. Jones' lawyers had offered her an out-of-court settlement entitling her to 1 per cent of the royalties – based on the nasal element of the pop star's total body mass – which so insulted her she had now decided to go public with her charges. Wrapping the piece up with a brief quote from one of Jones's many nose scouts to the effect that the pop star currently consumed new noses on a fortnightly basis due to tissue degeneration, he sent it off to the *Public Investigator* and went for a quiet drink.

One week later he was on the staff.

Six years and one chicken-fucking hick later, that inspiration had been drained from him again.

He found himself wondering if he hadn't already stayed in this motel. There had been so many, each so like the others, that he could no longer tell. For six years he had criss-crossed Atlantis on the trail of one daft story after another, and the longer he kept moving, the shorter his memory became. He had heard somewhere that there were indigenous peoples who would only travel a fixed distance in any one day because they believed they had to give their souls time to catch up. He wasn't one for New Age bullshit, but his own experience suggested that they could be on to something there.

He suspected he may have left his soul sleeping in some forgotten motel room two or three years back down the line, his body driving off at dawn with a coffee on the dash and the sting of morning cigarette smoke in its eyes. Wouldn't that be typical of his luck – no devilish pact, no trading of his eternal soul for earthly riches, youth and gorgeous babes, just a banal case of neglecting to leave a forwarding address? Maybe one day the two would meet up again in some highway diner, his spiritual self spotting his body sitting at the counter and gleefully slipping back

41

inside him, at which point he would slap the bar and shout, 'Damn, that's good coffee!'

Macauley Connor was inclined to think he'd made a real fucking mess of his life. He was forty-four years old and what did he have to show for it? One marriage to a fantastic woman with whom he had genuinely wished to grow old, lose his teeth and die – broken. One promising career in high-level journalism with a probable editorship of a newspaper somewhere in the future – ruined. One liver – wrecked. One soul – mislaid.

He didn't mind so much about the career or the liver, but he would never forgive himself for driving Rachel away. Why was it, he wondered, that men like him were only able to appreciate women in their absence? It must require some special kind of stupidity on their part, like children who have to have a toy taken away because they won't learn to stop maltreating it. How ironic that so many of them believed they needed to get in touch with their Inner Child.

Patently the blockage was with finding the Outer Adult.

At least he had the maturity to stand back, take a deep breath and acknowledge who was to blame for all his problems.

John Lockes deserved everything he got.

John Lockes may not have been more to blame for Macauley's problems than anyone else, but he symbolized what people were supposed to aspire to being, which was something approximate to the exact opposite of Macauley Connor.

Lockes was brilliant. Lockes was rich. Lockes was a self-made man. A man of progress with no sentimental attachment to the past, who had sold his vision of the future to the whole damn world. The man who had cheer-led a revolution in the way everyone lived and worked and thought and interacted. The man who had killed the past and made a fortune supplying funeral services. Tomorrow, tomorrow, always tomorrow, with no pause allowed for reflection on the state of things today, as if doubt in any form was unpatriotic. Dump the past and ditch anyone who hung around in it too long.

He was the Atlantian Nightmare masquerading as the Dream.

High Priest to the holy trinity of Faster, Cleaner and Cheaper.

But, Macauley knew, Lockes' god was a lie. His high-tech heaven would not be open to everyone, only to the new upper class he was helping to create, the tech-nocracy. Certainly it was not for the pathetically simple people that Macauley's work brought him into contact with – people so bewildered by the way things were changing, by seeing the future speed ahead of them, that their little minds sought refuge in absurd stories of alien spacecraft and global conspiracy.

Macauley understood these poor, gene-welfare cases better than almost anyone. He believed that their apparently idiotic beliefs were actually subtle self-defence strategies: because they no longer understood or felt in control of their lives, because the world was increasingly beyond their ability to comprehend, they sought an explanation that was beyond the realms of reason, and thus beyond the capacity of others to destroy.

In the end, Macauley suspected, it is more rational to believe one's life is controlled by aliens than to believe that one may be more than averagely stupid.

In a world of uncertainty, any belief that helps is rational.

Macauley's brooding was interrupted by the ringing of his mobile telephone. At first he felt too low to answer it, convinced that it would be Iago Alvarez, the *Public Investigator*'s editor, calling with some new story for him to follow up in the morning. He didn't feel like knowing how many hundred miles the morrow would add to his arse just yet. In fact, he didn't feel like going anywhere. A man has to stop running and face reality one day – just because you're going *somewhere* doesn't mean you're *going* somewhere.

The time had come to make a stand and lie on the bed of this motel room for as long as he damn well felt like it.

But then the sudden, wild hope that it might be Rachel overcame him. After a cooling-off period of three years, relations between them had gradually improved, warming back up to at least room temperature. They still hadn't seen one another, Rachel having moved to Petersburg on the coast shortly after the divorce, but they called each other once every couple of months. He suspected that it amused her to hear how sordid his existence was these days.

She, of course, had gone from strength to strength. There's always work for a good therapist on the coast, but she had some lawyer cousin out there who'd put in a good word for her with his friends. They were all lawyers too, naturally. Rachel was mining the mother-lode of self-hatred.

Macauley lunged for the telephone before the message service intercepted the call, falling half off the bed in his sudden hurry.

It wasn't Rachel, but at least it wasn't Iago either.

Instead, it was a call that would change his life. It came from a man he had never heard of before, a man with an unexpected proposition. The next morning, Macauley got in his car as usual. Only today he was excited for the first time in as long as he could recall.

After six years of going places, he was at last *going* places.

In two days, he would be in Entropolis.

III

'Don't shoot!'

It was a simple order, but in the split second that followed Washington's placing of the gun to Lockes' temple only one person had found their tongue in time to voice it. Uzi Washington turned slowly, his cesspit eyes darkening on Susan Summerday, the cause of all his troubles.

'Why the cock not?'

'Because . . . because . . . *Because!*' She threw up her hands in exasperation, suddenly unable to provide a clear rationale for something that seemed self-evident.

'Because what?' the gunman sneered, dark lips curling away from perfect-white teeth like the lid being flapped back on a piano.

'Because . . . you shouldn't kill!'

'Why not?'

'Because I say so, that's why!'

Not coming from God, the line lacked a certain authority.

Uzi Washington laughed, his hand stiffening on the butt of the gun again as Lockes sat statue-stiff in his chair, but Susan Summerday's intervention had bought others the vital seconds they needed to restart their mouths.

'Mr Washington, we do appreciate your point of view,' her husband picked up, keeping his voice unnaturally calm. 'You're clearly very angry. I respect that anger. I do.

But . . . how can you hope to get away with this?'

Washington's jaw muscles clenched, and he ground the barrel against Lockes' skin, shouting, 'Do you think I'm *stupid*? I'm not *tryin'* to get away with it! I don't care – I want his brains on the wall! How you gonna stop me?'

'Try two words, Mr Washington,' Bob Redwood intervened with the arrogant courage of the truly dim, ' "Death" and "Row".'

Washington let his eyeballs roll slowly in their sockets. His gun seemed to move with a life of its own, a third eye coming steadily round to bear on the Senator. Redwood watched wide-eyed as the barrel gazed curiously upon him for a few seconds before Washington's head deigned to turn his way. Even then, the killer seemed not to be looking at his face so much as at small spots upon it – a tiny insect crawling upon his nose or a crumb on his lip. Redwood managed to maintain his air of authority for a while, but his expression gradually collapsed under this clinical dissection until, by the time Washington began moving forward, bringing the third eye in for a closer examination, he was twitching uncontrollably. The Senator's throat began to constrict and spasm as the cold metal approached, narrowing its regard to the limited area occupied by his brain, forcing his own gaze to lift and cross with transfixed horror at the looming tunnel.

Once it was sitting dead-centre upon the by-now-gibbering Senator's forehead, Uzi Washington leaned down close to his right ear and bellowed, '*Hello-o?*'

Redwood had no answer to give. Unless one counts pee.

Washington yawped with laughter, his voice suddenly jumping several octaves as he exclaimed, 'You people are so fuckin' unreal! Death Row? Think all the brothers are real fuckin' scared of that one, huh? Well, check this – I got brothers sittin' pretty on Death Row 'cause they're gonna die *older* than their brothers on the street! That

46

ain't punishment, that's a fuckin' pension! How you gonna scare us? You ain't got no more threats! No more law! How you gonna scare a brother now?'

There was silence.

Apparently the man had a point.

'We're not your enemies, Mr Washington.'

Jefferson Smith's problem had always been not knowing when to keep his mouth shut. He tried, having discovered long ago that it seemed only to cause trouble, but his conscience was stronger than his reason. He even drank to shut himself up, dissolving his opinions in alcohol, but still they swelled up at the most inopportune moments, like teenage spots before a date. Washington cocked his head, voice dripping with sarcasm.

'Do tell.'

'No . . . nobody here *wants* a society where inequality and injustice exist, Mr Washington! We have all been active in the fight to integrate racial minorities. No one is saying that it's easy, or that there are any quick solutions, but progress *has* been made! There are Black Atlantians in government, a Black Atlantian on the Supreme Court, Black Atlantians in every profession and walk of life . . . What proof can we give you of our sincerity?'

The mountain of muscle contemplated Smith's bloated and wheezing body down his nose with the disdain of an art critic who has stumbled by accident into a sculpture evening class.

'I wanna fuck your daughter!' he announced finally. 'You got a daughter, fats? See, the only way a brother like me is going to get integration with *you* is by makin' babies!'

'As a matter of fact, Mr Washington, one of my daughters *was* married to a Black Atlantian. Satisfied?'

'*Was*, huh? Was as in was?'

'Yes. Was. But the fact that they separated is beside the point.'

47

'No *it ain't!*' Washington shouted, leaning down to grind the barrel into Smith's forehead. '*You know it ain't! Is it, greasedick? Tell me now!*'

Smith's soft cheeks stiffened, his eyes seeming to retract into his body as the surrounding fat winced.

'. . . No.'

'*Say it!*'

'No . . . it's not beside the point.'

'*Why not? Come on!*'

The liberal Smith groped for a delicate way of expressing himself. 'The inter-racial nature of the union placed certain specific strains of its own upon the long-term—'

'The inter-racial nature of the . . . *What the fuck are you talking about?* I don' know *what* that means! But I *bet* you didn't like the thought of black cock up your little girl, did you?'

Jefferson Smith seemed on the verge of tears. Why could he not learn to keep his mouth shut? Why did he always say the things that nobody wanted said? Forty years he had been in this town, and for forty years he had fought to restrain himself in the interests of getting things done, but still these unchecked thoughts haunted his tongue.

And the drink didn't help.

The trouble with Jefferson Smith was that he was a good man.

Was as in was.

'Mr Washington, I was only . . .'

The ex-waiter pressed the gun into Smith's fleshy forehead, slowly enunciating, 'You did not like the idea of black cock up your little girl, yes or no? Truth or Dare.'

Nobody breathed in the entire room. There was something in Washington's expectant leer that suggested either answer qualified as wrong. Smith saw it, and felt his throat close in terror.

The finger started to tighten upon the trigger, one

knuckle shifting under Washington's tight skin.

Suddenly Susan Summerday stood up. She was amazed at herself for doing so, her reasoning mind screaming at her to sit still and not attract attention, but something had snapped. Smith was her friend. He had been kind to her when she was new in town, and it felt as though the pathetically grateful young woman from half a lifetime ago had suddenly taken control of her body. She had no idea what she intended to do or say.

Washington's eyes twitched her way, the gun staying planted on Smith's forehead and his trigger finger still tensed.

'*I* like black cock!' she announced.

It was a desperate move, but it worked. Washington's finger relaxed and the gun moved slightly away from Smith's head, leaving a white ring in the flesh. There was an audible rush of wind as the whole table breathed in.

Washington laughed. 'Princess! Did you ever actually fuck a *nigger* or did the surgeon just fix a big black cock on your old man? Seriously – I been down so long that you rich folks can probably buy them in Accessories by now!'

A smile twitched across her mouth. 'Let everyone go and I'll show you.'

A low gasp united the table like a toast. Susan felt the glare of a hundred eyes upon her, but she didn't seem to mind. Her manner was calm, her body relaxed. Even the organic bits.

'What are you scared of?' she teased, pressing her advantage. 'Security? The doors to this room are solid oak – you'll even have time for a cigar before they manage to break the locks.'

Washington grinned, suddenly beginning to enjoy himself. 'Well, well, well . . .' he frowned, clicking his tongue against the roof of his mouth. For what seemed a minute he regarded Susan, standing confidently with one hand on her hip, and then he let his gaze travel over the rest of the guests as they sat in silent prayer. 'You're all hopin' I'm goin' to say yes here, ain't you? You're hopin' this kind white lady is goin' to save your fat asses! Go round tellin' us we in the same boat, but right now all you want is a chance to jump ship! Well, I just can't decide what to do now . . .'

He grinned viciously.

'So . . . let's see who votes I should let you go and fuck your friend here.'

The inspiration for Susan Summerday's extraordinary intervention came from a surprising source, and one that perhaps not even she was aware of at that moment. It lay in the writings of Li Pau, the great Baoist philosopher, which she had recently read.

Although written over 2,500 years ago, the teachings contained in the Bao Wa Yap have lost none of their relevance and, as Susan was demonstrating, are as useful in dealing with the problems of the world today – such as crazed men with guns seeking revenge on a society that cares less about poverty and inequality than it does about, say, dentistry – as they were in ancient times. As Li Pau taught, resistance only engenders resistance. The soft and weak can overcome the hard and strong by yielding as reeds in the wind. Thus, we can observe, Susan's Baoist path of yielding physically to the overwhelming strength of Uzi Washington's position produced results where argument and reason could not prevail.

Incidentally, the Bao Wa Yap is one of the few texts that defeats Infologix Abstractor. This is mainly due to the linguistic subtleties and ambiguities inherent in the original Sinosian, meaning that Abstractor tends to produce three alternative versions in the later stages of reduction. At 80 per cent, for instance, Abstractor renders Li Pau's work as meaning either '*All it is is all it is*', or '*It all is as it all is*', or '*All is it, it is all, all is all and is is is*.' Many Baoists find this quite a satisfactory condensation of Li Pau's wisdom.

Agreement collapses, however, on the merits of Abstractor's attempt to further refine the work by offering, at 95 per cent, either '*Shit happens*' or '*All things defecate*' or '*There's nothing like a good dump*.'

What is for sure is that the dinner guests were fortunate to have a Baoist such as Susan amongst their number that night, especially since she had only recently discovered the wisdom of the Bao Wa Yap. Prior to this she had been reading *How Big is Your Lifeboat?* by Faith Bangsputts.

'Well? I'm waitin' to see some hands here, people . . .'

The silent outrage was palpable in the seconds following Washington's ultimatum, a glowing hatred that seemed to thicken time itself. It was not just the obscenity of forcing them to vote on such an issue, it was the mockery being made of democratic procedure and all they themselves stood for.

A show of hands indeed.

Susan understood what the problem was when Washington didn't. 'I'll turn my back,' she offered. 'You all close your eyes. Mr Lockes can take the count.'

They looked imploringly at her, agonized by the horror of the situation and their guilt smouldering hotter the easier she tried to make it for them. At heart, Susan realized, they were decent people. Their innate sense of right and wrong rebelled against her sacrificing herself in this fashion, taking all the pain and danger upon herself and asking nothing in return.

Well, of course.

'Okay . . .' she announced, trying to harden her voice, 'this never happened. If ever it should turn out that it did happen, then it will be when I, and I alone, say so. Nobody breathes a word to the media. If and when it turns out to have happened, needless to say, I want the book rights, I want the film rights – *all* the rights, basically – on the understanding that names will be changed.'

She smiled as best she could and threw up her arms. It was the best she could do. She let her gaze settle on Jefferson Smith, fixing him hard and fast. Her old friend's face was white with nausea, lips mumbling something that may have been a prayer, but she just nodded softly. He understood, slowly submitting to her cool determination, and closed his eyes. One by one the others began to follow suit, and Susan turned her back.

When he announced the result, Lockes had the tact to deliver it simply as a majority in favour of her proposition, avoiding any mention of numbers. In fact it fell two votes short of unanimity, the sole dissenters being Smith – whose timid heart she had unwittingly enslaved all those years back and never let go of since, such that his drinking problem had worsened in direct correlation to her own slide into cocktail-party boredom and surgical tinkering – and her husband. Who, protective in his way, hadn't been able to resist peeping during the vote.

'Not so righteous now, people,' Washington sneered. 'Where'd your fine ideals go? You always talk morality at us like you know what it is, but you ain't got morality. You just got money. I ain't sayin' I got more morality than you – only as much as you do with a gun to *your* heads! But don't you worry none about that now – you all just go on home and keep gettin' richer, why don't you? You all just keep turnin' it all back to front and sayin' one thing don't lead to another. It don't really matter, 'cause your chickens'll be home to roost some day and we'll be square. See, maybe you think this is all gonna be over when you walk out that door, but it won't. Don't you *see*? It's closin' in on you!'

He looked them over disdainfully, almost pitying in the shake of his head. 'Why don't you walk down a street no more? Why do you have all this security around you? Can't you see you *need* valet parkin'? It ain't no luxury! But you don't wanna know, you just keep tightenin' up the laws and movin' further out of town to places where you can all make believe there's some kind of morality still around . . . but there ain't. You may be the last to know, people, but there *ain't*! You motherfuckers killed it! You sat on top of the heap for *so* long, talkin' hypocritical bullshit, that even the *good* folk down below started to figure out that you just wanted them to have morality *instead of money*! Ain't that the truth? Either you don't wanna believe this country is what you made it, or you just think everyone is so fuckin' stupid that they won't *ever* see the truth! Well, bad news, people! See, there's a point someplace where people can't *be* that stupid and still tie their shoelaces!'

He laughed bitterly, briefly, and then sucked in a deep chestful of air, his whole body lifting, and let it slowly out. 'The point is, I could have killed one of you if I wanted . . . and can any of you *tell* me why I shouldn't? Why shouldn't I do that? It ain't gonna change a damn thing! Somebody else will take the dead man's shoes, just the same. And you can fry me, but you *know* somebody will take my shoes. Just the same. So if it ain't gonna *change* anything, there can't be no right or wrong about it, can there? So what's stoppin' me doin' it?' He looked slowly up and down the table.

'Can't *anybody* think of a reason? . . .'

There was silence.

'See? Now you know what you dealin' with.'

For the first time since he started, everyone was looking at Uzi Washington less in fear than fascination. There was a part of them that was in some way jealous of the horrifying clarity with which he viewed his life, the kind of clarity that would allow him to kill without remorse.

'I can think of a reason,' John Lockes said.

Every head turned his way. Washington grinned. 'So, you goin' to share it with us?'

Lockes paused to look him in the eye, smiling back as if sharing a private joke.

'That gun's plastic.'

There actually is a man on Death Row whose crime was committed with a plastic gun. His name is Winston Loosum.

Winston Loosum didn't have the money to procure himself an honest gun for some crimes he had in mind, so he tried to hold up a gun shop belonging to one Avril Burkes using a fake Jeroboam .44. Burkes, who had a life-time's experience in firearms and being robbed, was not fooled for one instant by the imitation and calmly reached under the counter for his automatic rifle. He intended to teach the boy a lesson by shooting him dead, but at that very moment he tragically suffered his fourth and final heart attack. Unfortunately, he was holding the rifle at the time and the shock of the seizure caused his finger to depress the trigger as he thrashed and staggered about in the throes of death, killing four other clients who were in the shop at the time as well as a mother and baby who were passing by the window, but miraculously missing the stunned Loosum. Who stole the rifle just in time to get arrested.

Now Loosum was black, and his lawyer figured that with an entirely black jury he ought to have a pretty good chance of getting off, given that the forensics didn't contradict his story. But the white prosecutor argued that he just plain didn't believe *anyone* could be so stupid as to steal a rifle that had just caused the deaths of six people.

After much soul-searching, and even taking into

54

account the forensics, that black jury chose to send Winston Loosum to the chair. So maybe, in a funny way, justice is blind after all.

There was pindrop silence in the Presidential Banqueting Room of the Hotel Excelsior as John Lockes spoke. The politicians sat still, their natural outrage over the events of the last few minutes held in check by the billionaire's calmly forceful invitation for them all to sit back down and hear him out if they wished to retain his support. The wives were dissuaded from acting on their own instincts and storming out of the room by their husbands' urgent, meaningful stares.

Even Susan Summerday.

'I grew up in a little place called Farview. The richest man in town was called Hoover. Jay Hoover. Had the biggest house, and the smallest heart. Everyone hated him. He had a beautiful old apple tree in his front yard, but none of us kids were allowed to take the apples, even though all Hoover did was watch them rot. They were his apples, see. So naturally we all wanted to steal them. Only we couldn't, because although Hoover was old and feeble, others were guarding those apples on his behalf. There was Mrs Wayne across the way, and neighbours in every direction who must have had radars trained on that yard because we never got near the tree before someone caught us. Not that any of them liked the old coot any better than we did, but, you see – every damn one of them had grown up wanting to steal Jay Hoover's apples. And they never had because back then Hoover was looking after them himself. So they were damned if us kids were going to get away with it now just because he was old and half blind. I guess you could say it had become a point of morality.'

Susan sat in stunned muteness as Lockes paused, calmly feeding himself a piece of meat as he gazed

55

thoughtfully at the ceiling. It was true. The man had to be mad. First it transpires that Washington was holding a fake gun, but then, far worse, it turns out that the fake gun was being held by a fake Washington. He was actually an articulate and soft-spoken actor named Bryce Wilson, employed by Lockes for the evening to play a role in his little charade. And Lockes thought that was okay, as if his money gave him the right to humiliate them all. Which, of course, it did. But Susan wasn't standing for election, and she wasn't interested in his money. She had done what she had done to save his life, and how could he calmly sit there, masticating and talking about apples?

Anger and shame warred with one another for domination of her body. She had publicly offered to whore herself. She had been prepared to go through with it, if that was the price. And a few minutes ago she would have said that was possibly the worst thing that could befall her, but now she knew it wasn't. Far better to have done it for real than to feel as she did now, knowing she had stood up in front of all these people and said, 'I like black cock' . . . for an illusion.

Never before had she so wanted to kill someone. Only the thought that walking out would compound the injury done to her pride had persuaded her to sit back down along with the others when Lockes requested. Only her husband's imploring regard had stopped her tipping her plate over the man's head. She felt Jefferson's hand rest supportively on her arm, but it was almost as though the skin he touched had ceased to be her own. Her true self had fled deep inside, seeking somewhere to die, or at least hide safe from the eyes of other people.

'That's . . . fascinating, John,' her husband commented. She stared blankly at him, not sure if he was humouring a madman or still trying to ingratiate himself with a rich man. 'What happened?'

Lockes' gaze snapped back down to the table and he frowned. 'Sorry?'

'What happened about Mr Hoover's apples?'

'Well . . . nothing, Mr Vice-President,' he replied softly. 'Weren't you listening?'

'Ah, I *see*! He had an apple tree that no one *ever* stole apples from! I'd misunderstood. And this happened in your home town? Well, how about that? Hoover, eh?'

'Yeah. Well. He died eventually, of course.'

'*Ah!* So then what happened to the apples?'

'Mr Vice-President . . . nothing happened to the apples, okay? I thought I was clear about that. Who cared about them after he was dead? They were just apples. It's not as if he had a mango tree.'

People were looking from one to another around the table, agape with bemusement. Those unread *Public Investigator* reports were high in their minds.

'The *point*, Mr Vice-President, is that in the past a man such as Jay Hoover, and by extension all mean-hearted, wealthy people like him – and us – could rely upon those beneath to police their own kind. It may have been dressed up as morality, which made everyone feel better, but in fact it was an elaborate network of mutual spying that kept each community quiet and law-abiding. The *point* is that the system has collapsed.'

'Well, that is actually *debatable*, sir,' Redwood unexpectedly joined in. 'Hard policing has produced results. Total crime figures are actually on a downrising curve.'

Someone further down the table groaned audibly.

'And you are?' Lockes sighed. 'I wouldn't want to support financially a politician who thought me stupid.'

'Bob Redwood. But don't get me wrong, society is fried, John. I'm with you there. The question is why.'

'*Why?*' Lockes gawped. 'Surely that's the obvious part? Who in their right mind is going to find it amusing to watch Mr Hoover's *apple tree* when they can watch TV?

On the one hand you have a virtually unlimited choice of drama, scandal and action, and on the other you have some apples. This is not a hard choice to make. So nobody's spying on anyone else and all hell has broken loose. In the past people tended to notice if their neighbour was being hacked to pieces by a psychopath – now you might be screaming your head off and begging for mercy, but next door they'll be furiously zapping to find which channel you're watching.'

He popped another piece of meat in his mouth and sighed.

'At least television keeps them off the streets!' Redwood rejoined, mistakenly believing that Lockes was enjoying their debate.

'Oh, please!' Lockes sneered. 'They're doing research! They're finding out how the other half live! People could cope with being poor when the closest they came to the rich was getting soaked when we drove through a puddle; now they know what our kitchens look like better than we do! And do you know why that is the worst development of all?'

He paused, embracing the whole table with his gaze.

There was silence.

'Because it means they now know their enemy. True, the illusion of morality has totally collapsed. True, the poor aren't keeping each other in line any more. But worse, *far* worse, is the simple fact that they know their enemy. And deep down inside every one of us is scared of that. That was the point of this evening's little charade – I wanted to prove to you just how scared we have become; so scared that the idea of a complete stranger holding a gun to our heads at any time and place is now entirely within the realm of the possible; so scared that you did not for one minute doubt that your lives were in danger because you could not fault what your attacker was telling you; so scared, as the extraordinary woman sitting beside me here so bravely demonstrated, that we are already prepared to throw each other to the wolves.'

No one was eating.

'I ask you – how long have we got if we won't stand by a woman like Susan here?'

The fragile webbing of the great chandeliers sparkled brilliantly overhead, three vast bowls of crystal teardrops, and in the silence that followed it was just possible to hear the tyre-squealing, horn-blasting, siren-wailing chaos of the city below through the dark red thighs of the magnificent velvet curtains.

For all the luxury of the room and what being admitted into its wonders represented, it suddenly felt like a lonely place to be.

Lockes stared around the table without pity, without any doubt in his eyes. They were the eyes of a madman only in as much as the sane rarely think with such clarity.

'Now . . .' he asked softly, reaching into his pocket to produce a small, spherical object, 'what do you say we change the rules of the game?'

IV

A couple of days later, a man and a woman from Infologix arrived at Atlantis' toughest penitentiary bearing a hastily arranged congressional warrant. Strictly speaking, they arrived on top of it – all that was visible of the Parry Containment Facility as they parked their car being the visitors' refreshment centre, the deserted souvenir shop and the reception. There were no walls or fences, no watchtowers and no patrol dogs. There was no need. Parry was sixty feet below ground.

Parry was the latest thing in prisons. A fully automated facility requiring only a skeleton staff consisting of the warden, a small number of guards to watch the convicts on TV, plus catering and medical personnel. Except in extraordinary circumstances, they had no personal contact with the criminals, whose day-to-day life was regimented by computer. The entire facility was self-cleaning, cells and communal areas receiving a daily wash from the automatic sprinkler system. Meals arrived by conveyor belt connecting the kitchens to the dining area. Lock-up was effected by the prisoners themselves, in the knowledge that the steel-grille flooring of all communal areas was electrified after hours. The same panels could be electrified on an individual, chessboard-square basis in the event of a breakdown in discipline. There were no keys to any doors, everything being operated by remote command from the prison's central hub, and every inch of the complex was under video surveillance.

The impressive construction costs aside, Parry was theoretically much cheaper to run than traditional jails. However, unforeseen technical problems had meant that it had overshot its budget by around 250 per cent in every one of the four years since it opened. Teething problems, the experts called them – little hiccups like doors that seemed to open of their own accord or not at all, toilets that began their sterilization procedure while inmates were still inside, and rogue floor panels that remained permanently electrified.

Soon, the experts insisted, it would be working like it was meant to and all these stories of convicts being crushed to death by malfunctioning doors would be a thing of the past. The running costs would come down, and Parry-style containment facilities would become the cheapest way of dealing with your society's failures. Parry would one day be the template for a whole new export industry, they promised.

Frankly, as the government knew, it was a disaster. At the present rate, Parry would never be as economical as an old-fashioned penitentiary with armed guards and big old keyrings. But it didn't matter, and nobody openly criticized the facility's constant malfunctions or spiralling maintenance costs because they were all in agreement on the principle of the thing: Parry was pretty cool.

Nobody else had an automatic prison, anywhere.

Plus the public loved it. Having been hyped as the prison that would house *la crasse de la crasse* of the criminal fraternity, it had immediately entered popular mythology. Every movie criminal in recent years had been described as having done time in Parry to establish that he was really a seriously bad man. Parry convicts, in theory, were the ones that ordinary, old-fashioned prisons could not hold because they were either too violent, too ingenious or too influential.

61

It was true that other prisons could not hold the convicts sent to Parry. They were short of space.

So, myth though it may have been, Parry was the place that anyone looking for the very best the nation had to offer in the line of, say, armed robbery would think of first. Which is precisely what had brought the two young executives from Infologix here.

*

Chief Warden Sam Pelle finished looking through the congressional warrant the pair had presented him with and dropped it to the table, leaning back in his leather swivel chair.

'If I understand this correctly, I'm supposed to release four of the convicts we have here into your custody?'

The young man in the grey suit, apparently the senior of the two, nodded cheerfully. Adam Delapod, to Chief Pelle's intense irritation, had not stopped smiling since he arrived. 'The worse the better,' he confirmed.

Pelle's mouth twitched with the first stirrings of a sarcastic smile. Heel, boy, he thought.

'The worse the better . . .' he softly repeated. 'Well, we certainly have that in stock. Would sir be looking for something in a straight psychopath, or just a dumb, violent scumbag?'

'We need people with real experience in armed robbery,' the man's colleague, Lauren Patakio, explained calmly.

'Armed robbery? Oh, I think you'll find our range to be without equal, madam.'

Pelle looked wearily from one to the other, growling, 'Can I ask what the hell this is about?'

'I'm afraid we are not at liberty to reveal that, sir,' Delapod smiled.

'Why am I not surprised? Forgive me for saying this, but you folks don't look like you have a whole lot of experience dealing with sociopaths. Do you have any idea what you are taking on here?' He waved the congressional warrant despondently. 'I don't seem to have a choice, so you'll get what you want, but I'm just curious – you do appreciate that there is a big difference between someone who commits armed robbery and your average person with a negative attitude?'

Pelle did not like the two young executives. He had met them just five minutes before, but they were only too familiar to him as types from his four years as head of Parry – eager, confident young computer fucks. Ever since he had accepted this job his life had been plagued by these people. The kind of people who said there were no problems, only solutions. The kind who insisted on calling a disaster a challenge. It was no good talking normally to them, it was no good shouting, 'Your auto-fucking-matic toilets are flushing *backwards*! What are you going to do about it?' because they only smiled and replied that the toilets were a particularly exciting challenge in their lives right now. They were people who seemed to have been brainwashed into believing that a positive attitude was the answer to everything. They did not understand that shouting and cursing was sometimes the correct response to a situation.

'Yes, sir, we do appreciate that!' Delapod grinned enthusiastically.

'These are not *virtual* criminals, you know,' Pelle continued. 'They bite.'

'That's why we came to Parry, sir – we want the real thing!'

Pelle looked at their scrubbed faces with undisguised distaste. Shrugging, he swivelled his chair around to reach behind him for a huge concertina-file of jumbled papers, grunting as he lifted it up with both hands and dropped it on the table with a loud thud.

'Here's the menu, people. Take your pick – every single convict in Parry is in there.'

The two executives looked up at him in surprise.

'Haven't you got them cross-referenced by category?' Delapod gasped.

'Sure we do. On the computer system.' Pelle grinned. 'It's down.'

*

It took the two Infologix executives two days to work their way through the files, making an initial selection of possible candidates, then gradually narrowing it down and down until they settled on a final choice. Right from that first run-through, however, Lauren Patakio found one name sticking in her head: Lincoln Abrams.

The man responsible for his arrest, a certain Agent Winston Pepsi, had described him as having a pathological hatred of all forms of authority, but also as being exceptionally intelligent and endowed with a highly developed sense of right and wrong. He was right and others were wrong. She had greatly enjoyed a psychiatric report in which it was suggested that Abrams had never, from the earliest age, accepted the daily theft of his bodily wastes by the toilet. Basically, the writer seemed to be suggesting that, thirty years on, Abrams was robbing banks as a way of symbolically reclaiming all his stolen poo. Kind of gave her the feeling he had issues of his own to deal with.

She was not sure why her mind kept returning to Abrams, because he hardly fitted the profile she had of the ideal candidate. Whatever the reasons for Abrams' behaviour – he seemed to be one of those rare criminals who had made a conscious career decision to work outside the law – the fact was they were looking for a volunteer and he was not the type. Abrams wouldn't volunteer to win the lottery, let alone take part in this kind of project.

It was a shame, because they needed someone with his level of intelligence if the tests were to be valid. They needed the best, and Abrams, with a string of clever, original robberies to his name for which he only ever came under suspicion when he suddenly settled his child-support arrears, was ideal. Regretfully, however, she ruled him out and carried on searching through the dossiers.

Delapod and she ended up with a shortlist of twenty candidates. On the whole they had been disappointed by the quality of the choice Parry had on offer. The vast majority were simply stupid, brutal thugs who had ended up criminals for exactly the same reason other people end up as lawyers – earning a respectable living had simply never occurred to them.

They whittled it down to a dozen possibilities, after which point there really seemed nothing to choose between them. Delapod and she were on the point of picking one at random when suddenly she realized why Abrams had refused to leave the back of her mind. She dug his dossier back out and handed it to her colleague.

'He sounds great,' Delapod announced after due analysis, 'but he won't accept. Not in a million years. He would die first.'

'Perhaps, but let's just give him a shot,' Patakio urged. 'I have a suspicion that the very reason why we think he won't volunteer is why he just might.'

*

The parole-board hearings took place in one of Parry's more pleasant rooms. Being only five metres below ground, it had a slim light-shaft running down from the surface, bringing news of changing seasons through the occasional genuine smell. To men who had lived in an artificially lit environment for months or even years on end, a world that smelled of bleach, coming before the parole board was like a trip out in the country.

Lincoln Abrams did not know who the two young suits

were on the other side of the glass wall that divided the room, or why he had been summoned here. His sense of time may have become warped by living in the sub-terranean world of Parry, but not to the extent that finding himself in this room would suggest. He was not eligible for parole for another eight years.

He figured they must want something from him. They could be Bureau agents looking for information on an old associate, perhaps. They didn't look like the active service type, but they could be office cops. Maybe that son of a bitch Pepsi had sent them, knowing Abrams would never talk to him in person. But if they were hoping to cut a deal of some sort, he reflected, they obviously didn't appreciate who they were dealing with.

Abrams, contrary to society's opinion of him, considered himself to be a moralist. He was his own ideal of the honest man. To understand this, one would have had to see the world through his eyes – to see his father working himself to death in a factory that was closed and relocated to the Far East before he finished making the payments on their home; to see his mother sacrifice her beauty, laughter and eventually sanity for a lousily paid cleaner's job; to see his older brother, the proud soldier, get killed in the war that made that Far Eastern country safe, not for democracy, but for business.

He saw nothing honest in these things. No honour in letting others take your life and squander it. His idea of immorality was to sell your precious gift of life for a paltry salary and pension scheme, living for two days out of every seven. He held freedom too dear to settle for weekend access, as if life were the result of an acrimonious divorce between the stomach and the heart.

Abrams had chosen to break the rules because the rules were a lie. He knew that those at the top did not abide by them – they paid no taxes, feared no laws, and even death, who showed no indulgence with the poor, was prepared to negotiate with the rich. So he had never regretted his choice, not even when thirty men in bullet-proof vests had dragged him from bed one morning. In Parry, at least he still had integrity.

He regarded the Infologix executives through the two-inch-thick glass with a calm, arrogant stare. They had not yet said a word, and he was in no hurry to be somewhere.

'How are you enjoying your stay?' Delapod finally asked, smiling the smile.

'Just fine,' he answered flatly. 'You know, it costs you more to keep me here than you would ever pay me to work for you, so I figure you're in no position to smirk at me like that. Switch it off. You look like a cheeseburger being trod on.'

Delapod laughed. 'We're not the government, Mr Abrams.'

'Depends on where you think government ends and freedom begins, doesn't it? What you are or are not in *my* terms is not for you to say, mister.'

Delapod was more convinced than ever that they were wasting their time with this character. He was a sheer wall of obstinacy. But now that they were here they might as well go through with it.

'What would you say to a chance to get out of here?'

'I'd say, "How much?"'

'How much what?'

'Everything has its price.'

'We'll come to that in a minute, if you're prepared to listen.'

'You've already had a minute. I'm listening. Obviously you want me to do something; now tell me what.'

'We don't want you to do anything you don't like doing, Mr Abrams, believe me.'

'Somehow I doubt that. I like robbing banks.'

'Well now, that's where you're wrong, isn't it?' Delapod

smiled. 'Rob banks is exactly what we want you to do.'

For once in his life, Abrams was at a loss for words. Not that he was any less suspicious of this man and his silent female colleague – on the contrary, he was exponentially more suspicious of them after such a revelation – but he was no longer in control of the situation. He had no idea what this could be about.

'We can be flexible . . .' Delapod continued, beginning to enjoy himself. 'You can rob an armoured truck, for instance, or a supermarket. We don't really mind what it is, just so long as you get away with it. That's your end of the deal. In return, if you get away with it for at least one whole week, your criminal record will be erased and you will be a free man.'

Abrams, whose mind had yet to get back on its feet after having the rug pulled from under it, had settled on an alternative, emergency code of conduct to cope with the situation. He resolved to remain silent, thus forcing the other man to do all the talking.

Delapod paused, having expected some form of response, but Abrams kept his expression inscrutably blank. Not even his eyes moved.

'You will be allowed to pick a team of three people to partner you,' the executive continued, his smile diminishing. 'Like yourself, they must be presently residing in a penitentiary, be volunteers, and the same terms apply.'

He glanced briefly at Patakio, raising an eyebrow, and waited vainly for some form of communication from Abrams.

'We are testing a new crime-prevention system,' he admitted finally, unsettled by the silence. 'It is an advanced form of tag, capable of precisely locating the bearer to the nearest square yard. At any moment, you will thus be registered on a three-dimensional, virtual map of the city. The computer tracking you will automatically alert the police should you approach a location with obvious crime potential, and an emergency alarm will be triggered by any attempt to tamper with the tag, bringing law-enforcement officers to your location before you could ever hope to remove it. So the challenge before you is simple: you get one month to find a way of defeating the system. Commit a felony during that month, avoid arrest for one week, and freedom is the reward.'

Abrams remained still, his eyes narrowing a fraction of an inch.

Still no response.

Delapod reached into his attaché case and produced a thick manual. 'These are the technical specifications of the device. You will be given a copy of this manual on your release from Parry, to help you locate the fault in the system, should one exist. What do you say?'

Abrams allowed himself a small frown, but his mouth stayed firmly closed. He had been watching Delapod's eyes closely all along, and noticed he had looked very slightly to the left when he asked that last question. It was subtle, but telling. There was something more, he was sure of it.

The two men regarded each other in silence. Having already given away more than he had planned without any form of response from his candidate, Delapod was determined to sit it out before revealing the final detail of the deal.

The clock milled the seconds into a minute.

Lauren Patakio had chosen to remain silent until now. She had wanted to be able to observe Abrams' reactions, to see if her intuition about the man was correct. This dumb-act of his had been more revealing than he imagined.

'You know what I think, Mr Abrams?' she asked, finally rising from her seat and approaching the glass. 'I think you're about to tell us where we can stick our offer. It's a question of saving face, isn't it? If you don't accept

69

the challenge, you haven't lost. Accept it, and you might win if you're smarter than us, but you might just lose . . . and you can't bear to lose, can you?'

She smiled as his eyelid twitched involuntarily.

'You're right. Take the safe option, Mr Abrams, because my colleague here hasn't told you everything about the device in question. You've guessed that, haven't you? That's why you're so low on conversation all of a sudden – scared you might just be tricked into taking it up the proverbial butt . . .'

Patakio fished something from her coat pocket, holding her fist closed as her hand reappeared. She moved forward against the glass, unfurling her clasp to reveal a spherical object about half the size of a golf ball.

Abrams could not resist leaning toward the glass for a closer look.

'That's it?' he whispered.

'This is it, Mr Abrams. I imagine it would be very humiliating for a man like you to be defeated by such a little thing, wouldn't it? Especially since you would be *literally* taking it up the butt . . .'

His eyes snapped up her way.

'Told you you wouldn't accept, Mr Abrams,' she laughed. 'The state surgically implanting this device in your anal tract? You'd never, *ever* recover your self-esteem after a defeat like that, would you now?'

Abrams realized he was being manipulated by this woman, but it made no difference. She wasn't saying it, but she was right: if he did what he was inclined to do and refused the deal, he'd always know that he'd been afraid of being beaten. Morally speaking, the system would have won.

'Fuck you,' he snarled. 'And I will tell you where you can stick your offer . . . under the circumstances.'

'So we have a deal?' Patakio grinned.

'You can call it that if you want. I'll call it a battle.'

V

Someone once said, 'If you are tired of Entropolis, you are tired of life. So kill yourself.'

It was a tough, rude and neurotic city. Macauley Connor had avoided it for the last six years. He was not an Entropolitan by birth, and although he had managed to bristle and snarl with the best of them when he worked here, he had been more than glad to see the back of it.

Actually, as he had discovered, Entropolis was not so bad as the city's PR would have you believe. It's true that in its heyday it was the murder capital of Atlantis, but in recent years a combination of tough policing and un- usually wet summers had kept the lid on the situation. Entropolitans didn't like to admit it, because merely unpleasant cities are ten a penny whereas living in dystopia has a kind of apocalyptic chic, but even so these days you hardly ever saw the old bumper stickers proudly proclaiming SEE ENTROPOLIS AND DIE, SUCKER.

The offices of Janus Publishing, for instance, were situated on a quiet, tree-lined street with tall brownstone apartment buildings in which people were very rarely raped and murdered and discovered two weeks later as putrefying corpses by the concierge. Janus was a small, old-fashioned operation with a tastefully shabby re- ception in which Macauley felt instantly at home – he liked the worn leather armchairs and out-of-date maga- zines, the faded beauty of the middle-aged receptionist

71

and the fissured china of the coffee cup she brought him. He could tell at a glance that Janus was the kind of publishing house that wasn't supposed to exist any more now that they had all been scoffed by hungry media conglomerates: the kind that was mainly concerned with books.

The little research he'd done into the company since receiving the phone call revealed that it published quality works – history, biography, poetry and the occasional novel – which never shifted large numbers but apparently reached a small niche market of people with active brains. Twenty years ago it would have been considered normal – just a publisher publishing books like everyone else – but these days Janus was the literary equivalent of organic farming.

'Macauley Connor?' came a voice beside him.

He looked up.

'I'm Joel Schonk. We spoke on the phone.'

The director of Janus was not at all how Macauley had imagined him, judging by the offices. He was quite young – around the same age as Macauley himself – and had a bright-eyed, cheerful face. He had been expecting some withered sexagenarian in tweeds, pipe in jacket pocket, rather than the elegant, handsome man now facing him.

Macauley followed him into his cosily anarchic office. The wall-to-wall bookcases were full, books spilling over the floor, up on to chairs and across his desk, proofs and manuscripts slugging it out for space in a riot of reason. A coffee percolator was slurping noisily to itself in the corner, the caffeine-stained jug bearing witness to a thousand slow evaporations. Schonk hurriedly cleared some space on a chair, dumping galley proofs on the carpet, and got straight down to business as he poured them both a mug of brain lubricant, as he called it.

'Now, I believe I got as far as telling you that I want to publish a biography of John Lockes of Infologix. I take it you would be happy with the advance we mentioned?'

'Quite happy,' Macauley fibbed, his true feelings for the sum in question actually verging on infatuation.

'The question is, are you the man for the job, Mr Connor?' asked Schonk, turning round with a mug of coffee in either hand. 'I ran a media archive search to find the person who had written the most pieces on John Lockes in the past five years. Your name came up. Way ahead.'

Macauley smiled modestly.

'Then I took a look at the pieces . . .'

Macauley stopped smiling.

'Well . . . you have to bear in mind the public they were written for,' he defended himself, shifting uncomfortably in his chair. 'If you saw some of my other work—'

'I have,' Schonk interrupted. 'That's the only reason we're talking. I thought it strange that a man could go from serious journalist to . . . how shall I put it?'

'Hack?'

'I was thinking more . . . bullshit artist. It seems you got into some trouble a few years ago.'

'It was a misunderstanding. It's not what you've heard.'

'Oh no? What have I heard that was incorrect?'

'I was convinced she was lying, I was out of control, it looked like assault.'

Schonk smiled, nodding softly as if some private theory had just been confirmed. 'But she was lying?'

'It doesn't matter either way. I was in the wrong. But I know that come Judgement Day those breasts still won't need underwiring.'

Schonk chuckled as he sat down in the brown leather chair across the chaotic desk. He cupped his coffee in both hands and swivelled gently from side to side.

'How much do you actually know about Lockes?'

Macauley had been afraid this was coming from the

moment Schonk had questioned whether or not he was the man for the job. The fact was that he knew next to nothing about him. Certainly no more than the average person could pick up from magazine articles. His whole career of Lockes-baiting had been based purely on his mental image of the man. He wished he'd thought to research Lockes a little before coming to this meeting, but Schonk had pretty much given him the impression that the book was a done deal. Maybe that was before he read the clippings. Macauley felt the briefly proffered advance slipping from his grasp, and with it his dreams of escaping the endless parade of lunatics his work with the *Investigator* exposed him to, but there was nothing to be done about it.

He didn't even know enough to risk lying.

'I know what I think of him,' he sighed in defeat. 'But more than that . . . nothing.'

'Oh,' Schonk responded. 'Well . . . so what do you think of him?'

'That he's the devil's latest trick. He's defining progress, not as where we are going, but how fast we're going there. And everyone thinks he's a hero because he came from nothing, but they've yet to realize that all he is offering the majority of them as a future is still nothing.'

'Is that why you write these absurd lies about him?'

'I write stories in which Lockes is not an ideal, but an aberration, a creature as far removed from the readers as possible,' Macauley corrected, making it up on the spur of the moment. 'Is that a lie?'

'Biography is a field we take very seriously at Janus. Without claiming the credit for myself, I think I could safely say that we have published several works that will remain the definitive word on their subject. We pride ourselves on producing thorough, impeccably researched and perceptive books – works that will stand the test of time. Serious books.'

Macauley Connor shrugged, putting his coffee down on the table, and began to get up.

Schonk motioned for him to stay seated. 'But that's not what I would be wanting from you.' He stared slyly. There was a glimmer of something dangerous in his eyes. A wildness that had not been there a second ago.

'You wouldn't?' Macauley breathed.

'Absolutely not, Macauley. You don't mind me calling you that, do you? What I'm after, and this is why you appear to be the man for the job, is a sordid, tawdry, below-the-belt defamation of John Lockes' good name.'

Macauley sat up in surprise, unsure quite how to respond to such a compliment.

'Sorry,' Schonk smiled, handing him his coffee, 'that sounds rather derogatory, doesn't it? I don't mean to say that it doesn't *also* have to be thorough and impeccably researched! But let's be clear – I'm not doing this to increase his fan club.'

'May I ask why you *are* doing it?'

Schonk slumped back in his chair, his grimace suggesting Macauley had hit on a topic that was in some way painful. He winced as though wringing words from the pit of his stomach.

'*Ugh!*' he grunted. 'Why? Fair enough, fair enough. John Lockes . . . you're right, he may indeed be the devil incarnate. We live in the last days of the free spirit. The human brain is atrophying, inexorably being strangled of the oxygen of thought by devices that think for us. I believe that doubt is freedom. Uncertainty is the central condition of liberty. Fear, terror, dread of the unknown, these are the gifts of our geniuses, there to remind us that we are not just machines made of flesh and bone, but brief flames in the wind that must pass our spark while we can. Yet today all the delicately balanced doubts and questions our greatest mental architects have bequeathed us are being bulldozed and flattened, replaced by a key-pendant culture of pocket-sized digests by the likes of John Lockes.'

He searched on his desk for a slim paperback volume that he held up before Macauley's eyes: *The Lives of Ten Great Thinkers*.

'Do you know what this is?' he seethed. 'This is what passes for élitist reading today. This is what the person who *resists* is reading. The best of the rest are snacking on a Sunday-supplement diet of articles about *people* who write, *people* who read, *people* who think ... We are living in the theme park of our own history, taking rides on the high points of a cultural hit parade. And most of us are too anaesthetized to realize that *this* is why the real world of jobs and companies and currencies is becoming more and more like a fruit machine – a thousand employees axed over a share dividend, companies broken up to be sold as spare parts – because the ability to stand back from today has been lost. Our major purpose now in society is simply to have desires, to consume and so provide fuel for the new machine. Independent thought is not *useful*, because it leads to a splintered marketplace. Forces on every side are encouraging us to lose our memories, to live only in the present moment with today's news, today's fashion, today's celebrity and today's episode. History has become anniversaries – so-and-so died twenty years ago today, it is the fiftieth anniversary of such-and-such. More news, today's news. Politicians strive to say less, do less and lead less because the law of the lowest common denominator dictates everything, and the less one thinks and does, the closer one gets to becoming the ultimate brand that will be acceptable to everyone.'

'Is that Lockes' fault?' Macauley asked, surprised to find himself defending the founder of Infologix.

'Every religion requires a messiah. Lockes is that man – he has brought news of the new world, where

76

computers will contain the knowledge and we just press the buttons. He is rendering the human brain, the very organ that made civilization possible, obsolete. Logically, this path ends when we completely reverse the old order. The future, Macauley, is Mickey Mouse government and Big Brother entertainment . . .'

Macauley sighed with exhaustion. Schonk was worse than he was by far – not that he disagreed with what he was saying, but Macauley preferred not to think about such things before lunchtime. What kind of life did Schonk have if he was worrying about it by ten in the morning? How did he sleep?

'One biography of John Lockes, however vicious, won't change that.'

'What can I say?' Schonk laughed. 'I believe in books. I believe in the power of the written word. I have no choice, because if I give up my faith in books then I have been defeated. So I'm going to fight back the only way I know how, but I am not so naïve that I won't fight them with their own weapons – that's why the book must be scandalous. It has to engage the very hype machine that they have put in place of what used to be – forgive me – journalism.'

'Maybe Lockes has no dark secrets.'

'Everyone has secrets, Macauley, but half the art is in *making* them scandalous. Are you on board – advance paid up front, of course?'

He held up a cheque, already made out in Macauley's name and signed, and a contract. Macauley waited for what seemed like a decent interval – two, maybe three seconds.

'Can I use your phone?' he asked.

He knew the number by heart. The all-too-familiar voice of Iago Alvarez, editor of the *Public Investigator*, came on the line.

'Iago, Mac here. Bad news, I'm afraid.'

77

'You're already late filing your stories, Connor. That's the only bad news I care about.'

'Well, there's worse. I've been abducted by aliens.'

'What the hell are you talking about, Mac?'

'Figure it out, chum. Bye.'

He put the phone down with a smile, reached across to take the contract and took a pen from his jacket pocket.

'What if I *don't* come up with anything, though?' he asked, nib poised above the dotted line.

Schonk spread his arms messiah-wide.

'Seek and ye shall find, Macauley Connor . . . seek and ye *shall* find.'

VI

Lauren Patakio and Adam Delapod had been watching their volunteers' movements on computer for three weeks now, and were starting to think that they might have overestimated Abrams. As he and his three chosen partners moved about the virtual Entropolis contained on their screens, it was becoming increasingly clear that they were just using their month's freedom to have a good time. They'd gone their separate ways, returning home to wives and girlfriends, only occasionally meeting up in bars or round at Abrams' place. Their routines consisted of mundane trips to the movies, the supermarket, the swimming pool – nothing even remotely approaching a felony. Abrams, whose initial decision to stay at home might at least have suggested he was studying the Rectag manual, seemed to have given up. Lately he'd been spending time in sex shops.

Patakio pushed her chair back from the console and wandered over to get herself some coffee. Frankly, the project was turning out to be an anticlimax – it worked too well. She'd at least been hoping to see the system's capabilities stretched to their limits, but as it was there was little for her to do but sit and watch like some kind of virtual voyeur.

The signal being picked up by the computer told them a remarkable amount of detail about their subjects' private lives. The Rectag, the invention John Lockes had introduced to his gathering of the great and powerful that night at the Excelsior, was designed to operate in the anal tract for a specific reason: it could pick up an electro-chemical signature, the unique scent at the end of each individual's digestive system. They knew, for instance, that two of their four volunteers had taken drugs since their release from Parry. All but Abrams had got drunk on several occasions. Should they desire, they could even get the computer to analyse the signature and tell them what the wearers had eaten in the last twenty-four hours. The computer could accept tailor-made guidelines for each individual – some might have designated no-go areas, others might have curfews imposed on them. Any breach of the rules would be automatically revealed by the signal emanating from their behind. It was an extra-ordinary piece of equipment.

Rumour had it Lockes got the idea from dogs.

According to the version Patakio had heard, their boss had got to thinking that mankind had taken a disastrous evolutionary wrong turn when it stopped using the rectal snort as a method of social interaction. She supposed there was something in that – many problems of modern-day life might have been avoided had people not broken from their mammalian relatives on this point of etiquette.

For many thousands of years, while civilization was principally rural, this did not come to light: a lattice of social connections existed whereby each person knew *something* about almost every person they were ever likely to meet. As people became urbanized, however, the downside of rejecting the rectal greeting all those millennia ago became clear. Now more than ever, people needed a quick and simple method of making contact with each other. Would the city be home to so many lonely, single folk if men and women passing in the street stopped and took a brief moment to sniff each other's behinds?

She had trouble picturing it, of course, but logic dictated that, had human behaviour evolved in even a slightly different way, she would have had similar trouble picturing a society in which people intentionally breathed in the smoke of burning tobacco leaves.

The way Patakio imagined it, just as each person smiles in their own way, so would no two people place their nose to a butt in identical fashion. Between those who perfunctorily brushed their faces in the general direction of another's *derrière* and those who took long, thoughtful draws with their nose pressed right smack in the crack, there would be an infinite variety of styles. Some would seduce by the gracefully choreographic movement they made in leaning down, whilst others would be painfully malcoordinated, forever bumping their noses against belts and handbags. Sniffees, too, would reveal much of themselves in the process – some reacting calmly to feeling a gentle prod at their behind as they walked down the street, others making little clenched-butt hops. In so many ways, therefore, the streets would be animated places of exchange rather than the canyons of studied indifference they had become.

And after that first encounter – more informal and revealing than a handshake, yet not so intimate as a kiss – any conversation would surely begin on a deeper level, talking not of the weather but of one's day, of one's hopes and frustrations, of one's life, of love and, frequently, of dinner last night. Ideally, when the approach and the response was just right, one would talk of love at first snort.

Sadly, none of this would ever come to be, because man's evolutionary path had been chosen and there was no going back, but Patakio reflected that it would be nice to think of Infologix Rectag as a kind of hi-tech return to those simpler days.

She set her coffee down on the table and slumped back

into her chair, checking her watch to see how long it would be before Delapod came to replace her. Another two hours, she sighed internally, taking a sip of coffee as she gazed glassily at the screens.

When she screamed it was because of the coffee landing in her lap, but the fact that all four signals had disappeared wasn't exactly good news either.

*

'Fucking. No. Way,' was Dean Lewis' response when Lincoln Abrams explained his plan.

It had not taken Abrams long to find a way of beating Infologix Rectag – he actually hit upon the answer when he was only half-way through analysing the technical specifications he had been given. The device itself was faultless and the capabilities of the computer to which it transmitted were frankly awesome, but break the link between the two and the whole system was useless.

There was, he realized, a very simple way of doing this.

But he had then spent two weeks searching in vain for an alternative.

'No, man,' gasped Bob Crosby. 'Not possible. It can't be done.'

'It *can* be done!' Abrams insisted. 'I know people who've done it. Not for as long as we'll have to, of course, but the beginning has got to be the hardest part.'

'You *know* them?' Stan Hardy repeated.

'Not like you're probably thinking, but yes.'

There was an impressed pause.

All three were gazing at the four gargantuan, highly detailed devices Abrams had placed on the table before them.

'Anyone we know?' asked Dean Lewis.

These days you weren't supposed to talk about vibrators.

They were 'animated genital sculptures'. The four examples Abrams placed before his colleagues were precise replicas of the penis belonging to Fred Hammers, star of many classic genital dramas. There was a time, of course, when genital drama was thought of as 'pornography' and considered beneath the attention of serious critics, even though, in terms of volume output and financial return, it dwarfed all other forms of cinema. The turning-point was Pierre Foutiste's ground-breaking book *The Significant Udder*, in which he made the essential jump from analysis of 'pornography' in terms of traditional cinematic qualities to analysis of genital drama, where the dialogical tension of individual body parts, both on their own and in conflict with one another, revealed itself to contain dynamics of Shakespearean proportions. The essay '*King Lear* in *The Palace of Pervert Princesses*', in particular, shattered established opinion in its brilliant analysis of the crucial one penis/three vagina motif that so clearly dominates the work.

The new critical approach largely bypassed the general public, who remained mired in the classical paradigm of viewing drama as the domain of entire human beings. So there was widespread shock and outrage when Cornard University appointed Ginger Lovejuice, whose body parts had starred in over three hundred genital dramas, Vagina in Residence on their film studies course. The furore did at least have the positive effect of encouraging the public to re-examine the art in question, especially the five core works of the Lovejuice canon: *Night of the Slut, Butt Slut, A Slut Comes Back for More, Sins of the Vatican Nun Slut* and, of course, *I, Slut*.

These epic works, in which Ginger Lovejuice's vagina was principally partnered by a penis belonging to her real-life husband, Fred Hammer, commonly draw comparison with *Hamlet*, in that each of the many long and extraordinary soliloquies delivered by the penis is actually an attempt to penetrate deeper into the same core question, which might best be paraphrased as 'To be or to have been?' It is this tortured knowledge on the part of the penis – that resolution will, inevitably, involve its own demise – that drives the thematic unity of the whole canon. Although the theoretical stars of these films were Ginger Lovejuice's vagina, anus, mouth and breasts, the performance turned in by Fred Hammer's penis was outstanding. Here, at last, was a penis that could express the whole gamut of emotions – one moment gentle, the next raging like a pneumatic drill digging up tarmac. At turns pensive, seemingly vulnerable in its approach, and then raging like a pneumatic drill digging up tarmac again. It was a big, generous performance – certainly helped by the penis's domineering physique, but every inch of those one and half feet throbbed with the control of a true genius.

Fred Hammer, sadly, met an untimely death on the set of the unfinished avant-garde film *Are Rhinos Sluts?*, but the fame of his penis has never been greater, immortalized both on film and in a range of life-size animated sculptures such as the four purchased by Lincoln Abrams, who had correctly surmised that a suitably large and vibrating object placed next to the Rectag would block the transmission of a person's electrochemical signature.

*

One hour after the four signals had simultaneously disappeared from Patakio's screens, a downtown branch of the First National Credit was held up. The four robbers entered the bank slowly, marching with a stiff-legged, funereal step. As three cocked their guns, the fourth produced a loud-hailer from his bag and announced in an amplified whisper:

'*Every . . . body . . . get . . . down . . .*'

Sweat could be seen seeping through the nylon stocking on his head, and his breathing was tense in the loud-hailer's mouth. He had all the signs of a man on the edge. The handful of customers and staff obeyed immediately.

The man advanced with small, almost tentative steps toward the cashier's desk, like someone walking on ice, emitting strange '*Mmugh*' noises with each painful stride. His three partners were silent, but their bodies seemed to twitch and quiver so uncontrollably that they struggled to keep their guns trained on their terrified victims. The whole gang was unbelievably tense, it appeared, and hence all the more dangerous.

'*Mmugh . . . money*,' their leader grunted as he reached the desk, dropping a nylon carry-all on the cashier's prostrate body. '*Gah! . . . money . . . in . . . bag . . .*'

He spoke as though determined to use the minimum of breath, teaspooning words from the very top of his palate. She scrambled to her feet, little doubting that her assailant would not hesitate to shoot if she tarried a second too long, and began throwing fistfuls of notes into the carry-all. He clutched the edge of the counter with one hand as he waited, knuckles glowing white, and breathed through clenched teeth. '*Enough . . . bwoah! . . . money*,' he hissed when she had only emptied one till, sticking out his arm robotically for her to hand him the bag.

She obeyed unquestioningly and dropped back to the floor without even waiting for his command.

'*Stay . . . duhn! . . . down*,' he ordered finally, taking a step back from the counter.

The gang retreated as slowly as they had arrived, backing toward the door in a bizarre finale of *mig*s and *pah*s and *hoo-cha-cha*s until they closed the door behind them and escaped in their waiting car.

One week to the minute after they had vanished from the screen, the four signals reappeared. Brief blips had appeared on the monitoring screens over the days as batteries were replaced and dumps taken, but they were always isolated and in different locations. By the time anyone arrived on the scene, both the signal and the convict in question had disappeared without trace. This time however, all four signals were registered and they stayed on screen.

The teams who were sent dashing to the locations indicated found men who were shadows of their former selves. The cost of beating Rectag had come high, even for a person as determined as Lincoln Abrams. After a lengthy convalescence, they left hospital free men, but none would ever again know the simple pleasure of going to the toilet when and where they wished.

Their ordeals were over, but they could find no closure.

The gang went their separate ways shortly after their release, meeting again only once, and that some years later on the sad occasion of Dean Lewis' funeral. Lewis, who had separated from his wife not long after leaving hospital, was tragically killed in the back room of a gay bar when one of a group of men there with him at the time, in a desperate attempt to give Lewis the sexual satisfaction he craved, inserted a fire extinguisher up his anus and released the pin.

VII

It was four months later, and a glorious morning sun beamed through the windows as the Summerday family took breakfast together at the round pine table, golden light pouring over the big pitcher of orange juice, the wholemeal rolls, the honey, the jug of coffee and carton of milk, and making the little beads of condensation sparkle on the fridge-cool butter. In one window was silhouetted the familiar shape of the Independence Memorial in the distance.

Michael Summerday had shaved but still wore his soft, white bathrobe, as did Susan and Penny, their teenage daughter. It was a peaceful moment in which no one felt the need to talk, simply catching each other's eyes from time to time as they passed one another sugar or milk, and smiling as if sharing a private family memory. He finished reading the newspaper, the headline declaring *Atlantis Stands its Ground in Middle East Crisis*, and folded it gently, sighing:

'Well, guys, it looks like I'd better be getting to work.'

'Come on, Dad – it's Sunday!' Penny protested, stretching out her arms and yawning.

'I know, honey,' her father answered gently, 'but the world keeps turning, even on Sundays!'

Susan reached across the table, placing her hand softly upon his arm. 'Can't the Vice-President spend a little more time with the women he loves this morning?'

A flicker of pain crossed his face, and he squeezed each of them lovingly on the arm, looking from one to the other as he answered, 'It's because I love you that I have to work.'

The women hesitated for an instant, glanced at one another, and then smiled supportively.

'Go do what you have to do, honey,' Susan whispered.

Summerday got up from the table and kissed each of them lovingly on the cheek.

'And . . . *cut!* That's great, people. That was real.'

*

Susan Summerday looked at herself in the mirror as she removed the heavy camera make-up, and frowned. She kept expecting to see some outer sign of the deep ructions that were changing her inside, and yet the same old face would greet her every time, almost mocking in its placidity.

She did not feel like the woman she saw there any more.

It had started on the night of the Excelsior dinner, with that appalling shame she had felt after it turned out they had been duped by Lockes. The night her husband had done nothing to defend her humiliated pride, too desperate for their host's money to stand up for his own wife. It hadn't been a turning-point in their relationship, because she could see now that it had been rolling downhill with slowly gathering momentum for years: nothing could turn it from the path that had been set long, long before she realized anything was wrong. The difference was only in her – where once she might have felt anger, she now only felt pity for him and the ambition that had ruled their life together. The bigger he had become over the years, she realized, the smaller he had been getting in her eyes. He was now on a par with the simplest life-forms. He was a virus she had caught in her youth, whose long-term effects were only now starting to manifest themselves.

How could she feel anything but pity for a man who could choose Bob Redwood to be his running-mate in the election? The point, to her mind, was not whether Redwood would help reassure the more conservative, hard-line voters with his well-known views on criminals, the unemployed, single mothers and the poor. The point was that he was a moron, and yet her husband was proposing to make him second in line to the presidency. She wasn't the only one to be shocked by the choice. There were rumours of an emergency Secret Service plan being prepared to assassinate Redwood should Michael be killed after being elected President. That way the presidency would fall to Jefferson Smith who, as majority leader, was third in line. It was Jefferson Smith himself who had told her of it, of course, wryly observing that the spooks must feel that even a man who had drowned his brain cells in alcohol was preferable to a man who had never had any.

Yet, for all this, Susan did not know what she intended to do. She had considered withdrawing herself from the whole sorry stew of compromise, walking out on Michael and his career to start what was left of her life over again, but she knew she wouldn't do it. Certainly not yet. Some profound need for symmetry obliged her to see it through to the finish. One way or the other, the story would have its end after the elections. If she was going to close the book on him, she would do so having finished it.

Her husband didn't know that, however. She was letting him suffer for the moment under the threat of seeing his wife leave in the middle of a campaign. It was petty of her to needle him like that, she knew, but she didn't have many weapons at her disposal. In the mean time, she still publicly played the dutiful politician's wife – appearing at rallies and dinners, smiling for the camera, pretending to have a family breakfast. She didn't care about that. It was inside that the real Susan Summerday was slowly starting to make herself known.

The mirror gave nothing away.

*

Back in the studio, with its fake breakfast room looking out through fake windows on to a cardboard miniature of the Independence Memorial, Michael Summerday was in hushed but heated discussion with his campaign manager, Chuck Desane. They were trying to keep their conversation hidden from Orson Eisenstein, the director of the commercial, who was exorcizing his frustration by screaming at the lighting technician that his morning sunlight looked like pee.

'It's not that Orson's unhappy with it, Mike, but ... he's an artist, you know?' Desane was explaining. 'He's a perfectionist.'

Of all the aspects of running a political campaign that Chuck Desane liked least, shooting the commercials won hands-down. This was the one moment where the two ends of his job – the candidate and the creative talent – met and had to work together. Inevitably, both believed it to be their show.

'I don't understand, Chuck. That last one was *exactly* how he said he wanted it, right?'

'Absolutely, Mike, you all did a wonderful job. Especially Penny. I was amazed – I never knew she was so talented, seriously.'

'Isn't she?' Summerday beamed. 'She's playing the lead in her school play soon. So what are you saying, Chuck? What's the problem?'

Desane took a deep breath. He knew this couldn't have

come at a worse time, given that a butterfly whisper about campaign headquarters had it that all was not hunky-dory in the Summerday marriage, but there was no way round it. The campaign was at stake.

'It's Penny, Mike. She's the problem.'

Summerday's gaze narrowed. 'Uh-huh?'

'Penny is . . . I don't know whether you've noticed this, Mike, being her dad and all, but Penny is . . . a beautiful girl, of course, but like all of us at a certain age she is experiencing certain temporary . . .'

'Penny has spots, Chuck. I have noticed this. So has Penny, actually. We told her it's normal, and she's dealing with it very well. What are you saying?'

'Orson's never worked with skin blemishes before, Mike. He says they're hogging the camera. He wants to use Pixie.'

'What's Pixie – some kind of skin product?'

Desane squirmed with discomfort. This was a nightmare. 'We took the precaution of covering ourselves on this, Mike. Just in case. Pixie is not a what, but a who. She's a she.'

'She's a *she*, is she?' Summerday dripped acidly. 'What kind of a she would she be, Chuck?'

'She's . . . she's what is known in the business as a body double. All actors have them. The idea is that they—'

'I know what a body double is, Chuck. They make your butt look good. We're not filming Penny's butt.'

'No, but Pixie is Penny's body double . . . from the neck up. The only difference between her and your daughter is that Pixie's . . . Pixie's . . .'

'Not.'

'Not hormonally, no.'

'Not genetically, you mean? As in not at all.'

'I mean she hasn't got zits.'

'So now my daughter has zits. A second ago they were

skin blemishes, now they're zits. Thank you, Chuck – why not come right out with it and call them boils? "I'm sorry, Mike, but we can't put your festering, carbuncular child in our advert," is that it?'

'You called them spots yourself, for God's sake!'

'I'm her father, Chuck. It wouldn't alter my love for her if she had bubonic plague. You, on the other hand, appear to be suggesting that my daughter is too much of a dog to appear in a commercial about how much I love her.'

'But it *will* be her, Mike – in *principle*!'

'I really don't think you ought to bring a word like that into this conversation, Chuck. Do you have any idea what you're asking me to do? How am I supposed to explain this to Penny?'

'But that's the point – you don't *have* to!' Desane whispered enthusiastically, his energy and conviction suddenly returning as he picked up on the subtle implication behind Summerday's question. 'We film it again with Pixie once Penny has gone! Believe me, she'll never know because even *she* won't be able to tell the difference. We can use her real voice-track and she'll just be thrilled by how good she looks! You'll actually be making her a very happy girl, Mike!'

'We send Penny back home and secretly film it again?' Summerday gasped. 'And what do you think Susan will have to say about that idea, asshole?'

Desane nodded thoughtfully and lowered his voice still further.

'We . . . took the precaution of covering ourselves on that too, Mike. Just in case. Susan had better go home, too. We can use Mindy.'

'So now there's Mindy too . . . is Bill here as well?'

'Who's Bill?'

'I don't know. Ken, maybe. Joe. Buck. Someone must be here . . . *just in case*.'

'Oh, Derek! No; you're doing great, Mike.'

'Thank you very much, Chuck. Presuming you are Chuck, of course. So, let's see . . . you're asking me to make this ad, which is about home, and the importance of the simple things in life, and responsibility to the ones you love, with two total fucking strangers. Is that all of it, or is there more?'

'No, there's no more, Mike.'

Summerday gazed at his campaign manager in helpless, drowning amazement. 'No, Chuck. The answer is no, no . . . *no!*'

Desane paused, staring hard into his boss's eyes. He saw decision. 'Okay, that's fine . . . I understand you, Mike.'

'I won't do that to my family. I won't shoot it without them.'

Desane nodded. 'So that's it, then? I might as well tell Penny and Susan we're all finished here and send for their driver?'

'You do that, Chuck. Because we are. We're finished.'

'You'll stay, right? We need to have a meeting to discuss the Rectag project. With Chandra.'

'Discuss? Sure. Let's discuss. I don't mind discussing – but I won't *do*, Chuck; I won't *do* anything.'

Desane smiled, patting him on the shoulder. 'You're a good man, Mike.'

No doubt about it. He'd do it.

Once upon a time Michael Summerday had believed he deserved to be President because he had principles. Now that he was older and wiser he believed he deserved to be President because he had sacrificed principles. He had paid his dues. Supped with the devil. Done the dishes.

Few single acts of compromise could match the fact that he had accepted to become John Monroe's running-mate eight years ago, after all. Here was a man who represented the antithesis of all that he believed – a politician of pure style and pose who had never been motivated by anything other than personal advancement. Neither side had ever had any illusions about the nature of their deal – Summerday had been useful because he had a reputation for integrity, the quality that Monroe found hardest to imitate, and the kickback for his standing guarantee for Monroe's moral vacuum was that now, eight years down the line, whatever remained of him was in a strong position to take over the presidency.

The pact had been sealed one fateful night in the Carlton Pacific Hotel, when Summerday found himself battling a full-scale charm offensive from the man he had, only three months before, publicly described as 'cancer'.

'Between us is the ideal candidate, Mike,' Monroe had wooed him. 'You've got the morals, and I've got the looks. You've got the intellect, and I've got the intelligence. So far as the average voter is concerned, it's like mixing paint!'

'Possibly . . .' Summerday had resisted. 'But the smart voter is going to realize that one's oil and the other's acrylic.'

Monroe looked bemused. 'What?' he sighed, frowning impatiently. 'What are you talking about, Mike? Is that a joke? I don't get it. You know, *this* is why you don't connect with the public – someone makes a simple comment and you get all intellectual on him. Screw the smart voters! If the opinions of smart voters counted for anything in this world, Mike, we'd all be using Betamax. My advice is to keep away from them. Everyone else does.'

'So that's the platform, then – screw the smart voters?'

'Why not, Mike? They are anti-democratic.'

'I'm sorry?'

'You don't get it, do you? Smart voters want detailed, practical policies to improve society – their own sector of it in particular, I might add – and when you can't deliver, they punish you. But that is not what democracy is about! It is the art of manufacturing consent. Our mission as politicians is to make society hold together of its own free will at whatever cost. There is nothing cynical about that, and if it means we must insult the intelligence of a small élite then that's fine – those are the people who can look after themselves, Mike! They don't *need* us! The idiots need us!'

'I never realized you were such an idealist, John.'

'I'm an opportunist, Michael. I admit that. But in an unfair and imperfect world, the opportunist is the only practical idealist. And I'm offering you an ideal opportunity.'

Summerday had hesitated while Monroe excused himself in timely fashion to take a piss. He felt as though he were splitting in two – he realized that Monroe was right, but also that he ought not to be. Everything he knew about the man morally repelled him, and yet he was offering him the best chance he was likely to get of one day becoming President himself. Plus he had this disarming habit of being honest about his own shortcomings, which totally confused a man such as Summerday who could not stand back from himself in that way.

'How the hell can we be on the same ticket when only three months ago I called you "cancer"?' he finally protested when Monroe returned.

The other man smiled, immediately sensing that this was his prey's last line of defence.

'*Only* three months ago, Michael?' he laughed, pulling an unopened bottle of champagne from its ice-bucket. 'Do you realize how long ago that is in real terms? Call me simple, but three months is the difference between a summer and a winter. How many leaves turn on how many trees in between? How many birds fly south for the winter? Since you said that, all the flowers have died, all

95

the patio furniture has been put away, all the wardrobes have been reorganized . . . it's a different world, Michael, more profoundly different than any switch in politics or economics. A man is allowed to change his mind too. Not that anyone will remember what the fuck you said anyway.'

Put like that, it seemed to make sense.

Eight years later, refilming the commercial with actresses playing his own wife and daughter still cost Summerday a fraction of his soul. But since his soul was that much smaller than it had been before he clinked champagne glasses with John Monroe, it did not hurt nearly so much as he knew it should. And he owed it to the parts of himself that he had already sacrificed not to let them down now.

With five weeks to go until election day, Michael Summerday ought to have been in a commanding position. If nothing else, he had Chandra Dissenyake on his team. Prophet of the polls, guru of gurus, the one and only. A profoundly spiritual man in the ruthless world of politics, Dissenyake had three straight victories under his belt – Monroe twice, and before that Burgess. The legend of his infallibility dated from the second of these, the one where he switched his allegiances from the popular, eminently re-electable President Burgess to the rank out-sider Monroe.

It had seemed an insane move. Monroe was nothing but a liability, bringing with him both numerous skeletons in his ethical cupboard and a veritable Pandora's box of nubile, trashy young women claiming to have known him in the Biblical sense, most with particular emphasis on Revelations, but including at least one Genesis as well.

Yet Dissenyake, basing his decision on the private system that he used to predict election results, had never wavered from his conviction that Monroe would win, even in the midst of Stiffgate, the necrophilia scandal. And he was proved right. Monroe saved the situation with a live television interview in which he so earnestly denied ever having met the corpse in question that people began to have doubts about the testimony of the body-guards who claimed to have procured it for him. Then a closer study of the morgue records revealed that the body of a beautiful fashion model was in stock on the night in question, thus begging the question of why the body-guards would have come back with the mortal shell of a middle-aged cleaning lady.

But Dissenyake was behind the sensational turn-around. His channelling of Monroe's positive energy before the crucial interview had given the man the strength he needed to convince people of his sincerity. He said he had never met the corpse in question, and the public believed him. And he *was* sincere, remembering the guru's wise words: 'In spiritual terms you cannot *meet* a corpse, John, only encounter one.'

As a sitting vice-president with none of the scandals that had nagged the Monroe campaigns, Summerday ought to have been an altogether easier proposition for the guru. Furthermore, they were facing a weaker opponent in Jack Douglas than Tyrone Wheeler would have proved. Some would say it had been a dirty tactic for them to leak his medical records to the press, but, as Dissenyake pointed out, it was the negative energy Wheeler unleashed by lying about the third nipple in the first place that was truly to blame.

So Chandra Dissenyake ought to have been sitting on an easy winner, and yet Douglas kept climbing in the polls – slowly, undramatically, but relentlessly. Against all expectations, people were actually starting to listen to his critique of the economy. And now, to make things worse, his own candidate was not prepared just to let his campaign team make decisions for him, but had decided to start having ideas.

'May I speak my heart, Mr Vice-President?' the guru asked politely near the beginning of their meeting.

'Always, Chandra.'

Dissenyake rose slowly from his chair, partly for effect and partly because the little man's obesity was such that sudden movements could unbalance him. Straightening himself until he resembled a large, proud pear, he paused to collect his thoughts before giving them expression as:

'*Aargh! Aargh! Aargh!*'

He fell silent as people around the table slowly recovered their composure, then commented: 'Forgive me . . . I sensed some bad chi that had to be vented.'

'You see the adoption of Rectag as part of my electoral platform in mostly . . . negative terms, then, Chandra?' Summerday suggested.

'Positive and negative are but two sides of the same coin, Mr Vice-President,' the guru announced in a much calmer fashion. 'True, I see your body broken upon the wheel and your enemies dancing and making love amid your scattered entrails. I see the once-proud edifice of your candidacy shattered into a thousand pieces, your womenfolk weeping and your daughter licking the feet of a pagan idol, robbed of her rightful inheritance as offspring of a president.'

He paused for breath.

'But negative? No. All things are ordered for the best in the universe, Mr Vice-President. However, if you'll excuse me, I believe I must go on a retreat.'

'A retreat?' Summerday gasped. 'We have an election in five weeks' time, Chandra. For how long are you planning to go on retreat?'

'Not long. A year, maybe two. Time is immaterial.'

The little man turned and waddled out of the room, leaving the others gawping wordlessly at his back.

'He's quit?' the Vice-President demanded in a panicked tone once he'd left the room. 'Has he quit? I don't get it! What's *wrong* with Rectag?'

'With all due respect, Mike . . .' Chuck began in a cautious, soothing tone, 'it is a *very* brave issue to tackle during an election period.'

'Chuck. Can I just make a point here?' Bob Redwood intervened, smiling confidently and tapping his pencil against the table for emphasis. 'When the going gets tough, Chuck, the tough get going. Remember that.'

'Quite right, Bob. Yes!' Desane enthused, thrown by the way Redwood seemed unaware of the possibility that he might have encountered this concept somewhere before. 'But an election is not the time to do it. If you take a serious, challenging stand on an issue like crime control, you leave yourself wide open to attack by the opposition. The incumbent's role – and you are the nearest thing to an incumbent in this election – is always to occupy the steady ground, because inertia is his best friend. Douglas may be moving up in the polls, but if we stick our ground and keep pressing home the family values/character/no need for furniture removal angle, we'll still be home free – he's got a lot of ground to catch up.'

'Douglas has policies, though – why can't I?' Summerday protested. 'John Monroe had stacks of policies, for heaven's sake!'

'John Monroe had a huge libido problem, Mike,' Desane explained soothingly. 'Policies were necessary to prove that he didn't just think with his dick, but no one really cared what they were. No one here is saying you shouldn't *have* a programme, Mike, but why include something that is only going to incite debate? If you must have policies, something more along the lines of a middle-class tax cut would be much more appropriate, frankly.'

Michael Summerday hit the table with his hands. 'No! Douglas is talking about serious issues and people are listening! Rectag is the perfect counter-move – it's decisive, it's dramatic, and by making it a platform of my presidency I am identifying myself with the most important advance in crime control in the history of the nation! And don't you see that Rectag, by creating massive savings in the justice system, will *enable* us to deliver a middle-class tax cut?'

'Savings!' Redwood echoed, banging his fist on the table for emphasis.

'Tax cuts are great, Mike, so long as you don't get people involved in the mathematics. Why spoil everything? Would you try explaining to a child how Father Christmas manages to deliver *everywhere* on the same night if he didn't ask you first? The voters aren't asking.'

'The voters are not children any longer,' Summerday protested. 'They are adults.'

'True,' Chuck Desane agreed patiently, 'but they're not entirely happy about it and you should never bring the subject up with them.'

Summerday had not been expecting this kind of resistance to his suggestion. Rigorous testing of the new design had failed to bring to light any failing such as that discovered by the Abrams team. It worked perfectly. John Lockes himself had presented the final report on the programme to Summerday and the carefully selected group of congressional leaders who had been present on that strange night at the Excelsior. He made a great show of selling the idea, but more out of politeness than need. Everyone in the room had benefited from Lockes' financial generosity, and support for Rectag was the payback. Fortunately, they could support the scheme in all good conscience because its benefits were quite obvious and it worked. Rectag was effective, simple and safe.

There had been one isolated case of a Rectag exploding

during the tests, but the circumstances were exceptional and any repetition of the unfortunate accident could be avoided by warning convicts not to attempt short-circuiting the device by sticking live wires up their bottoms.

Best of all, it was incredibly cheap. Infologix was shouldering the cost of producing the Rectags and setting up the system, all of which could be done as soon as the government gave them access to the vital element on which the whole scheme depended: the one remaining location in space where a satellite could be placed in a geo-stationary orbit covering the entire nation.

Once it was in place, there would be a $5-a-day charge for each convict under surveillance. Compared to the $60 per day it cost to keep a convict in prison, plus the annual $100,000 cost of each prison cell and the $20,000 it cost to staff each cell, the savings were astronomical.

And yet Mike Summerday's decision to use Rectag as an election issue and personally announce it to the general public had just, apparently, cost him his campaign guru.

'What's wrong with you all?' he exclaimed in exasperation. 'I'm going to beat crime and cut costs – isn't that the ideal combination?'

'No, Mr Vice-President,' announced Dissenyake from the doorway, 'the ideal combination, in celestial terms, is an economic upturn combined with an opponent who is significantly shorter than you.'

'Or one with a Latin surname,' added Desane, his face lighting up at the return of the fat man.

'True, a Latin surname takes four inches off a man's perceived height.'

Dissenyake sighed and waddled back into the room.

'The signs get harder to read all the time. In days when men's hearts were simpler, it was easy to see the pattern of life in politics – the taller man won. But our physical forms are now traversing an age when the electoral soothsayer must divine all the hidden elements that add or subtract from a candidate's spiritual height. Policies, my friends, are the domain of the short. Subtract an inch for every policy not related to tax cuts. I'm sure you remember, Charles, the last time we had a real policy debate in an election?'

'Burgess versus Gold,' groaned Desane, shaking his head. 'Don't remind me.'

'You must face that pain, Charles. Haemorrhoids will ensue if you let it fester in your lower chakra. Gold, the sheep in your care, lost *despite* being taller, despite being Vice-President, and there were karmic reasons for this – the universe is never wrong.'

'Gold should have won! He was the better man!'

'Wuss,' Redwood muttered softly.

'I believe he was, Charles,' the guru continued, ignoring the Senator's contribution, 'but he was also the man with more ideas, and those ideas crushed him. How else did I predict a Burgess landslide against all the divinings of lesser pundits? As I recall, both men were roughly six feet tall in fleshly terms, but after profound meditation on their policies I saw that Burgess still stood at four feet seven inches tall, whereas Gold was an obviously un-electable three foot six. Nobody saw it coming because they listened to what the voters were *saying*, but no matter what a man may say, when his hand is poised over the ballot sheet his spirit is drawn to the spiritually taller man. It is a law of Nature.'

Those unfamiliar with the working methods of the legendary Chandra Dissenyake were gaping bug-eyed at him, convinced he must be mad. Others were smiling.

'Come on, Chandra,' Chuck chided him. 'There was more to it than that.'

'Of course. There always is. One must divine all the other variables, many of which exert opposite attractions according to the sex or age of the voter. Thin lips cost a

102

man half an inch with female voters, but gain him an inch with men. With fuller lips, the calculation works other way round. The seer must meditate upon every aspect of a candidate's face – size and shape of nose, eye colour and strength of eyebrow, ear deflection angles, distance from chin to nostril . . . his art is to see the truth in these things. To be sincere, Charles, I saw from the start that Gold was going to lose the female vote because of those droopy earlobes. All the commentators talked about how women approved of his maternity-leave proposals, putting women in the cabinet . . . nobody but me and the cartoonists saw that he had a profound earlobe problem. It is hard to see the truth sometimes.'

He sucked his teeth and looked at Mike Summerday. 'You are determined to go through with announcing Rectag before the election, aren't you, Mr Vice-President?'

'I have made my decision, Chandra, yes.'

'Despite the fact that you did a deal with Douglas not to discuss it?'

'How did you know?' Summerday gasped. 'That was a secret.'

'The bigger the secret, the more people it takes to sit on it. My weight was obviously considered a plus. How do you think he's going to react?'

'What can he do? He can't come out against it without offending Lockes, who has financially contributed to his campaign, and if he supports it he is implying support for me.'

'If only life were so simple! Well, what's done is done. Let us forget about crime control for a while, and meditate upon nasal hair.'

'But . . .' a bewildered Mike Summerday replied, 'I don't have any nasal hair.'

'No, Douglas does. This is significant. I cannot fathom why no one on his side has done anything about it, but it can only be a matter of time. We must use this gift the universe has placed in our path. A nickname must be invented for him that will draw the public's attention to the nasal hair, and then it will be too late by the time he clips it. Four inches will be lost.'

'I like it,' Redwood confirmed, nodding seriously.

Dissenyake sighed, suddenly exhausted by the weight of the task ahead of him.

'It's a little childish, isn't it?' Summerday groaned, having hoped to avoid these kinds of tactics in his campaign.

'Life is a schoolyard, Mr Vice-President,' the little man cut back, his voice tinged with sadness. 'What happens out there matters far more than what happens in the classroom. The schoolyard is where the laws of Nature apply, and who succeeds in that savage, name-calling rush of little bodies is the real test, not the spelling bee. That's why Rectag is a mistake. It is against the laws of Nature. The universe will resist it.'

'How? What is going to happen after we announce it?'

'In the corridor just now I looked long and hard into my soul to find the answer to that very question, Mr Vice-President . . .'

There was an anxious silence as they awaited his decision.

'And I don't know,' the guru finally announced. 'Somehow I cannot believe that members of the criminal community are going to react very kindly to the idea of having this device placed in their anal tracts. So, Mr Vice-President, I propose a deal – I'll stay for the moment, but if the shit hits the fan, I'm going on a retreat like I said I would and you are on your own.'

VIII

There were two things that had brought Macauley Connor to Petersburg. One of them was a promising lead for the Lockes book, which was good news as so far every avenue he had tried over the past months had proved a dead-end. No one was talking. Not that he was even beginning to regret having quit the *Public Investigator*, but it had been a hell of a lot easier making stuff up.

He had been starting to lose heart when he heard about the Global Village. It was a run-down cyber-bar where washed-up computer engineers hung out, whiling the days away over beers and reminiscences. Not much of a place, more what you'd call a tavern, but the Internet connection was free and the landlord didn't give a damn who you were or what you did so long as you didn't throw up on his keyboards. The regular crowd were all broken men – bright, schoolyard runts who had grown into proud and puff-chested high-flyers in the new world of information technology, only to have their wings clipped and be sent crashing back down to earth. Ugly ducklings who briefly became swans, but finally discovered they were turkeys.

They had few illusions about their futures. Once you ended up spending your days in the Global Village, you were no longer kidding yourself or anyone else that you were just between jobs. Most of them were single, having been downsized by their own families once things got really grim, and more than a few had little to their name but their crumpled clothes and the portable PCs in their bags, the last of their past they were going to hock. It wasn't wise to ask where they got their beer money from, but then you didn't have to be a detective to guess that some of the huddled conversations at corner tables probably weren't about job applications either. There were always ways for a down-on-his-luck software designer to earn some quick cash – a little back-street computer hacking here, a little virus-designing there. It wasn't something any of them were proud of, but it kept a roof over their heads and if they didn't do it someone else would.

The guy who called himself Don Benson was a little friendlier than most and didn't mind talking to Macauley for a little cash and a beer glass that stayed full. He was in his mid-thirties and already had the sallow-eyed gaze of the burned-out executive. He'd been with Infologix until a little over a year ago in some kind of high-ranking position, but he refused to specify exactly what his role had been.

'Can't discuss that with you, Mac,' he grunted, wincing as he gulped his beer. 'Got a confidentiality clause in my contract the size of *War and Peace*.'

'But you were a big shot, right?' Macauley pressed him, pouring more beer from the pitcher. 'So how come you couldn't get work anywhere else?'

'Usual story. Lack of experience.'

'What do you mean, "lack of experience" – you were a high-ranking executive with Infologix! How much experience do you need?'

Benson looked at him in pity, shaking his head. He snorted and took another slug of beer. 'You don't know anything, do you? I told you – I've got a damned C clause up my ass! Figure it out, spud!'

Macauley frowned in confusion, and Benson slapped the table with frustration.

'Listen. You apply for a job, they want to know what experience you've got, right? But what can you tell them if you can't say *what* the hell you've done for the last few years, Mac? The very most I could legally divulge was that I'd worked on an unspecified project, but now the project was over and so was my employment. They don't know what they're getting – you could be great or it could be you worked in some completely different field to what they're looking for! So they'll go for some bright young shit straight out of college, lock him into a C clause before they train him up, and by the time he thinks about changing jobs he finds out he's been working for X number of years but effectively has no experience! Eventually he winds up here. It's the classic scenario . . . and we're the Global Village idiots.'

He fell silent, peering broodily into his beer, and then appeared to shake off his thoughts, declaring, 'What the hell. Besides, I'm thirty-five, for God's sake! What goes around comes around, right?'

Macauley nodded sorrowfully, knowing from his own experience how these things happen, and then asked, with a hint of irritation, 'What's that supposed to mean, anyway? "What goes around comes around" – it's gibberish.'

'I never figured it out myself. But it sounds right. I just meant to say that sports became big business years ago, so it was only a matter of time before big business became like sports. Thirty-five is over the hill in my line of work. Way of the world . . .'

Benson leaned back in his chair and let his eyes drift off to the TV on the wall. It quacked away all day long in the Global Village, talking about a world that none of the people there were part of any longer, and Macauley had noticed a quizzical wistfulness in the expressions of

107

the regulars as they watched it that suggested some inexpressible form of distress. It took him some time to pin down what it was he kept seeing in their eyes, but then he got it and it occurred to him that it was probably the most awful comment on the horror of their situation that he could possibly imagine.

Is my life really so empty, each of them seemed to be thinking, that this isn't boring me?

'Let's talk about John Lockes,' Macauley suggested as he put a new pitcher on the table. 'Are you allowed to do that?'

'Sure.' Don Benson shrugged. 'So long as it doesn't have anything to do with my work. Neutral stuff is fine.'

Macauley poured out two new glasses, took a gulp from his own and began.

'What makes John Lockes tick?'

Benson raised his eyebrows slightly at the question, drinking from his own glass as he thought it over, and then replied, 'His watch.'

'I was speaking metaphorically.'

'I know. The answer's the same. The fundamental thing you have to understand about John Lockes is that he is in a hurry. And the speed just keeps picking up all the time – the bigger Infologix gets, the more he pushes the pace. I suppose with too much money there is a point when your choices are so unlimited that life gets absurd – on what grounds do you choose to do any one particular thing out of a million options every day? – so the only way of keeping any sense to your life is just to keep driving blindly forward, keep getting bigger and richer and never stop to think if enough is enough.'

'So fear, then?'

Benson thought carefully about it, his whole face contracting into the silently agonized expression of someone taking an oversized dump, until at last out plopped:

'No. It's not like he's running from anything. More like

he's struggling to catch up with his own thoughts. Like his mind is way ahead of his body, leaving invisible notes for him as it passes, and he's running along behind, picking them up and dealing with them. So he's stuck between two worlds – he's ahead of everyone else, but behind his own imagination. I remember one time we organized a surprise birthday party for him. He came in, we all shouted, "*Surprise!*" and started singing "Happy Birthday". He just stood there, looking totally confused as champagne corks popped and balloons flew up around him, and then announced, "But my birthday was last week!" '

'And was it?'

'The hell it was! Totally weird – the man is so far ahead of himself that he'd psychologically passed his birthday a week early . . .'

'Maybe that's what comes of being a genius.'

'I guess. Although you never feel like you're in the company of a genius, to be honest. Intellectually, he's not that impressive face-to-face. There were times when I'd walk out of meetings convinced that he hadn't understood a damn word of what I'd been saying. But then an e-mail would come from him that would just blow me away – I don't think he can think clearly *live*, you know? He can only express himself on computer.'

Macauley nodded, taking notes in shorthand. 'What do you think is his vision of the future?' he asked, immediately correcting himself: 'What I mean is, where does it stop? When is the overall plan realized?'

'I can't say.'

'Because of your contract?'

'Infologix is huge, Mac – there are dozens, maybe hundreds of projects in the works at any one time! Everyone works on their little patch and no one knows what anyone else is up to – so you don't even know how what *you're* doing fits into the grand scheme of things. It's like life, with John Lockes as God. I always suspected that was how he got his kicks – by being the only one who knows what the hell is going on. I don't think he cares about the money.'

'What does he do with the money?'

Benson shrugged in bewilderment. 'That's just it – nothing! You know he has his villa in the grounds of the Campus, right? Well – it's nothing special. I stayed there a few times and it's . . . a nice house, nothing more. Chain-store furniture – not the cheapest, but stuff that most people could afford. What do you make of that?'

'Maybe he's a miser.'

'No.' Benson was tapping a fingernail absent-mindedly against his beer glass. He hadn't taken a drink since they began talking about John Lockes. 'Either he's simply not interested in the money, or he's spending it on something else. God knows what. The man could practically buy a whole . . .'

Benson's voice trailed off as he became engrossed by something on TV. Macauley turned around to see what it was and immediately groaned – it was a repeat clip from Michael Summerday's press conference about Rectag.

'You haven't seen this? This thing is so—' he began, but cut himself short as Benson raised a hand for silence, his eyes locked on the screen.

'The Atlantian people . . .' Summerday was saying, as always pausing respectfully after mentioning the voters, 'have for too long suffered because of the few who refuse to abide by the rules of free society. Our great country . . . will no longer tolerate the cost of crime. Freedom . . . is too precious to allow the few to dictate to the many. Good people . . . should not have to pay for the corrupt few.'

Monroe could be seen standing behind and slightly to one side of the Vice-President, implicitly lending his support to the project. No mention was made of Lockes' involvement in the affair, or that it already had the support of the key players in Congress – Summerday was presenting it as though he was responsible for the whole thing.

'This programme is a great step forward . . . for freedom!' Summerday continued, trying his best to imitate the rousing oratorical style of his boss, but not quite managing to invest the key words with the same emotional resonance. Whereas when Monroe paused you genuinely felt the power of the last word, Summerday just seemed to have a loose connection. 'Freedom . . . from crime! Freedom . . . from fear! Freedom . . . from the billions of dollars wasted in taxes every year in policing our streets, running our justice system, and manning our prisons!'

He paused, producing one of the innocent-looking spheres from his pocket and holding it up between his fingers with a smile.

Macauley grunted in disgust, muttering, 'No thank you,' as he watched the scene again.

'Once in place, Rectag will not only bring crime as we know it to an end . . . it will put an end to good people having to pay to support the bad. Since Rectag enables us to release these people back into society, under foolproof surveillance, criminals will from now on have to *work* to support themselves and pay off their crimes . . .'

'Son of a bitch . . .' Benson muttered, his hands gripping the table.

'Tell me about it,' Macauley sighed. 'One big, happy chain gang.'

'That's not even the last model . . .'

'Had to happen eventually, didn't it? The criminals become slaves,' Macauley added.

Suddenly he froze in mid-sip of his beer. 'Sorry, what's that, Don? What did you just say?'

Benson flicked his gaze down from the screen, suddenly remembering he wasn't alone.

'Nothing. Don't worry about it.'

'No . . . *you* said, "That's not even the last model." What, Don? Do you know something about Rectag?'

Benson rolled his eyes to the ceiling, mouthing a silent curse. He leaned across, looking Macauley intently in the eye, and whispered:

'Yes. A lot. I know something. And I know nothing. But . . . I never told you that.'

'You didn't? Well, how else do I know?'

'You don't. You don't know the first thing about it, believe me.'

'So tell me.'

Benson's face froze over, his mouth setting firm like a kid refusing medicine.

'Come on, Don – it's not a secret any more! If Rectag was your big project then everyone knows about it now! And if John Lockes is behind it, then they have a right to know that, too!'

'I can't, Mac. It's more than my job's worth.'

'*What job?*' Macauley laughed. 'You're unemployed! You spend your days getting drunk in a bar!'

Benson pushed back his chair and rose from the table. 'At least it's an occupation. I'd like to keep it.'

'Don, please . . .' Macauley pleaded, 'I can keep a secret.'

The sallow-eyed designer looked pityingly down at him, shaking his head. He drained his glass, set it back on the table and whispered, 'Dream on, sucker. Thanks for the beer. And any time you feel like dropping by, don't.'

Macauley's attempts to elicit further information from Don Benson were singularly unsuccessful, a sizeable and unfriendly group of ex-engineers forming around him at a signal from their friend. He was shown the door. Very close up.

But at least, he reflected as he dusted himself down in the street outside, he was on to a lead. Schonk was right – seek and ye shall find. Lockes was not only behind Rectag, but Macauley was convinced that there was also more to it than anyone was being told. Back when he used to be a real journalist, he had prided himself on having a nose for these things, and there was far more behind Benson's sudden change in attitude than fear of breaking his confidentiality clause. Or maybe there wasn't. It depended on exactly what was in the clause.

Things were looking up. Not only was he on to a lead, there was also the second thing that had brought him to Petersburg.

*

Rachel was no longer the young woman he'd last seen six years ago, staring furiously after him as he apologetically backed away from the crowd shuffling into the theatre, called away by a lead on a story that had led him nowhere. The signs of ageing were there now – lines beside her eyes and mouth, and a subtle drying of the lips. She opened the door of her apartment to him in a pair of faded jeans and a loose white shirt, knotted in front and the buttons undone to reveal just the faintest hint of her breasts' swell, her ginger hair held back with a simple black clip. She had put on weight, or perhaps it was just that her muscles had lost some of their tension, but looking at her now he realized that they had both quietly crossed the threshold toward middle-age in these last few years.

'Good God, and I was married to that?' she smiled wryly, taking in his dishevelled clothes and unkempt hair.

He leaned forward, gauchely uncertain whether to kiss her or shake her hand, but she simply stepped back and cleared the doorway for him to enter, accepting neither.

Her apartment was modest and cosy, impeccably neat as always, and he was surprised to feel a pang of regret for the familiar objects that had once been part of their life together, in another time on another coast – her Chavin-civilization sculpture, half man half hawk, that had either been brought out of South Atlantis by dubious means or was fake; her antique tapestries and that damn pile of stones he was never allowed to approach; the shelves of psychoanalytical textbooks with titles like *The Detachable Phallus* and *Mapping the Mind Field*; *The Quantum Mathematics of Psychoanalysis*, light reading for executioners. The tropical fish were still there. There were more of them, it seemed. Maybe they were different ones entirely – who could tell? They were fish.

Even they probably weren't sure.

It was a single person's home, much like the one she'd had when they first met. Exactly like it, in fact. It was as if she had a sachet and just added water whenever she got to a new place: Instant Rachel. Now With Added Fish. Macauley mocked because that was his way with the world, but he still found whatever compound was in that packet attractive, even if experience had taught him that it was chemically incompatible with his own tastes and habits.

'This is all very familiar,' he commented, taking off his jacket. He was about to drape it over the back of an armchair when he caught himself and turned around uncertainly, looking for a coatstand.

There had to be a coatstand.

Rachel smiled affectionately at his attempt to please and took it from him, opening a cupboard just inside the doorway to reveal a line of coats on hangers.

'Even better,' he joked as she slipped it over a hanger, 'keep 'em in the dark.'

'You should see the bathroom,' she answered. 'Medicines in alphabetical order.'

'It's not your fault. There are drugs that would help, but you'd have to deal with men who don't use shampoo.'

'I know – tragedy of my life. I think marrying you was the only legal alternative I could find.'

He laughed, suddenly very happy to be here.

Their eyes met and a flicker of complicity passed between them that held both rooted to the spot. It was strange. They hadn't seen each other for six years, and hadn't even spoken for the first three of them, and yet Macauley felt it quite natural to find himself here, trading insults with her as if they were still in love.

He'd never been here before, but in many ways there was more of a sense of sanctuary about this place than in that unloved left-luggage depository he called home. And Rachel, for all the wearing of the intervening years, looked more attractive to him now than ever. He realized that he was aroused by the new lines on her face, etching a melancholy smile about her mouth, and the glare of sunshine in her eyes even in the evening lamplight of her apartment. Maturity suited her, blunting some of the prickles of her character and suggesting the underlying warmth whose release he had so rarely earned in the latter days of their marriage.

'Come, woman, I have to kiss you,' he softly ordered, holding out his arms.

*

'This does not mean you're forgiven, Macauley,' Rachel informed him later, her head resting on his shoulder and a hand idly fondling his dozing penis. 'I still think you're trash.'

He turned his head on the pillow and kissed her hair. 'Which is probably why you insist on liking me – you *need* some trash in your life, and you know it. I feel used.'

115

'Oh, I see!' she scoffed, closing her nails in a pincer movement around his balls. 'I am not a whole woman without your burping carcass on my sofa and your holed underpants in my washing machine, is that it?'

'Something like that,' he replied hoarsely, his testicles scurrying helplessly for shelter. 'Ask an analyst. There must be one somewhere around here.'

Rachel giggled and let her hand return to his penis, flopping it back and forth between her fingers like a warm roll of dough.

'I could get a dog.'

'I think you should. I learned everything I know about love from a dog.'

'I know. The dachshund.'

'Caesar was not just *the dachshund*. He was a human being born in a dog's body due to a celestial clerical error. Looked after my mother for years when my father was away.'

'God, if only you *had* been more like a dog! You can rely on dogs. You whistle, they come.'

'Not dachshunds. If they smell rabbit you can cancel your appointments for the rest of the afternoon.'

'My luck – I marry the one man who models himself after a ten-inch-high, bunny-chasing quadruped. Takes some doing. I suppose I should be grateful for the little you did pick up from him, though. Thanks to his influence you at least didn't pee on the carpet.'

'Except in the immediate vicinity of the toilet.'

'True. I stand corrected.'

Lying here in bed together like this, Rachel's cool fingers playing over his happy penis as if they had never been apart, Macauley felt a terrible longing to know this feeling every day. He didn't understand how he could have let himself lose her for the sake of stories about people he didn't really know, destined to be read by other people he didn't know, and forgotten the next day. It didn't make sense. What was there in his career that had ever brought him more happiness than being with this woman? Or more anger, of course. But that was as it should be – this was real, this was an actual person with faults and charms all of her own, not an actor in the never-ending soap of gossip and scandal. But even they, the celebrities, had real lives somewhere. And so did the readers. Only people like him lived in the virtual world between, thinking it counted for something to be the one in the know.

'Am I really not forgiven?' he asked in a more serious voice.

Rachel's hand stopped moving. She lifted her head slightly off his shoulder to look at him. 'Don't,' she warned.

'What?'

'We tried, Mac. It didn't work out, we split. Let's leave it like that. This is lovely, and I really am pleased you're here, but just because we're not mad at each other any more, and just because we made love, doesn't mean that it wouldn't be exactly the same story all over again if we got back together. You haven't changed and neither have I, so what's going to be any different? We'll just end up hating each other again, and I would far rather stay like this – friends who might occasionally screw. Isn't that better?'

'I could have changed.'

'Have you?' she asked doubtfully.

'No, I haven't . . . but maybe I'm saying that I *could* change. That I would be prepared to try changing. For you.'

'People aren't *like* that, Mac! You can't just change to suit someone else's tastes, not permanently. People's faults and virtues are the product of the same characteristics – you can't drop one side and not the other. And, anyway, it's outrageous to think that you should – of

117

course part of me would like to take you back to the shop and get them to fix the parts I don't like, but I can't and there isn't any shop to take you back to, and who says I'm right and you're wrong *anyway*? Some people are made to live together, and some people aren't – they might love each other but living together is about habits and tastes and a million mundane things that you don't ever think about when you fall in love. It's a tragedy that it has to be that way, and the world's a mess because of it . . . but there's no getting around it. Don't even think about it. We'd only end up hating one another again, darling.'

She stared pleadingly into his eyes. She understood perfectly what he was feeling behind the hurt expression on his face, because she felt the same way, but she had a rational streak that made it possible for her to limit her expectations. Macauley couldn't. She loved him partly for that romanticism, but prayed that it wouldn't mean they ended up with nothing because that was the only alternative he could envisage.

He stayed ominously silent, and her face began to crumple in misery until she collapsed back on to his shoulder, saying, 'Don't spoil it, please don't spoil it . . . this is so nice and why does it have to be more than it can be?'

They fell into a long silence, ten minutes passing without a word as each lay wrapped in their own thoughts. Rachel played disconsolately with his penis again, remembering from when they were married that at times like these it served no purpose to talk. It had been a lesson she hadn't learned in time, always trying to talk him round and creating an argument when she should have just waited for him to pull himself out of a sulk, but now she was determined to sit this one out.

The first sign she had of a softening of his feelings was when his head turned on the pillow so that his nose

118

was just touching her hair, and he sighed. She kissed him on the chest from the corner of her mouth and burrowed her cheek further into the hollow below his shoulder.

They still lay in silence, but his hand began to run slowly down her ribs to the valley between her chest and her pelvis. It was not so pronounced as it had been back when they were married, her nervous disposition no longer being so effective a diet as it had once been, but she still had curves. She grunted softly at his touch, feeling his fingers play over her hips, accepting with relief that the argument was over for the moment.

And then she felt a subtle movement between her fingers.

'Oh I see . . .' she whispered, moving her head down his body to address the stirring penis. '*You're* awake, are you?'

IX

As Chandra Dissenyake had rightly suspected, the criminal community did not react kindly to Michael Summerday's unveiling of Rectag. Nor, for that matter, did the legal community, who immediately saw that the device posed a serious threat to their livelihoods. Both sides reacted as their natures dictated – riots broke out in prisons and crime in the cities shot up overnight, and the legal profession filed a class-action suit for anticipated loss of earnings against the nation as a whole.

Nobody cared about the lawyers, of course, but the reaction from the criminals was another matter. It was like a larcenous equivalent of a panic buying spree – Michael Summerday had done altogether too good a job of convincing them that their whole way of life was about to end. Perhaps ordinary people in the street did not notice the phenomenon at first, and certainly none of the victims was surprised to find they could not get through to the police, but once the media got involved there was no ignoring it.

It was Kevin McNeil of the *Entropolis Daily Post*, one of Macauley Connor's old bosses from his time with the paper, who put a name on it as he examined the dummy of the morning edition three days after Michael Summerday's announcement:

'*Thirty Per Cent Rise in Crime in Entropolis* ...' he read aloud. His tone was thoughtful, an unmistakable sign that he was not happy, subsequently confirmed by his adding, 'Uh-huh.'

'Garbage?' tentatively suggested Ben Clarke, his sub-editor-in-chief.

'Well, Ben, no . . . it certainly tells us the facts,' McNeil commented distastefully. 'I like it in a way. It's a *Record Harvest in Wheat Collectives* kind of thing, isn't it? Something to get us all out of bed.'

'Okay! I'm sorry – I thought we could let the facts speak for themselves in this case. I was wrong.'

A small stroke shuddered the left side of McNeil's face. 'It is . . . *precisely* . . . not our job to let facts speak for themselves! What would be the point of journalists? People do not buy a newspaper for facts, they buy it for emotion! For stories! There's no story here!'

'Crime has gone through the roof since Rectag was announced, the cops are totally swamped, and that's not a story?'

'Of course it is! *Cops Swamped!* – *that's* a story! *Crime Wave Drowns Entropolis*! – *that's* a story! We see cops thrashing helplessly in a sea of larceny and pillaging, innocent women ravished, old ladies battered! Our role, Ben, is to tell people get-the-hell-out-of-bed-time stories: Once upon a time the world was a fucking mess, *Huge Ugly Dragon Rapes Maiden!*, and we all live crappily ever after . . . get it?'

'*Crime Wave Drowns Entropolis*, then?'

'Lovely, Ben. We know the day has started.'

Overnight, Rectag and the crime wave drowning Entropolis became the major issue facing the nation, just weeks away from election day. At first, both candidates kept calm. Douglas suppressed his irritation at Summerday's having reneged on their deal, and avoided coming out clearly for or against the programme whilst simply reflecting that Summerday had perhaps announced it somewhat prematurely. Summerday, for his part, maintained an air of breezy confidence, predicting that things would soon settle down again and the police would have things back under control.

Two days later, McNeil and Clarke were once again examining the morning's dummy front page. By now, however, McNeil was starting to have serious doubts about his sub-editor-in-chief.

'*Crime Wave Gets Thirty-five Per Cent Bigger* . . .' he read aloud, '*Crime Wave Gets Thirty-five Per Cent* . . . *Bigger* . . . uh-huh.'

'*Gets Huge*?'

'Is everything all right at home, Ben? You know you can always talk to me if you have a problem. How's Marion?'

'But it has! All the jails are full, the cops can't cope any more, and it just keeps growing!'

'I know that, Ben. Are the kids doing okay?'

'Fine. And it's Miriam. *Crime Wave Laps Higher*?'

'Well, Ben, that's the whole problem isn't it – what is this wave? Is it a little lappy-beachy thing, or is it a "O hear us when we cry to Thee for those in peril on the sea" kind of thing? *Crime Wave Gets Bigger* sounds like the surf's up, really, doesn't it? As for *Crime Wave Laps Higher* . . . I guess I'd better move the towel right now, Ben!'

'What then?' came the exasperated response. 'What do you *want* the damned wave to do?'

Kevin McNeil put his hands on his sub-editor's shoulders, squeezing him supportively. 'If the wave has got bigger, Ben, then it's a big wave, isn't it? What do we call a big wave? Stick with the imagery here – how can we tell people that this is now one fuck-off big wave they're dealing with here?'

Ben Clarke looked lost for a second, defeated, and then a spark of inspiration hit him so fast that his mouth started working before he could quite find the word he was looking for.

'Oh! Oh! Shit! Ts . . . Tss . . . *Tsunami!*'

'*Yes!* We are now dealing with a crime *tsunami*, Ben. This is a natural disaster – *Crime Tsunami Engulfs Atlantis!*'

'*Crime Tsunami Engulfs Atlantis* . . .' Clarke repeated, tingling at the sound of it in his mouth.

'Lovely, Ben. It's the start of a brand-new day, and the world is even worse than it was when we went to bed!'

Michael Summerday quibbled at the concept of a crime tsunami, but by now few people were listening. The nation was in crisis, and began turning to Jack Douglas for guidance. Douglas, suddenly no longer able to conceal his true feelings, revealed that he had been against Rectag from the very start. He even took a moral stand over the matter, returning the campaign contribution he had received from John Lockes.

Meanwhile, Ben Clarke's every waking minute was taken up with trying to prove himself equal to the task at hand. But it was hard, and each day, as the crime wave fed on itself and criminals of every stripe were whipped into an ever greater frenzy by the media stories, it just got harder. From the moment the *Daily Post* had chosen aqueous imagery for its headline, he had been doomed to stick with it. Yet the situation just kept getting worse and there weren't many things bigger than a tsunami to express it. But he tried, he really did.

One week after Michael Summerday unveiled Rectag, Kevin McNeil was sitting in silence at his desk, staring at the dummy of the morning edition. He looked up with what may have been a tear in his eye.

'God, this is beautiful, Ben,' he sighed.

'You like it? Really?'

'*Like it?*' the editor squawked. 'No, Ben. No, I do not like it. I *love* it! If there was ever a headline with which I would wish to settle down and marry, the front page that would bear my children, it's this one, Ben.' He looked back down with a smile and picked up the dummy, kissing it tenderly.

'*Crime Polar Ice-Caps Melt!*' he crooned. 'What a wonderful world we live in, Ben . . . what a *wonderful* world!'

The next day, Douglas overtook Summerday in the polls.

X

In the professional and personal opinion of his colleagues at the Global & Western Credit, George Bailey Jr was weird. Tall and lanky, with a kind of quizzical sensitivity to his face, he gave the impression of being adolescently out of place in his own body at the age of fifty-seven – as though nature had mistakenly issued him with a much larger physical shell than his personality felt able to fill. Chairs never seemed to be quite the right shape, and the distance between his shoulder and anything he reached for always turned out to be either longer or shorter than his arm, his fingers forever chasing after objects he had sent rolling off his desk in a misjudged attempt to pick them up. At the same time, he was polite and thoughtful and absurdly honest. He never swore, the strongest expressions anyone had ever heard him use being strange archaisms like 'Gee!' or sometimes, when under pressure, 'Darn!' All in all, if the police were to arrest him on suspicion of being a brutal serial killer, most of his colleagues would have testified that they had always suspected as much. He was too nice.

Too nice even to feel any hatred of John Lockes for ruining his life. Not that Lockes had personally singled out George Bailey Jr for punishment, but he was nevertheless responsible for the fact that George found himself, a few years from retirement, alone and lonely in Entropolis. Infologix Bankmanager had been John

Lockes' idea, after all, and for most of his working life George Bailey Jr had been a bank manager.

He had managed precisely the sort of small-town branch the big national banks were only too happy to replace with Lockes' automated computer terminals. Frankly, the work of a local bank was highly routine and in this day and age it hardly required a whole human being to manage the key decisions of a client's life. A centralized computer system could perfectly well judge whether a person was eligible for a loan or should have their house repossessed because they were behind on their payments, and do it extravagantly more cheaply.

People prefer a personal touch when it comes to such life-changing decisions, of course, which was why Bankmanager had not visibly affected working practices in major towns. City customers still expected to deal with a teller just as they always had, and so there were still employees in the big urban branches to provide a human interface between the client and the decisions taken by Bankmanager. There was no need for such extravagance in a small town like Bedford Falls, however, where clients did not have the luxury of choosing to take their business elsewhere.

George Bailey was fortunate in that he was promoted to executive assistant manager of the main Entropolis branch of Global & Western Credit as part of the 'structural changes'. Infologix Bankmanager had calculated that it would be more cost-efficient to keep him on the payroll for the few remaining years until he reached retirement than to pay him a redundancy fee. Since this was theoretically a promotion, with a small pay rise, George was faced with the unpleasant choice of leaving the home he loved for the big city, or resigning and submitting himself to the will of Bankmanager like all the other unemployed trash.

It was a sad end to a story that had begun two

generations before when George's grandfather had set up the Bailey Building and Loan, but he was a realist and chose the sensible economic option, rather than following the example of his father, who threw himself off a bridge when Bailey Building and Loan was bankrupted and taken over by the Potter Bank. As a child, George had sworn never to work for the Potter Bank, but a few years later it was taken over by Western National Banks, which released him from his oath. Western National subsequently merged with Global Eastern to create Global & Western Credit. And now Global & Western Credit was itself the target of a hostile takeover bid by World Wire Coathangers.

But George didn't much care any more.

The last time he had been back to Bedford Falls, he'd seen that the bank had now become a Ghetty's Burger Restaurant. Some of his old colleagues had even found new employment there as part of the energetic, motivated team of young, dynamic professionals with great opportunities for advancement in this rapidly expanding and exciting service industry.

The old foyer was now the dining area, the oak panelling on the walls had been ripped out and replaced with pine, the parquet floor had been tiled and the entire front wall replaced by glass. It pained him to see that, but at least he could be happy for his erstwhile junior teller, Julie Bell, who seemed genuinely thrilled by her new career managing the restaurant.

'Who would have thought, Mr Bailey,' she had enthused when he went in to say hello, 'that I would one day become a managing colleague with a real sense of target achievement on a daily basis, evolving in my own self in ways that I never envisioned possible? Just last month I took part in a Human Skills Seminar the company invited me to share in, and I thought to myself, Julie Bell, two years ago you were like a caterpillar who

127

didn't know that it would one day become an amazing and beautiful butterfly and flutter up into the sky!'

Julie took him on a guided tour of her domain, proudly showing him the kitchens – or food preparation consoles, as she called them – and introducing him to her food-preparing colleagues. His old office had become the Colleagues' Breather Area, where employees could relax between shifts. There were signs on the wall saying LET YOUR TEETH KNOW YOU LOVE THEM – SMILE! and A CUSTOMER IS A COLLEAGUE WHO JUST DOESN'T KNOW IT.

She insisted on paying for his lunch, although he had not been planning to eat in the restaurant, never having been entirely convinced that the old claim about Ghetty's Burger quarter-pounders containing 100 per cent prime beef referred to the entire burger or just the beef bits in it. Unable to refuse her offer without offending, however, he had hesitated between the Happy Bacon and the Funny Fish before eventually changing his mind altogether, choosing a Cheese Smiler and fries with Happle Pie for dessert.

To George's further distress, given that he considered elderly men consuming burgers to be a rather undignified spectacle, Julie sat down at his table and actually watched him eat. She had no idea of the discomfort this caused him, of course, being so energized by her enthusiasm for all things burgeroid that sharing his enjoyment in this way only seemed polite. He nodded his head and hummed in appreciation, desperate not to shatter her faith, but every mouthful stuck in his gullet.

But, once satisfied that the Cheese Smiler was entirely to his taste, Julie began to fidget in her chair.

'Will you still be in town next Monday, Mr Bailey?' she eventually asked.

George raised his eyebrows and nodded as he chewed.

Julie bounced with delight and leaned conspiratorially forward, lowering her voice to a whisper. 'Promise not to breathe a word to anyone, Mr Bailey, but next Monday is . . . New Big One Day!'

George frowned as he wiped mayonnaise from the corner of his mouth with his paper napkin.

'It's top secret,' she continued hoarsely, 'only managerial colleagues are supposed to know, but the recipe of the Big One is changing for the first time in over thirty years! I know I can trust you, though, Mr Bailey. It's been so hard keeping it to myself for the last few weeks, you understand?'

'It must have been,' George answered softly as he swallowed the last of his mashed cow. 'May I ask what is being changed?'

Julie's eyes flitted to either side and she leaned still further toward him.

'Poppy seeds,' she breathed. 'We're putting poppy seeds on the bun. Healthier, you know. It would be an honour for me if you were the first customer in Bedford Falls to be served with one, Mr Bailey. You will come, won't you?'

'Of course, Julie, it would be an honour for me too,' he responded graciously. 'At what time would you like me to come?'

'Seven a.m. – I'll prepare it for you myself!'

Seven in the morning. George could not have done a better job of keeping his smile in place if *rigor mortis* had set in.

Given that Ghetty's Burgers was now owned by John Lockes, indigestion was another thing he might have held against him, but George never blamed anybody for anything. He just believed in making the best of things.

For instance, for lack of any genuine responsibilities as sub-assistant manager, George tried to put his time to good effect by hosting visits to the bank by groups of disfavoured children. The directors of the bank had not been against the idea when he suggested it – it would keep the man busy, be good public relations and maybe translate into extra clients when the kids grew up. This morning he was showing twenty children from a local orphanage around in his usual clumsily gentle fashion.

Smallest of all the children in the group were Mary Walton, aged eleven, and her younger brother Joe, also aged eleven. (In most people's eyes this would have meant they qualified as twins, but Mary, as she constantly reminded Joe, had been born at 11.46 p.m. on 7 June, whereas Joe had not come into the world until 0.20 a.m. on 8 June, so obviously he was her kid brother. Joe felt there was something a little unfair about this arrangement, but he could not fault her logic.)

George, who had himself known the loss of a parent at a tender age, held little Mary and Joe gently by the hand as he led the group into the bank's central foyer, the difference in height obliging him to walk like a hunter following the trail of some very small animal. This was the part of the tour he enjoyed most, listening to the children's 'Wows' of awe as they saw the palatial grandeur of the building's architecture for the first time.

The head office of Global & Western Credit was a late-nineteenth-century construction whose architects had sought, successfully, to convey a sense of durability and confidence. The opulence of the materials used – the marble, mahogany and bronze – combined with the scale of the design, left one in no doubt of the power and strength of the organization into whose hands one was entrusting one's hard-earned savings. Great doric columns rose and rose around one to support the vaulted ceiling high overhead. There was a temple hush and intimacy to the exchanges taking place between clients and tellers at the mahogany counters below, their voices and the sound of footsteps swallowed up by the great space. Friezes on the ceiling depicted scenes of industry and commerce, of cargo steamers and railroad trains, of bountiful harvests gathered by cheap, happy labourers, of the peoples of the world shaking the hands of tall Western traders, and of decent, honest families with their bank manager watching proudly on as the finishing touches were put to their dream homes. The Standard Mutual Bank, for whom the building had been designed, may have been no more – long ago torn to shreds by the famished dogs of capitalism – but the place itself remained as reassuring and impressive as ever. The Global & Western Credit, it seemed to say, probably loaned Noah the money for a boat.

'Has it ever been robbed, Mr Bailey?' came Mary Walton's sweet little voice.

The tragedy of truth is that it is so rarely what people would like it to be. This is why polite people try to avoid it. George, who naturally faced this question every time he took children around the bank – although not usually so early on in the tour – was an honest man and would have liked the truth to be that the bank had foiled the best efforts of dishonest men. The directors of the bank, who had the company's reputation to think about, would have equally liked that to be so and had given George clear orders to pretend that it was. This left George, as someone who rather ambitiously aimed to please others *and* to be honest, in a difficult position.

'Gee, Mary . . . there probably aren't many banks that have *never* been robbed.'

This answer satisfied most children, whilst leaving both his honesty and loyalty intact. Just. But it did not satisfy Mary Walton.

'Did they have guns?'

'Wa . . . wa . . .' George stuttered, as he always did when unsure what to reply, 'well . . . that's kind of hard to say, you know . . . I mean, it depends, Mary.'

131

'Why does it depend, Mr Bailey?'

'Because there are all kinds of guns, I suppose . . . maybe they had guns, but maybe they didn't. I mean, I guess I don't know much about guns, Mary.'

She looked up at him in surprise, or suspicion.

'You *must* know about the AK48, Mr Bailey!'

'Well . . . gee . . . no . . . no, I guess I don't. That's a kind of gun, is it? I-I-I didn't know that, Mary, that's very interesting.'

'Did you know,' joined in Mary's brother Joe, breathlessly, 'that *all* the people with AK48s are going to have things put up their bottoms?'

'You don't say?'

'I do . . . it was on the news!'

'It's true, Mr Bailey!' Mary added. 'Everyone knows about it – up their bottoms!'

'Up their bottoms, huh? Well, how do you like that?'

'Not much, thank you.'

'Not much, huh? I guess that's about right. Say, kids . . . what do you say we take a look at the safe?'

The safe was normally the high point of the visit and saved until last, but as a diversionary tactic George was prepared to alter the order of the tour just this once. The suggestion was met with unanimous approval, but unfortunately they never got quite that far.

'*Everybody get down!*'

The shout came as they were still crossing the huge marble floor. Three men with guns stood in the foyer, pointing their weapons at the clientèle, who hurriedly obeyed. Only George and his party of orphans were slow to react, mostly because the startled children had strict orders from their supervisor, Miss Dowel, to do exactly what Mr Bailey told them to do.

Mr Bailey had yet to give them a clear instruction.

'*Eat floor, motherfuckers!*' one of the three men screamed, aiming at George.

132

Physically challenging, but clear enough.

'I think we should sit down, kids.'

He cautiously lowered his lanky form to the ground, sitting with his knees crossed. He was looking over at the kneeling children, smiling encouragingly, when he felt a dig in his ribs.

'*Pssst!*'

'Shush, Mary,' he whispered.

Mary tried to contain herself, but it was too much. '*That's* an AK48, Mr Bailey,' she hissed.

George had often reflected that it was strange how nobody questioned the high levels of security in big city banks. There were below-counter alarm buttons, booby-trapped cash clips, even ground-level buttons in the likely event that the staff would be ordered to eat floor, mother-fuckers. All of which meant that it was virtually impossible for criminals to rob a bank without the police being alerted. Which obliged them to work at maximum speed, entering and exiting in under two minutes. Naturally, the tension and pressure were such that they were forced to control the situation using brute force, which in turn encouraged a lower quality of criminal. So all in all, it seemed to George, if innocent people were more likely to be killed during armed robberies today than in the past, it was thanks to the banks themselves.

He had brought the subject up with his superiors on one occasion, but they seemed to think he was mad.

Obeying the bank's own rules for being robbed, the three gunmen who had just stormed into the Global & Western Credit – Julio López, Duey Martínez and Luís Alvares – had started cleaning out the tills within fifteen seconds of entering the premises. Julio López had already removed one of the booby-trapped money clips triggering the alarm connection with the 12th Precinct police station, but this was immaterial because no fewer than six alarm buttons had been pushed by bank employees on the crew's entry into the bank.

The 12th Precinct had immediately issued an all-points bulletin to its squad cars, but many of them were already occupied with two other robberies that were taking place at the same time elsewhere. George Bailey Jr could not have chosen a worse time to take a group of orphans on a guided tour of the premises.

So far the children were reacting well to the situation. They were keeping very quiet, and none of them had yet broken into tears. George tried to look protective and calm, smiling reassuringly at young Joe, whose lower lip was starting to tremble. He slowly raised a finger to his lips and winked, earning a flicker of a grin from the child.

This sort of thing had never happened back in Bedford Falls, but since coming to the city it was the third robbery the poor man had found himself involved in. The time always crept by at a snail's pace, but he knew the robbers could not afford to stay long in the bank and felt they must be on the point of leaving by now.

'*One minute!*' shouted one of the men to his colleagues. '*Nobody make a fucking sound!*'

Only one minute? The tremble in Joe's lip had spread to his jaw, and George could see the moisture beginning to well up around his eyes. In the periphery of his vision, he noted with mounting angst the nervous way that Luís Alvares was jerking his aim from one spreadeagled client to another, reacting to even the tiniest twitch or shift as if it were a potential attack. He prayed with all his might that the boy would manage to hold back his tears a little longer . . . just long enough to let the robbers finish their job and leave.

'*Okay! We gotta go! Fucking come on!*'

Joe's mouth started to open and shut like a fish, his cheeks wobbling furiously as the sound struggled to come up his throat. George was imploring him with his eyes to hang on just a bit more.

'*That's enough! Get the fuck away from the money!*'

The boy was starting to jiggle on the spot as if a great holler was ricocheting silently around his body, bouncing about his organs as it searched for an exit. The two men at the tills threw their bags across the counters and jumped over, finally finished. George held his breath as they walked hurriedly past him, money over one shoulder, gun on the other. They were going, they were going. It was going to be all right.

'*Everybody down!*'

The three men were half-way across the foyer when the shout came. They stopped in their tracks.

'*Hit the fucking . . . ?*'

The voice trailed off in confusion as the speaker took in the scene. There was a pregnant pause, then Luís Alvares found his voice.

'*What the fuck are you doing here?*'

George, his heart sinking, saw three more men with guns standing in the doorway. The children saw it too.

That was when Mount Joe finally erupted.

XI

Susan Summerday made her announcement as she and Michael were driving to a campaign rally in Redford. They had not spoken during the flight from the capital, Michael being busy with his campaign team, and she had waited until now, when the two of them were alone in the back of the limousine, to deliver her bombshell.

'Michael,' she announced, 'I've decided not to leave you.'

Summerday, who had been staring out of the window and dwelling depressively on his catastrophic slide in the polls since announcing Rectag, looked toward her with wan eyes. 'Okay,' he said, and turned back to the window.

Susan gasped, staring in amazement at the back of her husband's head. 'Okay?' she repeated. 'Is that all you have to say? I tell you that I don't want a divorce and you just . . . *accept* it like that?'

'What do you want me to say, Susan? You've made your decision, you've got your reasons, we're both mature adults, that's it.'

'Don't you even want to know *why* I've decided to stay?'

'You probably feel sorry for me,' her husband shrugged.

An indignant squawk escaped her lips. '*Sorry* for you? Are you insane?'

'Okay . . . so you don't. You're right – why should

you? I'm a fuck-up. I don't deserve you. You'd be right to leave me.'

'But I'm not!'

'Well then . . . there's nothing more to say, is there?'

They fell back into silence, Michael again staring out of his window as they passed through the post-industrial wastelands on the outskirts of town, Susan gazing in bewilderment at the back of the driver's head through the smoked-glass partition.

'You *want* me to leave you, don't you?' she suddenly snapped, turning back to her husband.

He did not respond.

'What's going on in your scheming little mind, Michael? Do you think the voters might feel sorry for you if I walked out now?'

Still he seemed not to hear her, his eyes fixed on the passing dereliction.

'That's it, isn't it? Poor Mike Summerday – kicked when he's down by his cold-hearted bitch of a wife! Look how well he's holding up! Jesus, have you really sunk that low?'

Summerday's head slowly swivelled her way, his face a blank sheet of pain and self-loathing. 'Hey . . . you can find lower.'

'In a biped?'

Summerday managed a small smile as he looked at his wife.

'I don't want you to leave, Susan. Contrary to what you may think, I do still love you.'

'Whatever that means in your case.'

'It means . . . I sincerely wish I was worthy of you. There's not a single other soul that makes me feel that way, Susan. So that must be love.' He shrugged and turned away. 'Frankly, though, I have no idea why you would want to stay with me – you're not even going to be First Lady, you know.'

'Do you think I care?'

'You must care. It wouldn't be human not to care.'

'Michael, listen to me!' she hissed, catching his arm and forcing him to turn her way. 'I *never* wanted you to be President. I never even wanted you to be in politics.'

'Well . . . good,' he smiled, 'because it looks like you're going to get your wish.'

'The hell I am!' she seethed. 'I haven't sacrificed myself for you all these years just to see you quit at the last hurdle! You are going to fight back and win this election just like you planned, Michael, or else I'll . . . I'll . . .'

'What? Leave me? I hope not, Susan, because I'm starting to get seriously confused over the grounds for divorce here.'

'We're not *getting* divorced!' she snapped, slapping him round the cheek. 'We're sticking together, just like we always have done, until you *achieve* this stupid, damned ambition of yours or die trying because I will not . . . *I will not* . . . let you throw away all the years I threw away on you, Michael Summerday!'

Summerday was speechless, not having seen such fire in his wife's eyes since the night at the Excelsior. He sensed not to cross her on this.

The limousine pulled up at the town hall where he was supposed to be talking. A large crowd had gathered outside, chanting and waving banners with various descriptions of what they would like to do to his rectal passage. Summerday's stomach cramped in horror at the thought of what awaited him in there.

Susan saw the fear in his expression.

'Don't even think about it,' she growled, pinching his thigh. 'Now – let's do this thing.'

*

138

What the polls had been saying was confirmed in the most graphic manner possible as they waited backstage, listening to the thunder of stamping feet and whistling. The events of the last few days had transformed the good people of Redford into a bloodthirsty crowd from a Roman arena, hungry to make Summerday pay for his error. There had been no increase of larceny in the quiet town of Redford, as such, but everyone there felt personally threatened by the famous melting of the crime polar ice-caps, nevertheless. The whole campaign team was terrified, Michael more than anyone. They could see the media out front, their cameras panning across the howling mob as the journalists shouted into their microphones, giving needless descriptions of the mood in the chamber. This was not a campaign rally so much as a lynching.

The Summerdays, Bob Redwood and Chuck Desane were huddled in feverish consultation as the moment of truth drew near.

'We can say you've been taken ill,' suggested Desane.

'Nobody will believe it,' Summerday groaned. 'They'll know damn well we chickened out.'

'Probably, but at least the networks can't show *pictures* of it. If you go out there, the lead item on tonight's news is you being crucified by the good citizens of Redford. Anything is better than that.'

Susan normally kept to herself during these discussions, knowing her role was simply to smile and look supportive, but not this time. This time she was actually going to *be* supportive.

'Michael is going out there, Chuck,' she announced flatly. 'If he chickens out, the election is lost right here, right now. You know that's true.'

'When the going gets tough, the tough get going, Mike,' mantra-ed Bob Redwood.

'Fuck what the tough do – the *smart* get the fuck out of the line of fire!' Desane exploded. 'Now that Chandra has gone on retreat, I have sole responsibility for this campaign and I say that we should let this one go – later we can regroup our forces and regain the initiative. We have exactly four weeks left until election day, and a lot can change in four weeks. For a start, there's always the chance that Douglas might screw up too! Did you think of that, Susan? And just listen to that crowd! Michael cannot go out there, it's as simple as that! Do you think they're going to let him speak?'

'Whether or not they hear him out is less important than whether or not he runs from them. It's a character thing.'

'It's not a case of running. It's what in military circles is called a tactical retreat, Susan.'

'Oh, sure!' she laughed. 'Which is what in business circles is called a negative profit, right? Bullshit! What this *really* is, Chuck, is a test of whether or not Michael's got what it takes to be President. It's that simple. And you can forget your news management – the cameras are already filming, and either way these images are going out on the news tonight.'

She turned to her husband, putting her hands upon his cheeks and forcing him to look her in the eye. 'You can't duck this, Michael! There is nowhere to retreat to except defeat! If you truly want to be worthy of me, you have to go out there. What do you say?'

Summerday stood rooted to the spot, the drumming of feet and choruses of whistles scrambling his thoughts. In his heart he knew Susan was almost certainly right, but even the faintest chance that they might be able to retrieve the situation at a later date in a careful, orchestrated manner was preferable to this nightmare of free speech.

'Susan, they won't listen . . .' he whispered, dropping his gaze in defeat.

He felt her hands slide from his face.

'They won't listen,' she repeated, placing her hands on her hips and looking from her husband to Desane and back again. 'Well, we'll just see about that, shall we?'

Before either of them realized what she was doing, she was out from behind the red velvet curtain that hid them from view and standing in the glare of the spotlights. A great roar went up from the crowd.

Meat.

'Oh my God ... Oh my God ..' Desane began babbling, 'we are all going to die ... crash and burn ... end of story ...'

Susan stood for what seemed like an eternity, squinting in the brightness as the howling and whistling shook the hall around her. She looked back offstage toward Summerday and Desane, a small smile playing over her lips and a near-psychotic glint in her eye, and then approached the podium, pulling the microphone down to her height.

The stamping and shouting was like a wall built of pure anger – unreasoning, unrelenting and unmovable. She must have waited a full minute, letting it wash over her as she took its measure, her gaze travelling over the twisted faces of the citizens and the blank stares of the cameras, and then, when she had accustomed herself to the fury enough that it no longer shocked her, she leaned in close to the microphone and spoke in a low, clear voice that soared out from the speakers to the back of the hall:

'I was raped.'

It was as though someone turned off Niagara Falls.

A single cough echoed like the last drip.

Susan was sensational. For twenty minutes she held the hall spellbound as she recounted the tale of a young sophomore's brutal introduction to the wickedness of the world – a tale of innocence broken, purity sullied, and

141

dreams lost. She described herself, the naïve young girl from a pampered background, her head filled with romantic ideals and fairy-tale ambitions, being ripped into reality by the random evil of one man whose path she had the bad luck to cross late one evening returning from a party, who stole her virginity then left her bruised and ashamed as he escaped into the night. She revealed how afterwards she had believed she would never be able to enjoy intimacy with a man, her first adult experience having scarred her for ever. She told them of her feelings of guilt and self-revulsion, of her fear, and of how her inability to share her emotions with a single soul began to drive her inexorably toward the waiting arms of a self-induced death.

She did not ask for their pity, reminding them how common her story was, how there were undoubtedly other women right there in that hall with them who had similar tales to tell and who had perhaps not known her good fortune in meeting a person who restored her will to live before it was too late, a person whose gentle strength inspired her with trust and whose tender care mended her broken wings, a man who promised to protect and cherish her.

'My God, she is sensational!' Desane exclaimed in the wings as another round of applause washed over Susan. 'This is the most incredible thing I have ever seen! It's brutally honest, it's heart-rending, it's gripping, it's . . . God, it's . . . how can I put this? . . . it's . . .'

'I think the word is "hogwash",' Summerday suggested, shaking his head in admiration.

'Quality,' Desane countered, unfazed. 'Quality hogwash. Hogwash champagne . . .'

His mind was starting to spin with possibilities. If Susan Summerday could reproduce what she had achieved here on a national scale, they were back in the race. Anything was possible. But they had to handle it right. They needed to give her confession the maximum possible impact. And he had no doubt where to go for that.

The snob in him didn't much relish the idea, but if progress was the ongoing process of mankind's burdens being eased – the wheel, the washing machine, the pizza delivery service – then Lola Colaco was the summit of human development so far. For millions of people she had removed the final burdens of thought and emotion. *The Lola Colaco Show* was said to have more influence on people's attitudes and perceptions of reality than all the principal religions and philosophies combined. Fortunately, she was a reasonably sane and well-adjusted woman who had never demanded that anyone sacrifice their first-born son or massacre the people of the valley. That was where he had to get Susan. But fast.

'Get on to ABS,' he whispered to the aide hovering behind them. 'Offer them an exclusive interview with Susan Summerday, future First Lady and rape victim, for tomorrow's show.'

XII

'I'm standing in front of the central branch of the Global & Western Credit, where a *horrifying* drama is unfolding, with twenty orphaned children, aged under thirteen, being held hostage by armed—'

'Whoa! Sorry, Vanessa . . . I'm not sure "orphaned" is the correct word here, are you?'

'Isn't it? Oh, okay. So I call them . . . parentally independent minors?'

'No, I mean it's . . . *technical* – the viewers have to understand that what makes these children special is that they have *no parents*. That's the story – no parents. "Orphan" may be too élitist.'

'Okay . . . I'm standing in front of the central branch of the Global & Western Credit, where a *horrifying* drama is unfolding, with twenty orphaned children with no parents, aged under thirteen, being held hostage—'

'Whoa! Whoa! Vanessa, you just said that none of the parents of these children are under thirteen years old!'

'I did not. How could I have said that, Ken? They don't even have any parents – they're orphans . . .'

'*You* said "twenty orphaned children with no parents aged under thirteen"!'

'No, I *said* "twenty orphaned children with no parents – *comma* – aged under thirteen – *comma* – tum-ti-tum-ti-tum".'

'Well, the problem is we can't *see* your comma there,

144

Vanessa. You have to change the order or it sounds like the story has this weird, under-age sex angle to it somewhere. I'm sorry.'

'All right, okay . . . I'm standing in front of the central branch of the Global & Western Credit, where a *horrifying* drama is unfolding, with twenty orphaned children, aged under thirteen, with no parents, being held hostage by . . . *what? What?*'

'Now their parents aren't being held *hostage?*'

'Ken. These are orphans. Little no-mummy-no-daddy people. *So get off my back about their parents, will you?*'

'Little no-mummy-no-daddy people! Can't we say *that?* It would be so much clearer.'

'It *is* simple, Ken: we have a word for orphans. It is "*orphans*". The reason why we have the word is so that we all know what we're talking about. I don't have a problem with that, as it makes my job a lot easier. But if you start telling me that some people out there are so pig-ignorant that I have to give them the word *and* the explanation of the word then I cannot be held responsible for what it does to the syntax.'

'I'm sorry, Vanessa – you're doing a great job, honestly. Could we just try to get it *one* time with "no parents" in there somewhere where it doesn't get in the way? Please? Vanessa?'

'I need a cigarette.'

'You're smoking again, Vanessa? Is that what you meant about the sin tax? Vanessa? What? What did I say?'

*

An hour prior to that, however, no one on the outside had known exactly what the situation in the bank was.

The Global & Western Credit heist was in deadlock. The stand-off between the two rival gangs – the Blade and the Blood – had wasted the crucial minutes that remained before the police arrived, trapping both gangs inside.

But that was the least of their problems. More important by far was settling the question of who was robbing the bank. Having arrived first, the Blade naturally considered they had dibs, but so far as the Blood were concerned what counted was who robbed the bank *last*.

It wasn't about money, anyway.

It was about respect.

The situation was all the more delicate because the Blade and the Blood were in the process of fragile peace negotiations to end the Lower East Side Crack Wars, and a hasty move now by one of the guys in the bank could wreck the progress that had been made, plunging the two gangs into a fresh spiral of reprisal and counter-reprisal which neither could afford to sustain. So both sides found themselves stuck, their weapons poised, as they wondered what to do next.

The only option had been for both sides to get on their mobile phones and let their chiefs hammer out a deal of some sort that allowed everyone to keep their respect. That was going to take time. The fact that the Blues were on their way, the sound of sirens growing louder every second, had been a lesser issue.

Nobody had to respect the Blues.

But they respected the Feds, and because the Global & Western Credit was insured by the Federal Banking Reserve any crime committed within it was a federal offence. The Feds arrived shortly after the Blues, immediately calling in a twenty-man SWAT team that took up positions on the rooftops opposite the bank.

This pissed off the Blues, who felt it showed a lack of respect. For them, this was now a hostage situation over and above being a bank robbery, and so they called in their negotiation specialist. However, the Feds argued that if it was a hostage situation they should call in their own crack Hostage Rescue Team, who arrived an hour later.

But the arrival of the Hostage Rescue Team pissed off the SWAT team, because the HRT thought everyone should defer to them when all they really knew about was rescuing hostages whereas the SWAT team had experience in bank robberies and violent crises of all kinds.

So it wasn't about law. It was about respect again.

Clearly in all of this someone would have to get hurt. If only to save face.

So far as the Global & Western hostages were concerned, the obvious choice was George Bailey Jr. George had marked himself out early on by being the first of them to speak to the gunmen, timidly raising his hand and asking whether it might be possible to organize a delivery of milk and sandwiches for the children in his charge.

That made him everyone's spokesman.

It was the story of his life – for reasons not clear to himself, George always seemed to end up representing the interests of other people. He was good at it, managing in his polite, apologetic way to get things done on their behalf that they themselves might have failed to achieve, but he had never understood *why* people assumed that he would do so in the first place.

They saw in George qualities that he did not see in himself and that would have made him a hero in a time of war. Heroes, contrary to the outrageous propaganda put out about them, are by nature meek, decent people. They don't do like everyone else and look after Number One. In peacetime, however, they usually get called suckers.

George had never done anything for himself. He'd never asked for a raise, or taken advantage of his position, or even made personal calls from work. This was why the Messiah warned that the only way the meek would get anywhere on this earth was through an inheritance.

George already had enough on his hands looking after twenty children, without having to take care of the twenty-eight adults in the bank as well, but he didn't see how he could turn them away if they came to him for help. He was exactly the kind of sucker who ends up taking the rap in a situation because his ability to stand up for himself and his ability to stand up for others are in exactly inverse proportion. This is why people like him get posthumous war medals while everyone else goes home to their wives and gets busy making the next generation.

Heroes are by nature expendable commodities, and so it is no surprise if they get fuck-all respect in peacetime.

A phone had been ringing in the bank. Special Agent Winston Pepsi waited vainly on the other end for a reply. All the bank's phones had been rerouted to patch them into the operations van across the street as the lawmen got ready to negotiate with the robbers. But something was wrong. Nobody had picked it up in over an hour.

Inside, the gunmen had stared coldly at George when he raised the sandwich issue. Two hours on from the initial attack, only two of the six gunmen were covering the hostages – Luís Alvares of the Blade and Ben Cage of the Blood. Julio López and Cray Jones were on the mobile phones to their respective leaders, while Duey Martínez and Sonny Day were covering Sonny Day and Duey Martínez respectively.

Alvares and Cage looked warily at each other, realizing that a sandwich treaty of some kind would have to be reached if the situation was going to remain deadlocked for much longer. Both, furthermore, were beginning to feel hungry. Sandwiches would be good. But they had to trust one another.

'You cool?' Cage asked, looking at Alvares while keeping his gun trained on the hostages.

'No, man . . . are *you* cool?' Alvares returned tensely.

'I asked first.'

There was a tight-testicled pause, conflicting emotions playing over Alvares' face. The ringing phone was getting on his nerves.

'Are you saying I don't look cool?'

'I ain't saying zip,' Cage answered, his eyes flicking back and forth between Alvares and the hostages. 'I asked a question. If I *knew* you weren't cool, I wouldn't have asked it.'

'Well, I'm cool,' Alvares announced finally. 'I'm always cool. Remember that. Are *you*?'

'Snow wouldn't melt if I pissed on it.'

They stared coolly at each other a while longer just to prove it, and then Alvares turned to George, snapping:

'Order some sandwiches, motherfucker. There's a pig on the other end of that phone – pick it up, order the food, but say anything, *anything* else to him, and you'll be so dead you'll think you're a fossil.'

'And no pig in those sandwiches, yeah?' Cage added as George started walking shakily toward the phone.

'Oh get real, man!' Alvares laughed. 'How they gonna hide a pig inside a sandwich?'

Cage looked at him as if it was a miracle that someone so stupid could hold a gun the right way round.

'Pig *swine*, not pig cop, asshole. I'm a Muslim.'

Alvares squinted dangerously, momentarily unsure how to avoid losing face without using his gun. Then he turned to George, shouting, 'Yo, *motherfucker*! And no nuts, neither!'

'You got an allergy?' Cage asked.

Alvares smiled triumphantly, confident that respect was about to be restored.

'Nuts *cojones*, not nuts nuts, asshole. I got more than any man needs as it is.'

Ben Cage smiled grimly. It was like he'd always said – there was no negotiating possible with these people.

'Hello? *Hello?*' a startled male voice leaped out of the receiver the second George picked up the phone.

'Hello,' he replied.

'*Yes!* Who am I speaking to here?'

'Bailey here.'

'Okay, Bailey, this is Special Agent Winston Pepsi. I want you to understand that even though we have enough firepower out here to put the *building* in hospital, we have no intention of harming you if you release the hostages and surrender peacefully. Do we understand each other?'

George glanced nervously over at Alvares and Cage, who were watching him intently.

'Um . . . no.'

'Come on, Bailey – you're in no position to play hardball with me. You'll only make things worse for yourself than they already are. Your best bet is to co-operate. You're up Shit Creek. I am the paddle. Work with me here, Bailey – what do you *want*?'

'Sandwiches.'

'Sandwiches, huh? Okay, Bailey, I could give you sandwiches, but there's no such thing as a free lunch. If I were to give you sandwiches, what would you be giving me in return?'

'Um . . . *money* for the sandwiches?'

'Forget the money, Bailey, it isn't yours to spend. Get with the reality here – you don't seem to understand how serious your position is.'

George looked apologetically at Alvares and Cage, pointing to the receiver and raising his eyebrows.

'On the contrary, Agent Pepsi, I don't think *you*

150

understand how serious my position is. My name is George Bailey. I'm not robbing the bank, I *work* for the bank!'

There was a long pause. George heard a distant, mumbled '*Shit . . .*' down the line.

'Okay . . .' Agent Pepsi eventually responded, 'sorry about that, George, but the situation wasn't very clear there, you know. You're a hostage. Right. Can you talk freely?'

'About sandwiches, yes.'

Again George could hear Pepsi's soft cursing in the distance as he thought the situation over.

'Okay . . . shit . . . okay . . . is anyone listening in to what I'm saying, George?'

'No.'

'Okay, good. Now I realize you're under a lot of pressure, George, but I need you to give me information. I'll get all the sandwiches you could want delivered, but what we're going to do first is have a coded conversation where I ask you questions about the situation in there and you reply in terms of sandwiches, do you understand?'

'I think so.'

'Okay, George, first of all – order a sandwich with a number of ingredients corresponding to the number of perpetrators in the bank.'

George frowned in concentration. His mind suddenly seemed blank of sandwich ingredients.

'Um . . . turkey . . . lettuce . . . and . . . potato . . . on rye.'

'Three! Is that right, George – there's three of them?'

'And onion . . . beef . . . and pickles . . . on white.'

'That's *two* sandwiches, George. I realize you're tense, but try to concentrate.'

'What kind of fucking sandwich is onion, beef and pickles?' Alvares was muttering in the background. 'Yo, mother! I don't want no pickles!'

'No pickles, sorry,' George relayed.

'*No* pickles!' Pepsi repeated. 'You were wrong about the pickles? There are five of them, not six?'

'Instead of pickles . . . tomato!'

'Tomato now! We're back to six. But we've still got two sandwiches. Let's talk about these sandwiches, George – one's rye, one's white . . . are you trying to say something about the ethnicity of your assailants here? Say olives for yes and . . . peanuts for no.'

George was starting to break out into a cold sweat. 'Olives . . . and peanuts.'

'*Yo!*' Alvares barked. 'I said *no* nuts!'

'Sorry . . . no peanuts. We don't want peanuts. Olives and potato crisps.'

'Olives and peanuts . . .' Pepsi recapitulated, '*no* peanuts . . . olives and *potato crisps*. So that's yes and no . . . not no . . . yes and *maybe*? I'm pretty confused here, George – do you think we could start again with one sandwich?'

'No.'

'Too many ingredients, huh? What about ordering a pizza?'

'No, no, no . . . I said rye bread *and* white bread. It's two completely different sandwiches. It's not a pizza.'

'What the . . . ? I don't get it. It sounds like you're being held hostage twice.'

'Olives!' George confirmed fervently. 'Black olives *and* green olives!'

'You *are* being held hostage twice! By two groups of assailants, is that it?'

'Stuffed olives!'

'Yo!' Cage shouted. 'That's enough fucking *olives*, man!'

'All right, now we're getting somewhere, George,' Pepsi was enthusing in his other ear. 'You're doing very well. Now I need to know about the other hostages –

numbers and gender. Order bacon sandwiches for males and tuna for females.'

George's heart sank. He looked at Cage, whispering down the phone, 'Haven't you got anything other than bacon?'

'I haven't got anything at all, George – I'm a federal agent, not a frigging delicatessen. What's the problem with bacon?'

'I'm under orders not to put pork in the sandwiches for . . . moral reasons.'

'No pork? You're being held hostage by Jews?'

'No-o-o . . .'

'Arabs! These sons of bitches are *terrorists*?'

'No . . .'

'*What* then, for heaven's sake?' Pepsi shouted, his temper snapping. 'Are you being held by militant vegetarians? By armed *pigs*? Speak to me, George!'

'Look,' George snapped, his own patience fraying under the strain, 'just no bacon, please. Turkey will do fine, okay? We want about fifteen turkey, fifteen tuna . . . *and* . . . twenty peanut butter and jelly . . . but hold the peanuts. Have you got that?'

'Peanut butter and jelly?' Pepsi gasped. 'I assume you're talking children?'

'Yes. Twenty.'

Pepsi whistled. '*Twenty* peanut butter and jelly without peanuts? Are you sure, George?'

'Radishes!' George offered in what he hoped was an affirmative tone.

'Yes? *Twenty* children?'

'Apples!'

'Are they with the tuna?'

'No . . . rollmops.'

'They're not with the tuna? Who are the rollmops? Is that like grandmothers or something?'

'Are you going to order dessert as well, man?' Cage

153

shouted. 'That's *enough* food, don't you think? Get off the phone.'

George nodded and sighed. He desperately wanted Pepsi to understand about the children, but he just couldn't think of a gastronomical metaphor for orphans.

'I have to go now.'

'No, George, wait – the children, who are they with?'

George had an idea.

'Eggs, but no *chicken*,' he said in parting.

'Wait! Wait! What about their weapons – handguns, rifles, automatics . . . what have they got, George?'

Cage and Alvares were staring menacingly at him as he hesitated, Cage motioning with his free hand for him to put the phone down. George began to comply, then whipped the phone back.

'*Maxi Cokes all round!*' he hissed, and hung up.

*

'Hello, George? Hello? Fuck!'

Agent Pepsi ripped the headphones off his ears and threw them in disgust against the console of the communications van.

'Well?' Detective Weiss asked. 'What do we know?'

'We know . . .' Pepsi looked down at the pad upon which he had been noting the lunch order, translating it into real terms as he ran over the list, 'that we have two separate groups of perpetrators. Armed with . . . well, maxi Cokes sound like fully automatic rifles to me, frankly. Plus approximately fifty hostages, of which fifteen are women, fifteen are men, and twenty are children.'

'Oh, wonderful,' Weiss commented, turning around on the spot and raising his palms pleadingly to the sky. 'This happens on my shift, does it? I don't get the nun rape-murder or the Ghetty's Burger Restaurant massacre. I don't even get the gang shoot-out with pregnant mother of two caught in crossfire. I get twenty kids being held hostage. We've got friends for dinner tonight but, hey, they can just catch me on the news, right? Thanks, Big Man.'

'It gets worse.'

'Good. Let's make this a day to remember.'

'What, if we're talking about children, does a reference to "eggs, but no chickens" mean to you?'

Weiss frowned and looked up. 'Orphans?'

'Right, that's what I figured, too. So I believe we should assume that we have twenty *orphans* in there, detective.'

'Orphans. Orphans.' Weiss tapped his lip with his finger as he weighed up the situation. 'Uh-huh. Don't hold back on me now, Pepsi – is that all of the bad news or is one of them, like . . . Orphan of the Year?'

Pepsi nodded grimly. 'I think we can safely assume that they each in their own, unique way has courageously hung on to their sweetness and innocence while leading a life of heart-wrenching tragedy, don't you, detective?'

'I would be shocked and disgusted to hear that they are anything less than angels, frankly.'

They looked at one another, the colour draining from their faces as the awful reality of the situation they were in returned, un-diminished by their attempts at cynicism. Pepsi's face hardened and he spoke in a low, grim voice.

'If only they turned out to be adolescents we could afford to lose a few of them. But anything under fourteen and it's our careers in the firing line here, Weiss . . .'

*

'No parents. Twenty children, aged under thirteen. Orphans. Two gangs of armed robbers. A bank.

155

Hostages. Children with no parents. A *horrifying* drama unfolds . . .'

'That was wonderful, Vanessa! We'll run it every five minutes in case they lose the plot. This is perfect, you realize – I was starting to worry that the whole crime tsunami story was running out of steam, weren't you? Do you want to break for lunch?'

XIII

The way some people are with chocolate cake, or klepto-mania, Jean Grey was with driving across bridges with her eyes shut. Lord knows how many times she'd promised herself she wouldn't do it again, but sooner or later she'd find herself alone in her car on a clear stretch of road leading on to a bridge . . . and the temptation was more than a girl could withstand.

When younger she was horrified by her peculiar desire, and her indulgence of it was a constant source of shame and self-recrimination. She had no doubt there must be something seriously wrong with her, the only question being whether she was actually insane. She could have sought the help of a psychiatrist, but was not prepared to reveal every detail of her private life just because one aspect of it was clearly abnormal. Instead, she learned to cope with it in her own way. Nowadays, at the age of thirty-four, she indulged her desire on a con-trolled, weekly basis at a location an hour's drive from her work where the passage of other cars was minimal. She was reconciled to it, reasoning that this periodical release probably made her overall a more stable, balanced person than she would be if she suppressed her peculiar need and lived in a constant state of frustration.

She shared her secret with no one, naturally, because to do so would be unfair on the person she told. How could one expect others to keep one's most intimate and shocking secrets confidential if one couldn't oneself, after all? And no matter how trustworthy some of her friends might be, it was a risk she could not afford to take. If word spread to the wrong people, the ramifications on her life and career didn't bear thinking about. The people who employed her weren't just looking for level-headed individuals. They wanted emotional pancakes.

Driving blind over bridges was not acceptable behaviour in an astronaut, period.

For a long time she had believed she had a kind of death-wish, probably due to her guilt over the suicide of her older brother, Scott, at the age of seventeen – a death almost certainly provoked by the turn their relationship had taken just prior to his jumping off the Tawnysuckit Bridge.

This seemed plausible.

But the more she looked into that dark period of her youth, the more she decided that it explained nothing at all, attractive simply because it is so easy to blame all your problems on a single trauma like finding your brother's broken body at the bottom of a gully and knowing that he was probably there because you had sex with him.

In her heart of hearts, however, she didn't really feel responsible for what had happened. It had been Scott himself who was to blame. She had resisted his advances, but when she did eventually give in she had done nothing to make him feel bad about it. She'd told him it didn't matter. She believed then, and still believed now, that it was just a physical act, just the bodies of two people – who loved one another, after all – doing something a little naughty. It was no more some hideous sin that entailed punishment by burning in hell than stealing magazines from the drugstore. Less so, if she were God. Had they married and had pig-nosed and web-footed babies then, yes, that would have been going too far.

She had loved him then, and loved him still, but her love did not cloud the real issue, which was testicles. It was testicles that pushed him into her bedroom, and testicles that pushed him over the bridge. Young males are like drug-crazed fiends, totally strung out on testosterone.

Barely a day went by without her thinking of him, but not with guilt so much as sadness, and the more years went by the more the one point of happiness within the sadness was that at least they had made love.

So, no. That wasn't it, she had decided, saving herself several thousand dollars of therapy in the process.

But such thoughts were far from the front of her mind on this fall day as she sped her black coupé up the mountain roads leading to her mother's cabin. She was thinking about the mission.

About the passenger.

Even though the leaves had already turned, the day was warm enough for her to have the top down, smiling as the wind whipped golden hairs against her cheeks. Glancing in the rear-view mirror, she saw the lines of breeze-blown tears trickling off either side of her sea-green eyes and wiped them away with her index finger, licking it absent-mindedly afterwards to taste the salt.

This is why life is so wonderful, she realized as if for the first time – just being able to drive alone through beautiful woods on a beautiful day. The woods might have thought the same thing of her, but Jean was genuinely not vain about her looks. Her nose, anyway too large, seemed to be in tune with the weather, constantly changing shape. Her skin was slightly rough with mysterious little imperfections that came and went, usually never resolving themselves into actual spots, although when they did they were of Krakatoan violence. She equated beauty with prettiness and so would never have called herself beautiful. Jean was not pretty, but she had something indefinable that made men look twice. Jean had IT. Old-fashioned IT, that is. She didn't own a computer.

She tried to avoid them outside work. Her colleagues at the space agency were surprised by her attitude, but Jean simply could not see what use she could have for one. There was nothing in her life that she needed a computer for, so why have one? She didn't need a dishwasher, either, but no one questioned that. Just because she worked in the most technologically advanced business in the world didn't mean she had to love computers. She loved space.

Emptiness.

Silence.

Which was why the passenger bothered her. They had no choice, since Infologix was paying for the mission and it was their satellite, but she thought of space as her temple, her great black temple, and astronauts as her fellow-pilgrims. She didn't want a damned tourist with her. The man was going with them for the sole purpose of pushing the button that launched the satellite. Like cracking a champagne bottle on a hull. Why did people have to cheapen everything?

They did not know who he was yet. Hell, until the Rectag programme was finally announced they hadn't even known what the satellite did. It still seemed odd to her that Memphis 2, the codename by which they still referred to it, should be so big. It was designed to track a few hundred thousand criminals, and yet it was the size of the largest telecommunications satellites she had launched.

She was briefly irritated with herself for thinking about it – she was on leave, she was supposed to put it all behind her. The road twisted up through a tunnel of trees, leopardskin light racing over her eyes. A few miles ahead her mother would be waiting with open arms, eager to

160

spoil her with home cooking. Actually, these days it was increasingly home reheating, but the crockery was still nostalgic. Poor mother. Jean felt guilty for not coming to visit more often, but although her mother's love was unquestioning, her company consisted of little but questions. When was she going to find a man? When was she going to have children? She would never understand why Jean wasn't worried by these things. Different generations. Her mother belonged to that generation who believed a woman's place was in the medicine cabinet.

But even if she had reservations about the coming week, it felt good to be away from New Toulouse. Her work at Star City took so much out of her that all she really wanted to do on her days off was stand under the shower until her skin was glowing and smooth, drink coffee in her dressing gown and pluck stray leg-hairs with her tweezers. That was almost half the day gone already. She needed a real break.

In fact that was another theory she had considered to explain the bridges: did she do it as a reaction against the extreme discipline and control her work demanded? Discipline and control had been the watchwords of her entire adult life, and even longer – it went back to the choice of subjects she had taken at college, knowing what would stand in her favour when it came to joining the Air Force as a necessary stepping-stone to becoming an astronaut. Everything had been planned with that one objective in mind from the beginning. God knows she would have preferred to study literature or art than engineering, but there was no call for a knowledge of Shakespeare in zero gravity.

And Jean had wanted space above all else. An infinity of blackness. Why, she didn't know.

Her dedication to the cause had been absolute and unswerving. She had denied herself relaxation, fun, and probably several possibilities of love in the process.

161

Had it been unhealthy to repress herself so thoroughly in the name of her ambition?

Probably, she eventually decided. But so what? The more she thought about it, the more it irritated her that people made such a big deal about their repressed desires and stresses.

What did they want?

Where was the value in doing something so easy that it didn't cost you anything? Didn't everyone have to repress themselves if they wanted to fulfil their ambitions? Did people seriously want their careers, and families, and lives, to be given to them free in cereal packets?

If everyone started to believe that every hardship left them emotionally scarred, then how long would it be before they all needed picnic insurance? How long before some lawyer successfully argued that his client needed to kill as a form of self-expression?

So, no, that wasn't why she drove blind over bridges either, she had decided, denying some poor therapist a new car in the process. Her foot unconsciously eased off the accelerator as the Tawnysuckit Bridge came into view, the car coasting to a stop just yards from its open mouth.

The afternoon sunlight leaned in solid beams from the road to the trees, pillars of a pagan temple. Just a breath of wind would shake their foundations and break the spell of the place, but it was still and silent, and Jean shivered. The road snaked uphill on the far side, climbing sharply through three hairpin bends until the track to her parents' cabin forked off to the left. This was the place they had come to all through her childhood, whenever her father's squadron leave permitted. It was the perfect antidote to the roar and scream of an airbase – no people, no cars, no rules; nothing but nature. She and Scott used to race each other down to the bridge on their bikes, skidding to a halt there where she now sat in her softly chuckling car. Every second of the downhill hurtle would

162

be pure, delicious terror, the tears so blinding her vision as she came out of the last bend that she would cross the bridge in a blur of water, trusting her bicycle as if it were a horse. It was a kind of torture, hearing the *thap-thap-thap* of the bridge's stanchions whipping past her, one that made her scream with joy as her brakes screeched burning rubber and she blinked to look for Scott.

Who always won. He was eighteen months older, after all, and bigger. Only by being that much braver or crazier than Scott was prepared to be could she ever hope to get there first. And Scott had never lacked in that department.

For a while she sat there in the motionless car, feeling the gas pedal's low throb beneath her foot, pretending she didn't know what was on her mind.

She knew all right, though. Just like she knew why she did it.

For the orgasms.

She closed her eyes with a languorous smile of antici-pation and began to depress the accelerator. She felt the car start to roll forward on to the bridge, a gentle breeze on her cheeks and a painful electric throb running up her legs from the pedals as her feet struggled with the desire to brake.

The light played over her eyelids as she let the car slowly pick up speed, then she took one deep breath, bit her lower lip and floored the pedal. As the car leaped forward, she pleaded with herself to stop or open her eyes, and the masochism of her own refusal only increased the waves of pleasure building inside her as the stanchions whipped *thap-thap-thap* in her ears, each knock on her eardrums rolling down her entire body.

She felt as though there was a dam between her legs, and with each *thap* little splashes of water spilled over the edge to land on a thirsty flowerbud below. And the dam began to crack as the flower unfurled, her body grew

163

taut, her legs straightening as she ground the accelerator to the floor, and *thap* and *thap* and *crack* the dam burst and her eyes snapped open, struggling to control the car as her muscles spasmed wildly.

She was heading full speed toward the far end of the bridge, seeing the road bend sharply up to the right ahead as she jerked and twisted in her seat. The car squealed deliciously as she snapped the wheel round, her eyes misting over and her body beginning to cry out for oxygen. She misjudged the second bend, taking it wide and spraying gravel behind her, but the pounding in her ears drowned out the clatter of the stone chips and the pleasure was so intense that she almost didn't care about getting the wheels back on to the tarmac. At last, as the road ahead straightened out, the shocks began to recede like a motorbike kicking down through the gears, and she breathed again, the mountain air making her dizzy with oxygen.

She eased off the accelerator and let the car roll to a halt, slumping forward on the wheel. Her breaths teetered on the edge of sobbing, her body battered and limp as a favourite teddy, her mind blank. After a minute or so, she flopped back against the seat, looked at herself in the rear-view mirror and began wiping tears from her eyes.

She looked a state. Not like she had just got out of bed so much as like she'd never been. No doubt her mother, waiting one minute up the road, would say this was why she didn't have a man.

The carphone rang.

'Jean? Where are you?' demanded Frank Baxter, her mission controller.

'On my way home. Why?'

'Turn around. The mission's been brought forward.'

'What about my leave?'

'Cancelled. This crime wave is killing the Vice-President in the polls, Jean. Result: we have to get the

164

satellite up and Rectag working before the elections. That means you're up for the next flight.'

'I don't need training for it, Frank! It's a straightforward launch. There's no reason to cancel my leave.'

'*You* don't need training, Jean. The passenger does.'

Jean's heart sank. 'Oh no, Frank. You're not saying what I think you're saying, are you?'

'I'm saying it, Jean. He's called Josh Cloken. We don't know anything about him except that he's aged thirty-nine and his only flight experience is on the kind of aircraft with a drinks trolley. That's why I'm putting him in your care – we need someone who's exceptionally . . . how shall I put it? . . .'

'Level-headed, by any chance?'

'Right! Level-headed!'

'Well, hey. I guess that's me, right?'

'Jean . . . you will be nice, won't you? I know how you feel about this, but these people are paying for the whole launch. They are customers.'

Jean felt the sun play over her eyelids, and sighed, 'I'll be nice. I can be very nice when I want to, you know, Frank.'

'Sure?' he insisted. 'Think you can handle it?'

'With my eyes shut, Frank,' she smiled, putting the phone down.

She sat for a couple of minutes longer, enjoying the peace of the woods, and then phoned her mother all of a mile away to explain she wouldn't be coming this time after all. Soon, she promised.

She wiped the last of the tears from her cheeks, turned the car on the thin mountain road, and cruised gently back down toward the bridge.

XIV

As always, Lola Colaco was dressed to suit the occasion.
Today she was a sober but sophisticated dark green –
smart and elegantly sexy – with a pair of silver teardrop
pendants in her ears and her blond hair swirled up in a
virgin-ice-queen-bitch-lawyer look.

They were talking about rape.

Or 'Wives of Famous People Who Have Been Raped',
to be precise.

Today's whole show had been built around Susan
Summerday's revelation of the day before, but they had
managed to get in some other celebrity victims at short
notice to make it more balanced. They had Teri Winston,
wife of the football star Crud Winston, who was news at
the moment because she was about to go to court against
her alleged rapist.

Her husband.

And they had Alice Chandler, wife of the actor Lewis
Chandler, who was apparently sort of raped by the
director when she had a bit part in a horror movie, but
the details weren't too clear. She said it was all going to
be in her autobiography *You'll Never Suck Dick in This
Town Again* just as soon as the lawyers had finished re-
writing it. Lola and her producers weren't too sure about
having her on if she was only going to imply strongly that
an unnamed party may have done certain unspecified
things to her, but they were short of guests and Alice had

promised to cover up the overall lack of detail by breaking down in tears as she talked about it.

It didn't really matter how those two worked out, anyway, because the meat in their sandwich was Susan Summerday. Lola had already heard what she was going to say and it was clearly a major televisual landmark given that her husband was a presidential contender. This was good for the show on every level – it gave her *gravitas* having the wife of a leading politician as her guest, and they hadn't made the headlines since she brought those twins separated at birth together live on air and one of them tragically stiffed it before he could say how he felt.

Lola still had nightmares about that. She'd tried to resuscitate him, personally administering the kiss of life, but he hadn't responded. In a desperate bid to save him she had administered the tongue, too, but the guy was a total corpse. Just checked out without paying his bill.

Not even a dying word.

Susan Summerday was in the make-up room having her skin tinted to compensate for the effect of the studio lighting. She had been grimly serious ever since she had arrived – not nervous, like most guests, but oppressive, with the air of someone who was about to go into battle. Lola wasn't often awed by the people she had on her show, usually expecting to find herself the object of their awe at the three-dimensional proof of her existence beyond the television screen, but there was something about Susan Summerday that commanded respect. She was that rare person whose sense of self was so strong that she did not need to appear on television to be sure of her own place in the world.

Lola couldn't imagine what it must be like to be that self-aware. To know who you were just by looking in a mirror.

The problem, however, was that people like that were always the most difficult guests, because they could not be relied upon to let Lola control the conversation. They

167

had their own ideas. They contradicted her. They wanted to say things in their own way in their own time, and didn't understand the need to keep the details of their lives short and snappy. Much the most interesting and rewarding people for her to talk to personally, but hell in the editing suite.

Lola stood in the entrance to the make-up room, expecting Susan Summerday to see her in the mirror, but she was engrossed in her papers, reading aloud softly as her hair was put into place.

'And I remember . . .' she muttered, 'Mike held me in his arms as I cried, and swore to me that one day . . . one day he would make this country safe for women such as myself. I didn't know then what he meant by that, and I was too happy just to be safe in his arms again to ask, but I think now that even then he had some idea of Rectag . . .'

*

'. . . that he's not just doing it for me. He's doing it for every woman who has known the horror of being attacked, for everyone who has felt terror walking the streets of their own neighbourhood, for everyone who fears for the safety of their children in this society.'

'Bitch! She's lying, damn it!' Presidential contender Jack Douglas threw a last disgusted glance at the screen and stomped over to the drinks trolley, plunging his hand into the ice bucket and dropping the cubes into his empty whisky glass. 'It's a scam, the whole story!'

'No doubt about it,' answered Travers de Lyne, his campaign manager, freezing the video on Lola's emotion-racked but nevertheless attractive face, 'but even if it isn't, the effect is the same. It's a smart move.'

'Smart!' Douglas spat, his throat burning from the hastily swallowed alcohol. 'What does it say about the state of this country when managing to debase the democratic process with perjury and cheap sensationalism is called "smart"?'

'That one has to be damned inventive to find new ways of doing it. Calm down, Jack – I'm not saying they are *smarter*. You're the one who has campaign workers out every night smashing windows to keep the crime statistics up, after all.'

'I know Susan Summerday, Travers, and I tell you – she's no more been raped than I have.'

'That's not the point, Jack! The point is that we cannot prove she's lying and were we to call her story into question, even in the subtlest manner, they would tear us to *shreds*! Can you imagine how it would look if we accused a woman who has just had the courage to talk about a deeply painful episode from her past of lying? Suddenly *we* would be the ones who were prepared to do anything for the sake of political advantage! Summerday's camp knows damn well that we won't dare question her story.'

'So what do we do?' Douglas growled bitterly as he paced the room. 'Politely offer our sympathies?'

De Lyne was quiet for a few seconds as he too refreshed his whisky glass. He answered in a quieter, more determined voice: 'It's an option we've been looking at.'

Douglas stopped dead in his tracks, his jaw dropping as the words hit home and his head slowly turning to face his adviser.

'Naturally you are kidding me. You are *kidding* me! We know it's a lie and you not only want me to play along with it, but to reinforce it? No way, Trav – there are limits to how low down in the barrel I'm willing to lick.'

'Think about it, Jack. Lie or not, the story is out there – by tomorrow the whole country will have heard about her appearance on *Lola Colaco*. There's no knowing how much having his wife raped will affect the polls, but we all know it won't do the bastard any harm. It gives him a new dimension. It gives the *election* a new dimension. Suddenly he's planted a flag for people to rally around. A well-judged message of sympathy from you could take some of the political sting out of it. Either way, there will be no avoiding the issue – it is all you will be asked about at your next press conference, believe me.'

'Don't you think I know that? I know that, Trav. I just feel pretty damn nauseous about handing them the moral high ground by pretending to believe this bullshit. It's obscene. It's like a guard dog rolling over to have his tummy scratched.'

'You don't have to hand them the moral ground. You can counter-attack, but not by questioning the sincerity of Susan Summerday's confession, that's all. That's a no-win battle.'

'Okay – so talk to me about counter-attacking.'

De Lyne chinked the ice cubes in his glass, watching the whisky swirl and then taking a gulp. He looked nervous.

'It's simple. You offer your sympathies, your deepest, most heartfelt sympathy with her in her pain . . . and say you can understand how hard it must have been for her to deal with what happened because your own wife was also the victim of sexual abuse.'

The campaign manager had thought of little else than how Douglas was going to react to this suggestion. Nobody who had seen the candidate get angry before wanted to be on the receiving end of that temper. He waited, every muscle tensed, for the explosion to come.

But it never did. Douglas was shocked into silence.

'Martha . . . raped?' he eventually whispered. 'My Martha?'

He was at a loss to know what to say. He could see the logic of de Lyne's suggestion, but the idea of abusing his late first wife's memory in that way was so utterly repellent to him that anger was not an adequate response. Instead he felt sadness. Sadness at the state of the country's political process, that it should become possible to wage election campaigns in this way, and sadness at the thought that he had ever got himself involved in this business in the first place.

'Don't you think that's actually a little suspicious?' he asked finally. 'Susan Summerday announces that she was raped and suddenly there am I saying exactly the same thing happened to *my* wife?'

'Not *exactly* the same, obviously,' de Lyne explained. 'You have to change the nature of it. We were . . .' He stopped, unable to get the words out.

'Come on . . . say what you were going to say.'

'We were thinking . . . she could have been sexually abused by her father as a child . . .'

'Uh . . . huh. And if tomorrow Mike Summerday's brother announces that he's on heroin, then what? Am I going to have to find a relative who injects bath-cleaner?'

'I know. I feel the same way, believe me – but in elections you have to play by the rules. You don't rob a gun shop with a knife, right? That's the name of the game.'

'Sometimes I think it would be healthier for society if the two guys running for President just climbed into a mud-ring in their underpants and wrestled.'

From the note of humour in his voice, de Lyne judged that Jack was coming round to accepting his suggestion. He hadn't said no yet, after all. 'But you'll do it?' he asked hopefully.

Jack took a deep breath and closed his eyes, like a man about to jump off a bridge.

'I have a feeling that this election is going to get very ugly.'

'Is that a yes? You'll say Martha was sexually abused by her father?'

'Sure . . .' Douglas exhaled. 'She never liked the old bastard anyway.'

171

XV

Macauley Connor's mood had darkened progressively throughout the hot morning drive until, by the time he stopped his car and started rootling around on the back seat, he was seething with aimless anger. He was thirsty, and his shoes had been sticking to the car's rubber mat since stopping at a Ghetty's Burger fifty miles back. He'd been brushing the unwanted poppy seeds off his Big One on to the floor of the car when he knocked over his cola. The lid popped off as it hit the floor and now everything was coated in a thin layer of sugary water. He needed to clean out the car, but then he had needed to do that for months now. The filthier it got, the less inclined he was to do anything about it.

He searched furiously through the mass of papers and dirty clothing on the back seat, snatching loose pages of his road atlas from the general anarchy and throwing them aside again with gritted teeth.

'Where are you, you little shit?' he muttered as he found himself picking up pages he'd furiously dismissed only seconds before. Page 128. He knew he should be somewhere on page 128. But where the hell was it?

'*Ha!*' he exclaimed triumphantly, peeling a six-month-old motel bill from the guilty leaf and scrumpling it into a ball. 'Don't fuck with me!'

He examined the sticky page with a sneer, searching for the town he'd passed through a few miles back. There it was. He was on the right road. He was only a few minutes' drive from his destination. Macauley tossed the page on to the passenger seat and got out of the car, slamming the door behind him.

Maybe it was the feeling that he was wasting his time coming all the way out here to John Lockes' birthplace that so angered him. It wasn't by visiting old school-teachers and nursery-school pals that he was going to get to the bottom of the Rectag mystery, but Joel Schonk had insisted on his getting the background research for the book finished first. Who cares where people were born or where they kissed their first girl? Macauley brooded. We only read about them because they grew up. He had argued his case passionately, but Schonk was a very stubborn man. And he was writing the cheques. So Macauley had ended up driving straight for two days to reach this piss-ant place.

True, not much was known about Lockes' formative years, but for a very good reason – he'd been born and raised out here, in a little town called Farview, and *nothing* of interest had happened until he left to attend a private school called the Welton Academy for Gifted Children, some eight hundred miles away.

Where he had made his first million.

Or maybe it was this landscape getting on his nerves, he thought as he considered the countryside around where John Lockes was born. Looking took about five seconds: where John Lockes was born it was flat. Very flat. Nothing but prairie stretching off into the distance wherever you looked. Not even a shadow, just the noon sun dropping vertically on to vertical, windless corn. Not a bird, not a plane.

He lit a cigarette, feeling duty-bound to give the spot a longer consideration but already bored. Maybe it was because he was a city boy, but Macauley had never had much love for the countryside. He was prepared to acknowledge that it could sometimes be attractive, in a dumb-blonde kind of way, but it was essentially boring. By definition, there was nothing to do there. As soon as there was anything to do, the environmentalists complained that it had been destroyed.

Actually, Macauley had a theory about environmentalists. They were dull. They didn't stand out from the crowd, so their solution was to say that crowds were unnatural. Instead, everyone should be divided up into small groups of hikers and dumped in the middle of nowhere where the only exciting thing that might put some perspective on their dullness was being eaten by a bear.

It was a brilliantly subtle conspiracy.

He'd got into a few arguments over this one. Not necessarily with the environmentalists themselves, but with people who had been brainwashed into believing their green-supremacist propaganda. Nature, evolution and science were on his side, however, because the objective proof of his theory was that good genes instinctively headed to the biggest gene pool to find a wider choice of mate. Therefore, good genetic material goes to the city, and bad genetic material stays in the countryside, where it will have a better choice of finding a mate simply because there is fuck-all else to fuck.

Therefore, country people were trash.

There was no arguing with this.

The countryside was a dumb blonde. The city, on the other hand, was dark-eyed and mysterious, supple with subtle intelligence. This was somewhat sexist, he realized, which was why he never brought it out in arguments on the subject, but still essentially true.

And by far the worst of all forms of nature was the prairie. God's parking lot.

'Let there be . . .' Macauley boomed as he looked down the straight road, stretching into the horizon like a dead man's cardiograph, 'let there be . . . let there *beeee*

174

. . . A VAST FLAT BIT! Yea, for know that the Lord your God is *bored* today! So in his infinite wisdom shall he make this land FLAT! And know ye that a day will come when one among you shall arise and say, "Behold! I have invented the Crunchyflake!", and there shall be much amazement among the beholders of the Crunchyflake for they shall know then that it was for *this* that their Creator made the vast flat bit upon the land!'

Strange how they were all so damned religious on the prairie, when all the evidence around them suggested that even God had off-days. Idiots. And Macauley hated Crunchyflakes too, for that matter. Not just for their astounding dullness, but for the things he associated with them – in particular those mind-numbing commercials that interrupted his Saturday-morning cartoons as a kid with their happy, blondoid families running through endless cornfields like that was about the most fun a person could have outside of a lynching. And the whiter-than-white milk being poured into the cereal bowl from so damn high that any fool could see it would all end up on the table – but maybe that was a prairie-dwelling Crunchyflake-eater's idea of being one devil-may-care son of a gun.

It was a world that should have died along with shoe-brush haircuts and electric shock treatment, but even now – after all that sex, drugs and rock and roll had done to save civilization – there were still people who ate Crunchyflakes, there were still Crunchyflake adverts, and nobody had done *anything* to get rid of the prairies.

It wouldn't be so hard, after all. Years ago now, Macauley had been struck by an idea of genius that would not only solve the prairie problem but also find a use for all the garbage society produced: dump it on the prairie. Build a few hills and valleys, for God's sake! Remove the topsoil first, then pat it back on top of the cheesepuff packets. Sure, the environmentalists would scream blue murder, but that was typical of their short-sightedness. In a hundred years, once trees had got their roots dug into the toptrash and covered the garbage with a good coating of rotting leaves, it would become home to all manner of beast and insect, probably even a bear or two, and the descendants of today's outraged environmentalists would demand the Connor Hills be declared a national park.

Finding supporters for his vision was a hopeless cause, of course. Even otherwise sane people seemed to have this weird reverence for the prairies, presumably because endless westerns had inculcated them with the idea that they were a place where decent, God-fearing folk raised children so wholesome and pure that you could use them to soak up oil-tanker spills. A place where women cooked simple, nourishing food because there wasn't a supermarket for a thousand miles around, and where men walked tall because their hats were, indeed, the highest point between them and the horizon.

It made sense, Macauley supposed as he stepped on his cigarette butt, that Lockes grew up here. What was the landscape of cyberspace, after all, if not prairie?

*

The sun was looking down hard on Farview as his car coasted slowly up Main Street (which in a more honest world would have been called Only Street). The sole shadows were those cast by the ledges of the windows, giving the buildings the exhausted, dreamless gaze of bodybuilders. Nothing much seemed to happen at noon in Farview, the town as still as if it were four in the morning. The shops were shut for lunch, although Macauley was impressed to find shops at all. Most towns this size had long since let their commerce, even their churches, die in favour of some distant mall, but Farview, to its

176

credit, seemed to have at least one example of each essential trade.

On the other hand, the fashions in the clothing-store window were so astoundingly out of date that it was possible to believe Farview hadn't *heard* about malls yet. A male and a female mannequin gazed blankly at Macauley from the window of Stella's Modern Fashions, each wearing clothes that last went on a date a few years before white boys got rhythm. The people they were originally designed for had now matured to the point where their clothing accessories included colostomy bags.

God, he despised small towns. It was like they did it on purpose. There was no other rational explanation for how they managed to stay so resolutely behind the times in an age when satellites made the same crap available to everyone – it had to be the product of some kind of joint decision to save money on calendars. There were Soviet peasants who were more hip than this.

He parked below a chestnut tree on the square, taking advantage of one of the few car-sized shadows in town, and stepped out to see if by rattling a stick in the openings of a few buildings he might be able to flush out some kind of life-form. The first place he tried was Delia's Food Restaurant, which looked as if it too was closed for lunch as he cautiously pushed open the squeaking door and poked his head inside.

'Anybody home?' he called to the bare Formica tables. 'Hello?'

He heard the sound of a chair scraping on linoleum somewhere in the back and feet shuffling his way. A thin, middle-aged woman appeared through a doorway at the far end of the counter, her curly blond hair so heavily permed that she probably didn't need pillows.

'He'p yew?' she asked, dabbing at her lips with a napkin.

177

'Could you tell me if there's anyone in town who knew a guy from here called John Lockes?'

'A guy from here called John Lockes, honey?' she smiled, frowning with puzzled amusement. 'You'd be talking about John Lockes, it seems to me.'

'Wel . . . yes.'

'John's folks're dead a way back, may they rest in peace. He ain't got no other kin left, poor boy.'

'It sounds like you knew him pretty well yourself.'

'Uh-huh,' she responded in a pleasantly unhelpful manner.

'I'm writing a book about him, see, and it would be very helpful to me to have some background information about his childhood here in Farview.'

'Well, yes, it would,' she smiled, still giving him no encouragement.

Small-town folk, he sighed internally. It was like they thought everyone from out of town had been sent to test them. No doubt Delia was worried that if she gave too much away about herself Macauley would have her smoking marijuana and dancing naked before Satan's altar before the day was out.

'What is your fondest memory of him as a boy?' he asked, hoping that the question would be inane enough to open her up a little.

'He ate my muffins.'

'Really?' Macauley exclaimed in fascination. 'So I'm standing where John Lockes ate his first muffins, am I?'

'Nope. You're standing in the doorway, honey. John sat at the stool there.' She indicated the last of the high stools at the counter, right by the glass-domed cake tray. Macauley looked at it as if the stool were blessed by Lockes' butt.

'Did he used to come here every day?'

'Nope. I ain't open every day.'

'But he came here most days – the days you were open?'

'Most days I was open he came.'

'And ate muffins.'

'Nope.'

'He didn't? I thought you just said—'

'I don't make muffins every day.'

'Ah! So what else did he eat?'

'Cookies. Brownies. Whatever.'

'Uh-*huh* . . .' Macauley responded, as if this were especially revealing, 'and what did he used to drink?'

'Milk.'

'Cookies and milk!' Macauley smiled with the sense of a profound insight into his subject's past. 'That's nice. It's so . . . average.'

'That's because a lot of kids have cookies and milk, honey. Are you sure people are going to be innerested in this?'

'You bet!' He nodded vigorously. 'It's all about giving them a feel for a person's life, you know? They only hear about John Lockes the richest man in the world, they never get to hear about him as a totally normal kid eating muffins. That's the kind of detail that makes a book come alive.'

'Well, darn . . .' she laughed, 'you better *eat* one of my muffins if they're gonna be a big part of your book, honey!'

'I'd sure like to – is today a muffin day?'

'Just so happens. Come on in and sit on the stool.'

He stepped inside, congratulating himself on his work, and went over to The Stool. He didn't sit down on it right away, pausing as if to clear his mind for this historic moment when he followed in the buttprints of John Lockes himself.

Delia – at least he presumed her to be Delia – strolled over to the counter and reached into the cakestand to get

179

him a muffin. It was neither chocolate chip nor blueberry, just your straight muffin. And it was dry, Macauley realized, as all the moisture was sponged from his mouth on first bite. He chewed the cake for some time, smiling, until it had the consistency of wallplaster, and then swallowed. Funny, he reflected, how even he tended to assume a country muffin would be better than those mass-produced by a global muffin chain restaurant on a busy city street.

'Could I have some milk as well, please?' he asked hoarsely.

'Boy, you really like to get into the feel of your subject, don't you?' she laughed, reaching into the fridge. 'I mean – milk's milk, honey. I ain't got a cow out back or anything.'

'So . . .' he continued, breaking off a small lump of muffin with his fingers, 'people here must be pretty proud of John Lockes being a local boy.'

She handed him his glass of milk, eyeing him a little cagily. 'Pride's a sin, Mr . . . ?'

'Connor. Mac Connor. Sorry, I didn't mean to suggest . . . I just meant you must be very . . . *happy* that a home-town boy made good like he did – it's not every town that was the birthplace of the richest man in the world.'

Delia was still smiling, but there was a hint of sadness to her lips, and Macauley worried he was pushing a little too hard.

'People here unnerstand that our John has done what he had to do, Mr Connor,' she announced carefully. 'Being the richest man in the world is the *burden* he has had to assume in his struggle to make the world a better place, not the reward. The real John Lockes knows that it's easier for a camel to pass through the eye of a needle than for a rich man to enter the kingdom of heaven.'

'But it's also a lot easier never to be rich than to give it all away once you are, don't you think?'

'It surely is. It surely is. The Lord chooses to test us all in different ways, some harder than others. John was given the gift of his genius, so now he must prove himself worthy of it.'

Macauley was unable to say anything while the last of the country muffin stuck his palate together like a clam, but he nodded and smiled in what he hoped was a sympathetic way. Delia looked at him, unconvinced that he understood.

'Or he must burn in hell for eternity, Mr Connor,' she added. 'Another muffin?'

'No. Thank you. It was delicious.'

'John always ate two.'

So . . . a pervert, too, he mentally noted.

'Then I must share the experience,' he smiled, and breezily added, 'Talking about burning in hell for eternity, though, I suppose you've heard that some people think John Lockes is evil incarnate?'

She dropped the second muffin on to his plate in shock, its hard crust hitting the china with a very unmuffinny *clonk*.

'John was always a good boy, Mr Connor,' she announced curtly. 'Only evil people would call him evil. *Who* says that?'

'Oh . . . just people. Nobody special. Some people don't think it's right that one man should have so much power, I suppose.'

Delia nodded sagely, narrowing her gaze. 'Is that so? And would you, by any chance, *be* one of those people, Mr Connor?'

'*Me?* What gives you that impression?'

'Well my, I don't know you at all, Mr Connor . . . but some folk might say it's a little strange for a person like yourself to turn up unannounced in a strange town and just start eating muffins. Does John Lockes know you're here?'

'Not . . . as such, no,' Macauley admitted, sensing he'd made a big mistake.

'Not as such, huh? Does he know you're writing a book about him?'

'Not . . . so far as I know.'

'Uh-huh. Does he know *you*?'

'Well, maybe . . . if he's read some of my stuff he might. But I've never actually had the chance of meeting him.'

Delia's hand reached across the counter and pulled the muffin plate an inch or two her way. It was a peculiar gesture – as if his muffin rights, while not completely revoked, were on probation.

'You say you're writing a book about him but you've never even *met* him, Mr Connor? That don't make a whole lot of sense to me.'

'Believe me, it happens all the time. And it's not my choice – I'd love to meet Mr Lockes, but he doesn't give interviews. That's his right, but people still want to know about him, so books are going to be written, with or without his help. Under the circumstances I don't have much choice but to turn up unannounced and just start eating muffins, as you put it. It's called research.'

Delia looked carefully at him, the seconds ticking by as she analysed him in that slow, country way, like she was trying to judge his weight. Eventually she reached a decision.

'Research, huh? Then you'd better talk to the Reverend Willis – he'll tell you all you need to know.' Without waiting for him to respond, she turned away and picked up the telephone, dialling the number from memory.

'Well hi there, reverend, this is Delia Jones . . .' she announced softly. 'No, reverend, they're still in the oven . . . That's right, no nuts just as you like 'em . . . but that's not what I'm calling you about. I've got a Mr Connor down here at the restaurant who's writing a book about *John* . . . that's right . . . Now, I told him that the best person to talk to would be yourself; I hope I did the right thing . . . yeah . . . Yeah? . . . Okay . . . well, that's great . . . okay, 'bye now.'

She put the phone down and turned back to face Macauley, saying,

'The reverend's coming to see you right away, Mr Connor.' She smiled and pushed the muffin plate imperceptibly his way.

For some reason, Macauley felt a strange sense of anxiety welling in his stomach. Maybe it was the muffin.

*

Even as an old man, and Macauley judged him to be somewhere in the eighty-plus region, it was possible to see that the Reverend Bob Willis had once been a powerfully built specimen – the kind more suited to hacking off heathen heads than dabbing water on babies. He walked with a cane now, but the way his large hand enveloped the handle suggested a man who could still do damage if someone tried to take it away from him.

He had a young man's eyes, full of promise and intelligence, and a smile that made you want him to like you. His hair, surprisingly, still retained traces of its original black mixed in with the white, creating a feline effect that was both attractive and disturbing. Looking as he did, he could probably walk into any electro-punk nightclub in the city and be treated with respect.

He made Macauley feel simultaneously immature and old before his time. Above all, it was instantly clear that no discussion of Lockes' childhood in Farview could neglect this man who must, back then, have been an even more domineering character.

'So this is the man who has come to pick our Lockes!' he grinned mischievously on entering the restaurant, offering Macauley his hand. 'Reverend Bob Willis at your

183

service, Mr Connor. Now, what can we do to help you in your . . . researches?'

His grip was firm and somewhat painful with old, protuberant bones. Macauley wanted to appear relaxed, sensing from the way Willis slightly emphasized that last word that he was under some kind of suspicion and it would not do to appear overly eager to unbury every aspect of Lockes' past.

'I don't know.' He shrugged. 'That's what I'm here to find out, reverend. So far nobody seems to know very much about John Lockes' childhood – everything I've read about him starts when he left Farview to attend the Welton Academy for Gifted Children at the age of fourteen.'

'Thirteen, Mr Connor,' the reverend corrected him.

'Was it? Well, there you go, you see!' Connor laughed, reaching into his pocket to jot the information down in his notepad, although he had known the correct age all along.

'And do you know, incidentally, that it was thanks to the kind contributions of the people of Farview that he was able to attend the school? His own dear parents could never have afforded the tuition fees.'

'Is that right? No, I didn't know that,' he answered, sincerely this time.

'If I'm not mistaken, Delia,' continued Reverend Willis, his sharp gaze settling on the woman, 'the restaurant was a particularly generous contributor.'

'Everyone was just as generous in their own terms, reverend. Me no more than those who had less to give.'

'Very nicely put, my dear,' he smiled, reaching out to place a hand briefly upon hers where it lay on the counter. 'So you hopefully understand something of your subject's background already, Mr Connor. Farview is not a wealthy town, but its heart is rich. We all know each other here, and we all help in whatever ways we can.

When it became clear that young John had been given a gift that could not be properly nurtured by his remaining in the local school, the money needed to send him to the Welton Academy was entirely raised from among my own congregation.'

'Is that most of the townspeople?'

'No.' Willis grinned. 'That is *all* the townspeople. I say that not out of pride, mark, but so that you understand that these are good, God-fearing people one and all.'

God-fearing, Macauley sighed internally. There you had the difference between the country and the city. In the country, where there was no danger, they worshipped God out of fear; in the city, with crime, poverty and rampant neurosis, they worshipped out of hope. Both were equally pathetic. If God existed, the only reason Macauley could see for worshipping him was the one about why mountains had to be climbed. Not that he'd ever understood why mountains had to be climbed.

'So if I understand correctly . . .' he wondered aloud, 'it was *your* initiative, reverend?'

'Do I detect a hint of disapproval, Mr Connor?' Willis frowned humorously. 'The town that obeys the preacher's orders? You both overestimate me and underestimate the people of Farview – John Lockes has repaid every cent of their money, and much more. It was an investment, as well as being the right thing to do.'

'What do you mean when you say "much more"?'

The reverend looked surprised. 'You didn't see it on your way into town?'

'See what?'

'Ah! You obviously arrived from the east! Well then – the best thing we can do is take a walk, you and I, and I'll show you exactly what "much more" means. Come, we can discuss your book along the way.'

He turned on his cane and strode out the door, leaving Macauley to scrabble for his change to pay for the muffins – a gesture politely refused by Delia – and follow him out.

*

The sun had slipped from its zenith as he joined the reverend on the square, shadows beginning to creep eastwards in the silence of the still town. He reached into his pocket for his sunglasses, and then decided against it, seeing the reverend's clear, unblinking gaze upon him. He didn't want to seem too much the city slicker in Hicksville.

Willis lifted his cane as Macauley drew alongside him, pointing to the simple, whiteboard building that looked over the square.

'Our church,' he announced. 'It's not much, but it was built by the people of Farview themselves some sixty years ago, after a cyclone destroyed the previous church. That was before I came here myself. But I sense that you're not a church-going man, Mr Connor . . . such things probably bore you.'

'Not at all. But you're right – I don't go to church. I never really understood . . .' he searched through all the things he had against religion and found there was too much to say other than, '. . . God.'

Willis laughed, beginning to walk across the square. 'Do you think I do, Mr Connor? Wherever did you get the idea that you were *meant* to understand God?'

'Surely that's the point of religion – to make sense of life?'

'Of course! Of *life*, not of God! It's very simple, really, Mr Connor – either one chooses to try to understand God, which inevitably means not believing in Him, and life makes no sense, or one chooses to believe in God without His making sense, without trying to understand Him, in which case everything in life makes sense. There's no mystery about it.'

186

'Isn't that a little absurd?' Macauley laughed.

'No, it's just practical. Only an idiot wouldn't see that it makes practical sense to believe in God, Mr Connor!'

'Except that some very intelligent people don't.'

Willis paused in his stride, smiling broadly. He leaned on his cane and raised a finger to emphasize his point.

'Extreme intelligence and idiocy are not so far apart.' He smiled, flicking his cane forward to continue the walk, and added breezily, 'Wisdom is the domain of the average man, Mr Connor, which is why everything true that has been said of life has been said so often that it has become a cliché.'

'John Lockes isn't an average man.'

They left the square and began walking along the main street, heading through the part of town that Macauley hadn't yet seen.

'No . . .' the reverend admitted sadly, 'but I believe he sincerely wishes to be, and that is what may save him in the end.'

'Save him from what?'

Willis glanced at him slyly, fighting to keep a smirk from breaking across his mouth.

'Why, Mr Connor . . .' he answered softly, 'from people like you!'

Macauley's mouth opened in silent protest, his eyes bulging as he searched for a reply.

'Now then, Mr Connor,' the reverend continued in a firm but not unfriendly tone, 'don't try to hoodwink me – I always speak frankly, and I will answer whatever questions you may ask truthfully, so long as you do not lie to me. *You* come to bury Caesar, not to praise him.'

There was no point in arguing – the old man had him pegged. And Macauley found to his surprise that he didn't really care to lie either, because there was something about Willis that made him want to earn his approval. He shrugged.

'Don't look so worried, Mr Connor!' The reverend smiled. 'I don't have many talents, but I'm a pretty good judge of men. You don't seem like a bad man to me.'

As their footsteps and the *clack* of the reverend's cane echoed around the quiet street, Macauley could hear signs of life behind some of the closed windows – conversation and the clatter of cutlery on plates, water running in basins and the sound of children playing in back yards. It was a relief to have some kind of evidence of other people being nearby, the oppressive heat of the day having started to play tricks on his mind so that he'd almost started to believe, looking at the shimmering road ahead of them and hearing their conversation swallowed up into the dry heat, that there was nobody in Farview apart from him, the preacher and a woman in a restaurant without clients.

'And so what would John Lockes have learned here?'

The reverend raised his eyebrows. 'Big question! I can't answer that, Mr Connor, I can only tell you what I taught John, which was what I have taught all the people of Farview since the day I arrived here from the city in the depths of the Depression: that God sees all, that He helps those who help themselves, and that the meek shall inherit the Earth. Nothing unusual.'

'You say that as though you don't believe it yourself.'

'I believe in belief. The art of the preacher is to preach the right god to the right people, so that they believe. God changes from one preacher to the next, and one place to the next, but we all preach belief. We're a little like . . . fashion designers. We clothe the hearts of men in whatever we can convince them to wear, whatever they feel good in. That is the vision I judged to be right for a small town such as Farview, lost on the prairie and forgotten by men. Something to help them live under such a big sky.'

Willis glanced at him again, those young man's eyes sparkling with a hint of mischief.

'You see, Mr Connor? I'm not keeping any secrets from you, am I? It's good to talk to someone like yourself – it helps me put my thoughts back in order to spend some time with an outsider. Sometimes it can become hard to keep one's sense of perspective, living for so long in a small town where little ever changes.'

'You're telling me!' Macauley agreed, relieved the conversation had moved on to different territory. 'It's like this town is stuck in amber.'

Willis laughed. 'You're a young man, Mr Connor. You grew up in a time when the ball had already started rolling, and so you have never known anything other than change, change and more change. But there have been moments of stability and respite. They are always short-lived, but they are the golden times, the moments that people will later look back on with nostalgia because their world briefly seemed to make sense. If you are very, very attentive, you can sense when you are in one of those moments, and in a small community like this it is possible to say, "Stop! This is it! This is where we want to be!" That's what we did in Farview. We have kept ourselves to ourselves while society has been pulling in all directions at once, every faction fighting its little corner, and will remain as we are until a moral order returns to bind the country back together.'

They were approaching the last of the houses, the road ahead breaking into open prairie. Willis raised an elderly hand and placed it on Macauley's shoulder, patting it gently.

'But don't go thinking we're some kind of cult, Mr Connor. We are all perfectly aware of the changes going on elsewhere, and we come and go from Farview as we please, but most of us find we prefer what we have here. I see from your smile that it is hard for an outsider such as yourself to understand that.'

'No – I was just thinking how ironic it is that no one is

doing more to keep society changing too fast for its own good than your boy Lockes. He's doing the very opposite to what you were just talking about . . .'

Willis did not reply. He just glanced at him, one grey eyebrow raised quizzically. They had reached the last of the houses in town, beyond which there was nothing but corn rolling in an imperceptible breeze. The reverend stopped, tapping Macauley's shoulder and pointing off to their right.

'That's what I mean by "much more", Mr Connor.'

It was set about a half-mile off the road – a huge, low structure in steel and glass. It seemed to shimmer in the sun, but not simply due to the heat-haze – the shimmering was like rain falling on water.

'Farview supplies all the poppy seeds for Ghetty's Burger's buns, Mr Connor,' Reverend Willis announced with pride as they approached the building. 'We may be small and off the beaten track, but thanks to John there isn't a town in the nation that we don't reach in our own little way! This factory is our insurance against whatever the future brings – fourteen per cent of the population eat at Ghetty's every day, and so long as people eat burgers we don't need to worry too much about the economy. Burgers are recession-proof.'

It had been immediately clear to Macauley on seeing it that Lockes' gift of 'much more' was a factory of some kind, designed in the why-pay-more school of architecture – one of those giant pizza boxes that seemed to appear overnight, littering the countryside like the remains of God's late-night munchies. A hundred yards off to the left, actually in the corn, was a large satellite dish. As they neared the building, Macauley realized that it was the reflection of the corn in the glass of the factory that made it shimmer like that.

And it was then that he realized what was niggling him.

'But this isn't a poppy-growing region.'

Reverend Willis grinned, his voice taking on the insanely chirpy tone of the dedicated corporate spokesperson:

'The poppy seeds in Ghetty's burgers are manufactured from extract of concentrated poppy seed, for a more satisfying poppy-seed experience, Mr Connor! Many people don't realize that real poppy seeds are not actually round – but we at Ghetty's Burger need a perfectly spherical poppy seed to enable an even sprinkle and avoid unsightly clumping. Unspherical seeds stick together and block the feeder tubes sprinkling them on to the buns, which allows the possibility of one customer feeling that his bun is not as well-sprinkled as that of the customer beside him. And, on a different note, poppy seeds are actually quite difficult to digest and get stuck in people's teeth. So we here produce a perfectly round, uni-form, saliva-soluble reconstituted poppy seed with flavour-enhancing agents to give you an even better poppy-seed experience than you get from Mother Nature!'

The old man winked, 'Isn't it amazing?'

'Totally . . .' murmured Macauley. 'Reconstituted poppy seeds. Who would have thought?'

'I'm afraid we can't go in because it's a hygienically controlled environment, but there you have it – John Lockes' gift to the town of Farview. This factory is built on part of the old Lockes farm, but it and the profits it generates have been made over to the town itself – the money it makes allows us to subsidize other aspects of Farview's economy that were becoming less and less financially viable.'

'Such as?'

'Everything. The farms, the shops, the restaurant – everything was in constant danger of going bankrupt without regular cash donations by John, but with this

191

factory he solved the problem on a permanent basis.'

In other words, Macauley realized, while Infologix technology provoked downsizings, mergers and rationalizations in every direction, hundreds of thousands of jobs disappearing with the application of a single computer program, here in Farview Lockes was subsidizing an outdated way of life that belonged in a black and white movie.

It was the hypocrisy of it that galled him.

No wonder Lockes never revealed anything about his past – not because there was anything shameful in it, but because if people knew about the existence of this cosseted little enclave, safe from the savageries of progress, it would expose his evangelization of change for the cynical lie it was.

Macauley had him by the balls. He had hit the jackpot. Here was proof that Lockes himself considered Infologix a menace to society! He smiled. This was bigger even than whatever was behind Rectag. He didn't need to uncover any private scandals or skeletons in the man's closet – the lie that would destroy Lockes was right here in front of him.

He could hardly wait to begin – another day or so in Farview, interviewing those who remembered him as a child and gathering testimonies about how he was supporting the community today, would give him all the background material he needed to complete the book. All he still needed was some kind of photographic record of Lockes' youth here.

'Thank you, reverend,' he smiled, turning to Willis, 'you've been a great help to me. There is one thing, though, that I desperately need – I don't have any pictures of John when he was a kid. Do you think there's anyone in town who would have one?'

Willis shrugged. 'I don't know about that. People here don't worry too much about that sort of thing, I'm afraid.

What's the earliest picture you have of him so far?'

Macauley reached into his backpack and produced the college-newspaper photo of Lockes when he first created Infologix. 'I've this one. He's about twenty.'

Willis took it and stared for a long time, reading the newsprint carefully, his frown deepening.

'Extraordinary . . .' he whispered finally.

'What?'

'I have some rather strange news for you, Mr Connor,' he announced, waving the photograph between his fingers. '. . . This is not John Lockes.'

XVI

On day two of the siege, everything was going fine in the Global & Western Credit until Ben Cage pointed out the joyous development in Sheila Lane's life.

'*Whoa, motherfuckers!*' he shouted when George Bailey was only half-way over to her. 'The bitch is pregnant!'

Sheila stiffened, staring imploringly at George as he stopped in his tracks. He smiled encouragingly at her, and turned to face Cage.

'She's not a dog, Ben, but yes, she is pregnant. Is this a problem?'

'Damn sure!' the gunman replied hotly. 'Pregnant counts double, right?'

'*Double?*' Luís Alvares squealed. 'What you talking about, double, asshole? We never said pregnant was double!'

'Yo, well I didn't see the bitch was packing, did I? How was I supposed to see that when she was sitting down, huh? Now I seen and she is *double*, motherfucker! Yo, George, a pregnant bitch counts twice, right?'

George sighed, his lanky frame sagging with exhaustion. Just when everything had been going so well.

Thanks to him the seemingly interminable phone negotiations between the chiefs of the rival gangs had finally produced an agreement that was acceptable to everyone. The main sticking point had been the money –

194

the Blade refusing to share any of their haul with the late-arriving Blood. Sensing that sooner or later someone was going to back their argument up with a bullet, George had timidly pointed out that there was money in the bank's safe – far more money than the Blade had stolen from the tills. If that was split evenly, everyone came out ahead.

That settled, there remained the question of the hostages. Since both sides were insisting on conducting separate negotiations with the lawmen surrounding the bank, each needed its own bargaining chips. With just under fifty innocent bystanders trapped inside the building, there were more than enough to go round, but so as to make sure that nobody had reason to complain about their particular hostages George had suggested they line everyone up and take turns to pick victims. Naturally the orphans had been snapped up first, being hostage gold. George had led them one by one to opposite sides of the bank, softly telling them not to be afraid and promising that he would let no harm come to them. The girls had gone first, then the boys. The last to be chosen was Bobby Shaw, a fat boy with glasses reluctantly selected by Ben Cage. Then they moved on to the adults, with first choice going to Luís Alvares, and that was when the trouble started.

'Excuse me for asking at a time like this, my dear,' George muttered softly to the terrified Sheila Lane, 'but exactly how many months are you . . .?'

'Six,' she whispered, choking back her tears.

'That's wonderful,' he smiled. 'Is it your first?'

She nodded, gulping hysterically.

'Well, don't you worry, dear – we'll have you both safely home soon, I promise. Just try and stay calm. It's not good for the baby if you let yourself get upset.' He patted her gently on the shoulder, then returned to the two gunmen. He motioned them close to him, rubbing his aching forehead as he announced, 'Legally the child has rights, gentlemen, so I have to concur with Ben on this point.'

'You have to *what* with me?' Cage growled.

George sighed, searching briefly for an alternative form of expressing himself and then giving up, explaining simply, 'I mean that a pregnant bitch counts double, Ben.'

'*Madre de diós!* No way, we *never* said nothing about this!' Alvares protested.

'You heard the man, asshole – the bitch is carrying, she's loaded, she's double. End of story.'

'You gonna stop callin' her "bitch", motherfucker? Show some fuckin' respect. How'd you feel if I called your mother "bitch"?'

'I do call my mother bitch – don't mean I don't respect her.'

'So if *I* called your mother bitch you wouldn't shoot my ass?'

'Damn right I'd shoot your ass.'

'For not showing her no fuckin' respect, right?'

'No. For not showing *me* no fuckin' respect, mother-fucker.'

'Gentlemen . . .' George interrupted timidly. 'These are fascinating points of etiquette, but let's not lose sight of the issue. *If* she counts double, which she does, we no longer have an even number of hostages.'

A simultaneous groan came from both men, their heads dropping as the implications of this development sank in.

'You happy now?' Alvares snapped at his opposite number. 'You really fucked it up, didn't you? We were *sorted*, man! We were in business! Then you start with your bitch this, bitch that, and now what the fuck are we gonna do? We're gonna have to shoot somebody!'

'Well, yes, that is an *option*, Luís,' agreed George hurriedly, 'or . . . *alternatively* . . . we could let her go.'

'Let her *go*?' Cage barked. 'What are you talking about, George? You can't do *that*, man! What are the pigs gonna think if pregnant bitches just start boogying out of the fucking bank? You've got to think about our credibility here. Hostages have to be *traded*!'

'Well . . . it shows good will, Ben.'

'George . . . you're fucking stupid, aren't you? We don't *want* to show good will! We're bad. We're Blood. We don't give away hostages for nothing!'

'She ain't *your* hostage, asshole!' Alvares shouted.

'She ain't yours neither, motherfucker, she's a joker. So back off.'

The two bristling either side of him, George searched desperately for a way to calm the situation again.

'Gentlemen, what if she were *my* hostage? Would that be acceptable to you both?'

'What you want with a hostage, old man?' Cage laughed. 'You want to be a bad motherfucker now?'

'I'm simply saying that if she were *my* hostage I could trade her without it harming your standing with the police. I'm just looking for a solution to the problem. She doesn't even have to be mine in particular, she could belong to all the hostages.'

The two gunmen paused, frowning. Cage and Alvares glanced at one another, each seeking the other's reassurance that this was not some kind of trick.

'So what are your demands?' Alvares asked finally.

*

He was totally unaware of the fact, but in the outside world, where the stand-off at the Global & Western Credit was dominating every news bulletin, the name 'George Bailey' was already synonymous with everything that was brave and good in the Atlantian spirit. Within hours of the police mentioning his name to reporters,

197

crack TV crews had descended on the sleepy little town of Bedford Falls and started interrogating the locals. Hard. The people of Bedford Falls were characteristically a soft-spoken and understated lot, but time was short and tongues had to be loosened. There were ways of making them soundbite.

'How would you describe George Bailey?' a reporter from News 24 asked Julie Bell in the local Ghetty's Burger.

'Well . . . he's pretty nice,' she smiled. 'He's real nice, I guess.'

'Nice, huh?' the reporter sighed, little appreciating how effusive Julie was being for someone from Bedford Falls. 'We heard he was a Communist.'

'You? A? Mr Bailey?' Julie gasped as a year was taken off her life. 'Well . . . well, I never heard *that*. George Bailey is as Atlantian as they come! Who told you a thing like that?'

'Thank you, Miss Bell,' the reporter smiled, glancing at his watch, 'I don't want to take up any more of your time.'

Half an hour later, the headline on the lunchtime bulletin ('A hostage hero – his home town speaks!') led with Julie Bell stridently announcing: 'George Bailey is as Atlantian as they come!'

None of this escaped the attention of the directors of the Global & Western Credit, preoccupied though they were by fighting off the hostile takeover bid from World Wire Coathangers. For the last twenty hours they had been gathered in a crisis conference with their stock-brokers, Sacker Leviticus Popsicle, at their offices on the forty-fifth and forty-sixth floors of the Bing Building.

It was said that the Bing Building was built on the very spot where, in the early days of the colonial period, Chief Sleeping Bull of the Longopshun tribe had sold half the lands of his great and proud nation for a rather fetching silk shirt with buttons. For a while, Chief Sleeping Bull's stock within the tribe had risen enormously on the back of the deal he had made, his silk shirt with buttons being the envy of all the young bucks, but soon, of course, more ships arrived bearing silk shirts and a seemingly endless supply of buttons, and the market collapsed. By the time Chief Sleeping Bull tried in desperation to re-establish his authority by massacring the settlers, the going rate for a button was fluctuating between a yam and a knuckle of tobacco, depending on the quality of the button.

Three hundred years later, the enemy facing Sacker Leviticus Popsicle's clients at the Global & Western Credit may not have been so physically terrifying as the enraged Longopshun tribe, but they were as ruthless, and nearly as well dressed.

The bank's defence strategy consisted simply in doing everything in its power to push up the market price of Global & Western shares, thus forcing World Wire Coathangers to keep raising its offer. It would work if there came a point at which the consortium backing their bid decided the price they would now have to pay to take over the bank was too high. That's why the last thing they needed right now was a public relations catastrophe like a hostage crisis in their main branch. Least of all one involving orphaned children with no parents.

'Who the hell is this Bailey creature they keep talking about?' demanded Lucas Berg when the lunchtime bulletin finished.

The chairman of Global & Western Credit was renowned for his irascibility. It was written all over his face in the fascinating bumps that had swelled up under his skin over the years, as if his body was not quite able to contain the energies that raged within him. His career over the last fifteen years had consisted of a series of chairmanships of companies that had been quite un-related except for the fact that they had all been in need of a vigorous shaking-down to rid them of the excess fat and inefficiency that had been allowed to clog their capitalist arteries by previous, lazy managements. The stock market loved him because he had turned around one company after another, ruthlessly hacking back staff and tiers of management, but unsurprisingly there was little affection found for him among any of the people who had actually worked under his stewardship. People called him 'Bumpy' behind his back, partly for his face and partly for the ride he gave. It was Bumpy who had imposed Infologix Bankmanager on the Global & Western soon after his arrival in the big chair.

'Has anyone here ever heard of him?' he continued. 'Is he one of ours, and if so in what capacity? Surely we have qualified PR people being held hostage in there who should be handling this situation, for God's sake.'

'We've been looking into that,' answered Mark Axmoor, a young and brilliant management consultant attached to Sacker's. 'At first we couldn't find any trace of him in your staff database, but then we thought of looking in Pending, and bingo – George Bailey Junior, fifty-eight years old. He's a branch executive sub-manager – garbage, in other words. Two years to go until he's naturally wastaged.'

'He's *garbage*?' Bumpy exploded, turning to his fellow-directors. 'Perfect! So every time our shareholders turn on their TV sets they hear the crisis is being handled by *exactly* the kind of useless human being we are currently paying the price for keeping on our payroll! Score one to World Wire Coathangers!'

'Except they don't *know* he's garbage, of course,' pointed out Axmoor.

'This is good news? Would we actually prefer them to think that this loser is the best we have?'

'Actually, Lucas,' cut in Larry Saxbloe, the suave Sacker's director heading the counter-attack on the takeover battle, 'and this is just an idea, I think it *may* be good news. Whoever this Bailey is, the Feds have been saying he's doing a good job. He's got twenty orphaned children in there under his care, plus all the other hostages, and two armed gangs standing each other off, but he's keeping it together. So far he's projecting a pretty good image of the bank – caring, responsible and calm. He's becoming a hero. We could maybe use that.'

Bumpy and the rest of the board were silent. They saw immediately what Saxbloe was suggesting – could they spin the situation to their advantage in the takeover battle by playing on public sympathy for Bailey?

'Sentimental crap,' Bumpy announced finally. 'We can't go up against World Wire Coathangers armed with nothing but a Bailey. This is about money and you're suggesting we offer them a damned *hero*? What's a hero worth to anyone? Nothing. Not ... a ... cent! So he's got courage, morals and integrity! You can't educate your *children* with that though, can you? They'll hang us out to dry!'

'Well ... hang on, Lucas,' Larry Saxbloe intervened. 'Bailey could become worth something if you could translate him into increased *business*. The punters love heroes. They hate banks. You could use him as a kind of company mascot – symbol of your dedication to client service and all that crap. Make him full manager of the bank. If you can increase business now, when the future of the bank is under threat, that will really impress the market. We impress the market, it puts up the share price. Put up the share price, and we save the bank. I know it sounds crazy, but there's a real buzz around this Bailey character right now. You should promote him. Use him.'

A storm passed over Lucas Berg's face at the idea of relying on someone like Bailey to save the bank. Bumpy had not spent the last three years savagely rationalizing the bank's operations, closing down unprofitable branches and dumping staff by the thousand only to be told that it was a clapped-out old fool they ought to have been shot of years ago who held the key to the future. He had integrity of his own, after all.

But they were up against the wall.

'Use him . . . how?' he enquired, with a visible shudder.

'Get out there and talk about him! The stand-off is only news so long as it continues – Bailey will be forgotten within days of its ending. Get on the news, get on the chat shows, buy advertising space, anything and everything that will push Bailey as a hero – and a bank manager.'

Bumpy seethed with irritation at the ridiculousness of the scenario, but he was not so stubborn as to ignore the advice of a man the calibre of Saxbloe. It might not be his personal way of doing things, but this was a crisis.

'Do the rest of you agree with this?' he demanded, looking around the directors. 'Should we get out there and tell everyone how proud we are to employ men like this George Bailey, a living symbol of all that we hold . . . of our dedication to . . . whatever it is the PR department does?'

The grim faces bowed in approval.

'And needless to say,' Larry Saxbloe added, 'the longer this hostage crisis continues, the more time it will give us to translate this into share value . . .'

*

Special Agent Winston Pepsi frowned as he listened to the strange tone in the familiar voice over the phone.

'Sorry, George . . . could you repeat what you just said?'

'You heard me, Pepsi. I said we want portable TVs – lots of them. Right now.'

'That's what I thought I heard. Are you okay, George? You sound a little tense.'

'Don't try messing with my brain, Pepsi. This offer is non-negotiable – get us the TVs and we'll release a hostage.'

'Yeah, I got that, but . . . who is *we*, George?'

'Who the heck do you think? We is us. The hostages . . . Dumbo.'

'Hang on a second here . . . the *hostages* are holding someone hostage?'

'Do you have a problem with that?'

'Well, frankly . . . yes. I'm a little confused, George. What exactly is—'

'Listen, *turkey*, just do as we say and none of us will hurt each other, okay?'

The phone went dead.

Sheila Lane and one other hostage were released shortly after a delivery of twenty televisions was made to the bank. The other hostage was necessary because, as George pointed out, if Sheila counted for two and they had an uneven number, it would still be uneven without her. Eventually he managed to talk Cage and Alvares into going back just two steps in the selection process, meaning fat little Bobby Shaw escaped at the same time.

Interviewed by on-the-scene reporters shortly after her release from the bank, Sheila said:

'It's been a terrifying experience and I'm just really glad that George Bailey managed to get me and my baby out of there. He's been doing a fantastic job of keeping everyone's spirits up in there. He's a hero. It's people like him who make Atlantis the great country it is . . .'

No doubt because she had by then had more time to recover and get her thoughts in order, her view of the situation had evolved somewhat by the time she appeared as a guest a day later on *The Lola Colaco Show* around the subject 'Pregnant Women Who Have Been Held Hostage at Gunpoint':

'It was a terrifying experience and I'm just really glad

that George Bailey managed to get me and my baby out of there. He's a hero. He's been doing a fantastic job of keeping everyone's spirits up in there, but I think that he really just sees that as part of his role as an employee of the Global & Western Credit, Lola. He's just applying the same caring attitude and integrity to a hostage crisis as he always applied to dealing with any ordinary client. It's people like him who make the Global & Western Credit the great bank it is . . .'

Sadly, Sheila Lane went into a post-traumatic depression shortly after her brief round of media appearances, which may be why her baby was born prematurely. In a moment of high emotion, she called the child George.

George was proud in later years to have been named after a hero, but it was still not the name she would have chosen for herself.

XVII

Two days later, Josh Cloken was up before the dawn for his first day's training in Star City. Neither the showers nor the coffee on the Space Agency's base in New Toulouse seemed to be very effective, and as he made his way across the tarmac to Building B his brain still felt as though someone had surreptitiously switched it for a cauliflower during the night. He checked his watch to make sure he was not running late for his six o'clock meeting, anxious not to make a bad first impression. It was only a quarter to, he saw, so he could have had that third coffee after all.

There was already somebody in Room B21 by the time he got there. He saw her first through the glass panel in the door, sitting with her feet on one of the tables, the chair balanced so far behind on its two back legs that it seemed poised on the point of collapse. The faded red of her Space Agency overalls, body-worn and soft, contrasted with the stark practicality of the room like a peach on a china plate. Her eyes were shut and her golden, shoulder-length hair swung in a neat crescent behind the precariously rocking chair. It wasn't just fear of startling her that made him pause with his hand on the door.

She was beautiful in a way that made him feel as though he'd seen her before. He knew he hadn't, but there was something so *right* in that profile – in the thick, dark eyebrows and the strength of her nose, in the wind-less sea-calm of her closed eyelids and the trace of humour etched beside her mouth – that she immediately seemed familiar. It was only the impression of an instant, a flash that was strongest on the moment of perception and faded the longer he regarded her, but it brought him up short.

Suddenly the coffee was working.

As though she sensed herself being watched, Jean Grey opened one eye and looked toward the door, catching him standing there. She tilted her head lazily and cocked an eye-brow, a faint smile playing over her lips as he started in surprise, suddenly fumbling with the doorhandle.

There was such a contrast between them in that moment – he stumbling into the room and she con-fidently lifting her feet off the table so that she was balanced momentarily on nothing but the chair's back legs, waiting as it began to tip forward – that he felt sure she must already consider him a fool before a word had been spoken.

'Mr Cloken,' she stated, rising to her feet and proffer-ing a hand, 'Jean Grey.'

'Josh . . . hi . . . Josh Cloken,' he stammered, stepping forward to shake her hand. 'I mean . . . call me Josh, please.'

'I would have anyway, Josh, but thank you all the same,' she announced, closing her fingers around his palm.

Seeing the surprise on his face, she explained, 'I'm under orders to be nice to you, Josh. I hope you will return the favour by not getting us all killed. Welcome to the Space Agency.'

He had been warned not to expect special treatment from the orbiter crew, for whom his presence could only make things more difficult, but even so he was taken aback by his first contact with a future shipmate.

'Thank you, Jean,' he laughed nervously. 'Just so I know – are you always like this at this time of the morning?'

'No-o-o . . .' she frowned. 'Usually I'm naked and in bed. But given that we only have three weeks to get you ready for this mission, Josh, I'll probably be like this.'

She stared hard at him for the briefest of moments, then winked. 'So . . . shall we get started?'

Josh liked her. A lot.

Five minutes later, he lifted his gaze from the plastic carrier bag she had handed him and asked, 'I don't get it . . . is this a joke? Some kind of initiation thing?'

'Not at all. This is your first training exercise.'

Josh pulled the object out of the bag. It was a brightly coloured plastic box, shaped like an old-fashioned cash till with a lever at the side. Only instead of numbers popping up, the box produced a row of large pegs in various shapes – a square, a circle, a star and a pentagon. It was called *Pull 'n' Play*, and manufactured by a company that went by the name *FunSkool*.

Josh lifted it up in bewilderment, turning it around to see if he wasn't somehow misunderstanding what the object was.

'"From six months to two years . . . Conforms to Safety Regulations,"' he read, finding the labels underneath. '"NEVER leave a child unsupervised with *Pull 'n' Play*. Children can CHOKE on detachable pieces. *Pull 'n' Play* is UNDER NO CIRCUMSTANCES to be used in conjunction with other toys. KEEP AWAY from all heat sources and from floors. DO NOT place *Pull 'n' Play* on tables. NEVER let a child walk, run or crawl with *Pull 'n' Play* or in the same room as *Pull 'n' Play*. *FunSkool* accepts no responsibility for any improper use of *Pull 'n' Play* such as BANGING, DROPPING, LICKING, SUCKING or PLACING PEGS IN INCORRECT HOLES."'

He nodded his head and whistled, adding, 'Guess that

pretty much covers them, huh? What are you doing walking around with this . . . *doomsday machine*, Jean? Have you got a licence for it?'

He looked up to check that she was smiling, and then put the toy back down on the table. 'Actually, you know, I have sort of mastered the trick with these things – the secret is that the square peg only fits into the *square* hole, right?'

'Right,' she grinned, 'so are you ready to try?'

'Actually . . . I was thinking we could move right on to exercise number two, if you don't mind.'

'Oh, you're not doing it *here*, Josh! You're doing it on the VC.'

'The VC?'

'The Vomit Comet. Zero-gravity simulation craft. I hope you didn't have too much breakfast, by the way.'

*

Crossing the runway toward the humming training-craft, Josh Cloken's stomach was already starting to cause him discomfort as he grew steadily more nervous. He was trying to take his mind off it by keeping up a ceaseless flow of talk.

'Society is in trouble when you need lawyers to write the instructions for toys, but it's all right to spell "school" with a K,' he sighed, holding up the bag. 'Hey, what about "UNDER NO CIRCUMSTANCES allow a child to PULL or PLAY with the *Pull 'n' Play*"? How did we get so screwed up?'

He shook his head. '"NEVER allow a child to be BORN. THIS CAUSES DEATH."'

'You're pretty nervous, aren't you?' Jean commented.

'It shows?'

'Somewhat. Don't worry, there's no shame in that. You're quite right to be nervous.'

208

'Oh, well, that's all right then.'

The plane was the size of a short-range passenger jet. It was unpainted, unmarked and had no windows except in the cockpit. In the early-morning cool, its four engines sent a shimmering cloud of heat across the tarmac toward them. Three men in red fatigues stood waiting at the bottom of the steps, waving sleepily as Jean approached.

'Wake up, guys!' Jean called with ironic enthusiasm. 'Morning has broken!'

'Yeah,' one yawned, sulkily eyeing the saffron-dusted horizon, 'and I'll be damned if I'm cleaning it up.'

'Guys, I'd like you all to meet our passenger on *Avalon*: Josh Cloken from Infologix. Josh, meet Troy Duncan, Ian Wells and Adam Gallaher. They will be doing other training exercises on this flight while you and I work on the *Pull 'n' Play*. Try not to puke on them.'

She set off up the steps while Josh briefly made their acquaintance. There was only time for a minimum of conversation.

'Josh, hi!' Ian Wells greeted him, shaking his hand in a bone-testing way. 'What *exactly* did you have for breakfast?'

'Crunchyflakes . . . two bowls. Orange juice and two coffees.'

'Uh-huh . . . can I give you a word of advice, Josh?'

'Sure – please do.'

Wells slapped his shoulder.

'Toast.'

The plane was already picking up speed along the runway as Jean adjusted the shoulder straps harnessing Josh to the wall of its empty, heavily padded hold.

'The cardinal rule is not to make any sudden or violent movements. Imagine you are under water – only slow, gentle actions. Every action will cause a reaction, most of which you won't want, so minimize your movements.

209

Channel your energy into the specific muscles needed to complete the task at hand. And if you lose control, don't try to compensate straight away, but wait until you achieve equilibrium. Got that?'

'Yes.'

'Bet you haven't,' she grinned.

The plane took off steeply, and she struggled to strap herself in between Josh and the three astronauts. Although there were no windows to see the ground receding, Josh's stomach gave him a fairly good indication of the speed and angle at which they were climbing. All his internal organs seemed to slip down, the very blood in his veins packing into his feet with the G-force against which he was being pulled. Breakfast was suddenly a heavier meal than it had felt at the time.

'When we reach maximum altitude,' Jean shouted over the engines' roar, 'the pilot will put us into free-fall. We'll have forty seconds of zero gravity before he has to bank and bring us round to climb again. When I give you the signal, release your harness, remove the pegs from the *Pull 'n' Play* and begin trying to put them back in their holes.'

Josh nodded nervously.

'NEVER,' she added, 'point the *Pull 'n' Play* toward your *EYES* when releasing the shapes in ZERO GRAVITY as this can BLIND.'

'And UNDER NO CIRCUMSTANCES have CRUNCHYFLAKES for BREAKFAST,' he groaned in response.

'*Already?*' Adam Gallaher winced, leaning forward in his straps to check Josh's skin colour.

'Hold on to it, Josh!' Ian Wells encouraged him. 'We're almost at the top.'

'Will that make me feel better?'

'No, but if you have to puke, always try to hold on to

210

it until we reach the bottom again. Puking when there is gravity on board is a lot less messy.'

Josh felt himself suddenly starting to grow lighter, the sound of the engines fading simultaneously. Had he not known what was truly happening, he would have sworn he was fainting. His vision blurred and he hazily saw the four others float away from the wall beside him.

'Come on, Josh!' Jean called. 'We don't have long.'

He released his harness, realizing with a start that his feet were no longer touching the deck. In one hand he held the bag containing the *Pull 'n' Play*, and with the other he pushed off from the cabin wall. Jean raised her eyebrows as he drifted past her and slammed into the wall opposite.

'*Gently*, I said! Now don't worry about your position – just try and remove the toy from the bag.'

The carrier bag, to Josh's surprise, was suddenly like a thing alive. It rippled and pulsed like a jellyfish, clutching on to the protuberances of the toy as he tried to pull it out. He tore at the bag in frustration, oblivious to the twisting spiral this produced in his own body's trajectory.

'Slow down, Josh! You're all over the place here!'

He looked around in surprise, having thought it was Jean who was moving, such was the sensory confusion that had washed over his body. His shoulder hit the padded deck and sent him on a new, more complicated, spiral trajectory down the length of the craft toward the spot where the three male astronauts were trying to arrange a boxful of parts into some kind of mechanical assembly.

'Coming through!' Jean warned, giving them just enough time to push gently inwards on their box, such that they each drifted out of his path toward the walls of the craft.

Josh took the machine parts with him as he crashed like a flailing daddy-long-legs through the spot where

211

they had been only a second before, still wrestling with his children's toy as he attempted to get the hold necessary to pull the lever without simply turning the whole device around itself.

'Precision, not force, I told you!' he heard Jean's voice shout. 'You're fighting yourself, for God's sake!'

He heard her, but a grim determination not to be defeated by a device invented for a six-month-old child had overtaken him, his teeth clenched as he wedged the toy into his stomach and yanked the lever. The little springs under the pegs, normally just strong enough to pop them up like pieces of toast, rejoiced in their turbo-charged power under zero gravity, flinging the plastic shapes out at high velocity. His forehead was struck by the pentagon, while the other three shot past him altogether and started travelling down the aircraft.

Suddenly he felt weight returning to his stomach as the plane began to level off, and looked down in panic as the deck rushed up to greet him. He gasped as he landed on the *Pull 'n' Play*, the machine parts following hard behind.

The plane resumed a horizontal flight path, banking widely to come round for the next loop, and he groaned as he rolled over on to his back, seeing the heads of the four astronauts looking down at him.

'*How was that?*' he whispered.

'Like being caged with an irate octopus,' Troy Duncan admitted. 'Don't worry – it was only your first attempt.'

'Don't let it get you down, Josh,' Jean added. 'You've got another twenty-nine passes in which to practise this morning.'

'*Twenty . . . nine . . .*' Josh gasped, holding his stomach. '*That's good to know.*'

The Vomit Comet finally lived up to its name on the tenth pass. Josh had just about mastered the trick of staying in

212

one spot, but was still far from getting around the problem of ideally needing a third, if not a fourth, arm with which to control the *Pull 'n' Play*. He was bruised and exhausted, and with each subsequent dive his stomach had rebelled more violently, the nausea spreading from his belly to occupy his whole body so that each and every movement seemed to have direct repercussions on the position of his breakfast.

He didn't know how much of it was caused by the nausea, and how much by his repeated failure to control the ejection of the pegs from the toy, but a deep despair had come over him. He felt as though none of the capabilities he had picked up over the last thirty-eight years was of any use to him in this new situation, and that he had little hope of being anything other than a danger and a liability to the crew of *Avalon*, if and when they actually found themselves in space.

This whole idea had been a mistake. He had no place being here. The important thing was that Memphis 2 be launched successfully – there was no need for him or anyone else connected to Infologix to actually press the launch button in person. The symbolic value it had was far outweighed by what he now saw to be the practical reality of the situation: he was not an astronaut, and travelling into space was not simply an extension of travelling by air, land or sea. Life there was governed by an entirely different set of rules. It was not for tourists.

And he was depressed because with that realization came the death of a boyhood dream of travelling into space, a dream whose possible fulfilment had inspired him to use his position within Infologix to force himself on to the flight.

These people did not want him with them. They were professionals who had dedicated their lives to achieving the ambition he was expecting to fulfil on a whim. His presence was an insult to them as well as an obstruction.

213

Maybe, he thought, that was why they had chosen to start his training like this . . . to show him in the clearest possible way that he was not cut out for this kind of work.

If so, it was succeeding. The idea of a further twenty-one passes in this plane filled him with absolute horror – solid ground seemed a lifetime away, a safe haven that lay on the other side of an experience he was beginning to think would leave him permanently weakened. Again, he felt his body lighten as the pilot reached maximum altitude and eased off the plane's power to bring them into free-fall. Again his stomach lurched, the feeling now become physically painful with repetition.

His mind clouded with nausea and pain, he was only dimly aware of the others drifting out past him. He moved like an automaton, his body doggedly following the routine he had developed for himself over the previous passes as he gave the softest of taps against the wall, using the straps to control the speed at which he drifted out into the cabin space.

Jean was watching him from further down the craft, muttering encouragingly. The task had been simplified, in that he no longer had to remove the toy from the bag, she having taken it from him after the chaos of his first attempt. He took shallow breaths, finding that anything more substantial only made his nausea worse, and began trying to manipulate the lever whilst keeping his left arm over the toy so as to control the ejection of the pegs.

'That's good – soft, small movements,' Jean complimented him, apparently not realizing that it was mostly his stomach that was dictating the pace and strength of his actions.

He pulled up his knees, placing the box on his thighs and wedging it into place with his left forearm. He gently pulled the lever, and felt the shapes pop up against his skin.

'Good . . . now gently remove them and leave them hanging steady in the air.'

He began to lift them out one by one, carefully placing them in the air before him. Alarm bells were ringing all over his body as his stomach began to spasm, his eyes all but shut with pain.

'Excellent, Josh!' she exclaimed as he successfully placed the last of the cubes in the air before him. 'Now start putting them back again.'

He took the square and was preparing to replace it when he stopped and started to take deep, alarmed breaths. Jean saw immediately what was about to happen.

'*Hold on to it!*' she warned. 'Wait till we have gravity.'

He lanced one pleading regard in her direction, holding his mouth shut, and then knew there was no hope of reprieve. His stomach cramped violently, at last deciding that whatever he had eaten for breakfast must be indigestible, and he jerked as the vomit raced up his throat like the ball on an old Test Your Strength machine at a funfair. He just had time to move his hand aside as his mouth was blown apart with the force, and watched as an orange and white missile of impressive proportions launched from his head, bearing straight down the plane toward the three male astronauts.

He saw Jean move, kicking against the wall of the plane, but didn't understand what she was doing as the vomit was not heading her way. It was only when he saw her produce the carrier bag from her pocket, blowing rapidly into it to fill it out as she raced into the path of the vomit, that he understood: in one seamless movement, she caught the cornflake missile in the bag, immediately beginning to lassoo it around her head to stop it rebounding back out, and brought herself to a controlled landing on the far wall of the plane.

'Close.' She smiled. 'Feel better now?'

Josh was so amazed that he didn't feel himself drifting back from the kick of the vomit until he hit the rear wall. The plane began to level off, but his newly emptied stomach didn't warn him until he saw his toys drop to the floor, followed a split second later by his own body.

*

Josh mastered the *Pull 'n' Play* five passes later, his mind having cleared immediately after his stomach. The depression had lifted, and he began to feel as though he might be capable of mastering the basic skills of space travel in the weeks they had before them.

Jean seemed to be impressed by the rapidity of his progress, but he suddenly found he had difficulty responding to her comments with anything other than a smile. In fact, he had not managed to get a full sentence out since the vomit episode.

It wasn't just embarrassment.

It was that Jean Grey's balletic dive to catch his vomit in zero gravity was the most awesomely graceful movement he had ever seen any woman make. As beautiful as she had seemed to him on the ground, she was infinitely more so in the air. She was like some kind of nymph, a spirit of the wind in human form.

Lying in bed that night, exhausted but far too stimulated by his day to find sleep, Josh Cloken would realize that it was not his stomach she had caught in that bag.

She had caught his heart.

XVIII

As the campaign entered its final three weeks, there was an extra chair at the meeting-room table in Mike Summerday's campaign headquarters. It had been put there shortly after the line on the wallchart tracking Summerday's performance in the polls had stopped its steep, catastrophic dive and begun to level out. Its occupant was the individual widely credited with bringing that turn-around about.

VOTE FOR SUSAN'S HUSBAND, as the latest pins said.

Chandra Dissenyake had cut short his retreat, even though his lower chakra was causing him gyp like he hadn't known in all his years of guiding lost souls through the political darkness. His chakra was still not quite all it should be – Susan's intervention in the campaign had caught him unawares, upsetting his spiritual equilibrium and throwing all his careful calculations out of the window. It was a question of balance: Susan currently towered at around six foot seven in spiritual inches, compared to her husband's five five. Douglas was six or seven inches taller than Summerday, but that was a difference they could hope to correct in the last three weeks of campaigning. The difficulty was that Douglas, crucially, stood above his wife. Summerday had to stand on a chair to kiss his. That was the kind of thing that would count heavily with the voters.

Yet Susan had also, the guru believed, given him a new

insight into this campaign. His retreat had been short, but he felt that he had achieved a deeper level of political spirituality nevertheless. Susan had single-handedly stopped the poll free-fall her husband had set off. The public could now relate to his motivation – it was all about avenging Susan's rape. They still thought it had been a dumb move, but dumb was okay if it was a case of a man having to do what a man had to do.

Now it was up to Dissenyake to get the line moving back up. The faces around the campaign table regarded him expectantly.

'I hope you can find it in your hearts to forgive me for not having been here these last days,' he began softly, 'but I have had much thinking to do. In the course of this campaign, a question has begun to trouble me and I could not fulfil my duties here without resolving it. I have searched my soul, and now, I believe, I see the answer. I believe I know how to lead this campaign to a successful resolution.'

He paused solemnly, closing his eyes. It was immediately clear to everyone in the room that a profound change had come over their spiritual guide. He seemed to be frailer than before, and yet lighter too, as though the great bulk beneath his suit was made not of fat but of air. He had attained a higher level of understanding. They waited respectfully for him to gather his energies, channelling them from around his body to give birth to his new vision in one clear pronouncement.

Dissenyake opened his eyes, spreading wide his arms as if to envelop them all in the warmth of his love, and smiled.

'Screw politics!' he announced.

The gathered heads leaned slightly inwards around the table, frowning as they tried to follow the thrust of his new philosophy.

'Who cares about politics?' he laughed. 'The

fundamental truth that binds together all the citizens of a democracy is one simple belief: that they could do as good or bad a job of running the country as their leaders do! So why try to convince them that we know any better? Why do we insist on lying shamelessly to our people, presenting them with unrealistic programmes that they know as well as we do ourselves can never be achieved? By so doing we not only insult them, we commit the far more heinous crime of *boring* them! Why else do the majority of people not even bother to vote? So the answer is clear – screw politics!'

There was an uncomfortable silence as the smiles he had been waiting for failed to appear. They were not following him.

'Don't you see, my friends? In this new age it is not our role to persuade people to believe in us! We are only human. We have no greater understanding of the world than they do! That is not what they *want* from us!'

'Chandra . . .' Michael Summerday at last spoke up, knowing that he was not alone in his doubts about the guru's grasp on reality, 'we're politicians. What else can we do? What are you saying they *do* want?'

'But it's so obvious, isn't it?' the fat man exclaimed. 'What do they always want? What is the great need that binds all levels of society together?'

'Money!' Bob Redwood exclaimed, believing he was the first to grasp the guru's argument. 'We offer them money! Either cash in hand for votes, or lower taxes for any state that swings our way!'

'Please . . .' Dissenyake sighed in disappointment. 'Do you think money is all that matters? I am talking about their *souls*! Did Susan save us from total catastrophe by handing out cash? No. Susan instinctively understood what we were all too blind to see! We have to . . . *entertain*!'

'You mean . . . like . . . sing?' Redwood gasped. 'I can't sing, Chandra.'

Susan shook her head pityingly, turning to her husband's partner. 'He means that it's a soap, Bob. My rape, the sexual abuse of Douglas's first wife . . . they like the drama.'

'Precisely!' Dissenyake agreed, hitting the table. 'From now on this campaign must be about pain! Tragedy! Susan understands what people want because she is a woman in touch with the goddess force of Nature. Listen to your wife, Mr Vice-President!'

'What are you saying I have to do?'

'You must suffer! We must see your body pulled from the wreckage of your car – bruised and bloodied, but miraculously unharmed. Your daughter must contract a terminal disease! Susan must battle with her inner demons and conquer her alcoholism! All the pleasure and comfort you might have derived from being born rich and connected must be ripped from you, Mr Vice-President, until your inner core is exposed for all to see – naked, battered and beaten to its knees! And then, when you stagger back up to your feet, they will vote for you. You will have their hearts, their souls . . . stop trying to win their minds!'

'Forgive me, Chandra, but . . . isn't it a little unbeliev-able? We have three weeks left until the election – I have a car crash, Penny gets cancer, Susan becomes alcoholic and subsequently reforms . . . isn't it a little much?'

A faraway look entered Dissenyake's eyes, the look of a prophet in the rapture of a divine vision.

'I have been on a retreat, my friends, and I have seen! I have had a vision of the future – not just ours, but that of all who come after us. We shall be the nation's binding force – the drama that they, the viewers, bring to a climax with their own hands by voting for the characters of their choice! The men who manage campaigns shall be artists, plotting new twists and shock developments to defeat their opponents in the agony stakes! People will

220

not only *follow* elections, they will buy the video!'

Summerday's mouth gobbled silently for a few seconds as he struggled to voice the turmoil in his mind, finally exploding:

'Chandra! What the hell do you *do* on these retreats?'

'I find my point of inner calm, Mr Vice-President, and I sit in silence. I become not Chandra Dissenyake, but all people. All the people out there whom we must reach. I become the blank sheet for them to write upon, listing their hopes, their fears and their desires. I watch TV.'

'That's it? You just watch TV?'

'And drink beer. I become one with the people, eating cheese puffs and ice-cream.'

Suddenly it was clear why Chandra Dissenyake was on the chubby side for a guru.

'TV is TV, Chandra,' Summerday pointed out gently. 'They won't buy it in reality.'

'Oh, but they'll buy a fiscally impossible programme of tax cuts and improvements in education, will they?' the fat man snapped with uncharacteristic anger. 'Do you think they believe that? The point is not credibility, but desire! If we make them want to believe, they will believe. All people ask of us is that we make them give a damn! And is that such a terrible lie?' He swivelled his chair around to face the TV, picking one of the campaign advertisements at random from the pile and slotting it into the VCR. 'Is it any more unbelievable than this?'

It was a copy taken from the agency's master cassette, with a clock on a blue screen counting down the seconds to the start of the film and the title of it written along the bottom of the screen. Michael Summerday's numbed stomach suddenly lurched into life as he read: 'Sunday Breakfast'.

Anybody who doubted Chandra Dissenyake's spiritual insight would no doubt have been converted to his philosophy had they known about the recent editorial meeting of a particular magazine. With the election only three weeks away, the huge machine of Atlantian media was finally turning at full power, every single publication finding its own angle on the contest, from journals of current affairs to fishing revues. Amid the forest of print, however, was one magazine that stood above the rest, its role in the great democratic circus being a matter of tradition and heritage.

Dream House magazine had recently been brought back from the brink by its new editor, Amanda Ely, hired in a last-ditch attempt to save it from dying with its eternally loyal readers. She had totally overhauled the moribund title, ending its traditional obsession with flower arrangements and perfect dinner parties in favour of younger, more urban subjects such as 'Tulips and Two Lips: How to Tell What He's Like in Bed From the Flowers He Brings' and 'The Perfect Pizza Delivery Boy'. She even changed the magazine's name to give it a more modern feel: *Dream House* was dropped in favour of the hipper, more challenging *hoUSe dreAM*. It was a high-risk strategy, bound to alienate the magazine's current readers, but it also generated huge publicity. As commentators pointed out, the metamorphosis represented a watershed in Atlantian culture: if even *Dream House*, that bastion of the pre-clitoral society, had been converted to sex then there was only one conclusion to draw: sex was obviously here to stay.

Of course, it had more than sex. Amanda Ely knew that the modern woman wanted a style magazine that covered every aspect of her life, reflecting and informing her tastes, opinions and aspirations while respecting her independence and unique personality. Sex was important, but so were work, travel, buttocks, design and sushi. 'The only taboo,' she liked to repeat, 'is to bore.'

And she was right: the relaunched *hoUSe dreAM* was

a hit with a generation of women who had just reached the age their grandmothers had been at when the magazine was first created. The middle generation had been jumped completely – they were the ex-radicals who had settled down to comfortably middle-class lives but still had a guilt complex about world poverty and tropical hardwoods: a lost cause to lifestyle magazines.

The editorial team met to brainstorm for new ideas on the first Monday of every month. Actually it was more of a brainwash. The ideas weren't ever new, just old ideas with a facelift and fake ID.

'Black,' announced Ursula Hoff, the art director.

'Uh-huh . . . uh-huh . . . What about black, exactly?' Amanda probed, intrigued but yet to be convinced.

'Black is Back.'

'Again? I thought Red was Ahead?'

'Red tried, it failed. Red is no longer the new black, black is. Red is Dead. But it's a New Black, a black that has learned from red and has evolved to reflect the modern *esprit* – it is purer, less cluttered and determined to be itself. Black black.'

'Uh-huh . . . what does that give in practical terms?'

'Black coffee in a black cup. Clean Caffeine.'

'Cream is unclean?'

'Exactly. Cream should not be seen. Cream is unseemly. Express Yourself With Expresso.'

'Are we talking about an entire Black Issue?'

'Not a Black Issue, but an issue about how Black *is* the issue. Nothing but black – black models, black furniture, black clothes, black type and black coffee.'

'Black and white photography?'

'No! Black is a *colour* now, that's the whole point! We have to show that, Amanda!'

Shelley Beech, the food editor, was looking alarmed. She was one of the few remaining figures from the old *Dream House*, having managed, after a career devoted to

223

suggesting easy ways to prepare a four-course dinner for six while still having time to drink a cocktail with your guests, to adapt to the new attitude of the magazine. Make the food section sexy, they had told her, and she had. Oysters, lobsters, mineral waters, defenceless little mango balls cocktail-sticked to a pineapple ice sculpture like a giant fruit grenade, pre-kindergarten chickens flambéd in tequila . . . her food pages were now less about sustenance than culinary foreplay.

'I have a problem with an *entirely* black issue,' she announced hesitantly. 'I can do coffee, obviously. I can do truffles. I can do squid-ink soup. But that's not the problem . . . the problem is the First Wives' Cookie Recipe Contest.'

'Oh spare me . . .' Amanda groaned. 'Do we have to talk about the bloody First Wives' cookies? It's so tan tights, Shelley.'

Shelley looked hurt. She had been with the magazine for twenty-eight years, through good times and bad, and felt no one appreciated how hard she had worked to adapt herself to the new look. She couldn't be expected to give up her moment of glory.

'The Cookie Contest has always been one of our biggest sellers, Amanda,' she replied sniffily, 'and it is, perhaps I should point out, an honour for the magazine. We are part of the great democratic heritage of Atlantis, whether that fits in with our new obsession with nipple rings or not. You can't just throw away a distinction like that – you don't spit in the face of history just because cookies aren't an aphrodisiac.'

'Shelley, relax!' Amanda consoled her. 'Nobody is talking about renouncing the role this magazine has always played in our presidential elections, but maybe we could bring the feature a little more up to date? I mean, does it *have* to be cookies?'

'Yes! Yes, it does have to be cookies! Cookies are

part of this country's cultural identity.'

'So is apple pie,' Amanda countered.

'Apple pie is . . .' Shelley winced. 'Apple pie is apple pie, Amanda. Apples in a pie. Cookies can be anything – pecan, chocolate, you name it. They can be sexy in their own way.'

'But philosophically you accept the principle – cookies are *not* the only cultural reference this country has?'

'Of course.'

'Guns!' exclaimed the new features editor, Mo Grace. 'Guns are as much part of our heritage as cookies! Why don't we have a First Wives' Firearms Contest?'

'Because guns are not culinary utensils!' Shelley protested, sensing an alliance forming against her.

'Not true. You hunt with guns,' Amanda pointed out, 'you hunt for food. So guns are actually *essential* culinary utensils, Shelley.'

'Especially today, when people of taste value authenticity,' Mo added. 'Fresh pasta, home-grown herbs, a double-barrelled shotgun – it's all part of the same movement away from pre-processed and pre-digested experiences.'

'This is ridiculous!' Shelley laughed. 'How many women keep a gun in the kitchen? The food section, surely, is at least about stuff you do in the kitchen, isn't it?'

'No it isn't,' Amanda contradicted her.

'I'm sorry? It's *not* about stuff you do in the kitchen? What are you saying – you want me to talk about bathrooms on the grounds that eating inevitably implies defecation, Amanda?'

'No, Shelley – but you don't *barbeque* in the kitchen, do you? Are you saying we can't talk about barbeques in the food section on the grounds that you don't do it in the kitchen? Where do you draw the line? Although, now you mention it, that bathroom idea of yours is pretty damn original. We ought to think some more about that.'

Shelley looked wildly around the table for a sympathetic regard. She saw only friendly smiles. The bitches were all against her cookies. 'Okay!' she snapped. 'Fine! Whatever you want! But how do you know either of the prospective first ladies even *has* a gun?'

This, they realized, was a valid point. A disappointed silence fell across the room as they contemplated a cookie victory by default.

'I suppose so . . .' Amanda thought aloud. 'Maybe it will have to be more of a First Wives' Self-Defence Contest instead – "Our Panel of Experts Decide Who, Out of Susan Summerday and Barbara Douglas, Kicks Better Ass?"!'

'Self-defence against what?'

'Rape, of course.'

'Rape,' Shelley repeated caustically. 'Rapist rape or oilseed-rape? Are we in the kitchen still or down dark alleys where shady people may occasionally barbeque?'

'Shelley!' Amanda exclaimed, genuinely excited, 'that's so brilliant! First bathrooms, now rape, and we're *still* in the food section! I love it!'

There was no point in continuing the discussion. Shelley knew she was beaten – but the longer it went on the less sure she became of whether she had been beaten or beaten herself.

'No cookies, then,' she relinquished sadly. 'Have it your way. "The First Wives' Self-Defence Contest – see Food".'

Amanda smiled, winking at her. 'And we title it *"If You Can't Stand the Heat"*. . .'

Following her furious departure from the meeting room, Michael Summerday finally caught up with Susan back in their private apartments. As he entered the living room her nose wrinkled, as if he brought with him an odour that would make a fart blush.

'Whatever you think, Susan, it's not how it—'

'*Ugh!*' she grunted, steadying herself on the mantel-piece. 'Stop! I can't stomach any more of your excuses, Michael. I'm getting nauseous just hearing you start. I neither know nor want to know who those two bitches are or how they came to be having breakfast with you, okay? This time you have gone too far. There is *nothing* you can say! You should be shot like a dog. Now leave.'

She breathed deeply, trying to keep a hold on her nausea.

'Susan, really, it's not so terrible a—'

'You are *relentless*, aren't you? You are determined to worm your way out of this! How can you bring yourself to even *think* I might forgive you? How can you excuse yourself . . . How can your lips even make the necessary *sounds*, Michael? Do you practise mouthing obscenities while you sleep or something? "Take me up the arse, O Beelzebub! The Madonna was a cheap whore who sucked off lepers' dicks . . . Vote for Mike Summerday" . . .'

She fell silent. Her free hand, the one that wasn't steadying herself against the wall, felt her forehead, as if to hold in the thoughts going through her mind. A smile began twisting her mouth.

'You know . . . I thought you were a scumbag, Michael Summerday, but I had it all wrong. There's no *bag*! Just uncontained scum! You actually care so little about us or anything but this election that you can happily stand there and . . . *vomit* on the truth. I knew that ad was a farce, but at least I thought we all cared enough for each other to play our parts! Did you think I wouldn't notice?'

Summerday frowned imploringly. 'I did it for *us*, Susan – so that everything we've already sacrificed to come this far will not have been for nothing!'

She pushed herself off the wall and advanced toward him, pointing her finger accusingly. Summerday began to retreat across the room as she exploded:

'Everything *we* have sacrificed? Michael, darling, I don't think you quite understand the concept. *I* have sacrificed, *Penny* has sacrificed, but *you* . . . you have bartered! It's not quite the same, is it? I can sacrifice my time, my career and my heart so that my husband can get ahead, but you, that husband – or you at least occupy his physical likeness even though you are actually an alien *pod-thing* – you have only exchanged your honesty, morality, courage and basic decency in return for becoming President. God knows I'm in no position to boast, because it was my own fault for not realizing the Michael Summerday I fell in love with and married was not a person but a marketing concept, but even so . . . *our* sacrifice? Just how insanely stupid do you think I *am*, you little virus . . . you . . . you *cancer?*'

Summerday's retreating heels hit the sofa and he dropped backwards on to the cushions.

'Susan . . .' he groaned, looking up at her pitifully. 'What can I say?'

She cupped her hands over her face, blowing into her palms and trembling as her body succumbed to the force of her anger, then lifted her head again, her fingertips leaving white trails as they ran down her flushed cheeks.

'I agree,' she gasped.

'Okay . . . okay . . . I *agree*! There. *I agree*. I am all the things you said, Susan, and probably more.'

She stopped breathing. For a full ten seconds she literally forgot to do it. Her mouth worked silently, trying in vain to find a sound that could express her feelings. Suddenly her instincts returned and she sucked in a huge, Hoover-lipped chestful of air, letting it out with slowly spat words.

'You make me . . . no, you're worse than that . . . you

228

make my *puke* puke! I meant I agree that there is nothing you can say, not that *you* should say *you* agree with *me*, you . . . *sponge*!'

'But I *do* agree! You're right! And at least . . . at least I have the courage to admit that to your face, Susan. So I must have principles of some kind, mustn't I?'

'Of course you do, Michael. You and your career. That's all there ever has been. That's all you are. You have no existence beyond your ambition. The devil himself could not tempt you. I don't believe you've ever loved me. I was simply the vessel you chose to prove your heterosexuality to the voters.'

Summerday closed his eyes. He was silent for a long time as he thought over the situation, and when at last he looked again and spoke, his tone had quite changed.

'There's no point in me saying anything. You don't even want to understand why I did it. Everything has to be personal with you, doesn't it, Susan?'

'*Hello?*' She laughed. 'I humiliate myself for you in front of the whole world, and when I am upset to find myself being played by some *actress* in an advert about our family life, you accuse me of taking it too *personally*? Where precisely does "personal" start in your warped imagination, Michael? Can I, for instance, take a hammer to your testicles and expect you to understand that I'm only presenting you with an objective definition of masculinity?'

'I only mean that you accuse me of selfishness because my actions don't suit *you* personally. But what about the 250 million other people in this country who have to choose, for better or worse, between myself and Jack Douglas – do they figure anywhere in your vision of things?'

'I am only human, Michael. I cannot comprehend horror on that scale. My tragedy was choosing you for myself. If tens of millions of other people make the same mistake then that's just . . . a statistic.'

'Very funny, Susan. But you avoided the question. A country needs leaders. It's all very well you seeing this from a personal point of view, but *someone* has to be prepared to do it! You're a very intelligent and talented woman – you could do the job just as well as me, but you're not willing to stand up and offer to take on that responsibility, so what gives you the right to criticize me simply because I am?'

'How noble of you. Nothing to do with ambition, then.'

'Of course ambition! But is it my fault you've always lacked ambition? I'm not saying that's wrong, but where would we be as a couple if both of us had lacked ambition? You *chose* me because you thought I had enough ambition for the both of us! You put the responsibility for our growth and evolution and change on to me, and without those things there is no point to life, or love, or even getting up in the morning, is there? I always understood that to be the case, and I believe you did too, so has it been so very wrong of me to do whatever I believed necessary to make it happen? It's not me that is the monster, but the world! You can't deal with it in any other way than I have done! So don't tell me that I have treated you as some kind of vessel . . . because I could accuse you of doing much the same thing! Don't you see that?'

It has to be said that Susan almost fell for it.

Five years ago she would have fallen for it without a doubt. Part of her wanted to think she was in the wrong. She was an old-fashioned girl at heart.

But not now. She'd fallen for Michael's line one too many times and she could see the hook – he sounded reasonable, but the bastard had just absolved himself of all blame again. And this time, she thought as a wicked idea formed in her brain, she was not going to let him get away with it. After twenty years it was payback time.

'You're quite right, Michael. I have been absolving myself of responsibility all along. Blaming you for my own guilt. I'm sorry.'

Summerday's eyes widened slightly in surprise, but he tried to look calm for fear of her changing her mind.

'That's all right, Susan. The important thing in marriage is for both of us to agree where we stand – everything else follows on naturally.'

'Absolutely. And you're right – it is time I started taking more responsibility upon myself.'

'Well, I'm glad to hear it, darling.'

'Do you really think I could be good at politics?'

'Are you kidding?' he laughed. 'Hell, you're more popular in the polls than I am!'

'Uh-huh . . .' A dangerous look came into Susan's eyes as she smiled at her husband. Summerday shifted uncomfortably on the sofa, suddenly not so sure he liked the way the conversation was going.

'They like me more than they like Bob Redwood, don't they?'

'Ye-e-es . . .'

'It's a pity you chose him as your running-mate.'

'Well . . .. Bob has qualities of his own, you know. He's much appreciated by certain . . . elements of the country.'

'Bob's an idiot, Michael. Everyone knows that.'

'Bob's not an *idiot*, Susan, he's just . . . impressionable.'

'I want to be Vice-President, Michael.'

'Yes, I guessed that, Susan. It's out of the question.'

Susan pouted mockingly. 'But, Michael . . . it's my ambition! And I only want to be *Vice*-President!'

'I have one already.'

'Ditch him.'

'I can't do that. You know I can't. Why are we even talking about this?'

'Because if you don't let me have my ambition, Michael, then I'm only left with having ... responsibility.'

'What do you mean?'

'Well, I think, if I'm to be really responsible, that I really should tell everyone it's *not* me in the advert ... don't you?'

XIX

What was the point of growing up, Macauley Connor wanted to know, if one wasn't subsequently right in one's opinions? Why go through all the pain of putting childish things behind one, learning to stand on one's own two feet and work for the little rewards life offered, if it turned out that you were still as clueless and misguided as you ever were back when your mother insisted she knew best? Children are cheated into becoming adults.

Of all the things he had lost that would never turn up at the bottom of a drawer or behind the cushions of a sofa, things like ideals, innocence and illusions, it was the lost certainty of what he knew that caused him the most grief. It was too depressing to think about. He didn't mind that he would never have an answer to any of the big questions in life, all the unfilled boxes on his metaphysical crossword, but he at least would have expected to be able to get the basic facts right.

John Lockes was not John Lockes.

Or, the John Lockes who presided over the world's largest software company was not the John Lockes who was born in Farview. He had resisted the truth at first, telling himself that Reverend Willis was old and may no longer be conducting a full orchestra, but the preacher had taken him from one person to another around town and they had all confirmed what the old man had said. The Lockes in Macauley's picture was not their one.

It made no sense to him whatsoever, apart from in the sense that it fitted in with his growing suspicion that his life was some elaborate joke being told for the amusement of whatever higher being was responsible for the mess of the universe. Just when he thought he had finally been getting to the core of his book, linking what he had discovered about Lockes as an adult with the research into his childhood, he found himself holding a male plug in either hand, unable to make a circuit.

He realized with a heavy heart that his work was just beginning. And from Farview, there was only one place to go next.

The Welton Academy for Gifted Children was housed in a huge eighteenth-century building set off from the road by a half-mile of tree-lined driveway. It was an impressive, palatial structure with colonnaded wings curling out on either side, and great wide steps leading up under a portico to the main doors, but Macauley instantly disliked the place. There was something about the big house that depressed him. Perhaps too many children had waved goodbye to their parents on those steps, their heartache being soaked up by the very stones of the building, or maybe the architecture failed in some subtle way to lift the spirit, but he had the sensation of entering a localized field of increased gravity.

The colonnades featured niches that must once have contained statues, but they and all similar trimmings had been removed, leaving only the raw architecture, like a wedding cake for pessimists. He imagined that the driveway must once have been loose gravel that crackled richly under the wheels of each wealthy visitor's carriage, but it had been paved over so many years before that even the tarmac was now cracked and holed, washed dirty white by the sun.

Looking up as he passed under the portico, he could see the plaster was beginning to fall off its underside, small patches having dropped away to reveal the wooden slats and caked straw behind. The doors were the height of three men, and even closing them carefully behind him produced a loud metallic *clang* around the marble hallway. The interior smelled of disinfectant applied with an old mop.

It was incredible how all such institutions, even when they were housed in palatial surroundings like these, managed to create exactly the same atmosphere of massproduced loneliness. How cold and alien this academy must have seemed to John Lockes, he realized, after the cosy claustrophobia of Farview.

Nobody was about, but a little wooden plaque painted with faded gold lettering pointed the way to THE SECRETARY, so he exited the hall by a corridor leading off to the left, the marble giving way to wheezing, polishedoak floorboards. He advanced slowly, sounding as though he were treading on mice with every footstep.

'Mr Connor?'

Macauley span round to see a man's head poking around one of the doors he had just passed. He nodded, a little too startled to speak, and offered his hand.

'The floorboards. Better than the best alarm system,' the man explained with a smile as he shook his hand. 'Dan Welton, director of the academy.'

Welton was much younger than Macauley had imagined from speaking to him on the phone – no more than forty on the outside. He wouldn't have been much more than twenty when John Lockes was here, which seemed an impossibly precocious age to be running a school.

'Second generation, I take it?' he asked as he followed the director into his office.

'My father passed away a few years ago. Coffee?'

Macauley declined the offer and Welton helped himself to a large cup from the percolator behind his desk, putting in three sugars as though the atmosphere of the

235

place were draining his energy, and sat down on the edge of his seat as if he may be going to get up again at any second.

'Now, Mr Connor . . .' he smiled, opening a fresh pad of paper and taking out a pen, 'tell me about your son.'

'Well, Jeremy is only six,' Macauley began, trotting out his prepared spiel. 'Obviously, it's much too early to know whether he will be talented enough to warrant a place at an academy such as—'

'Not at all,' Welton interrupted. 'Many parents put their children down for Welton at an early age, Mr Connor. And what's more, I should tell you, if you make a firm commitment to put your child with us now then he will not have to pass the entry test when he reaches the age of twelve. His place will be guaranteed.'

'Doesn't he have to be gifted?'

'All children are gifted, Mr Connor – it's just a question of us adults recognizing what their gift is. In the past, it's true, Welton tended to have a very restricted view of what was meant by "gifted", but times have changed – it may mean gifted academically, or athletically, or even in terms of personality. Some children are gifted with imagination, some have a gift for video games. All character is unique, and whatever is unique is a form of genius. So the important thing is to nurture whatever it is they have that's unique, don't you agree?'

Macauley looked a little surprised. He'd been imagining, in the vague plan he'd drawn up for himself, that he would discuss his Jeremy's fictional future safe in the knowledge that everything depended upon the little darling proving himself a mathematics genius or a budding astrophysicist.

'But surely, people imagine that if someone has been to an academy for gifted children, then that person is—'

'Yes.' Welton smiled. 'Well, obviously it can't do Jeremy any harm if people think that, can it?'

Seeing Macauley frown, Welton sighed and pushed his notepad to one side. He brought his palms together, the tips of his fingers touching his lips and a pained expression in his eyes. 'This is absurd. Look, I might as well be frank with you, Mr Connor. There's very little chance of Jeremy ever attending Welton.'

'He is unique in his own way, I asure you!' Macauley protested, suddenly feeling protective of his non-existent child.

'I'm sure he is, Mr Connor. And I would be very happy to have him here, but the truth is that I'm about one broken window-pane away from having to file for bankruptcy. I shouldn't waste your time.'

'But . . . but I thought Welton was the best?'

'Oh! We were!' The director laughed philosophically. 'We were the best, no doubt about it. John Lockes himself came here, you know. But these days . . . these days there are just too damn many special schools and not enough geniuses! It has become a highly competitive market. Gone are the days of cold dormitories and boiled potatoes, Mr Connor! Nowadays, if one school offers jacuzzis, the next has to offer jacuzzis and cranial masseurs. My father was too old to adapt and Welton, I have to say, suffered greatly as a result. We lost our star teachers because we couldn't match the salaries being offered by new academies, and the cream of the youth were lured away by the kinds of facilities that Welton simply couldn't afford. You wouldn't believe what parents expect these days. Little snotty-nosed geniuses have the right to demand state-of-the-art technology, Nobel Prize-winning teachers, Olympic sports facilities, five-star accommodation, corporate sponsorship deals, restaurant-quality food . . . it's a supplier's market. The competition for the talent is such that some academies are actually *paying* the families of the brightest children, rather than vice versa! We all know that with a few genuine geniuses at our school, the parents of other children will pay top dollar to have their own kids there. It's a status symbol. Welton didn't move with the times – until I took over we didn't even have industrial sponsors – and yet the cost of staying in the game has been constantly escalating. A big-name math teacher, for instance, can now be transferred for anything up to a million dollars.'

'Do they have to submit to dope-testing before classes?'

'It'll probably come. Most teaching contracts now leave the school the option of selling staff members to another school in the event of their needing to raise cash to cover some major investment, like a wave machine for the swimming pool. No one likes it, of course, but the only alternative is to fall into the downward spiral of dwindling funds. If you can't afford the best facilities and the best teachers, you don't get the best children, and if you don't have the best children you gradually find that you have fewer and fewer *ordinary* children. Pretty soon the roof is leaking and you don't have the money to buy a pot. Do you follow me?'

'How does anyone make money?' Macauley asked in bewilderment.

'Legacies. Tax-deductible donations from alumni who've made good. Plus, of course, you need some serious corporate backing – companies are desperate to secure the best talent for themselves for the future, so they are headhunting younger and younger individuals all the time. Most star children these days have already signed job contracts before they reach adolescence. It gets worse all the time – I've heard of elementary-school teachers being signed up as talent scouts. In a few years I wouldn't be surprised if we're seeing corporate reps in the crèches. Find a kid who's mastered going on the pot at an early age, get his parents to sign a contract option, and you could just get the next John Lockes on the cheap.'

'But you *did* have John Lockes! Haven't you approached him?'

A pained look crossed the young director's face. He threw his hands up in the air in exasperation and slumped back into his chair.

'Approached him?' He sighed. 'Frankly, I'm amazed they haven't arrested me for stalking yet, Mr Connor. I have written to him, faxed him, e-mailed him . . . zip. Nothing. The man obviously didn't enjoy his time here. It breaks my heart, Mr Connor, it breaks my heart. By rights we should be benefiting from that connection. We should be the best-funded school in the league with an alumnus like that . . . I just don't get it.'

Macauley wasn't sure if he was about to do the right thing. He had intended to find out what he could about Lockes' time at the academy without blowing his cover story, but he saw now that Welton was just desperate enough to be ready to hear the truth.

'May I be totally frank with *you*?' he asked quietly.

'About Jeremy?'

'Yes, about Jeremy. You see . . . Jeremy doesn't exist.'

Welton looked perplexed at first, and then, as if he were so at the end of his tether that everything had become a joke to him, he shrugged.

'Well in that case, Mr Connor, I can see no obstruction to him attending Welton, can you?'

'This . . .' Macauley continued, producing his picture of the young Lockes from his briefcase, 'is why I'm actually here.'

*

The dossiers on every boy who had ever attended Welton were kept in a small, windowless room in the basement. The files went back half a century, dating from the academy's inauguration, and were arranged in alphabetical order on shelves that stretched from floor to ceiling along opposite walls. Dan Welton was on his hands and knees, looking for Lockes' folder on the lowest shelf while Macauley trained a torch over his shoulder, since the room's one bulb didn't cast enough light to read the faded names on the files.

'One thing I'll say for my father,' Welton was muttering as his fingers ran across the cardboard dossiers until they closed over the one he was looking for, 'he was a stickler for good, old-fashioned filing. Never trusted computers, thank heavens, even once all the children were using them. With the way the equipment has changed over the years we'd have lost half our records had we kept them on disk.' He pushed himself up from his knees, dusting off his trousers with his spare hand, and waved the file proudly. 'Here we go! Everything about John Lockes' time at Welton – every grade, every medical report, every comment by every teacher.'

He slapped it a couple of times to knock off the thin film of dust and opened it up under Macauley's torch. 'Now . . . hopefully there will be an admission sheet somewhere near the back with a photo of him aged thirteen . . .'

He flicked rapidly through the report cards and carbon copies of every Lockes-related document that the academy had ever produced until he uttered a small cry of victory and pulled out a thick sheet with a photograph stapled to the top right corner.

The boy pictured was slim and healthy, his tanned skin and bright blue eyes suggesting someone who had led an active, outdoors childhood. He had sandy hair and his face, whilst still unformed, held the seeds of future good looks. He smiled in the fresh, seductive manner of someone who is by nature relaxed and confident, the kind of boy who would be the hero of the football team and narrowly avoid expulsion after getting a local girl into trouble. He seemed vaguely familiar to Macauley, but one thing was certain:

'That isn't John Lockes,' he announced. 'Not the person who calls himself John Lockes, anyway.'

Welton took a recent photograph of Lockes that Macauley offered him and compared the two side by side. It was true – there was no way this handsome young boy could have turned in later life into the bespectacled, geeky man who headed Infologix.

'I don't understand . . .' Welton whispered. 'Was it a totally different John Lockes who came to us?'

'No. Lockes came here all right. He designed his first computer programs while he was at Welton. But somehow . . . It's not possible there were *two* John Lockeses in that year, is it?'

Welton shook his head, still comparing the two photographs. 'No. The files would be right next to one another. This one was between Leary and Loomis.'

They flicked back through the dossier. Even at a cursory examination it was obvious that Lockes had a gift for all science-related subjects – his grades were consistently excellent and teachers' comments spoke again and again of his talent – and yet he seemed to be permanently falling sick with one virus after another, even though the boy in the picture looked strong enough to ward off most illnesses. It just didn't fit.

'Is there any way the photo on the admission sheet could be wrong?' Macauley wondered aloud.

'Not a chance – the parents of each student fill out that sheet before the start of the first academic year. Presumably they knew their own child. It just doesn't make sense . . .' He sighed. 'But at least I know why none of our appeals for donations from John Lockes got a response. God knows who we've been writing to.'

They stood in silence for a minute, each trying to find

241

some logical explanation for the discrepancy. They stared at Lockes' picture as though that might hold some clue, but the boy's happy face just grinned mockingly back.

'Hang on . . .' Macauley mused, taking back the photo of the adult Lockes.

Welton waited for him to continue, watching as he stared at the photograph, an idea seeming to run visibly across his brow – surging and being rejected, only to surge again. The journalist shook his head as if to dislodge the bothersome idea, the explanation that didn't explain anything.

'I don't quite know how this would work,' he admitted, holding up the photograph of Lockes, 'but why not approach this from the other direction? All the boys who came to Welton are in the dossiers, and they all have a photo on their admission sheet, right?'

Welton nodded.

'So how about we check whether *this* guy came to Welton as a boy?'

'Check *all* the folders, you mean?' the director squawked.

'Have you got a better idea?'

One hour later the good, old-fashioned filing system was in a condition that would have reduced Welton Senior to tears. Randomly stacked folders covered almost the whole floor of the small room, pages hanging out of them in testament to the impatient speed with which the two men had rifled through in search of their quarry.

And at last they had it.

Miles Cardew.

Same year as John Lockes. In his photograph he wore thick, black-framed glasses that overwhelmed his face, and his sickly, unformed features held only the rough genetic clue of the adult face to which they were comparing him, but the closer they examined the two, the

242

more Macauley and Welton became convinced that it was the same person. The boy in the file named Miles Cardew was the man the world knew as John Lockes.

Miles Cardew seemed to have earned himself a place at Welton Academy on the strength of his poetry, but his report cards showed a steady decline in his English grades over the time he spent there. He still got respectable results toward the end, but teachers repeatedly complained that he was not stretching himself to the full, sacrificing his academic work – and this was the give-away – in favour of his football training.

One only had to look at the picture of that spindly, runny-nosed creature to know that nothing short of a heavy diet of anabolic steroids would get him anywhere near a football field.

'I must have been wrong,' Welton announced. 'Obviously the photos were put on the wrong admission cards somehow. They must have been loose and my father simply put them the wrong way round. It's the only explanation. You only have to look at them to see that one is more the science type while the other has athletic potential.'

'Doesn't explain it, though,' Macauley responded. 'I have witnesses from Lockes' home town who say that the man shown in the photograph I have of Lockes looks nothing like the boy who left town to go to this academy. The admission cards are right, it's just the reports that are all mixed up. As though everyone in the school had their names the wrong way round.'

'That doesn't work either, Mr Connor. Even if everyone thought Miles Cardew was actually the young mathematical genius John Lockes, he wasn't. You can't fake talent. So how could he get such consistently good science grades?'

'Don't you see?' laughed Macauley. 'Everyone had them the wrong way round, yet they carried on putting their real names to their work! The academic grades are correct – these are really John Lockes' results, and these are Miles Cardew's in their correct folders – but everything else is wrong. John Lockes wasn't sick, he was out playing football! And Miles Cardew's work never suffered because of his bloody football practice, it suffered because the boy was permanently sick!'

'But why let it happen? Surely they *realized* people had them the wrong way round?'

Macauley gazed at the two pictures, shaking his head in mystification.

'I've no idea . . . no idea at all,' he admitted. 'Why did they let it happen in the first place? Why have they *never* – over two decades later – done anything to correct it? But what I really want to know is, if Miles Cardew is still pretending to be John Lockes . . . where the hell is the *real* John Lockes?'

XX

'We know where we're going here, don't we?' Josh asked, trying to sound calmer than he really was.

Jean Grey smiled without taking her eyes off the road. 'You said you wanted to go somewhere different. I'm taking you somewhere different.'

'Different I don't doubt . . .' he replied, squinting with discomfort.

The astronaut and her apprentice had long since left the parts of New Toulouse where parked cars still had the option of moving, plunging ever deeper into the twilight zone between man and nature where it was no longer clear whose laws were in force. The dark shapes of dead and dying industries loomed about them with cold chimneys and glassless windows. The only light came from occasional, sporadically functioning streetlamps and termite-mound housing blocks that seemed to have been thrown up at random, disconnected from any infrastructure beyond the occasional heavily grilled grocery store that cowered timidly under the overhang of a dozen layers of crumbling concrete. It was at once stark and chaotic – carcasses of cars stripped to the bone like dead animals picked clean in the wild – and yet the detritus of the century was strewn on every side in a sprawling junkyard of abandoned fridges, mattresses, chipboard cupboard units and unidentifiable pieces of moulded plastic. Bulging, neatly tied rubbish bags dotted their way in incongruous testament to the fact that someone was still, in the midst of all this, trying to guard an orderly space for themselves. And over everything lay a thin forest floor of paper and cardboard and styrofoam, stretching from sidewalk to sidewalk as though some mutated natural process was attempting to ferment this all down to a chemical soil.

'You are not seriously telling me there's a restaurant in this place?' Josh asked again.

It was not what he had had in mind as a first date.

By the time Josh Cloken felt he knew Jean Grey well enough to invite her out to dinner he was already in love. This wasn't the first time he had fallen in love, but it was the first time he had had no doubt that the feeling came from his heart – on the other occasions it had eventually become clear that what he had taken for love was actually just his penis being pretentious.

Which is not to say that Jean didn't bring out the romantic in his penis as much as any of the previous women. For several nights now, as thoughts of Jean kept sleep from him, his organ had been getting in touch with Josh's feminine side. A man's feminine side is located, of course, in his right hand.

Women, though, are more complex and subtle creatures than a man's right hand, which is why so many men have trouble comprehending them. To make matters worse, a woman's male side is not similarly restricted to her right hand. She can keep it just about anywhere, from the bathroom cabinet to a clothes drawer or even in the vegetable drawer of her refrigerator. So they are more highly evolved, too.

No wonder men battled for centuries to keep them barefoot and pregnant in the kitchen. Self-defence, pure and simple.

Returning to the subject of true love, one proof of the depth of Josh's feelings was that his penis arrived well back in the order of his priorities. Front of the queue were his eyes, because more than he wanted to make love to Jean he needed just to look at her, just see her dangerous smile. The way she squatted upon a chair rather than sat on it like normal people. The way she frowned when concentrating. Her gracefulness in zero gravity and the way she always caught his vomit in her bag. Then there were his ears, which longed to hear the sound of her voice and thrill to that raucous laugh. Somewhere in the queue were his hands, to touch the shoulder of her jacket, his nose, to smell the distant perfume of her shampoo, his feet, to follow where her feet fell, and his skin, to tingle at her proximity. In fact, Jean made so many demands on his mind and senses that the scene in his head was like a bad afternoon at the welfare office. His penis was probably regretting not having brought along a good book.

Jean made him feel like himself. That, he suddenly knew, was the mark of true love. This one woman made him like Josh Cloken.

Just when it seemed to him that if they carried on much further they should reach hell, the suburbs of which this must be, Jean took an unexpected right through a break in the high wire fence they had been driving alongside lately. The car dipped and groaned as the tarmac ended and they began rattling across a wasteland of some sort, strewn with piles of rubble that loomed up suddenly in the headlights, forcing Jean to meander her way between them.

'Oh my God,' Josh gasped. 'There's no restaurant out here. You've brought me here to rape and kill me, haven't you?'

Jean glanced across at him, keeping one eye on the unsteady way ahead, and growled, 'Shut up, bitch, I'm driving.'

Coming around another mound of broken

breezeblocks, they at last saw a lit building in the distance. It was a disused factory of some sort, squat and vast, with two great chimneys silhouetted by the distant lights of the city.

'Bingo!' she whispered. 'I was starting to get worried.'

'I can't imagine why.'

Their destination was insanely fashionable. The building in which it was housed had once been an asbestos factory. When the factory closed its owners had not even bothered to try selling the premises. If the idiot who would buy it had been born, he could never have survived long in a world with such dangers as open windows and kitchen utensils.

But they had not counted with the Riders of the Apocalypse, a chapter of Hell's Angels who began squatting the place. Rather than attempting to evict them, with all the cost and probable risk of violence that that implied, the owners were only too happy to make the bikers' possession of the health hazard official by selling it to them for the sum of $1. The Riders of the Apocalypse were well aware of the dangers involved in living in the building, but to give a damn would have been contrary to their philosophy.

It's not as if they called themselves the Riders of Cautious Optimism.

Worrying about asbestosis was like worrying about lung cancer. Go down that path and they'd probably end up thinking it was a bad idea to ride a motorbike at 120 mph without a helmet, for God's sake. Fuck, they might as well just climb into a coffin and wait.

The place was ideally suited to their needs, unexpectedly legal, and on top of all that they could cut their tobacco with the dust to make it go further when money was tight. For ten perfect years the chapter used the factory as a winter base vast enough to live in, work on their Harleys, test-drive them and even house their stolen eighteen-wheeler gasoline truck. Then disaster struck.

A tornado that wrought havoc throughout New Toulouse and all along the coast took the roof off the building. The good news was that the tornado provided precisely the kind of God-strength cleaning needed to remove all the remaining asbestos dust, but the bad news was that it also picked up their bikes and deposited them somewhere in the ocean.

The Riders of the Apocalypse had long been expecting a catastrophe of Biblical proportions to strike – hence their name – but this was worse than anything they had imagined.

They were pedestrians.

A group called the Riders of the Apocalypse could not undergo this kind of radical lifestyle change. For them to be without wheels was a sickening mockery of nature. It was like a bird without wings. A wet spark plug. A Ghetty's burger.

Not only had they no money to buy themselves new bikes, but each had put a lifetime's care and love into his lost machine, creating something unique and beautiful out of something mass-produced and beautiful. The bikes were as much reflections of their souls as a portrait is of the artist's. So when the tornado took their bikes, it took part of their very souls, and like the broken men they were they did not have the stomach to call themselves Hell's Angels any more.

They were nothing.

Flattened hedgehogs on the highway of fate.

Yet they could not quite bring themselves to disband and go their separate ways. Bikes or no bikes, they reasoned that they belonged together.

So they opened a restaurant.

Chez les Anges d'Enfer, as they called it, was a surprise success. The original idea had been to make it a place where Hell's Angels from other chapters could gather in threateningly large numbers, eat and take a digestive ride around the factory. Kind of a club. The pedestrianized Riders of the Apocalypse figured that at least that way they would remain in contact with their own people and with bikes until they got themselves back on their own two wheels.

It just so happened however that around the same time as it opened, journalists from the leading style magazine *Decline and Fall* were desperately looking for Hell's Angels. The artistic director's concept, which had come to him in a flash of inspiration after seeing a young woman being mugged on his way home, was to use real Hell's Angels in the magazine's next fashion spread. In the editorial meeting he had excitedly explained how he saw an eight-page montage in which models wearing the new season's colours were being brutally raped and humiliated by ugly, fat men with beards. How better to capture the bruised tints and dully throbbing undertones of the new collections?

Beer-gutted, unwashed slobs raping beautiful young girls.

It was right, it was now, and it was hip.

The concept was so brilliant and fresh that it had never occurred to *anyone* it could be so difficult lining up Hell's Angels to take part in the shoot, or even, indeed, to find out who their agent was. Amazingly, they *had* no agent. They didn't even appear to have anyone handling their PR.

'Fuck, darling,' Jac Jansen, the artistic director, screamed at his young assistant, 'they are a world-famous organization! *Someone* obviously handles them! Do you think they just became famous of their own accord?'

'Yes,' Sam Massudi, his assistant, replied. 'I've checked.'

'Oh, I see,' Jansen seethed, tired of dealing with

cretins, 'and no one set up the sponsorship deal with Harley-Davidson either, I suppose? Hmm, Samantha? I suppose they all have fucking great advertisements on the back of their jackets for *pleasure*, do they?'

'Yes!'

'Listen, you silly little tart, if you can't get me a dozen fat, hairy men on motorbikes by the end of the day . . . if you can't do a simple little thing like that, then what purpose do you serve in this world beyond your potential as a breeder?'

'But if there's no way of contacting them—'

'*Phone* Harley-Davidson. *Ask* where the slobs live. *Bring* me a selection. Is that clear?'

In the hysteria of the following week, it was perhaps not surprising that the only Hell's Angels anyone could find at such short notice were the Riders of the Apocalypse, who had the advantage of being without motorbikes. This essentially static aspect of the bikers, their bikelessness, only became clear once the entire styling team had arrived in New Toulouse complete with models, dresses and photographer. By which time it was too late to make alternative plans.

Sweeping in at the last minute, *Decline and Fall*'s artistic director listened with mounting incredulity as Sam explained the situation to him. 'Surely you jest, darling. I asked for Hell's Angels. I assumed it was understood that motorbikes – and not just any motorbikes, but fuck-off *big* motorbikes – formed part of that request. Now you tell me that these gentlemen use public transport?'

'Temporarily, yes. You see, there was a tornado and—'

'I don't care about some fucking tornado, darling. Don't you understand that this is a *disaster*? We have to shoot this today . . . *today*! Now, Frantz here is preparing his cameras to photograph the girls being raped on *some form of private transport*. Are you suggesting that we go out and buy these gentlemen skateboards?'

'There is another possibility, Jac . . . It's not quite what you had in mind, but—'

'Then it's obviously *not* a possibility, darling.'

'Listen! This place is some kind of a restaurant now. The Hell's Angels say they can serve the girls a meal instead.'

Jac Jansen looked nonplussed. 'Did I miss something? Did we talk in the editorial meeting about a back-up concept where the girls are raped by waiters? I don't really see the connection there – what are we saying?'

'Forget the fucking rape! They are in a restaurant. They eat. But the waiters are all Hell's Angels! That's got impact, hasn't it?'

Jansen looked doubtful, but he was at least unsure enough that he didn't rule it out immediately. Sensing the opportunity to resolve the problem, Tim, his husband, spoke up:

'I like it. It's *fin de siècle*. It's Raw. It's Food. Maybe even Raw Food, I don't know. It's *faim de siècle*, Jac.'

'Right!' Sam enthused. 'It's not the original concept, I know, but it's true to your vision. It's right!'

'It's now,' Tim announced.

Jansen wavered, stroking his goatee beard and wondering aloud, 'But is it hip? Girls, dresses, restaurant . . . fat hairy waiters in leather jackets?' There was a tense pause as he pictured it in his head, then he announced, 'I like it. It's hip. Tell them to cook aubergines.'

There were two ways of getting to Chez les Anges d'Enfer and Jean, partly to give Josh an even more interesting experience and partly because she didn't believe in always doing things the easy way, had taken the scenic route. The front entrance, the one normal people took, was easily accessible by taking the bridge over the river from the city centre and following the quayside for about half a mile. The restaurant looked out over the waterfront, with a pleasant view of the commercial district opposite. The post-industrial nightmare of social and economic meltdown behind was visible only as a hazily silhouetted skyline of chimneys, tower blocks and the occasional falling body.

On a Friday night it was always busy, the huge parking lot filled with luxury cars and loitering chauffeurs. A certain frisson of excitement was visible on the faces of the arriving diners, religiously thin women in their expensive slips of material feeling like gazelle on the savannah as they crossed the broken concrete lot. Their men walked tall, like they had just seen a movie and fantasized that the subtle bulges in their jackets were guns instead of wallets.

'Two, please,' Jean announced cheerfully to the grizzled, pig-eyed creature on the door.

He eyed her lean, athletic body up and down suspiciously, like some leather bear regarding a find in the woods that may or may not be a snack, then grunted to Josh:

'Does she eat?'

'I'm sorry?'

'Does your woman eat? We're running real short on space, so if she don't eat I ain't going to put you at a table for two. We got a table for one spare. She can have a chair. She can watch.'

'I think . . .' Josh started, laughing, 'I think she eats. I mean, she has a mouth. She lives. There must be a connection.'

'I eat,' Jean defended herself. 'I like food. Animals taste good.'

He regarded them a second longer.

'Just asking, you know. A lot of women in there ain't eating tonight. The chef's real pissed off. He's got meat cleavers. Keeps saying, "So the bitches want to lose weight . . ." '

253

'I will be eating a full meal,' Jean assured him.

He nodded, possibly smiling under his beard, and then straightened his back in a sudden show of formality.

'Would you like to follow me, please? I will accompany you to your table.' He turned and started up the three stairs leading to the first floor. 'Please do take care on the middle step. It is temporarily fucked.'

'Tonight's special is Voodoo Zombie Chicken,' growled their waiter once Jean and Josh were installed at a table for two.

'Uh-huh.' Josh nodded. 'And what does that come with?'

'A plate.'

'Right, I mean . . . *how* does it come?'

The waiter's moustache twitched with camouflaged irritation. 'I bring it to your table. On a plate. Are you making fun of me, asshole?'

'Absolutely not,' Josh assured him, seeing the man's grip tensing on his pencil. 'What I was trying to find out is what ingredients apart from chicken the Voodoo Zombie Chicken is prepared with. Vegetables, for instance.'

'Well, why not just say so in the first place? Do you think I'm psychotic? Anyway, I can't tell you that.'

'You *can't*?'

'Okay, I can tell you if you pledge your soul to Mantumba, Lord of the Undead. Or I cut your tongue out. It's an authentic voodoo recipe, see.'

'Oka-a-ay . . . and is there anything on the menu apart from the special?'

There was a long pause.

'I wouldn't recommend any of it.'

'Why not?'

The waiter put his hands on the table and lowered his huge bulk down until his moustache was almost tickling Josh's lips.

'Because the other stuff ain't *special*, motherfucker – why do you *think*?'

Josh leaned back in his chair and glanced at the neighbouring tables. All around the great expanse of the factory floor people appeared to have the same thing on their plates. In the cold neon light it was impossible to judge what was in it, but they did not seem to be having any difficulty consuming their food.

'Well,' he announced, 'I feel like the special. What about you, Jean?'

'Special sounds good to me,' she grinned.

'Two specials . . .' the waiter repeated, slowly marking it down on his pad, 'with plates. Do you want wine with your meal?'

'Sure, that'd be good.'

'Oka-a-ay . . . and do you want me to open it up at the table?'

'Ummm . . . does that mean we don't get to *choose* a wine? Is it like *special* wine?'

'I don't know. I don't do the wine. I'll send the wine waiter over for that. I'm *talking* about the chicken.'

It was this kind of authenticity – offering to bite the chicken's head off and anoint you with its blood at your table – that meant Chez les Anges d'Enfer was not just another damned theme restaurant. In a world where so much came packaged, pre-digested or in virtual form, discerning people naturally appreciated such a raw, genuine experience.

The exposure the fashion shoot gave the restaurant soon snowballed into a palpable buzz about the place. Chez les Anges d'Enfer was immediately adopted by *Decline and Fall* as a modern-day icon – computerization having massively speeded up the process leading to iconization – and every aspect of its style, attitude and design was discussed at length. Design, especially, was declared to be *passé* in light of the restaurant's rigorously authentic retention of the derelict factory space in which it was housed, and many of those who had spent large sums of money converting ex-industrial spaces into comfortable loft apartments suddenly started to feel an overwhelming urge to rip it all out again and just live in the rubble. Parquet flooring was out. Cracked concrete was in. Bare neon strip bulbs were in. Windows were out. Roofs were out. Drips and puddles were *de rigueur*.

Whilst interior furnishing was always the most simple aspect of fashion to predict and dictate, there was much less certainty about how far the look invented by the Riders of the Apocalypse would affect other domains. Most felt reasonably confident in proclaiming a big come-back for facial hair, worn long and dirty, but was fat back too? Certainly it was no longer cool to worry about health, but did this include a complete rejection of dentistry? And how, in light of the move away from hygiene and toiletries, were the big perfume companies expected to react? Above all, in the absence of Hell's Angelettes, what were the fashion implications for women?

The only certainty in all of this was that society was ready at last for a return to a more natural, old-fashioned idea of masculinity: neo-neolithic, as it was baptized.

'It's not what it used to be,' Jean sighed, looking around the tables. 'Back when hardly anybody knew about it except for the locals, the clientele wasn't so damn . . . *thrilled*. Not everyone came by the front entrance. It was more fun.'

'I don't get it,' Josh laughed. 'How do you find yourself in these places?'

'If you aren't a little scared then you aren't alive.' She shrugged. 'The sector of town we drove through there is called the Web. There's something exciting about that, don't you think?'

'Very, but it's not your *world*, Jean. I'm not saying they're bad people, but society is tribal – when you go to such places you are not protected by being part of the group. You could be raped and left for dead and no one would lift a finger.'

Jean leaned forward across the table until she was able to speak to him in a voice that was almost a whisper.

'Wrong. Society is far *more* tribal than that, Josh. Blacks murder blacks, and whites murder whites. Poor girls get raped by poor men. Nice college girls like me get raped by nice college boys like you.'

She sat back again and smiled.

Josh desperately wanted to swallow.

'That's not an invitation, by the way, just information.'

'Fascinating,' he replied, his voice a little garbled. 'Sounds like you wouldn't change a thing.'

'Maybe not. It's a better world than it will be once your satellite is launched, at any rate.'

'*My* satellite?' Josh started, finally gulping down his saliva. 'What do you mean, *my* satellite?'

'John Lockes' satellite, Mike Summerday's satellite, your satellite . . . you are on the same team. It doesn't really matter who has the idea, who puts up the money, who makes the law, who does the work, who gets the profits . . . it's all about one smart little tribe being more powerful than all the rest. The jungle. Just subtler.'

'Whoa, there! Aren't *you* on that side? You are taking the satellite up there, Jean. That makes you as much a part of it as me or anyone else.'

'Yeah . . .' she sighed. 'I've been thinking about that a lot lately.'

'And what conclusions have you come to?'

'None. Yet. But I will have to – and that's the problem, don't you see? Once Memphis 2 is up there all the people like me – all the nice, educated, middle-class people who make things tick for those in control but still want to believe that the object of democracy is to create a better, fairer society for all – we are going to have to stop kidding ourselves and decide whose side we are really on.'

'I don't understand what you're saying,' he frowned. 'Memphis 2 is the *result* of democracy.'

She closed her eyes briefly, sucking her lower lip, and paused before replying. When it was clear in her own head what she wanted to say, she leaned back over the table, placed a hand on his and spoke very softly:

'Look . . . I really don't bother following politics. We've got an election in, what?, a little under two weeks? I couldn't tell you a damn thing about the candidates except Mike Summerday nearly got killed in a car crash last week. Not that it matters, because we'll be in orbit. But anyway . . . it's all a charade, isn't it? Democracy is only the idea that we are all free and equal in society. That's all we have to believe – Free and Equal – and everything is all right. And if we lock a million men up in prison, or two million, it doesn't change anything because people in prison are *out* of society. Everyone *in* society is still free and equal. But tell me you're going to put a tag up their assholes and release them into the community as second-class citizens, who are not free and not equal, and then suddenly I don't feel so free *myself* any more . . .'

'But aren't they better off being able to live a normal life rather than rotting in prison? Aren't we better off if we end this climate of violence and crime?'

He was intensely aware of Jean's hand on his, her light touch sending a physically painful charge up his arm, setting the hair on the back of his head standing up. She was silent and sad, and the desire to kiss her was burning his lips. Slowly the fingers slid away, and she sat back with a sigh.

'I don't know what's best, Josh – I did math and science, not philosophy. But I suppose . . . if I try to ignore all the bullshit that Atlantis is supposedly founded on and look at it like a scientist, then I find myself thinking that all these grand things like democracy and freedom are only products of the Second Law of Thermodynamics.'

Josh looked at her impassively, his eyes slowly narrowing until he announced, 'I know I should know what that is.'

'Entropy, Josh. The tendency of all organized systems to break down. The urge toward chaos. Maybe totalitarian societies do not last because they are too rigid, not because high ideals win the day. Democracy is a naturally unstable system, and all freedom is a form of anarchy . . . so in a sense these things might just be inevitable products of the Second Law of Thermodynamics. Maybe democracy is what we end up with when the *true* human ideal of dictatorship runs up against the indefatigable law of the universe.'

'The true human ideal?'

'History would suggest, wouldn't it? We've had thousands of years of emperors, kings, Caesars, chieftains, tsars, kaisers and God knows what else on the one hand, compared to a few generations of democracy in a handful of countries on the other. Is that because we've been incredibly stupid, or is it ingrained in our nature? I *do* know that mankind is the building creature, always trying to impose symmetry and order on the face of things. That is our evolutionary vocation. So I guess we do it to ourselves as much as we do it to a pile of rocks or an acre of earth, but the Second Law of Thermodynamics dictates that everything we build will fall apart, run wild or break down. And thank God. If it wasn't for entropy we'd probably all be goose-stepping.'

Josh Cloken pulled down the edges of his mouth, stopping to think it over.

'Okay . . . but what is the problem with Memphis 2?'

She looked him hard in the eye, so hard that it was all he could do not to turn away. There was something in that regard that Josh Cloken could swear was seeing right into his every secret.

'It's a way of ordering society by computer. And I'm not sure entropy applies to non-living systems. That scares me.'

'I thought you liked being scared.'

'I *believe* in scaring myself. I never said I liked it,' she replied, still not letting go of his cornea. 'Know thine enemy, Josh, but don't love him.'

'Am I your enemy?'

The faint crow's-feet beside her eyes deepened slightly. 'I'm only trying to make conversation, Mr Cloken.'

Although the excitement about neo-Neolithicism was confined to the tiny élite at the cutting edge of fashion, the right people rushed to eat at Chez les Anges d'Enfer before each other, and the bewildered Riders of the Apocalypse soon found themselves serving not their biker brethren but a growing stream of glamorously dressed and coiffured creatures who were visibly thrilled by the surly, foul-mouthed reception they were given. The word spread through high society like germs on a tube train, and within weeks film stars, socialites and media figures alike found themselves rhapsodizing over this new venue where the staff genuinely *didn't* recognize them, and where – as more than one diner discovered to their extreme discomfort – they were expected to pay in cash.

You can't put a price on an experience like that, and many didn't, happily leaving behind jewellery and watches worth a dozen of the meals they had just eaten. It was a small price to pay for the later story of how they had narrowly avoided getting the shit kicked out of them by irate Hell's Angels. Before long the Riders of the

Apocalypse realized with total incomprehension that fewer and fewer people were coming equipped with cash.

Everything was meticulously put aside, barring the money they needed to buy the food, and the stash soon reached the kind of proportions that would have done the most ambitious armed robber proud. And it just kept getting bigger.

Which was a problem.

Everyone knew what the problem was, but the Riders had yet to mention it or discuss what they were going to do about it because none of them was sure if they *did* want to do something about it.

Because the stash was by now more than big enough for them all to buy new motorcycles, quit the restaurant business and go back to the old way of life they had loved for so many years. They could be free again, they could get their very souls back again.

But they had to want it more than that ridiculous, ever-growing mound of treasure they had unwittingly created.

The world only plays cruel jokes.

'Jean, I want to tell you something,' Josh announced hoarsely, barely able to believe what he was thinking of doing.

'Do you really?' she smiled. 'By the look on your face, I'm not so sure.'

'No, I want you to know something about me because . . . I think there's a chance you'll understand.'

He stopped, uncertain how to carry on. He hadn't been intending to tell her this – not yet – and, although he'd wanted to be able to tell her for a long time now, and although he had rehearsed the conversation a hundred different ways in his head over the last two weeks, he still didn't know how to say it. He just knew, after the discussion they had been having, that if he didn't tell her

261

now it would only become more and more difficult to do so with every passing day.

Their heads had moved together across the table as he struggled with his uncertainty. They were only inches apart, she silent and waiting patiently, he tense and all but paralysed with fear.

'I am . . .' he began, the rest drying on his tongue as he changed his mind. 'That is to say, a long time ago, I found myself to be in a situation where I was . . .'

Again he stalled.

'*Fuck!*'

Jean snatched back in surprise, more from the violence with which he'd cursed than the curse itself. Josh looked at her with alarm, obviously worried that she was offended.

'Cunt.' She shrugged. 'There you go. Now carry on.'

He looked at her tenderly, and then burst out laughing as he felt the tension drain away. He could tell this woman anything.

'Jesus, this is so stupid!'

'Take your time. Try saying it backwards or something.'

'Okay. No, I'm just going to tell you. The truth is that I'm—'

'*Hey!*'

Their heads jerked up in surprise. The bloodshot eyes of a Hell's Angel met their startled regards.

'Good-evening. I'm Napalm, your wine waiter,' the man said, holding up a leather-bound folder. 'Wine list. Do you want to choose something?'

'Oh . . . sure!' Josh answered, taking the folder. He opened it up and frowned. The interior was blank. One side a blank white page, the other red. 'Oh, I see!' he exclaimed. 'Which do you suggest would be best with the Voodoo Chicken – the red or the white?'

Napalm considered the question carefully, torn, and

was on the point of answering when his attention was drawn by a commotion over by the entrance. A small, suited man was barging his way in, flanked by a dozen police officers, some of whom were struggling with the doorman. The man in the suit opened up his briefcase and produced a sheet of paper that he held up in the air before him.

'This establishment,' he shouted in a thin, nasal voice, 'is operating in contravention of paragraph 9A of the state law regulating the sale of food and liquor, the said paragraph requiring any establishment intending to supply either food or liquor to members of the public to obtain a licence permitting the sale thereof from the regulatory body. In view of the said licence having neither been obtained nor applied for, this establishment is to be closed, effective immediately. All those persons involved in the preparation, provision and sundry related activities of food and liquor in this establishment are to be placed under arrest in accordance with the provisions in paragraph 9B of the state law regulating the—'

He broke off as a crash of breaking plates resounded from the kitchens and their doors burst open to reveal a massive, wild-eyed beast of a man. He stood for a second, heaving with aggression, and then began to charge, screaming:

'AAA!'

The police threw the doorman to one side and drew their weapons, taking aim at the crazed animal.

'AAA! AAA! AAA!' he shouted, throwing tables aside as he thundered toward them.

'Stop or we will shoot!' commanded one of the officers, dropping to one knee to steady his aim.

Still the creature rushed forward toward the tensing trigger fingers, until Napalm bellowed, '*AAA! Down!*'

The monster stopped in his tracks and looked quizzically at the wine waiter. There was still something human in that questioning regard, some mother's confused son, but it was buried deep beneath the unfathomable fury that had twisted his face into this mask of violence and hatred.

'Don't shoot!' Napalm called to the police. 'He's a fucking war hero!'

The police looked unsure, keeping their guns trained on the creature.

'Tell him to back off!' shouted the cop on his knee.

'*AAA! Kitchen!*' Napalm complied, pointing. '*Basket!*'

He stared sternly, jabbing the air with his finger to emphasize his point, and the creature whimpered softly. Slowly he turned and began to slink heavily back the way he came. The policemen lowered their aim once he was at a safe distance, but when he reached the kitchens he turned round briefly and eyed the man in the suit menacingly, growling, '*AAA . . . AAA . . .*' to let him know he was not forgotten, then barged open the doors and disappeared.

'If you want some friendly advice,' Napalm called over to the bureaucrat, 'I'd be leaving now. He'll be back, and I can't promise I'll be able to stop him a second time.'

'I will not be deterred from my work by threats,' the man announced petulantly, taking a step backward. 'This illegal establishment is to be closed.'

'I ain't threatening you, asshole. But he hasn't eaten yet and the next time he comes out you're probably going to have to shoot him. Now maybe that's covered in paragraph 9C of your fucking regulations and you don't give a shit, but that man is a war hero and maybe you ought to show some respect for the fact that he has done a little more for this country than defend it from illegal catering. All you have to do is back off and let us close up the joint our way. Nobody needs to get hurt. Stick around, though, and I guarantee you things will get ugly.'

There were murmurs of approval from around the

dining tables. Seeing themselves caught between the outlaw unpredictability of the Hell's Angels and the censure of the expensively dressed clientèle who still knew right from wrong, even if they were more usually involved in creating laws than breaking them, the police began to reconsider their situation.

'Maybe you ought to listen to him, Mr Smalkem,' muttered their chief. 'There are a lot of innocent bystanders here who could get hurt if things turn messy. We don't want to provoke a bloodbath over this now, do we?'

'The law is the law, captain,' Smalkem seethed, outraged at finding his position of power undermined on his own side.

'Yeah . . .' the captain sighed, 'but we're talking French fries here, not crack cocaine. The violence has got to stop somewhere.'

Mr Smalkem realized he had little choice in the matter. The raid had failed. All that he could hope to achieve now was to save face.

'Very well,' he announced. 'Under the powers invested in me by paragraph 9P of the state regulations governing the sale of food and liquor, I will take no immediate action. This establishment, under special dispensation of my authority, has until noon tomorrow to cease all further trading activities and all those involved in said activities should surrender themselves to the relevant authority, in this case myself, at that time.'

There was a pregnant silence.

Napalm frowned.

'So you're fucking off?'

'My work is done here,' Smalkem replied. 'Goodnight, ladies and gentlemen.'

He turned on his heel, replacing his mighty sheet of paper in his briefcase, and marched out, followed by the police. As they reached the door, a triumphant roar could be heard from the kitchen.

'AAA! AAA!'

'Wow . . .' Josh exhaled, turning to Napalm. 'That guy's really . . . what was the war?'

'*What?* That's AAA, dude! You've never heard of him?' Napalm gawked, shaking his head in disgust at Josh's ignorance. 'Space Invaders – that kid kicked more crab-alien butt in more towns than anyone alive, man. He was the best. I mean, most people figured AAA was a goddamned *legend*! And the fuckers didn't even give him a damn pension . . .'

He turned away, cursing, and went off toward the kitchens.

'What about the wine?' Josh called.

'Restaurant's shut!' Napalm answered over his shoulder. 'Get it yourself. No charge.'

*

Josh and Jean were among the last to leave, having scraped together some food in the kitchens and found a bottle of wine they cracked open on a window-sill. The Hell's Angels had got totally smashed trying to finish the stock before the night was out, and began throwing up over any clients who were stupid enough to sit still at their tables.

As they walked back out to the car, Josh's mind was still on their unfinished conversation. He desperately wanted to tell Jean everything, but the moment was no longer right and the greater part of him did not want to risk destroying the subtle way in which she had been getting closer to him throughout the evening: touching his arm as she talked, putting her mouth to his ear as if the noise in the restaurant were so loud that he could not hear otherwise . . . Each little trespass into each other's personal space was becoming a little easier, their heads brushing closer and closer to a kiss.

266

'Didn't you want to tell me something?' she asked, placing a hand on his thigh as they settled into their seats.

He turned to meet her eyes, his stomach churning with apprehension and excitement. She was smiling playfully, sure of her power over him at this moment and enjoying the last seconds of secrecy.

Josh leaned closer, his whole leg tingling from her touch. 'I . . .' he answered hoarsely.

'Uh-huh?' she breathed, moving a fraction of an inch closer.

'Jean . . . I have to tell you . . .'

He teetered on the cusp, knowing that the moment could go in two very different directions. Her lips parted ambiguously, expecting either an avowal or a kiss . . . and he chose the latter.

The moment was gone, another moment was here.

*

When the last of the last of the clientèle of Chez les Anges d'Enfer were gone, only the Riders of the Apocalypse were left, happily drinking the night away. They hadn't felt this good in a long time.

Their decision had been taken for them.

'Hey, dudes!' Napalm announced, staggering to his feet and holding a bottle high as he prepared to propose a toast. 'To wheels!'

XXI

The next morning, after much arguing and bluffing his way through layer after layer of Infologix assistants whose major role in life was to prevent people from getting through to John Lockes, Macauley had made it to the final, ultimate barrier: John Lockes' personal assistant, Maria.

'May I enquire with connection to what you wish to speak to Mr Lockes concerning about, Macauley?' she asked politely in the strangely colliding syntax used by employees whose function is to be unhelpful without being rude.

Macauley knew by now precisely how to handle this tactic.

'I'm afraid I am not in a personal position of being enabled to divulge that nature of information to you person-to-person, Maria,' he garbled fluently, having learned to fight fire with fire. 'The matter is confidential, for the ears of Mr Lockes himself only in the strictest personal sense.'

'Uh-huh ... I see ...' she answered, momentarily thrown by his expert use of gibberish. 'Well, I'm sorry to say that Mr Lockes is very occupied in a meeting situation at this moment in time, Macauley, and is not available telephonically. Can I take a message for him?'

He repeated his name, and gave her his contact number, finishing, 'And the message is that I have some urgent news for him about Miles Cardew.'

'That's it? Okay, I'll make sure he gets the message, Macauley.'

'Make sure you get the name right – Miles Cardew.'

'Miles Cardew,' she repeated, the name obviously meaning nothing to her. 'Don't worry, I've got the matter in hand.'

Macauley smiled – that was all he'd wanted. The message could do the rest of the work.

He didn't have long to wait before it produced a reaction.

'Mr Connor?' the unfamiliar voice asked. 'John Lockes here. I got your message about Miles Cardew. How is he?'

'You tell me.'

There was a pause.

'I don't know what you mean. I haven't seen or heard of Miles in years, Mr Connor.'

'Not having heard of him, I can believe. But not having *seen* him? That's tough. Don't you ever look in the mirror?' he challenged.

Again the line went silent. Eventually, a slightly panicked aggressiveness entering his voice, the man replied:

'Look, who are you? Who am I speaking to?'

'Now that's no way to address someone who at least has the decency to give you his real name, Mr Cardew. I'm who I say I am, okay? Now do you want to talk about who you say you are?'

For a third time Macauley found himself waiting impatiently for a response from his caller.

'Not now. Not on the phone. You'd better come and see me at my office . . .'

One of the sweetest sensations Macauley had ever felt in all his years of reporting began to flood over him. It was time to tell Rachel he was coming back out to the coast.

*

According to the popular myth that had grown up around the Campus, it was a pretty cool place to work. Within the security perimeter that hid the complex from view was rumoured to be a world where sharp young IT designers on fuck-you salaries came to work in battered jeans and sneakers, where rock music and free doughnuts were as much a part of the working environment as e-mailed memos and mission statements. The vending machines required no cash, an entire sports complex was at the employees' disposal, and there were relaxation areas where brilliant young things could rest their fizzing neurones and massage their knotted dorsal muscles on 'Magic Finger' recliner chairs as they listened to the sound of lapping waves or birds in the rainforest.

Set in a vast landscaped park, with every office of the futuristic buildings having a view over greenery, the Campus was supposed to be such a wonderful place to be that there was little reason for employees ever to leave, beyond the occasional need to spend some quality time with their children. Court orders permitting.

Macauley waited at the entry gate as the security guard ran his details into the computer, the man's polite and friendly manner being somewhat belied by the gun on his hip and the huge X-ray scanner under which the car was idling.

'That's fine, Mr Connor,' he announced, having received the necessary clearance.

Macauley existed.

The guard handed him a green plastic card on a clip, saying, 'Please keep this pass visible at all times. It will give you access to all green-coded areas. Please take care *not* to attempt accessing any door that is not green as this will create a security alert. Your parking spot is R42. Welcome to Infologix, sir.'

270

Macauley smiled and thanked him politely as the row of steel teeth blocking the road sank down into the tarmac and he drove forward into the gently rolling park.

The myth had it that Lockes had wished to create an Eden-like garden of contemplation for his employees when he ordered the two million tons of earth and ten thousand mature trees comprising the park to be re-organized into their present configuration. It was a pleasant place, all right – there were benches underneath bicentennial oaks, and stone rotunda in which one could picture young men soothing their frazzled brains in the early-evening sun after a hard day's wrestling with soft-ware, perhaps suddenly leaping up to shout, 'Eureka!' and run gaily barefoot down the hill to regain their desk. An office romance at Infologix would be positively bucolic with such Elysian fields for co-workers to stroll through hand in hand, sipping their free cans of soda, were it not for the gardeners who seemed to be at work in every direction, leaning on their hoes as Macauley passed and pausing to talk into the radios that hung from their belts.

It was easy to find spot R42 in the car park underneath the complex because it was the only empty space in the entire row. He found that disturbing. Everything was known here. He did not bother to lock the car, correctly reasoning that his vehicle could hardly be safer were he to place it in a safety-deposit box at the bank, and strolled off toward the elevator entrance that he assumed must be his destination, the door being green.

In his bag Macauley had placed photocopies of the documentation he had proving the link between John Lockes and Miles Cardew, his notepad, minicorder and mobile phone. He had taken the exceptional precaution of leaving the folder containing all his notes and original documents at Rachel's. She hadn't asked him what it was, and he hadn't offered, both of them knowing that talking about his work would only recall unpleasant memories and spoil the fragile happiness they had found together.

A pleasant yawning feeling in his groin reminded him of her now, and he smiled as he remembered how good it had felt to wake up beside her again this morning. It also made him sad to know she was right, and that there was nothing to be gained by their giving it another try. But neither could he feel satisfied with the kind of relationship that she had in mind for them. Macauley, for all that he had learned to the contrary, couldn't help clinging to the romantic notion that love should conquer all obstacles – and so far as he knew what love was, he still loved Rachel. Maybe people couldn't change, as she maintained, but surely it must count for something that he would be prepared to change if he could?

There was a slot beside the elevator, into which he fed his card, and the doors automatically opened to him. There were no buttons inside, the system apparently knowing from his card where he was heading. The doors reopened shortly on a broad entry hall in which two pretty, petite receptionists sat side by side at a great desk. Infologix was obviously an equal-opportunities employer because one was blonde and the other was black-haired.

'Good morning, Mr Connor, and welcome to Infologix,' smiled the blonde. 'Your meeting with Mr Lockes is on schedule. Please follow the pathway indicated by the doors with the flashing card scans.'

'Not the green doors?'

'Yes, sir, they are green doors, but only take the ones with flashing card scans. The system will lead you to the correct destination.' She indicated the first of the doors, already winking at him across the hall. He smiled at her and prepared his card.

As so often with technology, Macauley felt at once impressed and repulsed by the system that led him through the maze of buildings to John Lockes' office. On one level it was brilliantly practical, removing the need for secretaries to waste their time accompanying visitors from reception to wherever they were going. On another he felt like so much glass in a bottling plant, and found it deeply irritating to be greeted by name whenever he passed a secretary, his details obviously flashing up on their computer screens as he approached the door. 'Good-morning, Mr Connor, and welcome to Infologix,' they uniformly smiled at him, making him realize that the horror of technology was not the reduction of individuals to anonymous numbers, as everyone had for decades assumed, but just the reverse: theirs was going to be a world where anonymity was impossible.

The future was the nightmare of total strangers wishing you a happy birthday.

He suspected that if he stopped for a piss the entire building would know about it. The toilets might have the only doors that didn't require a card, but he would no doubt fall behind schedule on his computerized journey. His name would be there on the next secretary's screen with *Suspected Urination* flashing underneath it. It was not a world for claustrophobics. If he took a dump the toilet would probably thank him.

The office belonging to the man who claimed to be John Lockes was little different from any of the others he'd seen on his journey – it was light and spacious, with a view out over the park. There was a meeting room connected to it, but apart from that it was no larger than any of the others. Infologix was, on the surface at least, very egalitarian. All the differences of status and hierarchy were no doubt to be found on those little plastic cards.

Macauley surreptitiously opened his bag before reaching Lockes' office, fumbling nervously inside to turn on the minicorder.

Lockes/Cardew was seated in the meeting room, and

273

rose to greet him as he entered. He was somewhat taller than Macauley had imagined, and without his glasses on he had a gentle, clear-eyed face.

'Mr Connor' – he smiled genuinely – 'thank you for agreeing to come here like this.'

'Mr Cardew,' Macauley replied, shaking his hand.

Cardew laughed. 'Not one to beat about the bush, are you?'

'Do you deny that you're Miles Cardew, John Lockes' ex-roommate?'

'No, Mr Connor. I only laugh because it has been so long since anyone called me that.'

'How long exactly?'

'Is this an interview?'

'I don't know. Is it?'

Cardew nodded thoughtfully and invited him to take a seat at the table.

'Let me make a suggestion, Mr Connor. First of all, I shall answer all the questions you no doubt have in mind to ask me. Then, once you are satisfied that you know the whole truth, I shall make you a proposition. I agree to answer your questions; in return you agree to listen carefully to my proposition – does that seem fair?'

Macauley nodded, sitting down at the table opposite Cardew.

'Fire away, then,' the man smiled.

Macauley produced the two photocopied folders from Welton Academy, pushing them across the table toward Cardew.

'Can you explain this to me?'

Cardew reached into his breast pocket for his glasses, hooking them over his ears as he leaned forward to examine the documents with interest. He was silent for some time, shaking his head softly from side to side.

'Fascinating,' he announced finally, sitting back up. 'Fascinating. Do you know that I've never actually seen these, Mr Connor? My whole life has been dictated by the mistake in these two folders. You've obviously understood that John and I were confused from the moment we arrived at Welton, because people had an ingrained tendency to assume the mathematician would be the skinny kid with glasses whilst the poet would be the handsome young athlete. For me to see it on paper after all this time is . . . I suppose I feel rather like an adopted child meeting his birth mother.'

'But why did you let it continue? Why not correct the misapprehension right at the start?'

Cardew took a deep breath and let it out slowly, pushing the papers back across the table to Macauley.

'I can't give you the full answer to that, Mr Connor. You see, I was a very sickly child and spent much of my time at Welton struggling with one virus or another. I fell ill immediately upon my arrival there – I can't recall what it was that I had exactly, but I was in the infirmary with a fever for my first week at the academy and so was hardly a willing participant in the charade as it first developed. John was the one who let it take hold, for reasons that I don't to this day fully comprehend, even if I subsequently agreed to play along. I think it amused him, frankly – he was a mischievous boy, you know. *Extremely* intelligent, of course, and we were all to some extent pawns in whatever game he was playing in his head. He came to visit me once my fever had broken and explained the situation. I suppose I could have put my foot down at that point and refused to continue the farce, but . . . well, I don't know what you were like as a boy, Mr Connor, but all I can say is that at that age there are some who lead and others who follow. John was a natural leader – he was everything that I wished to be, everything that I admired, right from the moment I met him, and in my feebleness, both medically and in terms of character, it seemed to me to be somehow wonderful that this heroic character wanted me to *be* him, to take his name and the credit for his accomplishments. It's pathetic, I suppose, but for all my life until then I had been the runt and the kind of child that boys like John at best ignored, if not bullied. Yet *he* wanted me to be his partner in something. He promised to be my best friend. So I agreed. Does that make sense?'

Macauley sensed that this was the truth he was hearing. It fitted with the facts and he could easily imagine the man sitting in front of him as that unpopular child who would agree to anything a boy like John Lockes could ask of him for the sake of friendship. But it still didn't explain how the situation could have carried on so long.

'Surely you must have expected to be found out eventually, though? Your parents would know that the child on those report sheets couldn't be you – weren't you worried?'

'My parents?' Cardew repeated with a slim smile. 'I had no parents, Mr Connor. They died in a car crash when I was only five. I was raised by my maternal grandmother, but she could no longer cope with a child by the time I was thirteen as she was sick with tuberculosis. That is why I had to go to Welton – my intellectual gifts, while I had some talent for poetry, hardly qualified me to be described as a "gifted child". Welton took me even so, because there were always a few places for unremarkable children who could afford the fees. I don't know if my grandmother ever paid great attention to those reports, and if she had she would have found nothing peculiar about my supposed sporting achievements, because she always thought the world of me and would have believed almost anything possible. Grandmothers are like that. Anyway, Welton was an academic school – she probably assumed that even a sickly child such as myself could achieve sporting glory in that environment!

'As for John's parents . . . well, I never met them myself. He used to be brought to the school at the start of each term by a preacher of some sort – an absolutely terrifying man to look at, all sparkling eyes and huge hands. I never spoke to him, or even spoke much about him to John, but I always suspected he would not have approved of John's spending so much time on the football field had he known about it. John loved sports more than anything, of course, and so I think it was the fact that he could indulge himself fully in them under my name that made the arrangement so perfect for him. But to answer your question, we were worried about the whole confusion being discovered at first, but the longer it went on the more impossible it became to do anything about it, and after a year or two had gone by without anybody finding out we began to feel at ease with it. They had opportunities to find out, but somehow never did. Slowly it became clear to us that once people think they know a thing, they will go to almost any extreme of illogicality to avoid realizing they are mistaken. So, in the end, it's taken twenty years for someone to discover the truth, Mr Connor. Congratulations!'

Macauley was disappointed. He had expected Cardew to be devastated by the discovery of his secret, and yet the man seemed to be quite relaxed about the situation. He did not appear to appreciate that the news that the richest man in the world was an impostor was going to create an absolute furore.

'Why carry it on after school? Why didn't you revert back to your true identities at college?'

'Two reasons,' Cardew replied calmly: 'firstly, there were some other ex-Welton students there with us at college, so there was no opportunity for a clean break to be made, and secondly . . . neither of us particularly wanted our identity back.'

'Why not?'

'Freedom. If you've never changed your identity it is probably very hard to understand, but there is an incredible liberation involved in losing yourself in another persona. Have you never found it odd to think that you are Macauley Connor, for instance? You *are* this person, this name that was chosen for you at birth – Macauley Connor. You look in the mirror and you see Macauley Connor. You exist on God knows how many databases as Macauley Connor. Every person who has ever known you has known you as that – Macauley Connor. And yet is that *you*? Doesn't it ever strike you as being like a form of prison? Doesn't it bother you that you are forever being asked to supply your name so that people can fill in their forms?'

'Not particularly,' he lied.

Cardew smiled mischievously and swivelled his chair around to reach for five huge box folders on top of the filing cabinet behind him, picking them up one by one and dumping them on to the table with loud thuds.

'Do you know what this is? This is Macauley Connor – this is your life from birth to the present day: your medical records, your credit-card statements with all the purchases you have made, your tax history, your professional career with every article you have ever written, your marriage and divorce, your every address and phone bill and electricity bill, even a record of which magazines you have subscribed to . . . it's all here. This information is available if one knows how to get it by just entering the name "Macauley Connor".'

Macauley looked at the boxes of paperwork with a certain morbid fascination. He was at once amazed that he alone could generate such a quantity of paperwork, and horrified that his entire life could be contained in those boxes. He pulled one over to him, opening it up and flicking at random through the contents. It was all there, just like Cardew said: bills, purchases, parking tickets – his long, excruciatingly dull biography.

'This isn't *me*, though,' he announced finally, closing the box. 'That's not who I am.'

'My point exactly, Mr Connor,' Cardew replied softly. 'That's what makes it so irritating. It is everything about you, and yet it is not you at all. But looking at it all now, honestly . . . wouldn't it give you pleasure to know they had got the damned name wrong?'

Macauley paused to think it over. 'Maybe. Perhaps. But you are simply trapped in another persona – I don't see that's any better.'

'Isn't it?' Cardew smiled. 'Oh, it's not so bad being trapped in the persona of the richest man in the world, you know, Mr Connor! I don't know what I would have done with myself had I lived my own life, but I doubt very much that it would have been as much fun as being John Lockes! I head this company, I take decisions and chair meetings – my role is not illusory. I work hard and love every minute of it, and my reward is to live with all the trappings of extreme wealth – that seems infinitely preferable to whatever mediocre existence fate would have had in store for me otherwise.'

'But surely . . .' Macauley frowned, trying to figure out exactly how this worked, 'you are *not* the genius. Surely the real John Lockes is behind Infologix?'

'Certainly, to some extent. There are areas of the work – technical matters, conceptual matters – of which I have only a limited understanding. I can talk about them knowledgeably enough, but I could never take an active part in the creative work. John does that, but it is only a tiny part of the work of being John Lockes. The rest can be done by a competent person such as myself, just so long – and this is the ridiculous aspect of it all – so long as people think I am John Lockes! Being John Lockes is one part real genius to nine parts perception. He doesn't need to run Infologix so long as someone who is *perceived* to be him runs it! John never wanted this life for himself. I did. He was never in any doubt of how successful Infologix was going to be, but the idea of devoting all his energies to that success . . . well, it bored him, frankly. He had other plans.'

'Such as?'

Cardew raised one eyebrow, his forehead furrowing as if admonishing a naughty child. 'Now, now, Mr Connor – don't be greedy. I promised to tell you about myself, but we never said anything about discussing the private life of John Lockes.'

'But obviously you can't expect me to leave it there. I only know half the truth.'

Cardew's fingers began lightly strumming upon the table. He turned away to look out over the park, his eyes focusing on a gardener trimming the grass at the edge of one of the pathways.

'Actually, Mr Connor . . .' he sighed, 'I very much hope you will leave it there. You've done brilliantly. You can be pleased with yourself. But now I want you to call your investigations to a halt, for everyone's good.'

Macauley caught the unmistakable implication in those last words, and continued calmly, 'Including my own, I take it.'

Cardew's gaze turned back from the distant gardener to meet Macauley's.

'Everyone's. Obviously you are included.'

'May I ask why I would do that?'

'Certainly,' he smiled. 'Because you would be choosing to do so. I remind you that you have not yet listened to my proposition.'

'I assumed you would make it when you were ready.'

Cardew nodded and rolled his chair back from the table, his hand feeling underneath the seat for the lever that unblocked the back and brought him to a reclining position. He let out a deep breath of relaxation and lifted his feet on to the table, lacing his fingers behind his head. He spoke in a soft, somewhat sad voice, his eyes on the ceiling.

'They call this the Information Age, don't they? Stone Age ... Bronze Age ... Iron Age ... then you get the Classical Era, I suppose ... then the Dark Ages ... the Middle Ages ... the Renaissance Era ... the Industrial Era ... and now the Information Age. Pushing forward ever faster, always evolving. There was a time when it was possible for a man to know everything there was to know, but now there is so much knowledge that our poor, overloaded brains are forced to dump information on a daily basis, like taking the garbage out. For a while the news is filled with some horrific war, and everyone clamours for something to be done to end the atrocities, and then a few months later most of us can't remember even the name of the country where it happened. Our thinkers are forced to restrict themselves to ever more precise, ever more isolated areas of knowledge, to specialize like insects in the rainforest, and the ordinary man is left drifting in a sea of disconnected information, clinging for dear life to a log that bears his name. With each generation it takes longer for our children to reach maturity because there is so much more to learn, and our old die more in confusion than wisdom ... Perhaps that is why we call this an Age rather than an Era – Eras seem to be better neighbourhoods than Ages, wouldn't you say?'

'Maybe we'll get upgraded into an Era by future generations.'

'One must hope so. One must hope so. But personally I suspect that this time of ours will be seen something like we ourselves see the Old West – a hard, lawless period that is thrilling to imagine but hardly desirable to return to in reality. We build cars that can drive far, far faster than the law permits and all pile on to these thin strips of tarmac to battle our way past each other from one place to the next. We all have our drugs, even if our drug is abstention. We all gamble, we all drown ourselves in music and sensory delights, and those who consider themselves exempt from all of this are usually the most hopeless junkies of all, hooked on the search for a higher meaning. People still farm, and mine, and manufacture, but the real business is information. When to buy and when to sell. What to keep and what to throw away. Whom to know and whom to forget. Fortunes are made overnight, and lost in the morning. Individuals and companies and governments vie, cheat and spy for information. People will even kill for information. And next week it will be forgotten. And the faster things and people are forgotten, the more desperately we all try to do something that will make others remember us, if only for a brief time. If only for today. If only for fifteen minutes . . .'

He tilted his head in his cupped hands to look at Macauley. 'It's not sane, is it, Mr Connor? Where are we going?'

Macauley did not reply, assuming the question to be rhetorical.

'I know what you must be thinking.' Cardew smiled. 'You're thinking this is a bit rich coming from me of all people, the man who plays the part of John Lockes.'

'The thought had crossed my mind.'

'And you're right – it is pure hypocrisy. But the best generals don't love war, do they? I can be nostalgic for the quiet, steady world of my youth yet still fight tooth and nail to win the battle to shape the world of the future – there is no contradiction there, Mr Connor. And you may hate the power of Infologix and all that you believe we represent, but you must know that the war is not of our making – we are simply the winners. Surely it is better that it be won by someone on your own side?'

'Are there sides any more?' Macauley asked sarcastically. 'I thought we had ditched that kind of thinking long ago.'

'That's just media bullshit! Do you seriously think that the man who is born and raised in Atlantis, who rises to the head of a widget corporation and then switches all the manufacturing capacity to some foreign country with cheap labour, is *betraying his country*? Thanks to him Atlantis controls widgets around the world! Thanks to him the people of that foreign country earn money, and the first thing they want to do with it is buy a piece of the Atlantian Dream. They want the jeans and the cap, the movie and the album, the cola and burger – he is exporting Atlantis, not just importing widgets! A hundred years ago that same man would have been called a colonial entrepreneur and a patriot. Times have changed, however, and now he has the sensitivity not to plant a damned flag and demand everyone salute it. But he can't say that out loud, of course, and so the media come to their own dumb conclusions and make everyone think he's selling his own country short.'

'And Infologix is the same.'

'Damn right it is. Don't you realize what we've achieved? We have harnessed the biggest damn revolution the world has ever seen and brought it home! Ninety per cent of the world's computers use Infologix software! And you, Macauley Connor, are sitting in the head office of Infologix, talking in your own language to your own people! It could very easily have been otherwise, you know.'

'I don't see what any of this has to do with why I should discontinue my research into John Lockes.'

'Because information is power . . .' Cardew repeated slowly, emphatically, 'but *this* information is power to the wrong people!'

'From your point of view.'

283

'From yours too, if you had any sense! Look – what are you planning to do with this information? Finish writing your book, publish it and make a little money, right?'

'A lot of money, actually.'

'From your point of view. In reality you will be *giving* that information away – a certain number of people will actually read the book, but the entire world will learn the secret you have discovered for nothing! *Nothing!* Are you crazy? Intelligent people don't give treasure away, Mr Connor! Your information is worth more than the sales of any book can generate!'

To his consternation, Macauley realized that he agreed. As soon as Cardew had said it, he had begun to see his situation in a new light – he was so accustomed to being a jobbing writer, accepting a flat fee for whatever work he did, that it had never occurred to him to question the true value of his discovery. In his mind, he had accepted Schonk's advance for the manuscript and that was that.

But Cardew was right – he was giving it away at that price.

A kind of earthquake was taking place in his head as he thought it through: he knew that John Lockes was not John Lockes! Publishing that bare fact in a book was like finding the Holy Grail and then selling it as an antique cup.

'You know I'm right, don't you?' Cardew persisted, observing the stunned expression on his face. 'You're not an idiot.'

The exhilaration of Macauley's initial realization of what he held in his hands was already giving way to a sense of panic: what *should* he do with the knowledge?

Cardew could read the confusion playing over his face like a book.

'Sell it for what it is *worth*!' he prompted.

'How . . . how much is that?' Macauley stammered, all

pretence of being in control of himself collapsing.

Cardew smiled and reached into the breast pocket of his shirt. He drew out a folded cheque and held it up between them, opening it slowly with one hand to reveal the amount for which it was already made out in Macauley's name.

'I think that's reasonable, don't you, Mr Connor?' he asked softly. 'But feel free to ask for more if you disagree.'

Macauley stared in disbelief at the paper in front of his eyes.

It was not reasonable at all. It was insane.

'You would pay that just to stop me publishing?'

'No. I would pay that for the *information*.'

'What do you mean? I can't just hand it over, can I? It's in my head.'

Cardew frowned.

'That's where we have a small problem – it has to come out of your head, Mr Connor. Have you ever heard of Infologix Mesmer?'

Macauley Connor felt like a new man as he left the Campus. He was happy, he was at ease with the world, he was in love, and he had a fat cheque in his wallet.

He smiled and waved at a gardener as he drove through the beautiful gardens of Infologix, needing to share his happiness with somebody. Anybody. In fact, he ideally wanted to share it with everyone, because they were all wonderful human beings deep down inside and life was a miracle. You never knew what it held in store for you – only hours ago he had been an ordinary journalist, struggling to make ends meet, and then fate had intervened in the form of John Lockes.

What a guy.

It occurred to him that he should phone Rachel. They had to celebrate tonight. Then, in the morning, they had to get married and go on a second honeymoon. Didn't matter where, so long as they could have food delivered to their room – it wasn't too late for them to have kids, but they had no time to waste on sightseeing.

He took one hand off the wheel and reached for his phone. He felt around in the empty bag for the portable, trying to remember what her number was as he pulled it out. Then it occurred to him that hers had been the last number he had called so he just pressed Redial.

She wasn't going to believe the news he had to share. Even he had trouble believing, and he knew it was true.

He frowned as the phone failed to ring, and took it away from his ear to check he'd pressed the right button. The screen was dead. The battery was flat. Technology! It was a wonderful thing, but the old ways were still the most reliable. Hell, she'd be home soon anyway so he'd just drive straight to her apartment and tell her in person. It was better that way.

*

Rachel watched him with a strange smile on her face as he carefully hung his coat up in the cupboard, placing his bag neatly below it, and closed the door.

'You are not going to believe what happened!' he said for the third time, his face flushed with excitement as he removed his tie, folding it precisely in half and then half again until it was short enough to roll up and place in his jacket pocket.

'Try me,' she repeated.

'Okay, okay . . . no, hang on, I've just remembered I was meaning to do something. Stay right there.'

He went across to her desk, picking up the folder that was sitting there, and then strode into the kitchen, where he tidied it away in the garbage without even pausing to look at its contents.

'So . . .' he began, hovering beside her on the sofa. 'The most incredible thing in my life happened to me today, Rachel. You would never guess in a million years.'

'Don't tell me you were going to interview John Lockes at his office and saved his life by hitting him on the back when you found him in the last stages of choking to death on a sandwich? Don't tell me that he was so grateful that he insisted on writing an obscenely large cheque out to you on the spot, and you want us to get married and have children and live happily ever after?'

'Yes! *Yes!*' Macauley laughed, taking her hands in his. 'That's *exactly* what happened to me today! Isn't it amazing? So will you? Marry me, I mean.'

Rachel kissed him softly on the lips. 'Sit down, Mac. We have to talk.'

Macauley was down like a dog before her sentence was even finished. He did not lounge in the armchair, but perched neatly on the edge. Practically panting.

'Mac, you went to interview John Lockes, didn't you? Can you remember why?'

'Well . . .' Macauley frowned, 'because he's *John Lockes*! What other reason do you need?'

'But he doesn't give interviews, does he? So how come he granted you one?'

Macauley looked nonplussed.

'I'm writing a biography of him. Of course he wanted to talk to me. To put the record straight. He wasn't at all how I imagined him, you know. He's a nice guy.'

'Mac, this interview . . . did you record it?'

'Of course,' he announced breezily, reaching into his bag for the tape recorder.

'Let's hear it, shall we?'

Two minutes later, Macauley was still winding back and forth throughout the tape, refusing to accept that there was nothing on it.

'It doesn't matter,' he declared finally. 'I remember the

whole conversation perfectly. Odd, though . . . I have a clear memory of pressing the Record button before I went into the room.'

'Have you checked your phone since you left Infologix?'

'Yeah . . . I wanted to call you, but the damn battery's flat.'

'Right. So . . . ?' she invited him, raising her eyebrows.

'So . . . so I couldn't phone!' He laughed. 'Will you marry me, Rachel? I'll never leave my pubic hair in the bath again, I promise.'

'I know you won't, Mac, and . . . yes, I will,' Rachel promised, 'if that's what you still want, I'll marry you . . . but only if you do one thing for me.'

'Anything!'

She produced a pendant on a silver chain from her jeans pocket and held it up in front of him, letting it swing gently from side to side.

'I want you to concentrate on this pendant, Mac, and relax . . .'

It wasn't easy. Rachel occasionally used hypnosis with her patients, but she had never tried anything like this before. She knew the truth of what had happened to Macauley this afternoon thanks to the fact that she had arrived home to find her answer machine was completely saturated by the muffled conversation between him and Miles Cardew, relayed to her apartment from Macauley's bag. He had pressed the Call button on the mobile instead of the Record button on the minicorder just before entering Cardew's office.

Rachel had listened to the exchange in mounting amazement as the two men discussed the terms of their deal:

'You want to fuck with my *brain*?' Macauley had squawked at the first mention of Infologix Mesmer. 'Can't you just trust me to keep a secret?'

'Perhaps I could, perhaps not. I have no way of being sure, and if I pay you to keep a secret then we are not conducting a business exchange, are we? You would effectively be blackmailing me. Surely we both want this to be legal and fair?'

There was a pause on her answer machine as Macauley pondered his situation.

'But if I undergo hypnosis, what guarantee do I have that you will keep *your* end of the deal? You could simply wipe all memory of the money you offered me from my mind and I would never be any the wiser.'

'True, I could. The only guarantee I can give you is that for this to work on a permanent basis it is not sufficient to simply *suppress* the information in your brain – the danger would always exist that at some point in the future the memory would be triggered by an unforeseeable stimulus. To guard against that, we have to *cover* the true memory with a false one so wonderful that your brain will resist any attempt to dislodge it. For instance, if you have a memory of having saved my life and being rewarded with the cash sum in question, that is a wonderful memory. It is a dream come true. Your conscious and subconscious mind will protect that memory as precious, and in so doing keep the true memory suppressed. That is why it is in my own interest to keep my word on this.'

There was another pause as Macauley thought this over.

'Mr Connor,' Cardew insisted, 'I swear that nothing – *nothing* – will be taken out of that cheque. I am a man of my word, you know.'

'And if I refuse?'

Cardew could be heard sighing in the background.

'That would be unfortunate. Obviously I would be obliged to prevent the information from entering the public domain by other means.'

'What – are you going to have me killed?'

'Mr Connor!' Cardew laughed. 'You're not dealing with the Mob! I'm sure such things are quite easy to organize for the right price, but it's not something I would ever do – I have to sleep at night, you know!'

'So what *are* you talking about then?'

'There are many ways to destroy a man without killing him, Mr Connor. You've already seen how easy it was for me to get information on you that you assumed was private – that information can be changed in such a way as to make life very difficult for you and annihilate you as a credible source when you attempt to publish your information. It is not pleasant, but *that* I am prepared to do. I am offering you a very generous alternative partly so that my conscience will not be troubled by using such other means.'

'But what if I *accept* the deal and the hypnosis doesn't work – what if I remember the information at some future point anyway?'

'You won't.'

'But just supposing I did?'

'Then . . . I would be the loser, I suppose. The money would already be yours. What do you say?'

Rachel had listened with her ear pressed to the speaker on the answer-phone, her hands gripping the edge of the table with tension.

'I agree on two conditions,' Macauley had eventually decided. 'Firstly, for my own satisfaction, I want to know where the real John Lockes is before I'm hypnotized . . .'

'I can understand that. Agreed. And the second?'

'The second is personal – if you're going to fuck with my brain you may as well do some good while you're at it, so I want you to change certain personal habits my ex-wife hates in me.'

'Your *ex*-wife? Why does it matter what your ex-wife . . . Oh I see! You want her back, is that it?'

290

'Exactly. But she won't take me back with all my faults, so the faults need to go. Is it possible to hypnotize someone in that way?'

'It would be a pleasure to help in any way I can! How romantic! What are these faults?'

'I'm a slob.'

Cardew nodded, taking a note of what he had to change.

'And I'm not dependable. I promise to do things and then forget.'

'Uh-huh . . .'

'I don't listen to her suggestions. I take criticism badly. I drink too much. All the normal stuff.'

'Okay . . .' Cardew nodded, noting it down like a restaurant order. 'Is that all?'

'What about John Lockes? Who and where is he really?'

'Ah, John . . .' Cardew sighed. 'John amuses himself in many ways. He works here occasionally, as I said, pretending to be a freelance adviser to whom I turn on a regular basis. Otherwise, he has a variety of enthusiasms and indulges them under a variety of names – I don't believe that even I know them all. He likes to experience life from different points of view, you see. It's not a question to which there is any simple answer.'

'Just give me one, then. Where is he right now, for instance?'

Cardew must have paused for a long time, because that was where the recording had stopped.

One moment Macauley was looking at her with a glazed expression, and then, with a click of her fingers, thought entered his eyes.

They stared at one another, Rachel frowning apprehensively while she waited for some sign that her deprogramming of his brain had worked.

'Well?' she asked.

'I love you,' he answered. 'Well what?'

'Where is the real John Lockes?'

Macauley went to speak, but paused as he sorted through the rubble of true and implanted information in his brain.

'Josh Cloken!' he breathed finally. 'He's called Josh Cloken. It's an anagram. Cute. He's going up on the shuttle to launch Rectag in a few days. I guess billionaires have to go that much further to get their kicks.'

'Hi there.' Rachel smiled. 'Still want to get married?'

Macauley narrowed his gaze, as if suspecting a joke. 'Do you?'

'Hey, what sensible girl could resist a man who was willing to be brainwashed for her?'

'Plus rich!' he added with surprise as he remembered the cheque. 'In fact, *obscenely* rich. I may always be a slob, Rachel, but we can afford staff – take a look at this!'

He got his wallet from his pocket and fished out the cheque, admiring it briefly before handing it over to her.

'Not bad,' she admitted. 'Not what I had been expecting, but not bad.'

'*Not bad!*' Macauley exclaimed. 'Just how much do you . . .?'

He stopped and took the cheque back, looking at it again.

'The son of a bitch!'

'So he lied after all.'

'No . . . he didn't lie. He was just creative with the truth. There's nothing missing from this cheque.'

'Nothing?'

'In a manner of speaking. It had more zeroes before.'

He shook his head. 'Well . . . we can still afford a woman who does on a weekly basis, if you'll have me back.'

Rachel burst into laughter, slipping herself on to his lap and throwing her arms around his neck.

'I'll have you back, all right, Mac. But do me a favour – finish one thing before starting another. I can wait.'

'What do you mean?'

'Are you seriously telling me that you love me so much that you don't need the satisfaction of facing the real John Lockes? You're a romantic, Macauley Connor, but I know you better than that . . .'

XXII

President John Monroe, seated behind the big, president-size desk, observed Michael Summerday with barely concealed amusement. The two men had not been friends at the start of their association, but over the intervening years a bond had grown between them. Mutual dislike. Summerday found it almost impossible to disguise the fact that he considered Monroe to be an amoral, untrustworthy opportunist who was totally unworthy of holding the highest office in the land, even if he was very good at it. Monroe, for his part, thought his Vice-President was a prig, and made no attempt to hide it.

In the country's best interests, therefore, communication between them had been kept to a strict minimum. As the situation commanded, the public were offered Monroe and Summerday looking happy, Monroe and Summerday looking statesman-like, Monroe and Summerday looking grimly determined to balance the budget, but never Monroe and Summerday looking at each other. Behind the scenes of the presidential circus, they lived their lives completely apart in the big house from which the country was governed, a platoon of messengers keeping information flowing from one wing to the other. It is a tribute to the efficiency of these messengers that the entire Oil War had been planned, declared, fought and won before the two happened to cross each other in the corridor, Monroe saying, 'That went rather well, don't you think?' as he breezed past.

So if now, when his own presidential campaign was just ten days from its climax, Summerday had asked for a private meeting with his superior, there could be little doubt that he needed Monroe's help with something badly. Desperately. Hat-chewingly.

It was not a moment the President had any intention of spoiling by opening his mouth first.

'I need . . . John . . . I need your advice,' Summerday mumbled finally, his lips physically resisting the words.

Monroe was burning up with the urge to rub his nose in it by telling him that this was the whole problem with being a prig – in the end you always need help from precisely those you scorned. But Summerday would have taken it badly. Not because he would disagree, but because prigs can't help it. The only thing they didn't ever seem to take badly was other people's tragedies.

'I'm always ready to help, Michael, in any way I can,' he answered warmly. 'What's on your mind?'

Summerday had rarely hated him more, but had no choice other than to smile gratefully and explain the situation he was in. Monroe whistled when he heard the bottom line.

'Drives a hard bargain, dear Susan, doesn't she? My, my . . . she'd be good, you know, Michael. The public love her. She's got that common touch you've always lacked. But what the hell are you planning to do about Bob Redwood?'

'That's . . . what I came to see you about, John. I need to get him out of the way.'

Monroe raised an eyebrow. 'And what am I supposed to be able to do about it?'

Summerday grimaced still more uncomfortably, whispering, 'I thought you might tell me how to . . . *resolve* this kind of situation. Permanently.'

295

Monroe looked briefly troubled, frowning as he weighed Summerday's words in his mind.

'*Damn!*' he suddenly exploded, the laughter bursting forth as he understood. 'You want to assassinate the poor sap, don't you?'

It had certainly not been an easy decision.

Unlike Bob Redwood, Summerday secretly didn't believe in capital punishment. And even Redwood had not yet proposed executing the dangerously stupid. But then he wouldn't.

Nor had killing her rival ever been a part of Susan's demands, but it was hard to see any other solution. There was no way of ditching him at this stage without Summerday doing irreparable damage to his own campaign, and yet the damage Susan could – and apparently would – wreak if her demands were not met did not bear thinking about.

A tragic, senseless killing, on the other hand, could actually help his image. Indeed, it fitted in very well with the programme of drama and sensation that Chandra Dissenyake had been implementing over the last two weeks – Penny's disease, his own car crash, and Susan's revelation of her long but ultimately successful battle against alcoholism . . . all the show lacked was sudden death. Redwood's demise might almost have been in the original script.

It was an awful decision to take – in a sense it was murder, after all – but Summerday steadied his resolve with the thought that as President it might be his responsibility to send tens of thousands of young men off to war, or bomb hell out of some dictator's military-industrial-kindergarten complex, or even to drop the big one. In that light, he could see this as a test of his moral fibre.

* * *

Summerday's eyes bulged with horror at having the words spoken out loud – he couldn't believe that Monroe of all people would be so unsubtle about a matter such as this – but the President was howling like a hyena and slapping the table as his body convulsed with amusement. Each time it seemed as though his laughter might have peaked, Monroe caught Summerday's eye and was transported to a new level of hilarity by the sight of his Vice-President sitting – priggishly – as he waited for advice on how to assassinate his colleague.

'John, please . . . I don't see what's so funny about this,' Summerday muttered tensely.

Monroe's mouth worked soundlessly as he tried to reply, his body beyond his own control, jerking back and forth in his chair.

'*You don't, huh?*' he finally breathed hoarsely, the words apparently triggering off a fresh wave of hysterics. He gripped the arms of his chair as he struggled to regain some measure of decorum, finally whispering, 'You're something, Mike! That's priceless!'

'Listen . . . I know we're not close, but I at least thought we could talk about this in a mature fashion.'

'In a mature fashion? About how to knock off your running-mate?' Monroe began to bounce in his chair, as if a fresh explosion of hysterics was ricocheting around his body in search of an exit. He pinched his nose and waited for the feeling to subside, but it was no good – his mouth burst open as the laughter blew forth and he collapsed helplessly over his table.

Summerday's eyes narrowed in disgust. 'I knew you were cold-hearted, but apparently I misjudged you, John – I at least thought you retained enough of a sense of decency not to find killing outright funny.'

'Stop! Stop! Please!' Monroe begged from the table, the pain in his sides starting to become too much to bear. 'I can't take it any more – you come to me for murder tips and *still* manage to be a prig!'

'Well, I'm sorry about that, John, but maybe I just don't feel very good about this, you know.'

'I should hope not,' the President wheezed, pulling his face into an exaggerated impression of Summerday's disdainful expression. 'It's very badly brought up of you, Michael.'

Summerday sighed as Monroe's throat rattled with the agony of the spasms gripping his torso yet another time. To think this man led the most powerful country in the world.

Once Monroe had finally mastered his amusement, almost five minutes later, the two at last began to discuss Summerday's plan in practical detail.

'Mike . . . I appreciate you're in a difficult situation here, but I still don't really see what I personally can do to help.'

'Come on, John! Not you personally, but the people who you control.'

Monroe shook his head and spread his hands. 'Who?'

'Special ops. The fixers. The men in black . . . Tell me what you like, John, but don't tell me they don't exist.'

'Michael . . . they don't exist. I am telling you that.'

Summerday looked dubiously at him.

'Hey, listen,' Monroe continued, 'I was as surprised as you. Before I became President, I assumed we had all manner of secret divisions and dirty-tricks departments to handle this shit. Turns out not to be so.' He put his hands on his desk, quietly confiding, 'You know how each out-going president leaves a note for his successor on this desk, Mike? It's common knowledge, although the contents of the notes are never revealed, right? Well, do you want to know what the note said when I took over from Burgess?'

Summerday leaned forward, suddenly distracted from his problems by the tantalizing offer of being let in on a secret.

'It said – and this is what I would have written to you when your turn came, but now I guess I'll just tell you which of the interns give the best head – it *said* that there is no secret. I couldn't believe my eyes when I read it, but it's true and it is the single most useful piece of information the guy could have passed on to me. The secret is that there is no secret.'

'Do you seriously expect me to believe that the United States of Atlantis has *never* used trained assassins to do its dirty work? Bullshit!'

Monroe raised a finger, chiding, 'Ah-ah-ah, Mike! I didn't say "*never*". Apparently they did try it once or twice in the past. It didn't work out. The problem with trying to run an operation like that is that everyone who is involved has to be able to trust each other, but the bottom line is that you are relying on psychopaths. They are unreliable, to say the least. A conspiracy requires cool, level-headed individuals with a clear understanding of the issues involved, but these are not going to be the people who enjoy hanging out on rooftops with rifles, are they? Assassins are by nature *very* strange people, Mike – they are not what you'd call your dynamic, motivated individual who enjoys working as part of a team. Things tend to go seriously awry when you start involving them in anything. To my knowledge, no such operation has existed since the assassination of President Connolly.'

Summerday raised an eyebrow. 'So it *was* a conspiracy! Who was behind it – the Vice-President? The Feds?'

'Uh-uh!' Monroe grinned. 'The fact that those guys ended up being suspected of involvement just shows how wrong these things tend to go. It wasn't the V-P, it wasn't the Mob or the Feds, or *anyone* who has ever been fingered for it. It was Connolly.'

'*Connolly conspired to have himself assassinated?*'

'Well, no! That's the point, Mike! That's what I'm trying to explain to you! It's *why* we don't use these people any more! Nobody knows exactly what Connolly was trying to achieve – he may have been trying to stage a dramatic *attempted* assassination, or maybe they were supposed to shoot his wife, but the psychos messed up! The V-P, who was totally innocent of any involvement, just did his best to keep a lid on the disaster afterwards and the poor sap ended up being suspected of having masterminded the whole thing! Broke his heart, apparently. That's why he didn't run for a second term. Anyway, ever since Connolly got himself killed no one has wanted anything to do with special ops. The country's clean, Mike, believe me.'

'So how is it that the entire country still believes they exist?'

Monroe threw his hands up in the air and shrugged.

'Because everyone *wants* to believe it! Because nobody feels in control of their lives. Because they look at the politics of this country and see that the government is a mess, and they need to believe that someone somewhere is in control! So they start to suspect that there is a conspiracy behind everything, that the official organs of governments are just window dressing for the real power centres whose existence are never acknowledged. It's basic pyschology – if they believe everything they don't understand about their lives is the product of a massive conspiracy then their lives make sense! The struggle to see through the conspiracy and discover the truth actually gives their lives purpose and meaning – it's almost as good as religion!'

Summerday looked perplexed, unconvinced by this version of reality. 'But if none of it is true then why not *say* so? Why not prove it's all in people's minds?'

'How can you? How can you fight it? You *can't*

produce evidence proving the non-existence of something – it's a contradiction in terms! How can you disprove the existence of a *secret*, Mike? There is no point whatsoever in our denying conspiracies exist because that is *exactly* what everyone would expect us to do! So we'd only compound their suspicions, wouldn't we?'

Monroe smiled as he saw the very phenomenon he was describing played out on Summerday's face – doubt in what he believed battling with the belief that he was supposed to doubt it.

'Look, Mike . . .' sighed Monroe, 'think about it this way: so long as there's no *harm* in people thinking their way of life is being safeguarded by highly trained super-agents, why bother trying to disillusion them? If they *want* to believe that everything is part of some huge, incredibly complicated conspiracy, then where's the harm in letting them? It's better than them believing the truth!'

'Why,' Summerday asked softly, his eyes narrowing, 'what is the truth?'

'The truth? God, Mike! That it's all part of a huge, incredibly complicated series of *fuck-ups*, of course! Governing a country like Atlantis is an impossible task, and almost any attempt to control the way things happen is pretty well doomed to fail from the start. People just aren't clever enough! But between the public thinking their lives are in the hands of all-powerful, Machiavellian conspirators and them thinking we are actually just a bunch of incompetent assholes, which would *you* rather they believed?'

Summerday was starting to see the sense in this. Logically, if it was within people's capabilities to organize a smooth-running, effective conspiracy then it should also be within their capabilities to organize a smooth-running, effective government. Yet he knew the latter was not the case.

301

'So . . .' he frowned, 'in effect, there is a conspiracy to make people believe there is a conspiracy?'

'Exactly! You get the same results with none of the dangers – *real* conspiracies always fuck up like everything else, so it's much better if they only exist in people's imaginations. With a fake conspiracy there are still the same real fuck-ups, but at least some of your voters will suspect they are fake fuck-ups to cover up a genuine conspiracy! You can't lose – the more chaotic things seem, the more people are convinced that they're somehow missing the point and it's all a diversion! The irony is that people genuinely are free but still choose to live in a virtual dictatorship. So if you want a good reason why we don't bother having special ops, or the fixers, or whatever you want to call them, then the answer is really very simple: who *needs* assassins with a system like the one we have?'

Summerday tapped his forehead softly with the palms of his hands. He may never have liked John Monroe, but despite his lack of decency and morals he could be trusted in some things. This felt like it might be one of them. He groaned, because none of this helped him with the Susan situation.

'Right now . . . I do,' he sighed disconsolately.

Monroe looked at him sympathetically.

'I have to agree you would be doing us all a favour by getting him out of the way. It's one thing choosing a vice-president who's not going to upstage you, but there are limits, Michael! At least I figured you would be a safe caretaker if my plane crashed.'

'Thanks. I think. I know, I know . . . why did I choose him? I suppose I figured he would make me look more statesman-like. Idiot. But he's got to go – Susan's angry enough to bring me down with a snap of her fingers, and she'd be a better choice than Redwood anyway.'

'Try the Mob, chum. They do contract killings,

although I doubt you're their favourite person right now.'

'The Mob!' Summerday scoffed. 'You must be joking.' He paused, looking warily at the man he had worked alongside for all these years yet barely knew. 'You are joking, aren't you, John?'

'What's wrong with the Mob, Michael?'

'Well ... *ha!*' Summerday laughed. 'I don't know whether you've heard this, John ... but the Mob are *bad* people.'

Monroe rolled his eyeballs in despair.

'When will you grow up? We are *fortunate* in Atlantis to have probably the best organized crime in the world, because there is no power sector more committed to stability, prosperity and sustained economic growth. While never condoning it, a free country has to *accept* crime as a natural manifestation of the entrepreneurial spirit, and it is a sign of how decent and civilized our society is that we have the Mob at the top of our criminal tree. And God knows they do a good job, Michael! The rest of us are cursed to thrash about in the swamp of ideology – the executive, the legislative, and certainly the judiciary – but at least we have a rational criminal element which gets things done and thinks in the long term!'

'By breaking the law. Great. Why don't we all do it, then?'

'Well ... we all do, Michael,' Monroe pointed out softly. 'We all break little laws every day. We speed, we litter, we jaywalk ... all of us. Does that make us bad people?'

'Don't be absurd – there's no comparison between one thing and the other. The Mob break *important* laws.'

'The speeding laws are important, Michael – they stop innocent people from getting killed. The Mob has not killed so many people in its entire history as get killed every year by illegal driving!'

'So we're all bad people, then – is that your point?'

'No. I'm simply pointing out that all of us break the law and all laws get broken. But this is a *good* thing, Michael, because the law will always expand until it reaches the point where it is regularly broken. If a society is too restrained and law-abiding, it just becomes more and more repressive – laws are passed regulating how often hedgerows must be cut, what colour your house can be painted, and God knows what else. We need laws because we have criminals, but we just as badly need criminals because we have laws!'

Monroe looked expectantly at his Vice-President, daring to hope that he may have talked some sense into him, but Summerday's pinched expression showed all too clearly that he was doing everything within his power to resist the logic on offer.

'Michael . . .' he sighed, 'there are other countries – advanced, democratic societies such as ours – that have failed to develop a proper mob. They have as much crime as we do, but it is disorganized and wasteful by comparison. They look at us and take pride in the fact that they have managed to prevent the Mob getting a permanent foothold in their economy, but do you know what they have instead?'

Summerday shifted his head slightly to the side, his neck too tense to allow a genuine shake.

'Tea shops, Michael. Their middle classes paralyse society with crass sentimentality and suffocate progress with planning laws, historical preservation and half-baked environmentalism. Their rural communities sink into a neo-fascist nightmare of arts and crafts, antiques and pedestrianization. Their city centres are crippled by a myopic aversion to tower blocks, and their airports are gagged by noise-pollution laws. Gridlock follows as road-building programmes founder in the face of suburban snobbery, and business is encouraged to

304

relocate to ever more absurd areas by well-intentioned but ridiculous tax-breaks. All of this could be prevented by just a minimum of bribery, intimidation and blackmail: a healthy society *needs* people who will stop at nothing to make a profit, or the law becomes the lapdog of narrow-minded reactionaries. Is that what you want?'

It wasn't hard to see why Monroe enjoyed such powerful support to compliment his popularity with the public. Summerday realized that he had been guilty of misjudging him for all these years – in his own way Monroe was an idealist. He just had the extreme good fortune, for a politician, of having immorality as his ideal.

'Why do you say they won't like me?'

'Your precious Rectag, of course!' The President laughed. 'Not that the device threatens them directly – you won't find any wise guys being made to carry one of your transmitters up their arse, believe me – but you are going to make life very difficult for them nevertheless. The Mob is efficient because it is largely invisible. People know it is there, but it is camouflaged by all the petty crime and violence that dominates our vision of society. Take that away, as you intend to do, and suddenly the Mob becomes visible. I doubt they're very happy about that, do you?'

'So they won't help me.'

Monroe shrugged, sitting back in his chair and running his fingers through his hair. 'They are realists, Michael. You're not, so you may not understand this, but it means they believe in compromise. Talk to them.'

Summerday, feeling slightly nauseous, swallowed heavily and stared at the carpet with its big presidential seal. Monroe watched him from behind the big presidential desk, swivelling gently in his big presidential chair.

'Why do I feel that I will come off the worst in any compromise with the Mob?'

'Because at heart you don't believe in compromise, Michael. You're an extremist.'

'But I'm a liberal! How can you be a liberal extremist?'

'It's amazing,' Monroe chuckled, 'you people will never understand that there is *nothing* more dangerous than a person who insists on driving down the middle of the road, will you?'

XXIII

'Welcome back. Well, the Global & Western stake-out is now in its fourth week with no clear result in sight and we're talking "People Who Have Been in Bank Heists That Went Wrong and Turned Into Shoot-outs With the Police in Which Innocent Bystanders Got Killed". Jodah James, if I could ask you to join in here – you've had experience in this kind of situation and have served eight years for armed robbery . . . what do you think happens next?'

'Well, Lola, my guess is that the police and the feds are going to be coming under a lot of pressure to resolve this situation right now. The election is eight days away and Mike Summerday badly needs to bring the siege to a conclusion. If I was one of the guys inside right now, I'd be preparing for an attack.'

'How?'

'Well, Lola, I don't know if there is any way the Global & Western crews are gonna get out of there in one piece – they got the police, they got the SWATs, they got the HRT out there . . . that's heavy artillery, you know? But, if it was me, I guess what would be going through my mind is that the key to this situation has got to be the little kiddies. Personally, I'd demand a long-range chopper on the roof of the building – that way the HRT don't have the elevated shooting angle they'd get if you came out the front door, see? Then I'd demand some luggage-rack belts, you know?'

'Luggage-rack belts?'

'Sure. I need protection, right? So I need some way of getting me some of those orphan kiddies strapped on. I figure it probably needs three medium-sized kids – one hanging off in front to protect my chest, another off the back, and a third on my shoulders to make head shots too risky. Then I get two big ones to walk in front of me, and two more to walk behind so they can't take a leg shot, you know, and I get *them* to carry the money because I'm already packing a good 150 pounds of kid here, right? I have a handgun held against my chest-kid's head and forget the rifle – if it comes to a shoot-out I'm dead anyway, so I only need a light, compact firearm that will do for the hostages.'

'So, Jodah, we're talking three children strapped on, and four protecting your legs – that makes seven.'

'Yeah. Seven, Lola, right. But that's like *maximum* kiddie-shield, okay? Minimum is still three.'

'Well, I was going to say – we've got six perpetrators and twenty children here. We're way short on leg coverage.'

'Yeah . . . right. Well, you know, adults are just as good for that, I guess. They block your view, though, so the shorter the better.'

'Thank you. In a minute I'll be talking to the man who actually *shot* Jodah James in a stake-out five years ago. Stay with us.'

*

The atmosphere both inside and outside the bank was sombre.

With the hostage crisis in its fourth week, the news had come through that Lucas 'Bumpy' Berg had failed to save the Global & Western Credit from being taken over by the smaller World Wire Coathangers. The new bosses had wasted no time before putting into effect the sweeping programme of rationalization they had planned for the new company, promptly sending out notifications of severance to roughly one-third of Global & Western's employees.

Their approach, as recommended by their advisers at CN plc, was maximum pain immediately: along with hundreds of others across Atlantis, roughly half the hostages received brief letters in the daily postbag informing them that their services were no longer required. George Bailey was one of them.

It caused an uproar in the media, what with Bailey being a national hero and all, but more importantly it sent the share price through the roof.

Outside the newly renamed World & Global Credit, the mood was little better. Rumours had been building for the last month that the Bureau was going to start laying off agents once Rectag was up and running. Nothing was official yet, but it didn't take a genius to see that there would be no call for such a large organization once Lockes' computer was policing most of the criminal fraternity, and the Bureau's director had just confirmed everyone's worst suspicions by assuring them that 'no such plan exists at the present time'.

Which, if you read between the lines, simply meant they had not finalized their decision. Had he said no such *project* existed, that would have been different. But he didn't, he said 'plan'. So there was a project.

Suddenly, the one danger that no good agent had ever had to worry about had reared its ugly head, staring at them with cold, killer eyes more terrifying than any real-life gunman. Unemployment. How naïve they had been all these years, to think that theirs was the one profession proof against the periodic bouts of savage downsizing that had hit every other industry over the last two decades. There was no such thing as a job for life these days.

Naturally the older ones would go first. They would shave a thousand or so agents off in the first round – a fairly gentle start, almost all of the losses being accounted for by retirements and natural wastage. The retiring agents would simply not be replaced and nobody would suffer, so the outcry would be muted as the vast majority breathed a sigh of relief that the cuts had not been as drastic as they feared. But the real purpose of the first round would be to introduce everyone to the principle of downsizing. Once the mental jump had been made the real axework could begin.

Next, a year or so on, would come people five to ten years off retirement. They might even dare to stretch it all the way back to the Pepsi generation – guys in their mid-forties and below. They would be offered early-retirement packages – attractive, but not drop-dead gorgeous. The offer would be voluntary at first, but it would get more and more Don Corleone as time went by.

Then they would axe five thousand jobs in one go – straight severance pay, no frills, effective immediately. The move would meet resistance, but they would force it through by bringing out their trump card – a further two thousand redundancies. The new two thousand would make the previous five thousand seem like an old issue and resistance would break up as employees began thinking it was time to look after Number One and secure their own positions as well as possible. The younger ones would figure they should show some enthusiasm and sign the new, performance-related contracts to prove they had the right attitude to go all the way to the top.

Meanwhile, guys like Pepsi would be out there looking for a job suitable for someone with twenty-plus years' experience in crime and law enforcement. Only there wouldn't be any, because the police would be downsizing in exactly the same way, and so would the private security firms. They would be useless in any other profession, and so many of them would eventually come to the conclusion that there was only one realistic use remaining for their skills.

Crime.

And the last laugh would be had by all the pushers and pimps and frauds, who would meet their old adversaries waddling down the street, all of them with golfballs up their arses.

Agent Pepsi was not going to let that happen to him. In his twenty-one years with the Bureau he had never once taken a bribe, paid for information or cut a deal with a crook. He was as clean as the badge in his wallet, and proud of it. Unsurprisingly, many of Pepsi's colleagues hated him and his toothpaste morality, but he didn't care. He could look in the mirror every morning and know that that was a good guy shaving, which is more than was given to most people. He could bask in the knowledge that whatever happened, good or bad, *he* was on the side of truth, morality and justice. That's all he asked for from life. Which is why he hadn't joined the police.

But, that said, he had few illusions about his prospects if he was made redundant. For all his skill and experience, he would be just another coalminer in a nuclear world. Just another schmuck with a wife and 2.4 children, and neither salary nor safety net.

So it was as if God Himself had intervened in his fate when he got the call from Andrew Fox.

Pepsi didn't ask how Fox got his home number, or knew to call at 11 p.m., precisely half an hour after he got home, giving him time to take off his gun, get a drink and relax, but he had a pretty good idea. Money was already starting to talk with new oratorical prowess among nervous Bureau employees.

Fox was an agent too. A literary one.

The situation as he explained it was simple: George

311

Bailey was a hero, and a hero by nature has a story to tell. Right now, George Bailey's story was worth a lot of money – 'Two or three M, at least,' Fox had promised. But he had to do the deal *now*, when the drama was high in everyone's minds and its price was bumping the ceiling. George Bailey, of course, was in no position to sign a contract – but he could give a verbal agreement, recorded on tape and legally valid, that would serve almost as well.

That's where Pepsi came in.

All Fox needed him to do was use his position as point-man in the hostage crisis and the one man in regular contact with Bailey: convince Bailey to let Fox sell the book, film and TV rights on his behalf, record it on a fresh tape and hand it over. Nothing could be simpler.

Pepsi's cut would be ten per cent. A finder's fee, Fox called it. And it was guaranteed. Even if Bailey was killed and never received his share, Pepsi still collected.

It wasn't exactly corruption, more a mild breach of professional behaviour. Misuse of government material, conduct unbecoming in a special agent, that sort of thing. Pepsi was uncomfortable with it, but the timing was so uncannily perfect that he convinced himself that God must *want* him to do it. For his family's sake.

All morning he'd been waiting nervously for an opportunity to speak to Bailey, but someone always seemed to be in the van with him. By midday he could stand it no longer, and sent Agent Bukowski out for Chinese. The Chinese restaurant was two blocks away, which gave him a clear minimum of ten minutes to close the deal. As soon as Bukowski had gone, he put a fresh tape in the surveillance machine and called through to the bank.

'World & Global Credit,' the familiar voice answered politely, 'George Bailey speaking.'

It was incredible. The man had been a hostage for three weeks now and he was *still* doing it.

'George, I've told you a hundred times that the phones have been rerouted, haven't I? If it rings – if any phone *anywhere* in the bank rings – it's us.'

'I know that, Agent Pepsi. I'm just trying to maintain a sense of normality under trying circumstances.'

'Whatever, George. Whatever makes you happy,' he replied a little snappily, the tension coming through in his voice. 'Now . . . do you want to hear some good news?'

'No.'

'*No?* What do you mean, no?'

'I mean no as in . . . unyes. No as in absolutely not. I've had it up to here with good news. Why, if I have to hear one more piece of good news I swear I'm going to scream, Agent Pepsi.'

'George . . . are you feeling okay this morning?'

Pepsi heard a little sigh down the line.

'You don't much appreciate my sense of humour, do you, Agent Pepsi? Hasn't "Do you want to hear some good news?" ever struck you as kind of a *silly* question? When you get right down to it, it's rather like asking "Do you like having legs?" or "Do you think the sun is a good idea?", isn't it?'

'We don't have time for this, George.'

'Well, that's rather my point – why do we waste time on pointless interrogatives whose answer is inevitably going to—'

'Bailey!'

'Agent Pepsi.'

The names were out. There was a tense pause.

Business-Card Swap at the OK Corral.

'Let's start again. I have good news for you, George.'

'Oh . . . *good.*'

'Yeah. Very good. What would you say to a few million arriving on your doorstep?'

313

'"Some of you may have to stand," I suppose.'

Pepsi sighed. The pressure must finally be getting to the man. 'That's another of your jokes, isn't it, George? You see – I can spot the little critters. Dollars, George! Several million dollars. How would you like to be rich?'

To Pepsi's satisfaction, there was a stunned pause.

'How would I like to be rich?' Bailey repeated softly. 'Well, that all depends, I guess . . . what would I have to do?'

'Nothing. Just say yes.'

'Yes to what?'

'Yes to being rich. Yes to letting a certain Mr Andrew Fox, a leading literary agent, sell the rights to the George Bailey story. It's as simple as that.'

A low whistle wound down the line.

'Like a book, you mean? An autobiography?'

'Exactly – a book, a movie, a TV series, a T-shirt . . . you name it. Just say the word and everything else will be taken care of for you.'

'Well, I would love Mr Andrew Fox, leading literary agent, to sell the rights to my story, Agent Pepsi, but there is a problem – I can't write, and I don't think I would have anything of interest to say if I could.'

'You don't *have* to write – they'll get someone else to do that for you. All you have to do is certify it as the authorized George Bailey story. As for whether or not it is of interest . . . well, let me tell you, George, people are *very* very interested in you.'

'But that's just because I'm being held hostage by rival armed gangs.'

'Yeah. So?'

'It's not what I do for a living, Agent Pepsi. I'm afraid they'll be rather disappointed when they find out what I've been up to for the previous fifty-seven years.'

'That's *not* the point, George! The point is you're a hero!'

'But I haven't done anything heroic.'

'Look, George. You were there at the right time in the right place. That makes you a hero, okay? And that's worth a figure with a bucket of zeroes in it.'

'Is that so?' Bailey mused. 'I'm a hero, am I? And Mr Andrew Fox wants to give me several million dollars! They could call it *The George Bailey Story: From Zero to Hero With a Bucket of Zeroes*, couldn't they?'

'There you go, George! So are you on board?'

Pepsi's heart raced as he thought of the money that would soon be his. He smiled in anticipation, waiting for the precious word.

'No.'

Pepsi's smile stayed strangely frozen in place.

'*No?* What do you mean, no?'

'I thought we'd established this, Agent Pepsi – when I say no, I mean unyes.'

His smile was stuck. He tried to move it, but the muscles were jammed.

'This is another of your jokes, isn't it, George?'

'Unyes.'

'So is that, isn't it?'

'Agent Pepsi – we could go on like this all day. The answer is no. I feel it would be quite wrong for me to accept money for my story when it is not *my* story, being also that of all the other people here with me, and also, actually, *not* a story – this is real life, not a movie.'

A stuck cog somewhere in Pepsi's face suddenly broke free and his smile collapsed.

'George – what is your problem? Of course it's real, that's *why* it's worth so much money!'

'Because it's real, because people are truly in danger and truly suffering . . . it's worth money. There's something profoundly disturbing about that, Agent Pepsi. I don't think I want to become a part of that . . . industry.'

'Wait a minute, George,' Pepsi soothed him, glancing

nervously at his watch. 'You've been through a lot, and you're under considerable stress, so it is perfectly normal that you might not be thinking too clearly on this one. There is nothing *wrong* with being paid money because people are interested in something you have experienced – it's perfectly legal!'

'Just because something's legal doesn't mean it's morally acceptable. Laws are to protect people's belongings, not their souls, Agent Pepsi!'

'Autobiographies get published every day – are you saying that all those people are immoral?'

'Of course not. A little vain, perhaps, but this is different – this is not about my life, it is about this nightmare and all the people trapped in it. Why should *I* be paid a fortune for that and not the others?'

'Because you're the person that everyone knows. You're the hero.'

'I never asked to be one. I don't even *want* to be one.'

'So what the hell is *this* all about then? If you don't even want to be a hero, that's all the more reason to take the damn money – you're contradicting yourself!'

'No, I'm not. Taking the money would be immoral – as you just acknowledged, by the way. If being a hero means anything, it means doing the right thing.'

'The hell it does! Not these days, anyway. For an old man you don't seem to understand much about the way the world is, George.'

'For a law-enforcement officer you don't seem to understand much about the way the world *should* be, Agent Pepsi.'

'God damn it, Bailey!' he shouted, his patience lost. 'I've never taken a bribe or broken a single rule in my life!'

'Well . . . so what?'

'George, you are so far out they could bounce satellite signals off you, I swear . . . You don't think it's

316

an achievement to enforce *and* uphold the law?'

'That is as it should be. It's nothing to shout about.'

'Well, thank God most people don't think like you or there'd be piss-all motivation to be honest!'

He heard Bailey chuckling softly to himself on the other end. 'You must be right, Agent Pepsi. I don't understand how the world works at all.'

'Well take my word for it, George – it works the way I say it does, and I say that *nobody* turns down a no-strings offer of millions of dollars. Nobody.'

'Really?' Bailey replied, still apparently amused. 'Funny – *nobody* is precisely who I've always been led to believe I am.'

So saying, to Pepsi's horror, he hung up.

*

'Chinese no good or something?' Bukowski asked.

Winston Pepsi had been picking disconsolately at his deep-fried prawn dumplings for ages now, and it was starting to get on the younger man's nerves. There was something profoundly irritating about watching somebody lose their grip on a dumpling yet keep putting the chopsticks into their mouth regardless.

'Huh?' Pepsi replied, staring at the tape machine. 'No, it's delicious. Why?'

'Just asking. You've been going a bit heavy on the deep-fried air the last few minutes.'

'Have I?' Pepsi answered in a faraway voice. 'Sorry. Do you want some?'

Bukowski frowned at the proffered carton.

'You're not really listening to me, are you, Pepsi?'

'No . . .'

Pepsi's mind was miles away. It was so unjust. He had never taken the easy route, never given in to temptation or thought about himself, and the one time he decided to bend the rules just a teensy bit for the sake of his family and their future, he found himself dealing with Astronaut Bailey.

The man was insane. How could he turn his nose up at millions of dollars for a minor point of principle? It had to be the strain of being Head Hostage that was getting to him. He was unemployed, for Christ's sake! He needed the money. His behaviour simply wasn't reasonable.

Obviously, he was having a breakdown.

Pepsi wasn't surprised once he'd thought about it – Bailey was old, he wasn't used to the pressure of the city, and he'd been in this crisis for four weeks now. In his crazed state he probably blamed money for everything that had happened of late. Love of money is the root of all evil, as the man said.

He was on a messiah trip – suffer the little children to come unto me and all that. He was way out there in the weird part of his head.

So if he was not responsible for his actions any more, it was Pepsi's duty to think for him. He was responsible for the man's welfare.

That was his job.

The tape could be re-edited into a sane conversation. That was easy. All it needed was half an hour in front of a computer, cutting out all of George's wilder flights of fancy, and Pepsi could make a new tape with the conversation as it should have been, and *would* have been if George wasn't mentally unresponsible for his actions. 'I would love Mr Andrew Fox, leading literary agent, to sell the rights to my story' – he'd said that, Pepsi remembered. 'Unyes' could be trimmed a syllable.

It was dishonest. Even criminal, in the strictest sense of the term, but it was a victimless crime. And he would be doing it for George's own good. He would edit the tape, hand the corrected version over to Fox, and everything would be all right. George would be happy to have his millions once this was all over.

And Pepsi would have his 10 per cent.

He smiled as he brought the chopsticks to his mouth and felt something bump against his lips. He opened his mouth a little wider and popped a prawn dumpling in. It was good, much tastier than whatever he'd been eating for the last few minutes. He looked round in surprise as Bukowski started cheering.

*

'Welcome back. We're talking "People With Unusual Complexes Following a Hostage Crisis", and with me now is Dr Frank Cornucopia, author of the book *Hostages of Love*. Dr Cornucopia – children, hostages, what next?'

'Well, Lola, obviously years of counselling. My guess is that it will take that long for the trauma these young people have been through to manifest itself in a recognizable fashion. You know, the human psyche has the most amazingly complex defence mechanisms and I don't think any serious professional would want to predict *how* it will react to an experience such as being held hostage at gunpoint for several weeks, least of all in the case of a child at a formative age.'

'But if you *had* to make a prediction?'

'Some may find themselves suffering from severe, debilitating anxiety attacks in banks, or even in the presence of wallets, credit cards and other money-related objects. Others may find these same things intensely stimulating.'

'We're talking sex, I take it.'

'In layman's terms, yes. The proper name for it is fiscalonymphomania, and it is actually quite common in women who have had a life experience such as this at a

319

formative age. In my book I describe cases of female bank hostage trauma victims, for instance, who could subsequently only reach orgasm at gunpoint, or by physically *eating* money.'

'Eating *money?*'

'That's right.'

'Well . . . in a minute I will actually be talking to a woman who *does* eat money for sexual gratification. Stay with us.'

XXIV

To get himself on the list for the press conference with the *Avalon* crew before their mission launch, Macauley Connor had to swallow his pride and kiss, one by one, the butts of every contact he had in the business. He drew up a list of the people he knew who might be able to get him into the conference, with every one of whom he had at some point fallen out. These were the people who represented the story of his career, that slow drowning of promise as he clung stubbornly to his pride and let it pull him down. Basing himself in Rachel's flat, with a bottle of whisky and a glass on the table beside him, he worked the phone all morning. He listed the names carefully in reverse order of personal embarrassment, took a deep breath, and made the first call.

It was a humiliating experience. These were hard men, blunt-mouthed editors of mass-market dailies, but when it came to flattering their egos they behaved like the prettiest girls in the class. Butts like bowling balls, buffed to a shine and cold to kiss. Most allowed him to humble himself before their spread cheeks before rejecting him with a disdainful puff of wind; some haughtily promised to see what they could do. If they had time.

Macauley so wanted to be able to tell them to go fuck themselves. But his need was greater than his pride.

By noon he had puckered up and smooched his way down the whole list, reneging on more or less every single personal stand he had taken in his career. Throwing aside his list, with its crossings-out, question marks and obscenities, he felt drained. He was an empty vessel. In a way it came as a relief to be nothing more than a guy looking for a favour, almost as though this had to happen before his life could start afresh, but he was also painfully aware that he now had nothing to show for the past unless one of his question marks called back.

And one did.

He was lucky – with the election only seven days away, the journalist on the *Entropolis Daily Post* who had been scheduled to cover the *Avalon* press conference had been redeployed to cover Penny Summerday's battle with leukaemia. His timing was perfect and Kevin McNeil rang back to say he could take the reporter's place. Now he just had to get from one coast to the other in time for the conference tomorrow morning. Which meant flying, of course.

The only company that flew direct from Petersburg to New Toulouse was an outfit called EconoFly, a name which hardly gave him faith in their ground crew. He had a vision of an overworked technician in EconoFly overalls rubbing the sleep from his eyes at the top of a stepladder as he peered into the fuselage for an explanation of why he might still be holding a wire in his hand when all the terminals seemed to be connected. He imagined his boss shouting up from the ground, 'Yo, Dwayne! You finished already or what?'

He saw Dwayne sigh at the wire, figure that it was probably just the pilot's dashboard cigarette lighter or something, and stuff it out of sight up amongst the tangle of cables, shouting, 'Ready as she's ever gonna be, boss!'

On the other hand, he told himself as they took off for New Toulouse, maybe EconoFly was just cheap because they ran a tight, efficient operation and didn't waste money on frills like in-flight meals and free drinks.

This was also possible.

*

He was one of the last journalists to make it to the press conference at Star City. The conference room was already hot and overcrowded when he entered. The back half of the room had decided to stand on their chairs to get a better view, and Macauley found his view of the podium blocked by a forest of furry microphones and cameras.

The astronauts were late taking their places at the table. As they filed into the room, Macauley could only just make out the tops of their caps, even these disappearing as they sat down. He had not seen enough to spot John Lockes.

Because they were running late the press liaison guy started right off with taking questions from the floor, and Macauley realized he did not have much time to fight his way to a position where he could see Lockes' face. Quite what he intended to do if and when he did see it was still undecided: part of him merely wanted private confirmation of everything he had discovered, just so he would have a sense of closure. This was no longer about money, or revenge; it was simply about proving who was smarter.

Part of him had already decided to let Lockes and Cardew go.

But this was the part of him that occasionally ate bran for breakfast. The carnivore wanted the pleasure of the kill. He began hunting round for a chair to stand on, but they were all taken. He needed to push his way to the front, but his path was blocked by a solid wall of cheap jackets.

'Vanessa Chong, Channel 5,' the first of the journalists said. 'I'd like to ask Josh Cloken how he feels, emotionally, about going into space.'

323

'Very exciting. It's a boyhood dream come—'

Blood. Macauley scented it and the predator in him was tormented by its proximity. Without a second thought, he dropped to his hands and knees to see if there was any chance of crawling his way nearer to his prey.

It would not be easy. Ahead lay a jungle of chair-legs, tripods, bags and calves, but with enough twisting and pulling in his stomach it might just be possible to get to the front. He had not come this far only to fail now.

Pushing his bag in front of him, he began to crawl. Down at floor level, the sound of the conference was strangely muffled – he could barely hear the astronauts' voices through the canopy of belly and butt overhead, and what little he did hear was garbled by the creaking plastic of the chairs as they strained under the weight of the journalists.

A tangle of legs a couple of yards into his odyssey obliged him to wiggle left and scrabble his way to a small gap further along the row. Here he had to roll on to his side and slide slowly through the opening with little centipedal wiggles of his body. Dignified it was not, but Macauley was surprised to find himself having fun. He may no longer have been the right size or shape for this kind of activity, as the sweat seeping through his shirt proved, but the inner child was having a ball.

'Where do you stand on UFOs, Mr Cloken?' some prick was asking as he came out into a clearing where he could roll on to his back and take a rest.

'Who knows – on the ceiling maybe?' the reply snapped back.

The figures above him were silhouetted by a strobing storm of camera flashes as photographers pounced on the crew's laughter. Lockes liked to play with people all right, Macauley recognized with a grin.

Rolling back on to his front, he winced as he felt his keys dig into his hip and clenched his teeth to suppress a yelp. There were two ways forward from here – a relatively easy but circuitous route along the row, through a gap near the end, and back down the row in front, or the short route. Directly under a chair ahead of him. He hadn't been counting on doing this, but he figured that the space between the legs was no smaller than the gap between two chairs he had just passed through, and he had to start making better time or the conference would break up before he reached his destination.

Pushing his bag through the chair, he began inching his way through on his side with tiny pushes of the edge of his heel. It was painstakingly slow, like a baby who hasn't quite learned to crawl, but there was just enough room for him to pass through the legs without touching them. As Macauley passed through this row of chairs and then the next, Cloken's voice was getting clearer all the time, fielding one puerile question after another. Whatever happened to journalism? he wondered as the front of the podium came into view, as did the feet of the astronauts. One was jiggling his heels, and Macauley wondered if that might be his man, more nervous than his calm, dead-pan replies were letting on.

As he came through the last-but-one chair, Macauley saw a heavy camera bag bearing straight down toward him. He just had time to get his hands underneath it and pretend to be the floor before it landed on his head. Its owner let go of the shoulder strap and Macauley gently placed it on the floor beside him, hurrying along on his way before the hand came back down in search of it.

He could hear the PR guy warning that they only had time for a few more questions, and started feverishly wriggling his heel to take him through the last chair, clutching at the floor with his fingertips in a useless attempt to speed his progress still further. His shirt was sticking to his body and he periodically had to blow drops of sweat off the tip of his nose. His shoulders cleared the last pair of legs just as the PR guy called for one final question, and he scrambled to his feet just in time to raise his hand and shout:

'Yes! Macauley Connor, *Entropolis Daily Post* – I have a question for Josh Cloken!'

The PR guy's smile collapsed with surprise at seeing an overweight, sweaty and dishevelled journalist-creature surge up in front of him.

'Uh . . . okay . . . Mr Connor,' he acknowledged. 'And then that's it.'

Macauley wiped the sweat from his face with the sleeve of his jacket and turned to look for John Lockes. Had there been any doubt which of the four male astronauts he was looking for, the object of his search would have been instantly recognizable by the amused air of enquiry on the man's face as he waited for Connor's question.

But that was not how he knew which one Lockes was. As their eyes met and his mouth went to speak, the very air stalled in his throat and the question came out only as a low gurgle of incomprehension.

'I'm sorry, Mr Connor, could you repeat the question?' replied the man Macauley knew as Joel Schonk.

XXV

Michael Summerday's meeting with Mr Giuliano – he didn't know his first name – took place in the open. On a golf course, to be precise. They had no caddies and both had changed into their sporting gear within sight of each other in the club changing room, a tactful way of ensuring that neither was carrying any form of recording equipment.

They were the first out on to the course, a low mist still hanging over the rolling fairways and greens as they teed off. Giuliano offered Summerday a slug from his hipflask to ward off the morning chill. It was all very gentlemanly.

But then, if there were still people who believed the Mob to be comprised of thugs and hoodlums raised and hardened on the streets of the poorest neighbourhoods, they were probably living in log cabins. There still lingered the old stereotype of tight-knit family clans, each fiercely loyal to its don and sworn to silence on pain of much pain, but most people knew it to be just a nostalgic yearning for simpler days when such charming, honour-based systems could survive.

The truth was that, like any other industry, organized crime these days had to survive in a harsh, competitive global market. Powerful Asian, Slav and Latin cartels were challenging the Atlantian families both abroad and on their home territory, forcing them to unite and present a solid front if they wished to survive. The last generation of dons to use that term had buried the rivalries of the past and set about the process of mergers and takeovers that today meant the Cosa Nostra of old was no more than a fond memory. Wise guys these days signed contracts like anyone else.

They worked for CN plc, a global company with a stock-market listing. Although still involved in drugs, prostitution and construction, CN's affairs were increasingly focused on more profitable rackets such as accountancy and law. The company was well liked by dealers on the Stock Exchange because it had a very clear, far-sighted programme that it pursued with all the ruthlessness and determination that had traditionally been the corporate culture of the Mob, and because it always paid good dividends. Always. Whatever the price.

If CN's profits weren't looking good, there were always other companies who could be persuaded to lend theirs in return for protection. CN's methods were not quite so brutal as in the old days, when protection rackets were focused on corner shops and bars, but the system was basically the same. Now, instead of sending their goons in to smash up a recalcitrant grocer's store with baseball bats, they just played a round or two of golf with a few COs.

Golf, as Michael Summerday had heard, is a surprisingly dangerous sport.

'I always say the secret of a swing is in the way you clench your butthole,' Giuliano mused as he watched his ball drop beautifully on to the sixth green and dribble to a halt. 'Faggots can't play golf, you know.'

'Is that so?' Summerday responded, teeing up his own ball.

He had lost count of how many offensive remarks Giuliano had come out with in the short course of their game. On the first tee it had been how golf was the last nigger-free sport in Atlantis. On the second it had been how the secret of a good putt was to imagine the hole was a pussy. This had led him, as they teed off on the third, on to an explanation of how the secret of finding good pussy was to look at a woman's nose: women with small noses are lousy fucks, Giuliano announced. By the fourth he was revealing his more metaphysical side, pondering the question of whether a nose job – or a 'schnozz bob', as he called it – ruined a woman's sexual prowess, and on the fifth he decided that all plastic surgery was probably detrimental to sex. And now faggots couldn't play golf.

Summerday had kept his remarks fairly non-committal, his liberal sentiments making him reluctant to attack Giuliano as a racist, misogynistic homophobe. There was a time and a place for everything. They were here to talk business, after all, not ideology.

'You bet it's so,' Giuliano continued, frowning as Summerday's ball sliced off toward the trees. 'A man who takes it up the dirtbox has no strength left in his lower chakra. He can't focus his energy on it before the swing because the son of a bitch has been pumped into a thousand pieces. So there are no faggot golfers. Lucky for us, huh?'

That was it. Business or no business, Summerday wasn't going to listen passively to any more of this. 'Actually,' he announced stiffly, 'some of my best friends are golfers.'

Giuliano frowned.

'Faggots, I mean. *Gays!* Look, Mr Giuliano, can we change the subject? We're here to discuss business.'

Giuliano's face broke into a smile and he slapped Summerday cheerily around the shoulder. 'We have been, Mr Summerday! A common friend of ours warned me that you were a little ... uncompromising in your positions. I had to check you out for myself, didn't I? You seem pretty flexible to me, Mr Vice-President! But you *do* also have a breaking point. I like that in a man. I think we can work together.'

'You mean you've been . . . all that macho . . . you've been bullshitting? You don't really think gays can't play golf?'

'*I* play golf, don't I?'

Summerday stood blinking as his synapses ran this around his brain a few times to check that he had understood correctly.

'You're gay? A gay mobster?'

'We prefer the term "alternative capitalist" these days. And now who's being macho, my friend? Why do you all assume that just because a man is a wise guy he must be straight? It's weird – we're talking about a strictly guys-only club, all loyalty and brotherhood, bound to secrecy – we even *dress* well, for heaven's sake – and yet everyone assumes we're all straight as arrows. Why is that? It's not as though we've tried to make a secret of it, is it? Look at the St Valentine's Day Massacre – that's *so* obviously gay humour! Is it that people think gays are too *sensitive* to break a few legs? I blame the cinema industry – that town is the one place on the whole planet where nobody seems to be short of closet space, I swear.'

He contemplated the Vice-President's amazed expression with an air of detached amusement. Summerday's mouth was opening and closing softly as he searched for something to say. It seemed that the more corrupt he became, the more innocent he felt.

'So, Mr Summerday. You have an election in seven days' time. How can we help?'

*

'You should be told that CN does not do contract killings, Mr Summerday,' announced Giuliano on the tenth green. 'We've redirected our energies into management consultancy.'

Summerday was devastated. He guessed he shouldn't have been shocked – the whole problem with the modern world was that nobody wanted to do the dirty jobs any more, after all. Whatever happened to service? Whatever happened to taking pride in a job well done? No, these days everybody wanted to be a fucking lawyer or executive or artist, and nobody was prepared to stick their arm down the goddamn drain and pull out that ball of tangled hair and fat any more.

'I'm afraid that is of limited use to me under the circumstances, Mr Giuliano.'

'Well, hang on there – we *do* carry out audits.'

By the eighteenth green it was settled.

The audit of Bob Redwood was to be carried out by one of CN's best management consultants. With a long-range, high-calibre rifle. They decided to conduct the study – which would be thorough, exhaustive and penetrating – at a campaign rally four days from now. The Summerday-Redwood cortège would be driving through town in an open-top limousine, giving their man full access to the upper-level management from the rooftop of a nearby building.

It was to be just like Connolly, which would give the campaign a welcome frisson of glamour, and the bill for the entire consultancy was remarkably cheap. All Giuliano demanded in return was that CN have access to the Rectag criminal database once the system was operational.

'For a company such as CN, Mr Summerday,' he explained with a wink, after sinking his ball to take the match, 'the opportunities Rectag creates for direct marketing are very exciting indeed.'

XXVI

Two days later, the atmosphere in the bank was unusually sedated. The Blade and their hostages had eaten a large lunch from Chez Goran, the finest Franco-Serb restaurant in town, prompting the Blood to go one better by sampling the unique culinary experience that was Mama Lama, possibly the world's only purveyor of Tibetan pasta dishes. Bellies and taste buds satiated all round, most of the hostages had either settled down for a siesta or were quietly playing board games in burping little groups.

Ben Cage was counting the Blood's money again. He had done this more times than he could remember, but it still gave him pleasure to snap the crisp bills between his fingertips as he arranged the banknotes into neat little piles. For someone who had largely avoided mathematics during his brief flirtation with the school system, he was becoming an expert money counter. There was a job for him in a casino if ever he decided to quit the bank business.

Once he had the full sum neatly laid out in front of him in rows of ten piles of $10,000, he liked to contemplate them awhile before carefully stacking the piles on to one another and replacing them in the bag. It made him happy. His mother enjoyed cleaning the church, so something ran in the family.

George Bailey was content in his own way, too. One of

the compensations of being held hostage was that he had time on his hands to catch up with all the reading he had never got around to before.

'Yo, George!' Cage called across to him as he surveyed the haul of money before him.

'Ye-e-es?' George replied distantly, not taking his eyes off the page.

'What would you do if you had $1,210,723, huh?'

'Put it in a savings account at the bank.'

Cage frowned, disappointed by the banality of his answer. 'That's it, man? Put it in a bank? What you want to do that for – don't you want to spend none of it?'

'Nope,' George replied, still trying to finish his paragraph, 'I'd put it on deposit and spend the interest. At 4.9 per cent, the money would make around $60,000 a year, which would be more than enough for me.'

Cage grunted, unimpressed by George's idea of high living. He went back to his enjoyment of the cash, leaving George to carry on with his book. George still hadn't made it to the end of the paragraph, however, when a shadow fell across the page.

'Yo, George!' Cage whispered.

The older man's gaze at last lifted from the book, recognizing that there was no point in continuing while Cage was in a mood to talk.

'This interest gig, right?' Cage muttered secretively. 'If I put the money on deposit, it earns more money all the time?'

'That is indeed so, Ben.'

'So, like if I did that *today* . . . then it would already have earned interest by tomorrow?'

'In theory.'

'So then . . . we'd have more money than the Blade do?'

'Sure you would.' George frowned, starting to suspect what was going through the man's mind.

Cage looked down at the money in his bag and smiled. 'I want to open an account!' he announced.

*

Agent Pepsi had never known real fear until now. He had been scared often enough, his heart pounding in the moments before gunfire might begin, the last minutes as he and a SWAT team took up positions for a raid. But that was a controllable form of fear – the dangers were clear and there were equally clear ways of minimizing them. He could cope with that. That was his job.

But this was different. The fear he felt now was one for which there was no drill, no body armour or brave words to cushion the way it ate at your nerves.

He had not thought it would be like this to be rich.

There had been an initial sense of ecstasy when Fox handed him his $400,000 finder's fee for the deal he had just closed on *The George Bailey Story*, an immense release of tension as he realized that his future was now assured, but it had lasted all of ten minutes before the anxiety began to set in.

What if Bailey didn't change his mind about the money when he found out? What if he refused to accept it on the grounds that he had never given his agreement to the deal in the first place?

Then the truth about Pepsi's role in the affair would come out. The whole truth. Not only had he used his position to pimp for a literary agent, but he hadn't even been able to set up the trick right. He would be a laughing stock. He would be discharged from the Bureau in a sneeze – no redundancy package, no retirement plan and no employment prospects.

All because of George Bailey's absurdly over-developed moraloid muscles. The man was insane. Where did he get off saying it was immoral to profit from the fact that he was a hostage? How could it be wrong for something good to come out of something bad? Here was a nobody who had the good fortune to find himself in a position where he stood to get rich just by playing along, and it was not for the likes of him to question the Atlantian way in these things – in fact it was downright unpatriotic. Not so long ago the guy would have been suspected of having Communist sympathies, with an attitude like that. This great country was founded upon freedom and the pursuit of happiness, which normal people understood to mean money – so unless morality meant spitting on the Constitution, Bailey wasn't being moral.

Pepsi was beginning to realize that George Bailey was not the simple, decent fellow he seemed. In his own subtle way he was a dangerous man. He was a subversive. An anti-Atlantian element whose opinions ran contrary to the very foundations of society.

That was evil.

The irony was that Atlantians were such a warm and good people that even flag-burning scum like Bailey could be taken to their hearts and hailed as a hero. It brought a lump to Pepsi's throat to think how Atlantis was prepared to put its arms around everyone and welcome them into the fold. And most of the time it was an attitude that worked, because even bad guys responded to that love by wanting to be worthy of it. Even scum could be patriotic. But not George Bailey. He was too steeped in his twisted view of the world for there to be any reconciliation between his vision and that of Atlantis as a whole.

It broke Pepsi's heart to think how disappointed all the people who had made a hero out of Bailey would be when they learned the truth about him. Wasn't there already enough misery in the world without them having to be told that this man they so admired was secretly dedicated to the destruction of their whole way of life?

In fact, the more Pepsi thought about it, the more he realized that this was not about the book or his 10 per cent cut. It went way beyond that. It was about protecting Atlantis from scum.

And that, after all, was his job.

*

'What's the deal here, George?' Luís Alvares demanded half an hour later. He was in a bad mood, having lost to one of the children in their game of Cluedo 2000 (it was Colonel Mustard in the sauna with the chainsaw).

'Mr Cage here has just opened an account with the World & Global Credit,' George smiled. 'The account currently stands at $1,210,723.'

Alvares turned to Cage with a look of deep suspicion. 'What's the game, motherfucker?'

'No game. While you assholes sit around with your money in a bag, ours is going to be earning interest.'

Alvares laughed in disbelief. 'Yo, he can't do that, can he, George? That's stolen fucking money – you can't put it on deposit in the same motherfucking bank you *stole* it from!'

'Well, I agree it's a little unusual, Luís . . .' George replied hesitantly, 'but I don't see I'm in a position to argue, am I? And, strictly speaking, this isn't the same bank any more.'

Alvares looked from one to the other in consternation.

'That ain't fair!' he announced.

'Ain't *my* fault if you guys are too dumb to make your money get a job!' Cage sneered.

'There's no reason why you shouldn't do the same thing, Luís,' George suggested softly.

'Damn right I'm gonna do it!' Alvares snapped. 'You stay right here while I get the money!'

'Whoa! Whoa! . . . Hold it!' Cage said, grabbing his

336

shoulder. 'George and me ain't done yet.'

'Actually, Ben, we are,' George cut in. 'The money's on deposit. I can handle Mr Alvares now, if he wants.'

'Uh-uh,' Cage scowled. He pointed his gun at George, whispering, 'We *ain't* done, old man. Give me all the money!'

'The money you just deposited on your account?'

'Of course not! Why would I rob myself, George? Hand over the cash – I'm robbing the bank again!'

'But it's the same money!'

'Do you think I'm stupid, George? What we robbed the first time is on the account, so the *cash* belongs to the bank again! Now fill the fucking bag!'

George sighed and started piling the money back into Cage's bag.

'*The huh?*' Alvares gawped. 'What-what-what are you saying here, motherfucker? Now you've got two million dollars and we only have one?'

'Actually, asshole, we have $2,421,466!'

'So, then what? You deposit the cash a second time, and steal it right back again?'

'Sure. Why not?'

'Because it doesn't make any sense!'

'You're just jealous,' Cage sneered. 'Tell him, George – does it make sense or doesn't it?'

'In strict legal terms . . .' George admitted dejectedly, 'all cash becomes property of the bank once an equivalent sum has been credited to a customer's account.'

'Fuck this!' Alvares screamed, waving his gun at Cage. 'We're doing the same!'

Cage's eyes narrowed, and he turned his pistol toward the Latino. 'You haven't got an account with the bank, asshole!' he hissed, putting the barrel to the other man's belly.

'So I'll open one!'

'You need an appointment!'

'Oh yeah? Oh yeah? Fine, smart guy! I'm making an appointment, George! Right now! You got that?'

'George is busy with a client, asshole – can't you see that? A client of the *bank*, not some fucking greaseball who just walked in off the street. So if you want to make an appointment you get in the fucking queue!'

'What fucking queue? You?'

'Yeah!'

'Oh I'm sorry, could you excuse me, motherfucker?'

The crack of his gun was muffled by Cage's belly. The taller man's eyes bulged momentarily, and he gasped, 'You stupid spick no-brain!' before raising the barrel of his own gun to Alvares' head and making the insult an objective reality.

Both men dropped away from the counter, crumbling heavily to the floor with a thick *crack* as their heads thwacked the marble, and a horrified George looked ahead to see four guns pointing his way.

'Does one of you gentlemen wish to make a deposit?' he whispered hoarsely.

XXVII

Macauley did not stay to watch the *Avalon* launch from the press enclosure. Pity, because seeing a space ship blast off had been a boyhood dream of his, but the climate was warm enough at this time of year without the heat his cheeks would be giving off if he had to see any of those journalists again. Instead, he had caught the morning Econofly bucket back to Petersburg, glad to put the humiliation of New Toulouse as far behind him as possible. Every time he thought about it, his stomach lurched with embarrassment.

Perhaps that was why he suddenly felt such affection for the flight stewardesses – they were friendly, smiling and, above all, did not have a fucking clue who he was. He felt sad for them because they were clearly at the end of their careers, forced like whores to work ever less salubrious airlines as their figures filled out and their skin dried. It was comforting to think they were obviously very experienced, but experience was equally obviously of secondary interest to the airlines for whom they worked. Useful, but the shorter the CV, the firmer the butt.

He was seated in the very front row, sole occupant of three seats. Across the gangway two businessmen were deep in conversation, their voices hushed lest unseen ears hear sensitive information about spreadable processed ham.

They had paid no attention to the hostess as she went through the flight safety procedures. This irritated Macauley, because for him the demonstration had little to do with knowing how one was supposed to react in the event of a crash – who ever heard of survivors? – and everything to do with voodoo. The hostess, holding the bright yellow oxygen mask up by its little rubber tube and gesticulating toward the emergency exits with traffic-cop exaggeration, was actually a high priestess of Luck performing the sacred dance of Not Crashing. It was a holy rite, to be followed with respect and humility no matter how many times one may have seen it performed before.

Something about those yellow oxygen masks bothered him, but he'd never been able to put his finger on what it was. The hostess looked a little bored going through the routine today, which was worrying as he felt sure the sacred dance was more effective if performed with the utmost seriousness, but at least she was doing it live. The last time he'd been on a plane he'd found to his horror that they had replaced the live demonstration with a video played over the aircraft's TV screens. This struck him as outright blasphemy, like baptizing babies with Coke.

For once take-off came as a relief, because his inevitable terror took his mind off the press conference. As always, he pretended to read his newspaper, but behind his air of nonchalance were eyes that just kept sliding over the same paragraph without making the words connect in any meaningful manner. Only once they were safely in the air did he find the sentences begin to make sense.

He looked wistfully up at the NO SMOKING light above his seat. In the past he used to wait, packet of cigarettes in his hand, for the *ding!* as the light was turned off. He remembered how that simple rush of nicotine to his blood would help reconcile him to the fact that he was miles above the ground in a metal structure weighing several hundred tons, calming his outraged sense of physics. These days, of course, the light never went off.

The irony was that cabin air used to be healthier when there were smokers, because it was constantly replaced by fresh air from the outside. Now the airlines shaved a percentage point off their fuel bill by constantly recycling the same air, along with all its germs. But then Macauley suspected tobacco fascism had never been about health so much as it was about subconscious jealousy: why should some people have an easier, more relaxing time on Earth just because they were prepared to accept tar in their lungs?

Almost an hour after take-off they were served a bun and drink – Holy Communion, basically – and he began to calm down, re-assured by the knowledge that buns and drinks are almost never served on aircraft that are failing to fly normally. Plus it was a statistical fact that the vast majority of accidents happen in the minutes surrounding take-off and landing, so he could reasonably expect to live for at least another three hours. With relaxation, however, his repressed memories of the press conference returned in all their horror. He closed his eyes as he relived the laughter of the day before, suddenly so wrapped up in his thoughts that he didn't even notice the little jolt that broke the smoothness of the plane's flight.

At first all he had managed to do when he found himself face to face with his own employer in the guise of astro-tourist Josh Cloken was gargle.

'I'm sorry?' Schonk had asked with a smile. 'You're not being very clear, Mr Connor . . .'

Macauley's brain had stalled; the carb was flooded, and no matter how long he kept the contact on all that came out of the exhaust was a sputtering gibber. He was aware of journalists beginning to snigger behind him, and the tight-lipped pain of the astronauts as they struggled to contain their amusement. Finally a spark caught and the air in his lungs combusted into language:

'You!' he bellowed. 'Are you . . . *you* . . . him . . . you?'

That was it. The last restraint snapped and the entire room flooded with hilarity at the incoherent idiocy of the question they had waited so long to hear. Macauley looked behind him, wild-eyed, and proclaimed, 'He's not! How do you *know* he's him?'

A renewed gale battered the walls, and he felt tears of frustration prick his eyes as a coherent explanation of what he was trying to say continued to escape him. The only people not laughing were Schonk, or Cloken, or Lockes, or whoever the hell he was, his own eyes betraying a kind of pitying tenderness as he watched the journalist flounder, and the woman sitting beside him, whose regard flitted rapidly between the two of them with an alert frown on her brow.

'Mr Connor . . .' Schonk announced gently over the roar of mirth, 'these are fascinating philosophical questions you seem to be raising, but this is neither the time nor the place to explore them. We have a plane to catch.' He winked and rose from his chair, the other astronauts following suit as he began to exit the room.

'That's all, folks!' the PR guy proclaimed, holding up his hands.

The conference broke up in shambles, the astronauts rapidly gone but the gathered journalists reluctant to leave the room, forming happy little groups who studied the weird, sweaty creature at the front and wiped their streaming eyes as the laughter dragged on.

Macauley had to escape in a hurry, exiting the room on a wave of ridicule that seemed to follow him all the way back to his hotel, tattooed on his eardrums. He retired to the bar, proceeding to down three whiskies in quick succession as he waited for his racing heart to settle down. Nothing made sense any more. The more he thought about it, the more the implications of that insane connection threw the last few months of his life into confusion.

Schonk was Cloken was Lockes. The very man who had hired him to write as damning and sensational a biography as possible turned out to be the subject of the biography. That was why the boyhood photo of John Lockes had struck him as strangely familiar, he realized, excusing himself for not having made the connection on the grounds that it was so outrageous that his own sense of logic had prevented him from doing so. His brain hurt from trying to square the circle.

Clearly Schonk must have wanted him to find out the truth, which was why he had kept rejecting drafts of the biography and telling him to keep on researching. But if Macauley was the victim of some kind of set-up, just where did it begin and end? Had Schonk/Cloken/Lockes expected him to be at the press conference, or was he supposed to be still blissfully going through life with a washed brain? Except was that part of the plan, or had Cardew acted on his own initiative? And if Cardew had been involved, how many other people were too? Was Reverend Willis in on it? Was Delia? Dan Welton? Had every lead and snippet of information that had come his way over the last few weeks been planted carefully in his path?

But screw all of that. The real question was *why*? What could Lockes conceivably hope to achieve from all of this? Was it some grand scheme in which Macauley had been chosen to play a role of some sort, or was he just the victim of an absurd practical joke?

Over the next hours, seated at the bar, he turned the possibilities around in his head a hundred times and got nowhere. Every time he seemed to be settling on a possible explanation, some factor would occur to him that threw the whole scenario into doubt.

'And I thought only God fucked you up like this,' he muttered into his eighth whisky tumbler.

The phone rang in his pocket. He knew it would be Kevin McNeil from the *Entropolis Daily Post*, ringing to find out where the hell his copy was. Macauley was tempted not to answer, but then figured that he was going to have to face up to his failure at some point and may as well get it over with. Things could not get worse than they already were, after all.

'Macauley Connor,' he announced in a whisky drone.

'Well, I'm glad to hear you're still sure of *that* much, Macauley,' a familiar voice teased.

'You . . .' he hissed, eyes narrowing.

'Me, him, indeed. I just thought I'd check in with you one last time before the launch, Macauley. How's it going?'

'*How's it going?*' Macauley slurred. 'How is it *going*? Is that a joke? It's *going* down the toilet. There. Happy now?'

'So long as you've got your humour, you'll always be a wealthy man, Macauley. Believe me, I know about these things.'

'And how will your sense of humour hold up when I go right ahead and publish *The Secret Lives of John Lockes*, asshole?'

'Mmm. Good title. But am I that different to anyone else, Macauley? You think you know a person, but they are always more complicated than that, aren't they? The deeper you go, the less sense they make until eventually you aren't even so sure you understand who you are yourself! That's why all psychiatrists are insane. It's a fine example of chaos theory – every time you seem to be getting to the heart of what makes a person, a whole new stratum of detail opens up. Biography should be sold in the fiction department.'

'Is that what this is all about? Are you just trying to prove that what I do is pointless and deceitful?'

His tormentor tutted patronizingly. 'There you go again! Always trying to reduce things to a simple formula! "Is that what this is all about?"! Haven't you been *listening*, Macauley? I know you don't believe in God, my friend, but you do insist on trying to play Him, don't you?'

'You're a fine one to preach about not playing God.'

'More true than you know. We are both guilty of the same faults, but I happen to be in a better position than you to appreciate what those faults are, my friend.'

'Stop calling me that.'

'I can't help it if I like you, Macauley! I see you as a friend, even if you see me as an enemy – I'm afraid that's one more thing you can't control.'

Macauley had the unpleasant impression that everything he said was complying with a script that had already been worked out by the man on the other end of the phone. There was something altogether Pavlovian about his own end of this conversation.

'You've fucked with the wrong person, Lockes. I don't need all of the answers to be able to publish the questions. People are going to hear some unpleasant truths about the man in charge of Infologix.'

Lockes/Schonk hummed doubtfully. 'Publish? I'm your publisher, Mr Connor. You're under contract.'

'And you never intended to publish, did you?'

'On the contrary, I still do. But your book isn't finished yet.'

'Oh, but it is. I'll just put it out on the web. You can't stop me.'

'Of course you have that option,' Lockes laughed. 'Only you will be taken no more seriously than all the other sad lunatics swapping insane theories across their computers. It's a wonderful medium for people to let off steam, Macauley – total freedom of speech. The only problem with total freedom of speech, of course, is that nobody listens! Benevolent censorship has its advantages, as I'm sure you appreciate.'

It seemed that whichever way Macauley jumped, a fence sprang up in front of him. He was being artfully penned into his own little prison, carefully designed to match the exact shape of his head.

'Why are you doing this? Why pick on me?'

'Oh, I'm sorry . . . I was under the impression that *you* were picking on *me*.'

'That's different. You're rich and your company affects the lives of everyone in this country – that makes you a legitimate target. I'm nobody.'

'So you're saying that because you have a low opinion of yourself you are entitled to attack me? That's nice.'

'Someone has to keep an eye on people like you.'

'And who watches the watchman, Macauley? Who ever elected you to this position of guardianship, and who checks the objectivity of the things you write? You've written some nasty things about me in your time, you know. Not because I ever did you any harm, but because you resent my very existence. This is not and never has been about me or anything I have done – it is about *you* and the things you secretly despise about yourself. The world is riddled with problems, society groans with injustice and cruelty, but you choose to ignore all of that and devote your talents to sniping at people whose only crime is to rise above it all in some way. You *could* try to be constructive, but you're a glass-half-empty guy! You bitch and bitch and end up feeling even worse about yourself than when you started, so can you honestly blame me for deciding to make you see things another way?'

Macauley seethed at the attack, hating its author all

the more for the fact that there was some truth in what he was saying.

'Now who's playing God?' he spat.

There was a heavy silence down the line.

'Well . . . it doesn't seem as if God is prepared to do it any more, my friend, so someone else has to, don't they? I just happen to be the best equipped to do it. A time will soon come when you will understand what it is I am trying to achieve. Until then, you should think about what I have done and ask yourself if I am really your enemy. Hopefully you will decide that I am not, because despite everything I have great respect for your intelligence. And then I hope you will raise your voice in my defence – I want it to be you precisely because you have until now considered me your enemy. That's why I chose you. That's why we have been playing this game. I have a purpose that goes beyond you and me. You will see that soon enough.'

'This plan of yours, whatever it is, will just have to go ahead without me. I'm not playing.'

'I'm afraid you have no choice, Macauley. Everyone will have to play. Everyone will have to choose a side. You know more about me than almost anyone else, so you will be in a better position to judge my motives. It's actually a great gift I've given you – you're going to be the Man of the Moment!'

'Maybe I won't feel like being the Man of the Moment. The news, the media, the talking heads . . . right now I really don't care. A moment is like a bus: there'll always be another one coming along right after. Moments are like burgers.'

'This is different.'

'It's always different. That's what makes it a moment, asshole! They come, they go, nothing changes. You can't change the world.'

Lockes laughed.

'So everyone says. But you can. The world isn't such a mysterious place. The mistake we always make is to appeal to people's heads. But people rarely know what is best, and they lack the heart to act upon it when they do. Only by reaching men's hearts can you make a difference, even temporarily. I'm told the best way is through the stomach.'

Macauley was about to reply when he stopped to think, realizing that Lockes had lost him some way back in the conversation. He rubbed his sore eyes and sighed. 'I have no idea what you're talking about, you know.'

'You'll just have to figure it out for yourself. You've got all the ingredients. It's simply a matter of putting them together and digesting them, Macauley.' He laughed a brief, sad laugh. 'Got to go, my friend. Flight to catch, you know.'

He paused, as if unsure how to end the conversation.

'If we don't see each other again, Macauley – it's been fun and I wish you all the best in the future. If you want my advice, take care of those you love, and let God take care of those you don't.'

'You already said God wasn't doing the job.'

'Yeah . . . but I'm hoping He'll get back to work any day now.'

He hung up, leaving Macauley no wiser than he had been at the start.

The first Macauley knew of something being wrong with the plane was when a hostess hurried past him, ditching her tray of used cups on the floor in a manner that was just a tiny nuance away from throwing it aside in panic. He was so wrapped up in his thoughts that for once he forgot to be afraid, and was merely curious as he watched her open one of the lockers in the galley and begin feverishly hunting for something inside. When a second hostess joined her, also ditching her tray, he began to think one of the passengers had been taken sick and they were looking for the medical kit. Which, on Econofly, was probably small and heavily reliant on aspirin. But then they stepped back from the cupboard and he saw what it was they had been hunting for: each held a small oxygen bottle with a breathing mask attached.

This was not good.

He was still struggling to absorb this information when the cabin resounded with a loud *chonk*. Suddenly everything started to drop – people dropped whatever they were doing and looked drop-jawed overhead as the plastic flaps under the luggage racks dropped open to let the oxygen masks drop out. Then the plane itself got caught up in this sudden counter-culture movement that was all the rage on board and began to drop out of the sky.

'Ladies and gentlemen,' one of the stewardesses spoke into the microphone, 'please place the oxygen mask to your face, fasten the elastic strap around your head and breathe normally. Parents should fasten their own masks first before attending to their children.'

Nobody screamed, nobody whimpered. The plane was uncannily hushed. It probably helped that they hadn't gone into a tailspin. But neither had they hit an air-pocket – the plane was not in free-fall, it was just very rapidly losing its superiority over pigs.

His every cell bristling with horror, Macauley reached for his oxygen mask and did as instructed, pulling down firmly on the plastic tube like they'd always said he should in the voodoo dance. Two heartbeats later, looking at the tangle of rubber tubing in his lap, Macauley realized that either he had misunderstood what was meant by 'firmly' or Dwayne had checked over the flight safety gear.

As he reached for one of the other masks, a hostess took the empty seat beside him and buckled herself in, holding her oxygen bottle to her mouth. Macauley looked at her, eyes wide with interrogation. She met him half-way, carrying the same question in her eyes.

That was when he knew for certain they were crashing.

They were crashing. To his surprise, he found that he had already accepted that simple truth: they were crashing, and he was going to die. Every muscle in his body was pumping with adrenalin and life, but he did not appear to be afraid of death. It would be quick and so catastrophically violent that he would feel no pain. Oddly, there did not seem to be more to it than that – the Reaper had simply settled into the seat behind him with a nod and small smile of greeting.

And he was acceptable company. Death was not ugly, and he did not smell. He kept his elbows under control and didn't listen to a Walkman. Death was happy to talk, but he would wait for Macauley to speak first.

This was not at all how he had imagined he would feel when his time came. Especially in a plane crash. Instead of succumbing to hysteria, he found himself calmly reflecting that in general his life had been interesting and largely enjoyable. He wanted it to continue, indeed he would have accepted any price for one more day, for a chance just to say farewell to Rachel. Yet, at heart, he could accept that this was the end like he could accept a traffic light turning red.

Only one thing bothered him. The oxygen masks.

They were the wrong shape.

Round instead of triangular.

Oxygen masks for people without *noses*, basically.

No matter how he tried pressing the mask against his cheeks, the flimsy rubber just popped into a figure of eight, gaps appearing either side of his nose and chin. Even with both hands over the damn thing he couldn't get a fit.

Then he glanced across at the two businessmen, both

dealing with the knowledge of something bigger than spreadable ham, and realized what was so undignified about dying like this. It wouldn't matter, given they would all be *dead*, of course, but the idea of the rescue teams finding them all wearing these fucking useless bits of rubber bothered him. He could see what the two ham-spread men looked like in their bright yellow masks, and knew he must look the same.

So this was how it all ended.

Macauley Connor, already duped and humiliated in life, was now going to die looking like Donald Duck with a nose job.

XXVIII

The final decision on what to do about the World & Global Credit crisis fell to the Attorney-General, Tom Hagen. It was the part of his job he did not like. Only he could decide to send in the Hostage Rescue Team, and only he would take the blame if they fucked up and got innocent people killed. Innocent children at that. Orphans.

It could have been worse, of course. But not much. The Dalai Lama might have been in there.

Or Bambi.

The pressure was mounting on him to do something decisive. It was no use arguing that keeping one's cool and letting the negotiators do their work *was* decisive; that was not what people meant by 'decisive' in this context. They meant dramatic.

Were it truly up to him alone, he could stick to his guns. But the election was three days away, and it had been made quite clear to him, now that Michael Summerday had clawed his way back to within a whisper of Jack Douglas in the wake of the revelations about Susan's heroic battle with alcoholism, that he had to bring the siege to an end if he wanted to keep his job under a possible Summerday administration. There was the public to think about, and the public were getting restless. They were bored with the siege. To make matters worse, the media had run out of sensible things to say and had started affecting outrage at the way the gunmen seemed to be living in luxury-hotel style inside the bank. It was true that things had got a little out of hand on that level, but this was an unusual situation in that they were dealing with rival gangs – if one gang chose a 1970 vintage from the wine list, the other automatically chose 1969. It hadn't started out like that, of course, but after four weeks of negotiations they were running out of ways of expressing their superiority over each other.

The positive side of this was that their victims were being better looked after than any hostages in living memory. Mattresses and bedlinen had been supplied by Darcy's, the department store. Clothes were delivered fresh on a daily basis. Towels, soap and a full range of bathroom products were supplied freely. Every day food was delivered from some of the best restaurants in the area, dishes being chosen from a variety of menus faxed through each morning to the bank. A full book and video library had been built up by each side to entertain the adults. The children had been showered in comic books and toys picked from the catalogues of the city's leading stores. There was even a rumour of them throwing rival one-month-anniversary parties.

On the other hand, neither side was prepared to leave the bank on the same terms as the other – each was determined to cut itself a better deal, and so it was impossible to satisfy both simultaneously. But the longer the crisis carried on, the less inclined they were to leave the bank anyway.

All in all, life in there was not bad.

But everyone, Tom Hagen most of all, knew that it could not last. As he found himself increasingly isolated within and without the government, the effort it required to keep a level head was costing him more and more. He had hoped that the people on the ground would have reached a consensus on how to tackle the situation by now, but they remained as divided as ever between the negotiators and the action-men. And their opinions were held with the passionate conviction of people who would not ultimately take the blame if it turned out they had been wrong and had caused a bloodbath.

Every day he held a meeting with them, and every day it was the same. The negotiators, led by Agent Pepsi, were adamant that with time and patience a solution would be found, but the cost in both financial and public-relations terms was escalating daily. The city was already being sued by dozens of local businesses for the lost earnings caused by the need to block traffic off from the area, and there were rumours of a class-action suit being brought by the relatives of the hostages, claiming millions of dollars in terms of mental anguish and trauma caused by government inaction. On the other side were the rescue teams, who had proposed a series of plans to release the hostages, all of which had only one thing in common: they could not guarantee how many of the hostages would make it out alive.

Tom Hagen tried to remember that he had not become a lawyer all those years ago so that he would one day be in a position to order a massacre. He had wanted to change society for the better, to help those who were least able to defend themselves.

Strange how, the more power a man gets, the fewer choices he has.

*

George Bailey looked at the AK48 in his gentle hands and asked himself if he had what it took to be a hero. And if that was what being a hero was about.

Everything had changed since Cage and Alvares had killed each other, and he was no longer sure that he knew what he was doing. Before those poor young men died he had been under the impression that he was on the right track – he had established a relationship of trust with his captors, helping to keep the situation calm and safeguard the other hostages. He had resolved more conflicts and soothed more tensions over the last four weeks than he could remember. It wasn't dramatic or heroic, but it was what he was best at.

And then everything had collapsed when those shots were fired. The insanity of his situation seemed to have increased exponentially over the ensuing hours until now, almost a day later, he was the one holding a gun.

'Does one of you gentlemen wish to make a deposit?'

Four gun barrels and eight eyes had twitched between George, the bodies and each other. A cough was all that was needed to make it rain steel there and then. At one moment it looked as if Martínez would shoot Jones, Jones would shoot López, López would shoot Day, and Day would shoot Martínez. Then everyone twitched again and the sequence was reversed. And again, faster, like a gyroscope losing its balance.

That was why George said what he said. In the heat of the moment he was gambling that what they needed was a metaphorical cold shower. 'Does one of you gentlemen wish to make a deposit?'

The guns all turned his way.

'Security?' he suggested. 'Money in the bank?'

Their eyes were flicking from side to side like executive toys, but the barrels stayed trained on him. He had broken the connection.

'I'm just thinking of your families. Banker's instinct, you know. You have all the time you need for reprisals and shooting one another, but shouldn't you consider your loved ones first? Do any of you have funeral insurance, for instance? I don't know whether you're aware of this, but it can be cripplingly expensive if one wishes to bury someone dear with even a minimum of dignity.'

He was babbling now, trying to keep talking long enough to let the adrenalin wear off just that tiny amount needed to bring them back from the brink. He turned to López, supplicating:

'Let's take you, for instance, Julio. You have a baby daughter, I believe? Now, she needs new shoes every what – two or three months? And that's just the start. There will be schoolbooks to pay for, toys, bicycles . . . all that needs money. With a fixed-interest, long-term deposit account paying dividends into a separate current account, your wife can cover all these expenses over the coming years simply out of the interest *without* ever touching the capital sum, which is, of course, stolen and therefore illegal. Think about that. You'll say you're busy right now and can't afford to fill out the paperwork, but what if *I* were to hold your gun and cover your back for half an hour? Following that, I could do the same for the rest of you. Who shoots whom is no concern of mine, but can't we *at least* have this situation on a secure financial footing before anyone else ends up like poor Ben and Luís here?'

A temple hush fell on the bank as he let them reflect on the financial implications of their situation.

'Call me old-fashioned . . .' he urged finally, 'but oughtn't you gentlemen to start taking your responsibilities a little more seriously?'

And that was how George came to touch a gun for the first time.

López didn't go so far as to lend him his own weapon, feeling more secure with it hanging from his shoulder as he filled out the forms to open the account. Instead, he gave him Luís Alvares' bloodstained AK48, showing him how to stand to absorb its kick, how to hold it so that the weight was taken by the strap rather than his arms, how to fire with a spraying pattern to be sure of hitting Sonny

Day if the need arose. All this with the ease of a car salesman.

At first George found contact with the weapon a chilling sensation, deeply uncomfortable with the feeling of his finger against the little death-dispensing lever on its underside. And yet there was a sense in which the machine was so refined in its adaptation to the human form that even he began to bond with it. Each time he put it down to complete his side of the administrative work involved in opening accounts for each of the men, he found it easier to pick up again afterwards.

It began to excite him to feel its weight upon his elderly shoulder. And when the work was finally done, George did not automatically put the weapon aside.

But then, nobody told him to.

Something odd had taken place and it no longer seemed illogical to any of the gunmen that one of their hostages should have a gun. Without anything having been said a tacit understanding had grown that each side trusted him better than they trusted the other. George was a good man. They could rely upon him to referee the situation, a neutral element who would automatically support the victim against the aggressor if either side made a move to break the fragile ceasefire. So whoever shot first would always be outnumbered.

It was an unusual arrangement, to say the least, but it was vital if anybody was going to sleep. One person on either side could rest while his partner mounted the watch.

Which worked fine, until emotional exhaustion got the better of them in the early hours of the morning and all four fell asleep.

Leaving George Bailey to look at his AK48 and wonder if he had it in him to kill four men.

*

'Let me guess, gentlemen,' Tom Hagen announced as he strode into his office in the morning: 'there has been no breakthrough in the negotiations, Agent Pepsi, but you are continuing to consolidate the foundation of trust that you have established with the sons of bitches. And you, Lieutenant Schwarzkopf, want to be given the green light to send a small group of men into the building via the plumbing system, bringing them out through the toilet bowl in the rest room, from where they will launch a surprise attack of devastating odour upon the gunmen. Am I near the mark?'

Pepsi and Schwarzkopf shifted uncomfortably in their seats. Relations between them had been impeccably polite over the twenty minutes they had been awaiting the Attorney-General, neither having spoken a word, and they were no more forthcoming now, as if it seemed a shame to break the peace.

'I really don't know why I bother having these meetings,' Hagen sighed. 'I'm bored of hearing the same thing. Aren't you bored? Isn't one of you tempted to try something new before Alzheimer's claims us all?'

Pepsi cleared his throat and opened his mouth as if to speak, but then apparently thought better of it, glancing across at Schwarzkopf. The lieutenant raised an eyebrow, signalling his willingness to see their treaty broken.

'Well, Pepsi?' Hagen demanded.

Pepsi cleared his throat again, and announced, 'There may be . . . I myself am of the opinion . . . a reasonable basis on which to envisage some form of alternative engagement as a viable strategy within the present operational context . . . sir.'

Hagen eyed him coldly. 'What?'

'I of the opinion am that there may be a reasonable basis on which—'

'Shut up,' Hagen snapped. 'Where do you people learn to speak? It's one thing talking like that in court, but it won't wash with me. Did you just say what I think you said – you've actually changed your opinion?'

It seemed too much to hope for after weeks of stalemate, but he was sure that his ears had not deceived him – Pepsi seemed to be talking about ending negotiations.

'Under the present operational circumstances.'

The Attorney-General frowned. Talking to policemen was always tedious, but it was worse when they actually had something important to say. The more you tried to speed them up, the more garbled and portentous their language became.

'Today, you mean? Why today?'

Pepsi looked pained, his eyes sliding toward Schwarzkopf to check his reaction. The lieutenant was fighting hard to keep his composure as he listened to Pepsi's announcement.

'Certain possible factors requiring consideration have come to my attention regarding the individual upon whom our negotiating strategy has been based up until the present moment.'

'Why? What's wrong with Bailey?'

'Bailey . . . that is to say, the individual in question may not be . . .' Pepsi shifted his position in his chair, suddenly unable to find a comfortable way of sitting, 'motivationally unidirectional.'

'Motivationally unidirectional . . .' Hagen repeated, struggling with Pepsi's crescendo of technobabble, 'motivationally unidirectional . . . you mean he's . . . ? No, I give up – what the hell do you mean, Pepsi?'

'I believe he may not be an impartial intermediary. His allegiances are questionable.'

'He's gone over to the other side? He's got Geneva Syndrome?'

'I believe that not to be the nature of the situation.'

'Not Geneva Syndrome?' Hagen wondered aloud. 'So

that must mean . . . Oh my God! You think he's the inside man!'

Lieutenant Schwarzkopf's eyebrows cranked up in amazement despite his attempts to control them. This was the first he had heard of this.

'You mean he's the inside man, right?' Hagen repeated.

Pepsi could stand it no longer.

'Yes, God damn it!' he shouted. 'George Bailey is scum! He's the criminal mastermind behind this entire situation – that's why we've got nowhere with the negotiations! Doesn't it strike you as a little *too* convenient that Bailey happened to enter the bank with a party of orphaned children just minutes before the robbery? It was a ploy to ensure they had the perfect negotiating position if anything went wrong with the robbery! The man is so low that he actually used orphans! He is *scum*!'

'Can you prove this?' Hagen demanded.

'*All* the circumstantial evidence points to Bailey's involvement! How come *he* was the one to initially answer the phone? How come all communication still goes through him? Isn't it obvious that he, an elderly employee approaching retirement, tried to arrange a nest egg for his twilight years by organizing a robbery of his own bank? That's why two gangs were involved – he didn't trust either one to keep their end of the bargain and give him his cut of the stolen money, but he realized that two rival gangs would stop each other from breaking the deal, don't you see?'

'So there is no more point in negotiating?'

'Screw negotiations! We've got to get those kids out of this monster's clutches by whatever means necessary! He's dangerous, he's probably armed, and he's leading the whole set-up – we take him down, then the other gang members!'

'Shoot first, ask questions later?'

'Screw asking questions later!'

'That's actually what the saying . . . oh forget it,' Hagen sighed. 'It seems we have a consensus then, gentlemen?'

Schwarzkopf could hold his natural urges back no longer, leaping up from his seat to punch the air with a resounding, '*Yes!*'

*

As the sound of machine-gun fire and ricochets faded up into the vaulted ceiling of the World & Global Credit, George Bailey Jr staggered slowly forward, the AK48 falling from his shoulder to the marble floor with a clean steel clatter, and dropped to his knees as his legs suddenly lost their strength.

It was done.

He looked at his gentle hands, the imprint of the gun still visible on his skin, and asked himself if they would ever again take pleasure in the touch of anything, living or not. These hands that had killed four men in their sleep.

It was no use telling himself that they had been bad men, for the only significant difference between them and himself was that he had life and they no longer did. There was no relativity in that equation.

George was well aware that no one would damn him for what he had just done. Legally, it was self-defence – not just of himself, but of all the hostages. Indeed, he would be a greater hero than he already absurdly was in the public's eyes. But that would comfort him nothing each time he went to wash his hands and felt the stain remain. George was a mass-murderer now – if not in their terms, then in his own and those, he felt sure, of any god worth worship.

He had done it for the children, because it was his fault

that they had been there in the first place and so it was only right that he accept the burden of guilt involved in releasing them. But the guilt was the same. Realizing he was going to be sick, George did not move his killer's hands from before him, letting the vomit burst over them as his stomach choked on his own soul.

At least for the others it was over now. Their screams had subsided, the tears of the children had dried, and the bank was beginning to tinkle with soft, disbelieving laughter as people realized, one by one, that their ordeal was over.

Not his, though. His had just started.

Had he the courage to do so, George realized that he could without regret end his own life now rather than face the years ahead with the knowledge that everything he had once believed about himself was a lie. He did not have the strength for that ordeal. The battle was lost already.

He heard footsteps approaching softly behind him, and a woman's voice softly telling him:

'You did the right thing, Mr Bailey.'

'There is no right thing,' he answered, his voice a faint echo of its usual self. 'There is nothing.'

'That's not true, Mr Bailey,' she insisted. 'That's just so untrue, I promise you.'

George Bailey shook the last of his own vomit from his hands and lifted his head, slowly turning to look her way. Roughly half of the hostages had gathered in a semicircle behind him. Those nearest, like her, held guns.

'At the very least there is the money,' she smiled, 'isn't there now?'

XXIX

At the same time as George Bailey Jr was coming to terms with the fact that his nightmare was far from over, a man was staring out of a window some 180 miles above the planet's surface.

The man unknown as John Lockes was not aware of Jean Grey approaching behind him until tresses of her blond hair tickled past his neck, floating with a life of their own now that they were released from gravity. At the same time he felt a hand close on his shoulder and turned with a start to see her face beside his own.

How she managed to move with such silent ease and grace in these conditions still mystified him.

'Dad's checking on baby, is he?' she grinned.

They were alone on the flight deck. When *Avalon* had passed round on to the dark side of the Earth and there was nothing to see but the static, speckled blackness of space, the crew had dispersed around the ship to continue their routine tasks in the spacelab and on the flight deck, leaving their passenger to gaze out of the aft window at the fat satellite sitting in the floodlit cargo bay.

'I thought you were busy with the flight operations,' he explained, seeing her amusement at having startled him so.

'That I am. I have to prep the arm to move Memphis 2 out of the cargo hold.' She gestured toward the aft control station before them. It was from here that she would conduct the delicate operation of picking up the satellite with the twenty-metre mechanical arm. Once she had positioned it above the ship, they would move *Avalon* to a safe distance and then fire the satellite's small rocket to lift it up into its permanent orbit position.

That was his part of the mission. His one duty on this voyage and the sole reason he was up here, 180 miles above the planet's surface: to push a button. In purely financial terms, given that Infologix was covering the entire cost of the mission to the tune of over $1 billion, it was almost certainly the most extravagant button one man had ever pushed.

And he could have done it from Mission Control, for that matter.

He felt sure that Jean must think the self-indulgence implicit in that to be obscene, but if so she had never given any sign of it. Instead she gave the impression of understanding that there was more to this than he or any-one else was letting on, but it was impossible for him to know exactly how much lay behind that softly teasing smile. John Lockes was unaccustomed to being at a dis-advantage in his dealings with anyone, but now that he was, for the first time in his life, he had to admit that he liked it. And there was an undeniable symmetry about the way that it was only now, as his life's work approached completion, that he had found the one woman who he felt could not only understand him, but even outwit him.

He wished he knew exactly what she thought of him. Obviously she liked him – her kiss on the night of the restaurant had proved that – but were her feelings any stronger than that? She switched between intimacy and professional detachment with disconcerting ease, always catching him off guard and a step behind. Could she do that if her feelings approached anything like the strength of his own? It was agony not knowing where he stood, and yet he had never felt more vibrantly alive than he did in her company.

Jean was tantalizingly close, his every sense of her – her body heat, her scent, the sound of her breathing – magnified tenfold by the lack of gravity. She didn't need to be so close. Her hand was on his shoulder as if to steady herself, but there were a dozen other anchors that she could use within reach. His blood seemed to roar in his ears, boiling with the desire to kiss her, but Lockes was all too aware of the fact that for all his training over the last weeks he still moved with the clumsiness of a toddler. If he went to meet her lips, he would probably just break her nose.

'I'm sorry – am I in your way?'

'I don't know,' she whispered, locking his eyes. 'Are you?'

Damn her. They had not been alone together since the press conference, and her manner had been impeccably professional at all times, but now she was doing it again. His body began to tremble as if being electrocuted.

'Jean,' he groaned, 'what is this?'

'Why don't you tell me?'

'But I don't know! I know what it is for me . . . I think you've guessed that . . . but what about you? I've no idea what to make of you.'

'Well, Josh, then we're equal . . . aren't we?'

A glitter of suspicion dusted her irises.

He had to answer. He could not know for sure what it was she suspected, or what she wanted to hear, but he had the intimate conviction that everything depended upon what he said next.

'Ask me any question,' he ventured, 'and I will answer it. No secrets, I promise.'

It was a fudge, and she knew it. Her head moved just an infinite inch backwards.

'Very well . . .' she responded neutrally, 'who was that

man at the press conference and what didn't he say and why?'

'Jean, I tried to tell you, okay? Just bear that in mind. I did try.'

Jean raised one perfect eyebrow. 'I believe you, Josh. But then my next question will be' – the neutral tone vanished as her eyes flashed with passion – '*how hard*?'

John Lockes had never had to explain the choices he made to anyone, not even himself. He knew what his reasons were all right, but so long as he'd never had to spell them out clearly then he could pretend they didn't really matter. He was just living from one day to another like anyone else, and the things that touched him were ordinary things. The light when the sun went down along a long city avenue. The sight of commuters swirling through a station concourse at the end of the day, salmon pushing home. Fresh newspapers in string-bound stacks beside a kiosk in the early morning. The streetlamps lighting at dusk, street by street; flowers of the night closing their amber eyes come dawn. The lights of a distant apartment block, the shimmering blue of someone watching television in the dark, and the sight of a blind being lowered against the world. The epic poetry of petty things.

What struck him again and again, always with the same thrill, was the unrecognized fragility of life. The way most things happened for the stupidest of reasons, and what made the difference between a good and a bad day was so often a stranger crossed or a whim of the weather, set against the persistence with which people sought to control their lives, refusing to admit that they could never control anything that really mattered. And yet if only they could bring themselves to learn a little humility they might see enough wonder to make their wildest dreams seem dull and tawdry.

All that was wrong with the world, Lockes believed, was a lack of recognition for what was right.

He did not know how to explain to Jean what he had always known to be the case, because there was no reasonable explanation of it: for as long as he could remember he had been aware that it was his destiny to be reviled. Logically, he did not believe in destiny, and yet his sense of it was so acute that it seemed, impossibly, to lie behind rather than ahead of him. He felt it behind him in the way that one can be conscious of another person's eyes upon one and turn to catch them look away. The gifts with which he had been born, which he could no more refuse to use than a poet can avoid seeing the metaphors around him, were inexorable in their weaving of his purpose. Had he felt that purpose to be wrong he might have been able to deflect his destiny, but he could not, for two reasons: it was right, and anyway he loved life too much ever to bring it willingly to an end.

But he was realistic enough to know that others would not understand or accept what he had to do until long after it was done. That was why he knew he would be reviled. Why he had tried, for as long as he could, to delay his destiny. And why he had decided to live as much of his life as possible as someone other than John Lockes.

The reasons for his deception, which he now tried to express in a way that he hoped Jean Grey would not find totally insane, came down to one thing: he had simply wanted to taste a little freedom first.

Jean got more truth than she had bargained on. He was taking a risk telling her all that he did, revealing secrets that went way beyond the trivial question of his false identity and touched right on the heart of what this mission was all about. If she was shocked, she did not show it – her expression was unreadable as he finished and she floated silently before him, absorbing the implications of what she had just heard.

He waited nervously for the inevitable questions to come: What gave him the right to do this? How could he know what was for the best? How could he expect her to do nothing now that she knew?

But, in the way that Jean always managed to confound his expectations, she did not ask any of these things. Her question, when it finally came, took him completely off guard:

'Why "Memphis 2"?'

John Lockes frowned. He would never understand how this woman's mind worked. 'No reason really,' he shrugged.

Her red lips pouted mockingly. 'Somehow I have trouble believing you are capable of doing anything for no real reason.'

'Seriously, it's just a name!'

Jean turned and began prepping the mechanical arm as she should have done half an hour ago. Which had its desired effect on Lockes:

'If you must know, Memphis was the name of my dog.'

Her hands paused in their rapid sequencing of the switches on the aft control station.

'Your dog?'

'My dog.'

'What kind of dog?'

'A dog dog . . . a hound-dog I had when I was a kid. No particular kind.' He shrugged. 'Didn't ever catch a rabbit.'

Jean didn't reply, finishing her preparations at the control station. Finally, she shook her head in amazement and turned to face him, her face betraying more shock now than at any point in their conversation.

'You've named that thing in the cargo bay . . . this device that will for ever more change the lives of every man, woman and child down below us . . . after a *dog*? One of no particular kind that never caught a rabbit?'

Lockes thought it over. 'I suppose . . . I hadn't really thought about it, but put like that, it's a little outrageous, isn't it?'

Jean Grey's hand reached out to touch his shirt and he felt himself being pulled toward her until their faces were only an inch apart.

'Two things,' she announced. 'First: of all your many secrets, Mr John Lockes, *that* is the one I think we should keep to ourselves at all costs.'

Lockes' heart leaped in his chest. 'We', she had said.

Her expression melted into a smile and her lips closed upon his. He understood, as the blood fizzed around his body, that this was her way of telling him that she had accepted his explanations. Her kiss, soft but insistent, was the seal on the pact. They were in this together.

'I love you,' he softly confessed, breaking slightly from her lips.

'That had better not be another lie, Mr Lockes.'

'You know it isn't, don't you?'

'Mm-hm,' she admitted, kissing him again.

The longest minute of John Lockes' life was in that kiss. All the lives he had lived seemed at last to meet and all his personas end their differences. None of it mattered compared to this woman.

His eyes sparkled moistly as they broke again, Jean moving his floating body back from her.

'But there's the second thing,' she warned.

'Which is?'

'The cargo-bay arm isn't working.'

XXX

While John Lockes was absorbing the catastrophic implications of a malfunction in *Avalon*'s arm, a slightly overweight and balding man was cleaning his car in Petersburg.

Contrary to his own recent expectations, little had changed about the man in the last day. He was still recognizably humanoid in form – limbs, torso and head all very much connected, rather than dangling from separate trees on some desolate mountain. Any changes were on the inside: Macauley Connor had spent quality time with the Reaper and lived to tell the tale. It was what they call a growing experience.

He was not sure how close Flight EF101 had really come to making like a big JuiceMatic with their bodies, but he suspected it was a whole lot closer than the pilot let on when he finally came over the speakers and explained that he had been obliged to drop altitude because they had lost cabin pressurization. There had never been any real danger, he assured them. Sure, which was why he hadn't said anything for ten minutes. And even if his excuse was true, Macauley was suspicious – he might not know much about aircraft design, but it seemed to him that they shouldn't lose pressurization without the luggage-bay door dropping off or something.

Then things got insulting. In lieu of the year or two

they had lost off their lives, they were all offered a complimentary drink. (Except for the one of their number who had suffered a minor heart attack – possibly stress-induced in the short term, but probably also not unrelated to working in the ham-spread industry, frankly. The man no doubt had arteries a sandwich away from gridlock before he ever stepped on board.)

After they had limped into Petersburg there was talk on board of filing a class-action suit against Econofly, but Macauley had not stayed to attend the meeting called by one of the other passengers. A lawyer, of course. Maybe the man was right and there was a goldmine in this situation for each of them, but at that moment it seemed enough to Macauley that he was walking out of the deal alive and on legs – anything else was small change.

It was only once he was comfortably installed at Rachel's that evening that Macauley realized how shook up he was by the experience. Literally. The ice jangled in his whisky as if he were the epicentre of a small, extremely localized earthquake. When they went to bed that night, he found the image of the dropping oxygen masks returned each time he closed his eyes.

And the next morning was no better. After Rachel had left to go to work, he lay listlessly on the sofa – if one can tremble listlessly – still seeing the masks raining down. Eventually he realized that the problem was chemical. When he had believed he was going to die, his body had automatically flooded his whole system with adrenalin. Unfortunately, nature is way behind the times. Strength in hand-to-hand combat, or an exponentially increased ability to duck, run or jump is all very well, but not much use when death comes while one sits strapped into a cushioned armchair. These days what was needed was a *sedative* equivalent of adrenalin, to cope with modern forms of death.

He had to do something to burn off the unused drugs in his body, so he decided to clean the car. It might not sound like much, but this was Macauley Connor's car – tens of thousands of miles on the clock since it last saw a sponge, the wrappers from months of junk-food stop-offs, the tar from hundreds of cigarettes, and a trunk full of God only knew what.

The collected litter of his life on the road filled two large garbage sacks. Newspapers, plastic bottles, burger packaging, chocolate wrappers, old T-shirts, bills and receipts, motel soap and shampoo – he swept it all into the sacks without pausing to check if anything was important. He wanted it all gone, definitively out of his world. It was not hygiene, it was therapy.

Next he drove around to the car wash and began hoovering out the interior, ramming the vacuum pipe into every cranny and nook of the seats. He worked with such energy that he began to sweat, pumping coins into the vacuum cleaner in his determination to remove every last microscopic trace of the past.

The worst part was the rubber floor mat in front of the passenger seat where his cola had spilled a week back. He ripped it out roughly, draping it over the trunk of the car, and fished around in his pockets for enough change to work the spraygun.

He was still standing at the back of the car, counting out the coins in the palm of his hand, when he saw something glint from the corner of his eye. He looked up, but there was nothing there. Then, lowering his head, the flashing returned, distracting him from his counting.

He looked up again, more slowly this time, and saw that something on the mat was sparkling when the sunlight caught it at the right angle. He frowned, putting his hands on his knees and approaching the mat at a low level, keeping the sunlight shining on whatever it was.

It was only when his nose was just inches from the

rubber that he began to be able to make out the source of the flashing – the mat was coated in hundreds of tiny dots, small as grains of sand, that sparkled like chrome steel. At first he thought they *were* grains of sand, but looking closer he could see they were too round for sand – they were tiny spherical objects, hundreds of them, sticking to the dried cola.

Curious, he dabbed at the rubber with his forefinger, a half-dozen of the shiny little spheres coming off on his skin. He held them up to the light, squinting, but still couldn't make out what they were. Getting the magnifying glass from the glove pocket, he examined the enlarged objects on his finger, but they still made no more sense: they were perfectly round, and smooth, and shiny, like ball-bearings. All were exactly the same size, and they were definitely *not* grains of sand.

Macauley tried to think what he could have done or where he could have been to have these things all over the floor of his car, and it was only a matter of seconds before an answer occurred to him.

He rushed back round to the mat with the magnifying glass, crouching down to examine it for all the poppy seeds he had brushed off his burgers over the last weeks. There were none, but logically the mat should be covered with them, stuck down by the cola.

There were none. But there were hundreds of these mysterious metallic spheres. Suddenly beside himself with excitement, he bundled the unwashed mat into the trunk of the car and sped back around to Rachel's. She had just got back from her morning consultations and was unloading her shopping bags on the kitchen table when he burst in, carrying the carefully folded mat.

'Microscope, Rachel!' he shouted. 'Do you still have your microscope?'

She turned to him, carrots in hand, with a lopsided smile on her face, saying, 'You may be a slob, Mac, but my, when you decide to clean a car, you really clean a car, don't you?'

He strode over and held the mat under the kitchen light.

'See it?'

'Car mat,' she replied. 'To my trained eye this is clear without even a microscope.'

'No, look!' he insisted, tilting the mat so that the balls caught the light. 'See them shining now?'

'Sand?'

'*Not* sand! *Not* sand!' he repeated excitedly. 'I have to see one under a microscope *now*!'

She giggled with incomprehension and put the carrots down on the table, going to get her microscope from a cupboard in the living room. 'What is this all about, Mac?' she sighed, setting it up on the table and plugging it in by the fridge.

'The poppy seeds on the burgers aren't poppy seeds!' he announced triumphantly. 'They are something else, coated black to *look* like poppy seeds, but the cola I spilled on the floor must have stripped off the black coating to show what they are!'

'Oh please . . .' she sighed, pausing to scrape a few of the sparkling grains on to a slide, 'do you have any idea how ridiculous this is sounding, *even* as far as conspiracy theories in general go?'

'Absolutely! He must have loved it! Even *I* would never have concocted something so downright unbelievable, because the readers would never have bought it, but it's true – in Farview there is a factory that produces reconstituted poppy seeds for Ghetty's burgers, that much is fact. But if the poppy seeds are fake anyway, it's only one step further to using them to disguise . . . I don't know, to disguise . . .'

'A microchip?' Rachel suggested, looking down the microscope.

374

'A microchip, for instance.'

'No for instance about it, honey – take a look for yourself.'

Macauley froze, hardly daring to put his eye to the microscope.

'You can see that?' he gasped. 'For sure?'

Rachel shrugged. 'I have no idea what I can see down there, Mac, but I know what it means.'

'Uh-huh?'

'My ex-husband, Mr Macauley Connor, is no doubt not home for dinner tonight because in about ten minutes' time he will be on the road to this Farview place again.'

XXXI

At dawn the next day, two days before the election, a tired but proud Ellen Henry, chair of the Portsmouth Summerday-Redwood Campaign Committee, took a last ride along the route the candidates' limousines would be taking when they arrived in town later that day. Ellen had worked feverishly to get everything ready over the last week, too busy overseeing the preparations to take care of the kids, the house or even her own body. She had not even had time over the last two days, she realized, to visit the bathroom.

But even her guilt over neglecting her family could not detract from the pride she felt in her achievement. Portsmouth was only a small town – pleasant and maddening, in the way small towns are when they get as good as they are ever going to be – and she had fought a long, hard battle against the modest, defeatist mentality of the townspeople and even the party organization to convince them that they could bring the pomp and razzmatazz of the Summerday campaign to their quiet little corner of Atlantis.

Portsmouth was heavily pro-Summerday, but for that very reason it seemed to everyone around her that he would never include them on his campaign trail. Ellen alone had the energy and enthusiasm to push the idea up through the party hierarchy, promoting Portsmouth as the ideal showcase of the Atlantis their presidential candidate sought to celebrate. She had telephoned, faxed, written, e-mailed and waiting-roomed her way through the last months – all on her own time and out of her own pocket – but she had succeeded: Portsmouth was chosen as one of the last campaign stops.

Michael Summerday was told he had chosen it because it symbolized everything he believed in, which he was glad to hear.

Even then there had been the question of cost, the town council gagging collectively when she told them precisely how much organizing the event would set them back. Again it was enthusiasm that won the day. This would put Portsmouth on the map, she argued, giving its people something they could be proud of instead of meekly accepting that, for all their qualities, they did not matter one iota on the national scale. Ellen believed they mattered, and slowly others came over to her opinion: they mattered and it was worth whatever it cost to show the world that they too existed and could be mentioned on the news.

Then came the whole logistical nightmare of organizing the rally – equipping the town for a media event, with extra power cables, satellite links, catering and toilet facilities for thousands; draping the streets in red, white and black, festooned with streamers and balloons; building a podium for the speeches and laying on microphones, speakers, amplifiers and security. It was huge and unlike anything Portsmouth had ever before attempted. And little Ellen Henry had done it all.

And now, as the sun rose on their clean little town, she was well pleased with the result. A big day was coming, possibly the biggest in Portsmouth's history, and all of her work and exhaustion would be worth it if these good, unassuming people with whom she had lived all her life ended this day a little prouder of themselves. She really had done it for them. For the town she loved. Ellen Henry was the kind of Atlantian who had made the country great.

So it was really, really unfair that Portsmouth should have been the town selected by Summerday and Giuliano for the audit of Bob Redwood.

As the cortège entered the thronged streets of Portsmouth in the blinding noon sun, Susan Summerday was thrilled and a little overwhelmed to witness the scale of the townspeople's admiration of her. Young, bright-eyed girls in tight T-shirts waved WE LOVE YOU, SUSAN banners and threw flowers at the limousine, mothers with babies on their arms blew kisses and smiled, men wolf-whistled playfully and laughed when they caught her eye.

She was a heroine to these people, she realized, suddenly ashamed of her part in their deception. They were good people, they deserved respect. But democracy, sadly, was not and never could be about respecting people as individuals. It was about respecting them as faceless members of the mass or, put another way, finding the least insulting point of consensus.

On that score, Susan genuinely believed that her participation in the creation of the myth around her and her family was forgivable, if it saved Atlantis from the insult of a Redwood vice-presidency. Michael had not told her how he was planning to remove the man from his current position, saying it was better she didn't know, and Susan was inclined to believe him. She was confident both of her ability to know when her husband was lying and of the fact that he was now sufficiently scared of her not to try any form of double-cross. At any moment she chose up until polling began, she could bring this campaign down in one interview.

And if he still had any doubts that the exchange would work in his favour, they should have been settled by the scene around them now. The impromptu banners in her

praise outnumbered the official SUMMERDAY FOR
PRESIDENT and I LIKE MIKE placards by an easy two-to-one
margin. Some people had even written SUSAN on top of
the first of these.

The local campaign office had done a good job,
Michael Summerday reflected, thinking with a twinge of
guilt that it was a damn shame their efforts were going to
be ruined by the imminent assassination of Bob
Redwood. It would put the place on the map, mind.

The open-top stretch limousine they were riding in
rolled slowly through town to give the people time to
have a good look at the candidates, the four police bikes
in front of them wobbling slightly as their riders
struggled to keep them steady at such a slow pace. Mike
and Susan were both standing, smiling and waving to the
cheering throng, Bob and Mary doing the same in
the row behind.

Summerday had not warned Susan what was going to
happen because he wanted her behaviour to be as natural
as possible. When the moment came and the rifle shot
rang out across the main square, he wanted the cameras
to capture the horror on her face in all its natural force.
There were to be two bullets fired – one to his shoulder,
the other to Redwood's head. If the marksman was as
good as he was supposed to be, Redwood would never
even know what had happened to him. There would be a
momentary pause as confusion reigned, and then the
cavalcade would speed up and head straight for the
hospital. They would arrive too late for Redwood, of
course.

The extent of Summerday's own injuries would not
initially be clear, giving the media time to whip themselves into a frenzy of speculation about the future. In the
event of both candidates dying, the baton theoretically
passed to old Jefferson Smith, the party leader in the
Senate. For all his remorse about Redwood, Summerday

had to admit that he was rather looking forward to seeing how Jefferson took the news that he may be obliged to step in at the last minute. It would be a miracle if he managed to face the press sober.

This was the moment when Susan had to rise to the occasion and start acting presidential. She had to show fortitude under extreme personal stress, calling for calm in her blood-spattered suit – it should be blood-spattered naturally, but if not he was planning to roll over her way and rub his shoulder against her – as the media howled for information. She would be the one to make the announcement about Redwood's death, her words – probably spoken on the steps of the hospital – leading the evening news bulletin the world over. Solemn, dignified and strong.

Finally, after a suitable delay, she would give the good news about Summerday himself – his injuries were not mortal. She would be joyous, but humble. She would thank God for his mercy in not having denied Atlantis the leadership of her husband. If she played her role right – taking command of the situation and becoming the voice of reason amid the chaos – then people would subconsciously begin to see her as the new vice-presidential candidate long before the official announcement was made. They would be momentarily surprised by the suggestion, shocked even, but almost immediately they would begin to see her as a natural choice to fill Redwood's shoes.

Atlantis would have its first husband-and-wife presidential candidacy. Officially, that is.

For all that he'd thought Susan insane when she initially stated that as her price, Summerday had come round to seeing the idea as utterly brilliant. The public already loved her, and the idea of a husband and wife working together was bound to capture their imagination. It was different. Not the usual marriage of political convenience, but a genuine marriage. Why, it would almost be like they had a royal family. And Atlantis, like all long-term republics, had a romantic fascination with royalty – what could be better than having a royal family without the guilt? If they got tiresome, they could be ditched at the next election – best of both worlds.

And on a personal level, what could be better for his marriage? Susan and he would finally be on the same wavelength, as united in their moral sacrifices as in their work. It was perfect.

It would be like a second honeymoon.

The cavalcade approached the town centre, and Summerday's heart began to race faster as the critical moment approached. Although still waving and turning, he slowed his movements so as not to mess up the marksman's shot, his left shoulder as still and as relaxed as he could keep it under the circumstances.

Under his shirt he was wearing a bullet-proof vest, just in case the man's aim was a little off. Even if this information leaked, nothing odd would be seen in a presidential candidate wearing one to a public event. Few fashion-conscious Atlantians did not own one since Vermani produced their designer version in homage to the murdered fashion guru, after all.

The limousine slowed as they entered the main square. A podium had been constructed in front of the town hall, from which Summerday and Redwood were to address the crowd. Any second now, Summerday thought, he would feel the bullet tear through his shoulder muscle. He had known that pain before, back in the Army, and it had been several minutes before the agony really set in. By then he would have been given something to kill it.

A sudden wave of guilt overcame him as he realized he had not said anything to Redwood before they got in the car. Obviously he couldn't have said goodbye, but he should at least have told him that he appreciated all the work he had put into the campaign – it was not much under the circumstances, but it might help to have said it once this was all over. He fought against the urge to turn round in the car and say something, knowing it was not the moment, but it was stronger than him. He turned slowly.

'Bob!' he called over the cheers of the crowd.

Redwood squinted, barely able to hear him, and leaned forward toward Summerday. Suddenly his body span back, immediately followed by a loud *crack*. Summerday saw his mouth open in shock as he fell back against his seat, clutching at his chest.

Michael Summerday frowned. That wasn't right.

He turned in the direction the shot had come from, just in time to receive his own bullet smack dab in the middle of his forehead.

It was, needless to say, the worst day of Ellen Henry's life.

XXXII

Just as Summerday's body was crumpling over in the limousine, Macauley Connor arrived in Farview. He sensed with a sinking feeling that he was not the first person in Atlantis to have discovered something not quite kosher about the poppy seeds on a Ghetty's burger.

Farview was no longer the sleepy little town he had seen two weeks ago. There was a traffic jam on the main street as cars from every state in the union searched in vain for parking spots, their movement being further restricted by roaming gangs of TV cameramen and journalists doing vox-pop interviews of any stray towns-people they could lay their hands on.

There was probably little point in him pursuing the story now, but having driven through the night to get here, he could hardly just give up and turn around, so he crawled through town and out the other side, ditching his gently overheating car on the side of the road a few hundred yards on from the Infologix plant. He saw a major concentration of journalists gathered around the entrance to the factory, a forest of microphone booms reaching forward toward the familiar white-and-black-haired figure of the Reverend Bob Willis.

He could not get close enough to hear what was being said, but he gathered from the comments of the journal-ists listening in over their headphones that it was pretty much as he had suspected – Memphis 2 was much more than simply the observation satellite for Atlantis' criminal community.

Memphis 2 was designed to observe *everyone*.

The poppy seeds were miniaturized versions of the same technology that went into the Rectag, but whereas Rectag emitted a unique, immediately traceable signal, the poppy seeds were designed to operate in conjunction with one another. Each emitted one of a thousand basic signals, meaning that, once they were randomly mixed, the poppy seeds on any given burger created a unique combination that allowed Memphis to isolate the individual who had eaten it and track his movements. The black covering was removed by the digestive juices in the stomach, uncovering and activating the transmitter hidden inside. This was coated with a heat-activated adhesive that slowed the transmitters' progress through the intestines, whilst their miniaturized form encouraged them to become lodged in the ripples and folds of the digestive tract. As more burgers were eaten by an individual, the computer on Memphis automatically noted the change in that individual's overall call signal.

All of this information was subsequently downloaded from the satellite via the factory's dish and was accessible by Internet.

The applications of this boggled the mind. Should a crime be committed, for instance, all the police would now have to do was enter the time and place of the crime and let the computer find the signals of the individuals who had been there at that moment. Once that was known, the computer could simply trace that signal to the present and inform the police where their subjects were to be found now. A missing person could be located by working from the last time and place their location was known, the exact sequence of events in a car crash recreated to establish responsibility.

In the future there would only be perfect crimes:

those committed without anybody realizing.

But that was just the beginning, because the information Memphis produced would not just be available to the police, but to anyone equipped with the necessary Infologix search engine. A wife could check on her husband, and vice versa. A lost friend could be found by simply working forward from one's last meeting with them. The clumsy fumblings of dating agencies would become a thing of the past as lonely-hearts dared to match their own tastes, lifestyles and hobbies (as reflected in their movements over previous months) against the database to produce a list of precisely kindred spirits. Celebrities had nowhere to hide.

The journalists, unsurprisingly, were outraged. Memphis was a direct, devastating attack on individual freedom and privacy. Yet Macauley found himself laughing as he looked around the faces of the people who were saying this. He knew most of them by reputation, if not intimately, and he instinctively understood that not one of them was there by chance. Each had been hand-picked by Lockes – or Schonk, or Cloken, or who knew what other personas he might have – for the simple reason that they were among the most relentless invaders of other people's privacy in the country. To hear them holding forth about protecting the individual's right to privacy was like watching Marines preach Buddhism. What really irked them, he suspected, was that John Lockes had just created a system that could do what they had always done, only infinitely better – he had just made them obsolete.

But that wasn't how they saw it. In their eyes this was an attack on the constitutionally protected rights of the individual. It was not, Macauley knew. He did not know the Constitution well enough to be able to say *why* not, but he didn't need to – he simply knew John Lockes well enough now to be quite certain that he would have

385

anticipated any such problem and have made sure it did not exist before putting his plan into action.

Memphis, whatever the journalists said now, would turn out to be within the Constitution.

Memphis, however much they swore to the contrary, would go ahead. There would be trouble at the start, of course, and the backlash when its existence was revealed would be phenomenal, but it didn't matter. John Lockes would have allowed for everything.

And, to his surprise, Macauley found that he was glad. He suddenly had faith in Lockes and his plan. Something had to be done to restore a sense of scale to this country, and it might well be that Lockes had found the answer. The man had been right about everything else so far – somehow he had managed to play all these people so skilfully that they had each made it to this precise place, on this precise day, simply by following the clues he had strewn in their paths. And for the first time in his life Macauley found himself believing that Lockes truly was acting in what he perceived to be the interests of the greater good.

If power had been what he truly wanted, then he could have had it. Memphis would have given him power on a scale no dictator had ever dreamed of – access to information on every man, woman and child in the country. He had only to keep control of the system for himself.

But he hadn't done that. He had set it free.

He had given it to the people.

Not that the people were going to want it initially, of course. They would react just like the journalists were now, demanding that the system be destroyed. They would succeed in little ways – the poppy seeds would be removed from the burgers, the factory destroyed perhaps. But it wouldn't make any difference. Macauley had not a shadow of a doubt that the poppy seeds were only one of many systems Lockes had put in place to feed his transmitters into society. There were probably dozens of other outlets whose existence no one yet suspected, and if they were ever discovered there would be others waiting to be activated behind them. They could destroy the Farview transmitter, but there would be other transmitters hidden elsewhere – whatever they did, and whatever happened tomorrow and in the days and weeks following the revelation of Lockes' plan, people were going to live with the system long enough to get used to it, and once they were used to it they would be half-way to accepting it, to realizing that its benefits far outweighed its negative aspects. Soon, when justice reigned absolute and crime was all but extinct, they would not be able to imagine a world without it. It would be impossible to uninvent.

Macauley had to hand it to him – Lockes had achieved what he had promised: he had changed the world. It would be a world where answers were available to all who sought them – they had only to ask the right question. It was not a police state, but a state without secrets.

God, just as he had promised, was back.

Macauley moved slightly apart from the other journalists, suddenly too tired to keep standing in the noon sun. He watched from a distance as Willis brought the impromptu press conference to an end, and the first of the journalists broke from the pack as they decided they would learn nothing more and should now try to be the first to get the news to their employers. Within the space of two minutes the first trickle of departures had turned into a panicked stampede and the factory was suddenly still.

Macauley was in no hurry to leave, closing his eyes and listening to the sound of the heat. He had no editor waiting impatiently for his report, no article to write up or footage to edit. He had only a book that would probably now never be published, and a seat in the shade to laze upon while he waited for the day to cool down.

'I'd thought you were going to be the first, Mr Connor.'

Macauley looked up to see the smiling figure of Reverend Willis leaning over him. 'Turns out I'm the last, though, doesn't it? My wife left me for that sort of behaviour.'

'You were so close the other day,' Willis continued, shaking his head sorrowfully. 'John had put so many people on to his trail, but you were ahead of the pack! Standing here right by this factory before a single other journalist had ever heard of Farview – the truth was only the right question away!'

'Because you would have told me the truth?'

'Of course. I had given you my word. I would not have liked it, because the plan was always that the truth should only come out once John was in orbit and the satellite was about to be launched, but a man is only as good as his word, Mr Connor.'

'The plan being yours or John's?'

Willis narrowed his gaze, as if momentarily blinded by the sun.

'Or God's, Mr Connor, don't forget that it might be God's. Grand schemes and little ones alike rarely come about because somebody sat down and planned them out; they evolve gradually over time from a thought here, a comment there, bubbling up through the subconscious until by the time you are actually aware of what you're thinking, most of the thinking has already been done. We're not in control of that, so you could say it's God's domain. Beyond that it is John's vision, but then I admit to having had a certain influence over him when he was a child. We see the world in complementary ways. What I achieved in Farview, he is trying to achieve in the country as a whole.'

'What did you achieve in Farview?'

'I gave the people of this town peace of mind. I found a community that had lost direction and hope because the world had left them behind and I gave them what they needed – knowledge that there was a god who was looking down on their every action. Not a vengeful god, and not a merciful god, simply a god who saw them living their lives. That's all people need in the end, Mr Connor – to know that someone, somewhere is paying attention. That's all! It's not much to ask, is it? They don't expect miracles, or the Garden of Eden – they just need something to help them live under the sun. Now people think that's a city problem, but I tell you it's even harder out here with this goddamn sky and endless wheat to contend with – how are you meant to see yourself against all of that? How are you meant to have *any* sense of life having a purpose when you're out here on the prairie? You're *nothing*! So you need a god to be there for you, Mr Connor – He doesn't have to *do* anything, He's just got to be there. My job is to make Him be there for the people of this town, to talk Him into existence. John is doing the same for the whole of Atlantis.'

'Memphis isn't a god, though. However powerful it is, at the end of the day it's just a satellite, designed and built by men.'

'Of course. And if that's all it remains then it will still be doing a good job. But give it time, Mr Connor – people have put their faith in lesser things than Memphis before. It is not a question of what the thing *is*, but what it represents. Memphis represents the dawn of a new age. One day, when the world we live in today is but a memory, and not a particularly pleasant one at that, the people of the new world will reach out for a symbol . . . and they may choose Memphis.'

'With John Lockes as the new messiah?'

'Who knows, Mr Connor? Maybe John *is* the new

messiah. He's just a man, but so are all messiahs – the Messiah is simply the man who changes things. Maybe one day they will end up sending prayers in John's name. You can't force people to believe, but equally, you can't stop them either . . . There's something for you to speculate upon in your book.'

'My book is a little dead in the water, I'm afraid, reverend. The main story just got hijacked and driven out of town in a dozen RVs. By this time tomorrow it's not going to be news any more.'

Willis shrugged and carried on drawing patterns in the dirt with his stick.

'Except *they* still have the wrong John Lockes . . .' he muttered.

Macauley jerked upright.

'You mean *none* of them . . . ?'

'None of them. That was kept back just for you, Mr Connor. His gift to you in recognition of all the amusement your stories have given him. Only you know the real John Lockes. So you can attack him like you were planning to, or come to his support like he hoped you would, but either way you still have a best-seller on your hands . . .'

XXXIII

Avalon was at that moment in stationary orbit at the point from which Memphis 2 was supposed to be launched. But the huge satellite still sat in the cargo bay, its systems up and running while a solution was desperately sought to the malfunction with the deployment arm. Once every imaginable system had been checked on board in a fruitless attempt to discover why it was not responding, there remained only one alternative – a spacewalk, to see if the problem could be located on the arm itself.

Troy Duncan and Jean waited patiently in the airlock for the long depressurization process to finish. Under their two-piece spacesuits they wore all-in-one bodysuits woven with liquid cooling tubes to protect them from he heat of the sun. The cooling system, as well as all the other life-support systems, were contained in the backpack of the hard, fibreglass torso section of their suits. Putting it on, even on Earth, Jean always felt as if she were donning a suit of armour, white and strong, like knight and princess rolled into one.

And the dragon?

The dragon was everything else. It was the airless extremes of space, burning 250 degrees in the sun and freezing –250 degrees in the shade. It was the zero pressure that would boil her blood and bodily fluids in seconds were the armour's own pressurization to fail.

It was the unknown.
It was herself.

*

Josh Cloken, as he was still calling himself up here, was waiting impatiently on the flight deck as everyone else busied themselves with preparations for the spacewalk. He had been discovering one of the more frustrating aspects of life in space over the last few hours.

You can't pace.

The very thing that sets you free from the dominant law of all human life, escaping from the gravity that pins you down and slowly beats the strength from your body over the years, traps you instead in the infinitely more restrictive cage of your own emotions, offering you nothing to fight against. Lockes was boiling with tension, but he couldn't even hit anything to let off some steam, as doing so would only send him ricocheting around the cabin. He had no choice but to wait passively until something was done to resolve the situation.

If something could be done. For if the arm was definitively fucked, he realized, the launch could not take place. And if the launch could not take place now then it would never happen, because his entire project depended upon facing Atlantis with a *fait accompli*.

A new launch would be subject to debate, and given the choice no society would willingly go down the path he had mapped out for them. Humans were too stupid, too selfish and too scared to make that kind of change. They would rather stew in the fetid broth of their own weaknesses, generation after generation visiting the same ills upon one other in a vicious circle of vice, than dare to bring it to an end once and for all, choosing the devil they did not know over the one they did. They would beat him, destroy everything he had tried to build, and then

392

still be stupid enough to think they had won a battle for freedom as they danced upon the rubble of his dreams.

That was not something John Lockes could accept.

*

Two handles, both protected by flip-guards, had to be turned through 480 degrees to engage the purge system that vented the last of the air overboard, bringing the pressure in the airlock down to zero. Once that was done, no power short of a bomb could open the hatch leading back into the living-space of the craft, held shut as it was by the simple mass of air at normal pressure.

It always seemed to Jean that she could feel space like a physical presence as she opened the outer hatch on to the nothing beyond. Every astronaut tried to describe the quality of space, and all failed, but the closest anyone had come in Jean's opinion was the cosmonaut who said, 'Space is a shout you hear with your eyes.' That was almost it – the darkness had a texture, and the silence echoed for infinity.

The glare shield descended automatically over her visor as she floated softly up through the hatch, yet still the sunlight made her squint. The side of her arm that caught its rays seemed to burst alight, while the shaded parts were simply no longer there. She looked suddenly two-dimensional.

Jean exited first, fastening her security line to the ladder rungs outside, and Troy followed behind. It bothered her not to hear the reassuring metallic click that her instincts demanded as she fastened the clip, and she checked it twice before letting go and floating back toward the hatch to pull it shut.

The cargo bay gleamed below her in the floodlights. No beams coned outwards from their bulbs to the objects they lit because there was nothing – no air, no dust – to catch their light. Objects seemed to glow of their own accord. The payload-bay doors, sixty feet long, were folded back along the length of the spacecraft – a white book upon a vast, black table. The satellite waited silently in the centre of the hold, awake and only needing the final push of the ignition activation button to fire the burners that would lift it into its pre-programmed orbit.

Jean had not responded to Lockes' explanation of the purpose this device really served because, in all honesty, she did not know what to think. She understood the implications of its capabilities, and could appreciate all the arguments he had put in its favour, but she felt unable to say whether it was right or wrong. She realized that she was neither for it nor against it. Jean's peculiarity was that she lived only in the moment, truly in the moment as very few people ever do or can, and in the end philosophical questions about the nature of life, or freedom, or dignity did not matter. She would be as free in a dictatorship as in a democracy so long as she breathed the same air, saw the same land and felt the same shadow of her own death creeping behind her.

She did not understand why everyone she had ever met seemed to think that life could be analysed, organized and judged along logical lines. She could *apply* logic and reason to the tasks set before her as well as anyone, but these things were not life. They were simply adult continuations of the games and puzzles she had played with as a child. Life was the thing she dived into when she opened her eyes again after driving blind across her bridges. Life was what her brother had no doubt seen as he plunged from his.

That, she suspected, was what had attracted her to Josh Cloken. Even when she had not known the truth of his alter ego, she had felt a desperate hunger for life in him. They were utterly different people, born on opposite poles, but they shared the one thing in common that had ever mattered to her. She could never imagine a tomorrow, but she could imagine someone like him being there.

*

Lockes watched anxiously from the aft window of the flight deck as the two astronauts went about their work below. He knew that it was Jean who had put on the jet pack to go to work on the arm while Troy stayed attached by a line to the cargo-bay wall and examined the circuitry on its base unit, but only because he had been told. The two figures were utterly unidentifiable in their dark-visored suits.

Nothing in his life had prepared him for the sense of impotence he felt now, watching the small, instantly dispersing clouds from Jean's nitrogen jets as she travelled back and forth along the huge arm, stripping back its layers of insulation to reveal the aluminium below. This was the first time he had ever been faced with the extraordinary knowledge of not knowing – not knowing what he would do next if they failed to locate the fault; not knowing what the purpose of his life would be if Memphis 2 was never launched; not knowing, indeed, what its purpose had been until now if that were the case.

He was adrift in God's sea, no land in sight, no compass, no stars. And it was a feeling that every cell in his body, his very genes, rebelled against. Before, there had always been some way of mastering the situation.

Below them right now – presuming everything had worked according to plan down there, at least – the people he had chosen to do so were discovering the truth about this satellite. Soon it would be common knowledge, blasting out of every television, radio and bar across the land. The politicians who had made this possible would be realizing that the entire Rectag programme, although genuine, had simply been a bait to lure them into granting him the orbit he needed for Memphis 2. The Ghetty's Burger Restaurants would be hurriedly closing their doors as the news of their secret ingredient came out.

He knew there would be panic, and anger, and violence – but so long as what was done was done, it would spend itself and achieve nothing. And no one even knew of the other outlets he had arranged for the transmitters – the ice-creams, the chocolates, the candies, the health bars, the muesli and more. There was, in all probability, no one down below who had managed to avoid them altogether. Statistically speaking, at least.

The minutes dragged painfully by as he heard Troy running through the circuits on the base unit, checking each one off as it responded exactly as it should under verification, until he finally closed the doors on their housing and gave up.

He watched with increasing agony as Jean travelled back and forth along the arm, checking it for any abnormality.

'It's not looking good, I'm afraid,' Adam Gallaher muttered, watching out of the window beside him.

Lockes' stomach was knotting, and he could not even manage a reply, simply shaking his head sorrowfully as their eyes briefly met.

And then Jean suddenly stopped.

She seemed to be focusing on something in the lower joint of the arm, leaning forward and reaching in with her gloved hand.

'Have you found something, Jean?' Gallaher called over the radio.

There was a pause as she straightened up, moving back with a little puff of nitrogen, and replied:

'Mmm . . . no . . . it's nothing, I'm afraid.'

'All right, folks, that's it.' Gallaher sighed. 'Put

everything back together and come home.' He turned to Lockes with a despairing regard. 'I'm sorry, Josh – the launch will have to be rescheduled.'

'*The launch can't be rescheduled!*' Lockes snapped through gritted teeth.

'It can – it will just take time. I know it's a blow, but we've had this kind of problem before. Nothing in life is totally reliable, you know? Sometimes shit just happens.'

'Not to me.'

'I'm sorry, but what can we do if it just can't be done?'

Lockes turned to him with a strange, sad look and whispered, 'Just do it.'

And then he hit the ignition on the satellite's burner.

XXXIV

For the last twenty-four hours, Agent Winston Pepsi and his team had been too occupied with the preparations for the raid on the bank to pay any attention to the news. They did not know, therefore, that with the election just one day away politics had been shunted into the background by the revelation of the true function of the Memphis 2 satellite and the real nature of the poppy seeds on the Big One's bun. They had no idea that the nation's initial shock had rapidly been replaced by a sense of outrage that was silently building with every hour, a dark energy beginning to charge the air, flexing across whole cities like telepathy as strangers' eyes met on the street, on the subway and in every public place, and each person saw their own simmering anger reflected back at them. Pepsi and his team fondly imagined themselves and their imminent attack on the bank to be the most dramatic development in Atlantis at that moment, little realizing, as they furtively set the charges that would blow out the bank's doors and windows, that the entire nation had become one huge tinderbox of repressed fury, waiting to explode.

The attack had been set for just after dark, when the building's power would be cut just as he and the others blew out the doors and windows of the bank. They would be wearing infra-red masks, flooding in on all sides while their targets floundered in the dark. Every man on the team had been issued with a photo of George Bailey, issued by his ex-employers at the World & Global. He didn't stand a chance.

They began to take up their positions as the sun went down along 5th Avenue, synchronizing the explosive charges at their various entry points and preparing their weaponry. Pepsi's own team was positioned by the huge main doors, which alone required ten charges, one for each hinge. They worked in silence, each squad checking in over the radio in whispers as they completed their preparations.

Now they only had to wait until dark.

The power cut had been set for fifteen minutes after sundown, and Pepsi found it hard to keep his eyes off his watch as the minutes dragged slowly by toward the resolution he so desperately needed. With five minutes still to go, he was waiting with the radio in his hand and his finger on the call switch when he was distracted by the sound of alarms some way up the street.

'What the . . . ?' he whispered, looking up 5th Avenue to see a large crowd of people some way beyond the barriers that sealed off the block where the bank was situated.

At first he didn't understand what it was – with the last rays of the setting sun silhouetting it from behind, the crowd seemed to swirl and twist upon itself like smoke as those in the front were pushed out to the sides by others charging up from the rear. It was rolling down the avenue like a slow, dark mist that curled into every window and doorway on the ground level, setting alarms off wherever it passed.

Then he understood.

It was a riot.

A big riot, heading straight toward the barriers that no one had crossed for over a month now. Heading, in other words, toward him.

Pepsi used the telescope on his gun to size up the situation. For the most part the mob seemed to be composed of ordinary-looking people, well-dressed men and women who would normally be on their way home from work but who had instead found themselves caught up in some kind of hysterical rush-hour of violence. The cross-hair in his sights settled on one figure, marginally in front of the others. He was running, exhorting the crowd over his shoulder to follow, his eyes burning with an air of righteous conviction.

Something about the man seemed familiar, but Pepsi had no time to search his memory for where or when he might have seen that face before. He struggled with his conscience, desperately wanting to deny that this was really happening, now of all times, but there was no getting around the fact that the mob was going to be on them before the power was cut to the bank.

'I don't know how many of you can see what I'm looking at down here,' he shouted into the radio, 'but the ball game just changed. This is now an urban pacification situation, people! Take up positions facing the street and prepare to fire a warning volley on my command.'

He ran back down the steps of the bank to the mobile HQ and ordered them to turn on the loud-hailer system and broadcast him at full volume.

'This is Special Agent Winston Pepsi of the Bureau!' his voice boomed down the street toward the streaming mob. 'You are an illegal gathering heading toward an armed force. You are to desist – I repeat: *desist* – in your current progress!'

The mob momentarily seemed to slow, growing denser and darker as the front lines of the crowd braked and brought those behind piling into their backs. It quivered, the two forces struggling for supremacy as it moved forward in jerks. Slightly ahead of the pack there was still that frustratingly familiar lone figure, exhorting them forward.

'Desist!' Pepsi commanded. 'Do not cross the barrier. Do not cross the barrier or I shall give the order to fire!'

Suddenly the tension broke – the front was no longer able to restrain the back, and he saw the limp silhouettes of those who had been restraining its movement flail as they lost their footing and were trampled underfoot by the suddenly rushing crowd.

Pepsi just had time to order a warning volley to be fired before the barriers were knocked down and disappeared under the stampeding citizens, but it had no effect. The riot had found itself a target in the little armoured agent standing by the communications van and he saw the faces of the front-runners twist with anger as they bore down on him – blind, unreasoning fury deafening them to his threats. He dropped the microphone and prepared to defend himself with his pistol, taking aim at the nearest of the mob, but each time he looked down the barrel at an individual target he found himself unable to pull the trigger.

These were not the scum and hardened criminals he was used to pointing his weapon at, they were ordinary men and women in suits and designer clothes. They were the people he was supposed to be protecting, only now they were carrying sticks and lengths of pipe, bricks, baseball bats and even the occasional gun.

Pepsi understood that they were out for blood, but he did not understand why, nor could he defend himself, because they were civilians, not the enemy his training had prepared him to face. He searched for the leader, knowing that he was the key, but he was lost amid the rushing bodies. Pepsi hesitated fatally, his aim skipping from one ordinary face to another until it was too late and they were upon him in a flurry of blows that came from so many directions at once that he was kept on his feet by the very pounding that sought to drive him to the ground. He covered his face with his arms, feeling his pistol being wrested from his grasp, and held his breath.

The mob was still moving, and he could feel his heels dragging along the tarmac as he was kept pinned in place by the crush, the jabs and cracks still raining down upon him. As his mind started to cloud over, he was dimly aware of sliding down the surrounding bodies. Then his trailing feet were trod on by other feet and suddenly he was ripped to the ground, the fists and sticks now replaced by a flurry of kicks and stamping heels as the mob flowed past directly over him. He heard his ribs cracking, felt his mouth fill with blood and his neck twist to an impossible angle, and suddenly the pain in his body was no longer there, a smile forming on his misshapen face as he fled into the warm embrace of death's protective arms.

He remembered who that man was.

EPILOGUE

Who Laughs Last

As she gazed at the imperceptibly receding planet before her, Jean Grey calculated that she had about seven hours to live. She had begun distancing herself from *Avalon* the second she saw the burners on Memphis 2 ignite, using the maximum thrust on her jet pack to escape the inevitable explosion. The shockwave had caught her about thirty seconds later, propelling her forward at a speed which, with a little luck, would be sufficient to take her out of Earth's gravitational field altogether.

Although she would be long since dead by then, of course.

The horror of that thought had not lasted very long, considering. It wasn't such a bad way to end – gently losing consciousness as the air in her suit turned to carbon dioxide, entering a coma and eventually dying. And there was comfort in the thought of her body travelling on after her to some unknown destination, perhaps millions of years hence. Everyone has to die, but to achieve some sort of immortality is . . . nice.

That's what John had probably wanted so much that he had destroyed *Avalon* to achieve it. Immortality.

Men had a thing about that.

The irony was that he needn't have done it. She'd lied. She'd fixed the problem with the arm. Once back on board, she'd been intending to go through the charade of testing it one last time and finding – surprise! – that it worked.

Jean had been expecting to find some technical problem with the arm, a hitherto undiscovered design weakness such as most missions revealed about some aspect of the shuttle. So when she saw the true cause of the fault she had been strangely touched by the incongruity of it.

There was a spanner in the works. Literally. Probably what had happened is that it had fallen down between the arm and the insulation when a ground technician had been preparing *Avalon* for the mission. Forgotten, it lay there until they reached orbit, at which point it had floated back up and got lodged in the arm's gear train, snagging it when she first tried to operate the mechanics.

It was a cheap, three-sixteenths spanner with *Made in Kando* clearly visible where the sunlight caught it. The kind you might get free with a tank of gas. Ridiculous.

Perhaps it was that which had moved her to lie – the absurdity of this cheapo little tool derailing the operations of a $1.7 billion spacecraft. All the technology, all the military precision of their preparations, set against this one act of carelessness, this human touch reaching into the cold wastes of space. A dime dropped in the cup of a Wall Street bum.

And probably, she had realized, some technician below them in New Toulouse was asking, with a lurch in his stomach, whether the catastrophic malfunction of the arm mightn't be related to the spanner missing from his toolbox, desperately trying to remember if he had used it since working on that part of the shuttle.

The lie had escaped her lips without her having taken any conscious decision. It was instinctive. From the moment the truth was known, the problem would be immediately traced to the individual responsible. Whoever he was, his entire life would be turned upside-down for a spanner made in Kando – his career, and with it everything, from the next instalment on his house to his children's education, paying the price of his carelessness. His humanity.

There was something in the situation that made her warm to that poor man. Maybe it was the fact that the satellite and their mission had cost this astronomical sum of money and yet he was given a tool made by some semi-slave worker in Kando to do his work. It seemed unjust. So she had covered for him, whoever he was. She had removed his spanner, and lied.

And John Lockes, believing all hope lost, had taken the decision to launch his satellite from the belly of the ship itself.

Men.

And now here she was, sole survivor of *Avalon*'s destruction as the satellite blasted murderously off from the interior of the cargo bay, a lone sack of soul speeding off into the darkness.

The ghost in the machine.

Just shows what you get for trying to help people.

*

Jean, almost alone among the people of this Earth, would never know about the riots. No doubt there are jungle tribes, hermits and individuals with advanced Alzheimer's who managed to avoid any knowledge of or involvement in them, but they don't register on the statistics.

When it was all over, when the last of the fires were long since put out, the rubble cleared, the glass replaced and the bodies given decent burials, no one would be able to establish when or how the riots had started. When it began, it began everywhere – within minutes of the violence breaking out in Entropolis, news had spread to other cities and the pattern repeated itself. When it happened, it happened with immediate, maximum violence. The great illusion of Atlantian civilization crumbled as if at the snap of a god's fingers. But actually that god was an ordinary mortal, and the man who threw the first stone in the first window, who turned to the people on the street around him and declared, 'So what are you waiting for?', had a name. It was the name that had come to Winston Pepsi's mind as the crowd trampled him to death.

Lincoln Abrams, the man he had put in Parry. The man who had beaten Rectag. Lincoln Abrams, finally triumphant.

There was no possible resistance to the energy his action had finally unleashed. The few isolated, short-lived stands made by the police and Army no more affected it than an umbrella affects the rain. Soon they too were shedding their uniforms and joining the mob, the interior of the riot being the only sanctuary left. The reporters followed suit, the television stations switching over one by one to a pre-programmed menu of sit-coms and adverts as the society outside their deserted offices collapsed. But no one was watching anyway, the vortex of the riot having sucked them in. So long as one did not resist, so long as one let the destructive energy flow through one's hands – smashing, burning, looting – there was no real danger or fear at the heart of the riot. Only those brave and foolish enough to resist, or even just stand apart, became victims.

Civilization does not end when enemies clash, it ends when neutrality becomes dangerous.

For two days and two nights the mobs roamed the towns and cities, seeking out all symbols of authority. Police stations were targets. Government buildings were targets. Traffic lights were targets. Wherever one mob had passed, destroying all in its path, another soon followed behind to stamp upon the pieces and burn the remains.

It was anarchy in many ways, but not entirely – the fact that the uptown districts were always the first to be looted suggests that a certain consumerist dynamic was still in place. But the longer it continued, the more random and widespread the riot's targets became, until whole cities wailed like vast babies as their alarms screamed in unison throughout the night.

And there was, of course, one true enemy that gave the destruction a particular focus whenever any symbol of it was encountered. Infologix . . .

*

The Campus, being situated several miles outside Petersburg, was not attacked until all the branch offices of Infologix had already faced the full fury of the mobs. Their last communications were hastily written e-mails as the panicked employees fled before the enraged citizens. One by one they ceased to exist, the permanent electronic links between them and the mother office breaking as every last terminal in every building was torn from its sockets and smashed.

Realizing it could only be a matter of time before the Campus itself came under attack, John Lockes' dedicated executives made an undignified scramble for the car park – junior employees tearing Infologix stickers off their cars and billionaire directors bumming lifts off people whose vehicles did not have INFO in the numberplate.

Only the man they believed to be John Lockes elected to stay. Miles Cardew knew it would cost him his life, but he had to do whatever was in his power to save the company. He had to transfer all the vital data to safe locations at Infologix's foreign offices, hold a meeting of the branch heads to decide the company's future structure in light of the total destruction of its Atlantian operation . . . He did not know how long he had, but even once the mob arrived he felt sure he could hold them off for some time by magnetically locking all the doors in the Campus. They would be forced open eventually, of course, because they had not been designed with a riot in mind, but it might slow the mob's progress long enough for the essential work to be done.

He saw them arrive from his window when the work was only half done. Rock-festival numbers suddenly started to flood across the Elysian Fields toward the building, breaking into a trot as they saw their destination lying below them, each wanting to be among the first to strike at the heart of their anger. From the unnatural calm of his office, he listened as they broke into the building – the distant sound of breaking glass and cheers sounding almost like a party. He focused himself on the task at hand, shutting out the ever-swelling sounds of destruction, of computers smashing, hard disks being hurled from windows and cables ripped from the walls.

And when it was done, when Infologix was safely resituated abroad, he sat calmly in his chair and listened to the last doors being beaten down, staring at the swirling patterns of Infologix Mesmer upon the monitor in front of him . . .

*

The only reason why the Entropolis Stock Exchange didn't crash was that it didn't reopen. It couldn't. There was no exchange left. It was gone. Destroyed. Although unintentional, this was actually a brilliant ploy. Instead, the fall-out from the Atlantian riots spread over stock exchanges everywhere else in the world, each of them entering meltdown from the moment they opened. With

Atlantis apparently descending into total anarchy, people's belief in liberal capitalism simply evaporated as if they had always been secretly of the opinion that it was all an illusion anyway. The crash was sudden and complete – share owners no longer caring about the scale of their losses in the scramble to salvage whatever cash they could in a frenzy of destruction that mirrored the riots themselves. For two days the world's exchanges crashed and crashed until they could crash no more, multi-billion-dollar conglomerates dissolving into the ether like alcohol. Cash was no more secure a form of wealth, as the dollar and all other traded currencies fell like cheerleaders' pom-poms after the quarterback breaks his neck.

Even to ordinary people, who owned no shares and had no investments in currencies, it seemed as if the world had suddenly ground to a halt. Without the reassuring knowledge that their way of life was underpinned by the limitless greed of a small minority who owned all the capital, they concluded that it was now a case of every man for himself and rushed out to secure whatever supplies they could lay their hands on. Supermarkets attempted to control the crush by operating a nightclub policy of one-in-one-out, but the hysteria of the crowds soon overpowered them and their entrances were stormed, their shelves pillaged and their cashiers overwhelmed, screaming a final 'Have a nice day!' before running off with the contents of the tills. The banks closed their doors until further notice, the insurance companies issued a joint statement to the effect that they were considering the current situation to be one of civil war and would thus honour no claims, and in every theatre in every city the show did not go on.

But then, late on the second evening, just when it seemed that the anarchy had achieved a kind of perverse stability and lawlessness had established itself as the new status quo, the rioting in Atlantis stopped. Exhausted of energy and targets, it melted away as suddenly and mysteriously as it had begun – the orgiastic, end-of-the-world appetite for destruction giving way to quieter but ultimately stronger urges, such as taking a warm bath, getting a good night's sleep and feeding the cat.

A strange quiet descended on Atlantis that night, the streets as empty as if after the passing of a plague. With nothing left to loot and nowhere to go, the country decided as one to rest.

At first people believed it was only a temporary reprieve. Although their own lust for chaos might have been spent, they imagined that others would again take to the streets come morning, consolidating their new-found power and liberty. But the streets were still quiet long after sunrise. The few people who ventured out walked softly, avoiding each other's gaze for fear that they'd find themselves being lured into a small attack on a parking meter or a vending machine. They were like hungover teenagers waking up to wander through the mayhem left by a party, half repentant and half proud of their excess.

By midday, it became clear that the mood had changed – there was no flux in the air any more, beyond a dawning realization that cleaning up the mess would require even more effort than creating it had. The first people to return to work were the journalists. Rapidly, and without any comment on their own output over the last twenty-four hours, the TV stations replaced their wall-to-wall sit-coms with non-stop coverage of the chaos left by the riot.

Things were back to normal: it was on TV. It was official. No serious attempt was made to explain what had happened, let alone to moralize about it, because everyone understood that it surpassed reason and even the few talking heads they dug out had the exhausted air of ex-rioters. The point was that the riot was now definitely over because TV was talking about it in the past tense.

A cheerful and upbeat Lola Colaco returned to their screens later that day with '*Couples Who Met and Found True Love While Rioting*'.

It was also, as the journalists pointed out, the day Atlantis was supposed to elect its new president.

The election took place with an all-time record low voter turn-out, but was valid nevertheless. It was won by the late Michael Summerday and the equally late Bob Redwood, the riots having somewhat suppressed the news of their demise.

Senator Jefferson Smith, the majority leader, automatically took the murdered man's place. Susan Summerday, whom he had long loved from a distance, was named as his choice for Vice-President. Neither the assassin himself nor the person or people behind the killing were ever identified. Numerous books have been written on the subject, with speculation fingering everyone from Jefferson Smith and Susan Summerday themselves to John Lockes and even the Reverend Bob Willis.

Many years later a killer on Death Row tried to bargain his way into a stay of execution by confessing to the assassination. Although the detail with which he described the event suggested that he may indeed have been the assassin, his absurd attempt to buy his life by claiming that the conspiracy was led by Summerday himself, whom he had mistakenly shot, was rejected as an obvious fabrication and the fucker fried.

Slowly, in the days following Jefferson Smith's proxy election to the presidency, the great clean-up began. Enough of the communitarian spirit of the riot remained for residents to begin spontaneously clearing – or at least rationalizing – the mess in their own streets. Within a day most people had returned to their places of work, anxious to distance themselves from their own actions, but no company could account for all of its employees straight away. Most of the missing people would gradually turn up over the next few days, but even once Atlantis was back to work in normal fashion and the last traces of the riot had long since disappeared, there remained a statistically significant proportion of the urban population who were unaccounted for.

Some were dead, the burned buildings all having their share of charred, unidentifiable corpses, every river its share of floating bodies, but most of them had simply disappeared.

Among the more famous of the missing people was George Bailey. Speculation over what had become of him was mostly restricted to the employees of the World & Global Credit. The media didn't get around to following up on the story that had so obsessed them in the weeks prior to the riot until most people had long forgotten George's name and the mystery only rated a small piece at the end of the evening news bulletin on a slow day.

The first people to enter the bank after the riots found a peculiar scene – the detritus of the hostage crisis had been cleaned up into neatly tied garbage bags and placed near the door. The mattresses had been stacked and the sheets and blankets folded, apart from six mattresses lying in a row, each carrying the body of a man respectfully laid out under a sheet, his gun upon his chest. When the vault of the bank was opened, they found all the cash safely placed inside, meticulously counted out into piles of $1,000 each. But there was no George Bailey, no orphan children or any of the other hostages, and nor would anything ever be heard of them again.

The bank doors had been locked from the outside.

Little effort was put into locating them because there was no evidence of any crime except for the six corpses, who checked out as being the gang members who had initially robbed the bank. Forty more missing persons on top of the thousands on the police records was no big deal, and the file was closed in a job lot along with tens of thousands of other cases under which the police decided to draw a line.

There was no mystery, however. In a former age, when these things were dealt with by hand, the location of George Bailey and the children would have been discovered almost immediately. But in their place these days there was only a computer software program called Infologix Bankmanager, which every month mindlessly issued bank statements to twenty-one millionaires living in Bedford Falls, all but one of whom were children.

The fortunes created by George Bailey on behalf of all the hostages, who had each taken their turn to rob the bank and deposit the cash, were chickenfeed compared to the astronomical debts left by the riots. The destruction was such that no figure could ever be put on the total cost of the episode, but strangely enough it didn't really matter. The money was all hypothetical anyway, and so long as people regained their belief in the system behind it, so long as they were prepared to invest in the businesses which immediately restarted the process of rebuilding the nation, nothing had really changed. The Entropolis Stock Exchange, when it reopened, recorded its biggest ever rise in a single day of trading as money from all over the world, from countries whose own exchanges were still staggering from the crashes they had experienced during the riots, flooded into Atlantis.

A country in need of complete rebuilding was clearly a great investment.

*

The mystery of what became of *Avalon* was never resolved, and the various theories in circulation were only further confused by the revelation in Macauley

413

Connor's best-selling biography, *The Secret Lives of John Lockes*, that Lockes himself had been on board.

The celebrated author's remarriage to his wife was widely reported, not least by the *Public Investigator*, which claimed that their ex-reporter's spouse was in fact none other than John Lockes himself, who had secretly undergone a sex-change. Macauley gave up journalism and writing altogether, using the money he had earned from the book to buy a large tract of prairie and set up a waste-recycling business that turned him into a billionaire. The couple now live in a charming house on the peak of the highest of the Connor Hills, the one mainly built from burger containers, and the forests and streams are coming along nicely. Despite their vast wealth, they live a simple life in the company of their children, their dogs and the chicken that was sent as a wedding present by a mysterious, or perhaps illiterate, well-wisher.

Many months after it had been forgotten about, incidentally, a rogue satellite was detected. It turned out, to everyone's surprise, to be Memphis 2. The blast of the shuttle's explosion had knocked it fractionally off course as the pre-programmed rocket burst lifted it into geostationary orbit, and it was now patiently trying to collect Rectag data from a large section of the Pacific Ocean.

There is currently talk of using it to monitor whales.

*

It is perhaps fitting to end with the one person who learned something, who advanced one small step forward in their understanding of the world and its people as a result of all of this.

Jean Gray died a peaceful death on her meteoric journey out of the Earth's gravitational field, but as the carbon dioxide in her suit inexorably began to overcome her, she was briefly startled back to consciousness by a revelation that had struck her dying brain.

She had been drowsily thinking about life, and what purpose it served, and where it came from, when an answer of sorts suddenly came to her. The mistake people had always made, she realized, might be in thinking that there was any mystery at all to Creation. Why couldn't life, the universe and everything exist simply because logic demanded it?

What was the alternative, after all? How could there be nothing, just one endless nothing, without that in itself being something? How could there be just a giant zero without that zero being a singularity, and therefore . . . *one*? One and zero implied each other, and in between them lay a space for infinity.

She smiled to think, as she slipped once more into death's soft and loving arms, that it may *all* be powered by this simple paradox locked in the heart of things, this unsolvable equation that vainly tried to work itself out in an endless span of galaxies and black holes, suns and planets, seas and mountains, plants and people. And they all carried the paradox in them, and the paradox gave them life, and took life away, and the questions they asked themselves would go for ever unanswered.

Or so we should hope.

And her breathing became shallower and shallower as the air in her spacesuit grew thinner. And even as her mind relinquished its fight against the encroaching darkness, her lungs still struggled to carry life one breath on, and one further, and one more, until they scraped the last crumbs of air, her own death sounding strangely in her ears like a person scooping urgently for breath at the end of a long, hysterical fit of laughter.

And after the last laugh, when her heart had delivered its punchline to resounding silence, she still looked out, and could still hear with her eyes, out here in the endless tracts, the single shout of space.